Critical acclaim for Peter James

'A well-paced thriller that delivers maximum emotional torture' *Chicago Tribune*

'Grippingly intriguing from start to finish'
James Herbert

'Too many horror stories go over the top into fantasy land, but *Dreamer* is set in the recognisable world . . . I guarantee you more than a frisson of fear'
Daily Express

'A thought-provoking menacer that's completely technological and genuinely frightening about the power of future communications' *Time Out*

'This compulsive story is a tale of the search for immortality . . . I cannot remember when I last read a novel I enjoyed so much' *Sunday Telegraph*

'Gripping . . . plotting is ingenious . . . in its evocation of how a glossy cocoon of worldly success can be unravelled by one bad decision it reminds me of Tom Wolfe's *Bonfire of the Vanities*' *The Times*

'Peter James, Britain's closest equivalent to Stephen King' *Sunday Times*

'The suspense holds on every page, right to the end . . .'
She

1

The scream was carried towards her by the gust of wind, then whiplashed away, leaving her face smarting with the sting of grit and shock.

She stopped and listened. Another gust shook a few more early autumn leaves down from the trees, and dealt them out across the field. Then she heard the scream again.

A single piercing scream of utter terror that cut through her like a knife.

Go, it said. Get away.

Go while you have the chance!

Run!

For a moment, Sam hesitated. Then she sprinted towards it.

A small girl, slight, a few days past seven, her fringe of dark brown hair slipped down over her eyes and she tossed it back, irritated, then tripped over a flint stone in the dusty track and stumbled.

She stopped, panting, and stared around at the furrows of brown soil that stretched away from her across the barren field, at the woods that bordered two sides of it, and the barn beyond the gate at the far end, listening as the fresh gust came, but it brought only the sound of a creaking hinge. She ran again, faster this time, dodging the loose stones and bricks and ruts, the sandy soil kicking up in spurts under her.

'I'm coming,' she said, slowing again, catching her breath, stopping and bending to retie the lace of her left sneaker, then sprinting again. 'Nearly,' she said, 'Nearly there.'

She paused a short distance from Crow's barn, and hesitated. Huge, dark, in a state of neglect, with half its door missing, she could see through into the blackness of its interior. It was OK to go in with a friend, but not alone. Alone it was scary. When she played around here, and visited her secret places, she kept a safe distance from the barn, sufficiently far that nothing lurking in that blackness could leap out and grab her. The half door swung out a few inches and the hinge creaked again, like a wounded animal. There was a bang above her, then another, and she jumped, then breathed out again as she saw a loose flap of corrugated iron above lift and drop in the wind, banging loudly.

Slowly, nervously, she stepped past a strip of rotting wood, past a buckled rusted bicycle wheel and through the doorway into the black silence. The air was thick with the smell of rotting straw, and a duller, flatter smell of urine. There was another smell too, some smell she could not define, but which made her flesh creep, made her want to turn and run; a strange, frightening scent, of danger.

She felt as if the scream she had heard was still echoing in here.

She peered around in the gloom at the empty trough, the obsolete threshing machine and a section of an old plough lying on the floor in a shaft of dusty light. An old ladder lay hooked in place up to the hayloft, and as she stared up into an even blacker darkness, she heard a noise coming from up there; a whisper.

Her head spun in terror.

Then she heard a whooping sound as if someone was inflating a dinghy with a footpump, a strange tortured whooping, then a low pitiful moan.

'Noo.'

Then the whooping again.

Sam ran to the ladder and began to climb, ignoring its bending, its flexing, and the fear that at any moment it might snap in two; ignoring the blackness into which she was climbing. She reached the top and scrambled out onto the rough wooden joists and the thick dust, wincing as a splinter slid deep into her finger.

'No! Oo! *No!* Please no. Please . . .'

The voice turned into a strangled choking. She heard the pumping sound, much louder now, and a human grunt that accompanied it, and she heard a girl's voice hoarse, struggling for breath, pleading.

'Stop. Please stop. Please stop. No. Oh – h. Oh – h'

Her hand touched something round and hard, something plastic with a cord coming from it, something that felt like a switch. She pulled it and a bare bulb lit up inches above her head. She blinked and saw straw bales piled high in front of her with a thin dark gap like a corridor running between them.

For a moment, there was complete silence. Then a whimper, cut short. Shaking with fear she followed her shadow slowly down between the bales of dry acrid straw that stretched to the ceiling, stepping carefully on the joists, until her shadow became indistinguishable from the rest of the darkness.

There was another gasp, right in front of her, a sharp snapping sound, and one more terrible gasp that faded away into complete silence. She froze, her heart thumping, petrified as a figure rose up out of the darkness and began stumbling towards her, his hands reaching out for her, and she began to back away in slow steps, finding the joists, trembling, touching the rough straw to steady herself as she went, staring wide-eyed at the figure that followed her out of the shadows and was getting clearer with every step.

So clear she could now see it was not shadow that hid

his face, but a hood. A black hood, with slits for the eyes, the nose, the mouth.

She could see his hands too now; could see the deformed right hand, with just the thumb and the little finger, coming out of the darkness at her like a claw.

She tripped and fell backwards underneath the light bulb. She rolled, scrambled to her feet and tried to step back, but stumbled again, and felt a crunch as her foot went through the rotten flooring.

'You little bitch. What the fuck you doing here?'

She felt his hands clamp around her neck, felt the hand with just the thumb and finger, strong, incredibly strong, like a steel pincer, and her face was filled with the stench of onions and sweat; old stale sweat as if it had been in his clothes for weeks and was now being released, and fresh, raw onions, so sharp she could feel her eyes water from them.

'I – I was—' She froze as the grip of the hands tightened around her neck, squeezing the bones, crushing them. She jerked back, then she stumbled and he stumbled with her and they crashed to the floor. There was an agonising pain across her back, but she was free, she realised. She rolled, heard him grunt again, rolled some more and struggled to her feet. She felt his hand grab her sweater, pulling, and she wriggled, trying to tear free, then tripped again and fell.

As she tried to get up, his hand gripped her shoulder and spun her over, then he was lying on top of her, knees either side, pinioning her body down, and she felt the stench of his breath, the raw onions like a warm foul wind.

'Like to be fucked, would you, little one?' He laughed, and she stared up at his black hood, lit clearly by the bulb above it, seeing the glint of his eyes and his rotten broken teeth through the slits. He leaned back

4

tugging open his belt. The loose corrugated iron flap lifted above them in the wind, lighting them up with daylight for an instant, then banged loudly back down. He glanced up, and Sam sprang at him, clawing at his face with her hands, jamming her fingers into his eyes. The fingers of her left hand sank in deeper than she had thought they could, and she felt a hideous damp gelatinous sensation, then heard a rattling from the floor, like a rolling marble.

A hand crashed across her cheek. 'You little fucking bitch, what you done to it? What you done?'

She stared up, trembling, pulling her hand away from the sightless socket that was raw red, weeping, the eyebrows turned in on themselves. She felt him lean back, groping with his hands, and as he did so she pulled a leg free and kicked him hard in the face. He jerked his head back sharply, smashing it against the bulb which shattered, and they were in complete darkness. She rolled away, scrambling feverishly towards the hatch, then she felt her shoulders grabbed again and she was flung backwards, felt him jumping onto her. She kicked again, yelling, thrashing out, punching, feeling his breath closer, until his face was inches from hers, and a sudden shaft of light came in as the loose flap above them lifted again, lighting clearly the red sightless eye socket that was inches from her face.

'Help me!'

'Sam?'

'Help me!'

'Sam? Sam?'

She thrashed violently, and suddenly she was free of his clutches, falling, then rolling wildly into soft ground, in different light; she tried to get up but fell forward, and rolled frantically again. 'Help me, help me, help me!'

5

'Sam?'

The voice was soft. She saw light again, from beside her, from an open door, then a figure standing over her, silhouetted.

'No!' she screamed and rolled again.

'Sam. It's OK. It's OK.'

Different, she realised. Different.

'You've been having a bad dream. A nightmare.'

Nightmare? She gulped in air. Stared up at the figure. A girl. She could see the light from the landing glowing softly through her long, fair hair. She heard the click of a switch, then another click.

'The bulb must have gone,' said the girl's voice. A gentle voice. Annie's voice. 'You've been having a nightmare, you poor thing.'

She saw Annie walk towards her and lean down. She heard another click and her bedside Snoopy lamp came on. Snoopy grinned at her. It was all right. The baby-sitter was looking up at the ceiling, her fair hair trailing below her freckled face. Sam looked up too, and saw that the light bulb had shattered. A single jagged piece of glass remained in the socket.

'How did that happen, Sam?'

Sam stared up at the socket and said nothing.

'Sam?'

'He broke it.' She saw the frown on Annie's face.

'Who, Sam? Who broke it?'

Sam heard raised voices downstairs, then music. The TV, she realised. 'Slider,' she said. 'Slider broke it.'

'Slider?' Annie looked down at her, puzzled, and tugged the strap of her corduroy dungarees back over her shoulder. 'Who's Slider, Sam?'

'What are you watching?'

'Watching?'

'On the television.'

6

'Some film – I don't know what it is – I fell asleep. You've been cut. You've got glass in your hair and on your forehead. And your finger. It's everywhere.' She shook her head. 'I left it on. It must have—' She stared around again. 'Must have exploded. Don't move a sec.' Carefully, she picked the glass out of Sam's hair.

'Are Mummy and Daddy back yet, Annie?'

'Not yet. I expect they're having fun.' She yawned.

'You won't go until Mummy and Daddy get back, will you?'

'Of course not, Sam. They'll be back soon.'

'Where've they gone?'

'To London. To a ball.'

'Mummy looked like a princess, didn't she?'

Annie smiled. 'It was a lovely dress. There.' She walked over to the wastepaper bin, stooping on the way and picking something up from the carpet. 'Bits of glass everywhere. Put your slippers on if you walk around. I'll get a dustpan and brush.'

Sam heard the light tinkle of the glass dropping into the bin, then the sharp shrill of the front door bell. It made her jump.

'It must be your parents. They've forgotten their key.'

Sam listened to Annie walking down the stairs and the sound of the front door opening, waiting to hear her parents' voices, but there was a strange silence. She wondered if the film on the television had finished. She heard the click of the door closing, and there was another silence. Then she heard the soft murmur of a man's voice; unfamiliar. There was another man's voice as well that she did not recognise. Puzzled, she slipped out of bed, tiptoed across to her door, and peeked cautiously down the stairs.

Annie was talking to two policemen who were standing awkwardly, holding their caps.

Something was wrong, Sam knew. Something was terribly wrong. She strained her ears, but it was as if someone had turned off the volume, and all she could do was watch them mouthing silent words.

Then Annie turned away from the policemen and walked slowly, grimly, up the stairs while the policemen stayed down in the hall, still holding their caps.

She sat Sam down on the bed, pulling the blankets up around her like a shawl. She dabbed Sam's cheek with a handkerchief, picked some more pieces of glass from her hair, laid them down on the bedside table and then stared at her with her large, sad eyes. Sam saw a tear trickling down her cheek. She had never seen a grown-up cry before.

Annie took Sam's hands in hers and squeezed them gently, then she looked Sam directly in the eyes. 'Your Mummy and Daddy have had an accident in the car, Sam. They aren't coming home any more. They've – gone to heaven.'

Sam did not dream of the hooded man again for twenty-five years. By then he was only a dim memory in her mind. Something that had been a part of her childhood, like the toys she had forgotten and the rusting swing and the secret places that now had housing estates with neat lawns built all over them. Something she thought had gone for ever.

But he had not forgotten her.

2

Sam tapped out a row of figures onto her computer terminal, then sat back wearily and closed her eyes for a moment, the insides of her head banging and crashing like the vacuum cleaner in the corridor outside. She looked at her watch. Six-twenty. Wednesday, 22nd January. Christ, time went fast. It only seemed a few days since Christmas.

She swivelled her chair and stared through her own reflection in the window at the fine needle spray of rain that was falling silently through the darkness of the fast-emptying streets of Covent Garden outside. The wettest rain of all, the type that seemed to come at you from all sides, got inside your clothes, inside your skin, it even seemed to come up out of the pavement at you.

A draught of cold air blew steadily through the glass onto her neck and she hunched her shoulders against it, then rubbed her hands together. The heating had gone off and the office felt cold. She stared at the story board propped up beside the VDU. One coloured frame showed a sketch of a palm-fringed beach. The next showed a man and a woman in designer swimwear and designer suntans bursting out of the sea. In the next frame the woman was biting a chocolate bar which the man was holding.

'Castaway. To be eaten alone . . . or shared with a *very* good friend.'

The office had white walls and black furniture, and a skeletal green plant cowering in the corner that resisted all her efforts to make it flourish. She'd watered it, talked to it, played music to it, bathed its leaves in milk – and it stank foul for days – moved it closer to the window, further away from the window, moved it to just about every position in the room where it was possible to put a plant; but it never changed, never actually died so that they could throw it out, but never looked how it was supposed to so that it was worth keeping. Claire, with whom she shared the office, told her she reckoned it was a *house* plant, not an *office* plant. Claire had strange views on a lot of things.

The walls were covered in schedules and pinboards with memos and Polaroids and product shots and there were two desks, her own which was vaguely orderly, and Claire's, which was neat, pristine, irritatingly tidy. Claire always arranged it like that every evening before she left with a smug expression on her face, almost as if to imply she might or might not be coming back.

Sam heard the cleaner coming closer down the corridor, clunk, bang, thump, and she squeezed her eyes shut against her headache which she could scarcely distinguish from the banshee howl of the vacuum cleaner. The door opened and the roar became a thousand times worse. She looked up fit to scream if Rosa was going to try and come and vacuum in here, then she smiled as her boss, Ken Shepperd, came in and closed the door behind him.

'Hi. Sorry, I'd have been down earlier, but I had a—' He waved his right hand in the air, then circled it around as if he were winding a ball of string.

'It's OK,' she said. 'I just need to know who you're going to have to light the Castaway shoot.'

'You look pale. Feeling OK?'

'Bit of a headache. I think it may be this VDU. I'm going to get one of those filters for it.'

'I've got some aspirins.'

'It's OK, thanks.'

He walked across the office towards her, a restless man in his mid-forties in the clothes of a college student, his steely hair tousled, permanently in need of a cut, his face comfortable and creased like his denim shirt, his sharp blue eyes smiling good-naturedly. He stopped by Claire's desk.

'Tidy, isn't she?'

Sam grinned. 'Is that a hint?'

'How are you finding her?'

Claire had only been with them a few weeks. Lara, her predecessor, had left without any warning. One Monday she failed to appear and sent in a letter the next day saying she was suffering from nervous strain and her doctor had advised her to work in a less stressful environment.

'She's all right,' Sam said. 'She doesn't talk much.'

'You complained that Lara nattered too much. Maybe Claire'll cope better with the pressure.'

Sam shrugged.

'What's that look on your face mean?'

She shrugged again. 'I thought she was nice when she started – but – I don't know.'

'Give her time. She's quite efficient.'

'Yes, sir!'

He walked over and stood behind Sam's desk, staring down at the story board. 'Joncie,' he said. 'I want Joncie to light it.'

'Shall I book him?'

'Pencil him in.'

'Who do you want if he's not available?'

'I've mentioned it already to him.' He squinted down at the board. 'Castaway. Daft name for a chocolate bar.'

'I think it's all right.'

He glanced down the sequence of coloured frames, and read out aloud. 'Like a coconut, Castaway has the goodness on the inside.' He stepped back, patted his stomach and repeated the line again, in a deep bass voice. Sam laughed.

'Castaway,' he boomed. 'The chocolate bar that won't melt in the sun . . . Castaway, the world's first pre-digested food. You don't even need to eat it – just buy it and throw it straight down the lavatory.'

Sam grinned and shook her head. Ken lit a cigarette and the sweet smell tortured her. She watched him prowl around the office, staring at the schedules on the walls; eighteen commercials already booked for this year; they'd made forty-three last year. Ken charged a fee of ten thousand pounds a day for directing and the firm took a percentage of the total production cost. If he weren't still paying off his debts and his wife, he'd be a rich man by now. And if he could keep his temper and his eye for the changing fashions, he would be eventually.

'You're going to behave at the meeting tomorrow, aren't you?'

'Behave?' he said.

'Yes.' She grinned.

He nodded like a reluctant schoolboy.

'Big bucks, Ken.'

'Done the budget?'

'Just going to print it out.'

He looked at his watch, a heavy macho brute of a watch festooned with important-looking knobs, water-proof to five hundred metres (handy for the bathtub, Sam once told him). 'Fancy a quick jar?'

'No thanks. I want to get back in time to bath Nicky. I was late last night.'

'Only a quick one.'

'Hot date?'

He pointed a finger downwards. 'Snooker. Got a couple of new lads from Lowe Howard-Spinks coming over. Business, Sam,' he said, noticing her expression.

'Business!' she mocked.

The wipers of the elderly E-Type Jaguar smeared the rain into a translucent film across the windscreen, making it hard to see. She drove fast, worried Nicky might already be in bed, straining forward to see the road ahead, past the Tower of London, its battlements illuminated in a bright fuzz of light and mist, into London's docklands and slowed as she turned into Wapping High Street, trying not to shake the twenty-five-year-old car too much on the cobblestones. She passed a block of dark, unfinished apartments, and a large illuminated sign which said SHOW FLATS, and another which said RIVERSIDE HOMES – RIVERSIDE LIFESTYLES. Buy a lifestyle, she thought. I'll have a pound of salami, two melons and a lifestyle please.

She drove down the dark street, so dark it could have been a hundred years ago, and turned right past a warehouse into an unlit parking lot. She smelled the oily, salty tang of the Thames as she climbed out, hitched her briefcase from the passenger seat and locked the door carefully. She hurried across the lot through the driving rain, glancing warily at the shadows, and flinched at the sudden rattle of a hoarding in the freshening wind.

She climbed the steps into the porch and the automatic light came on with a crisp, metallic click. She punched in the code on the lock, then went inside, closing the door behind her. Her footsteps echoed as she walked in the dim light across the stone floor of the lobby, past the exposed steel girders that were painted bright red, and the two huge oak casks that were recessed into the wall. Warehouse. You could never forget it had once been a warehouse, a huge grimy Victorian Gothic warehouse.

She went into the lift that you had to go into in darkness, because the light only came on when the doors shut. Creepy. Creepy and slow. She leaned against the wall of the lift as it slowly shuffled up the four floors.

Lucky there weren't any more, she thought, or you could eat your dinner going up in it. Then it stopped with a jerk that always unbalanced her, and she walked down the corridor to her front door, unlocked it and went into their huge flat. Nicky came racing down the hallway towards her, his shirt hanging over the top of his trousers, his blond hair flopping over his face.

'Mummy! Yippee!'

She bent down and hugged him and he put his arms around her and kissed her firmly on each cheek, then he looked up at her solemnly. 'I'm a 'vestor now.'

'A vestor, Tiger?'

''Vestor! I got a porthole.'

'Porthole?' she asked, baffled.

'Yeah! I made three pounds today.'

'Three pounds? That's clever. How did you make three pounds?'

'From my porthole. Daddy showed me how.'

'What's your porthole?'

He took her hand. 'Come on, I'll show you.' He looked up at her, triumph in his wide blue eyes. 'We're going for it.'

'Are you?'

'Yeah!'

' "Yes", darling, not "yeah".'

'Yeah!' he teased, tugging his hand free and running down the corridor, turning his head back fleetingly. 'Yeah!'

She put down her briefcase, took off her coat, and followed him across the huge hallway and down the corridor to his bedroom.

'Daddy! Daddy! Show Mummy how much money we've made.' Nicky stood beside his father, who was kneeling on the red carpet in front of his little computer, a cigarette smouldering in the ashtray beside him, holding his whisky tumbler in one hand and tapping the keyboard with his other. A tall, powerfully built man, even kneeling he dwarfed the cluttered room. He turned and looked at her and smiled his nothing-has-changed-has-it? smile. 'Hi, Bugs.'

She stared at him for a moment, at his handsome, almost old-fashioned face, the sort of face that belonged more to Forties Hollywood than Eighties London, his slicked-back blond hair, his pink shirt opened at the collar, his checked braces and pin-striped trousers. Stared at the man she used to love so much, who now felt almost like a stranger.

'Good day?' he said.

'Fine.' She leaned down, more for Nicky's benefit than for anything else, brushed her cheek cursorily against his, feeling his evening stubble, and mouthed a blank kiss, like a goldfish. 'You?'

'Bit slow. Market's a bit cautious.'

'Show her, Daddy.' Nicky put his arm around his father's back, and patted him excitedly.

'We've made him a little portfolio. Put a few shares in and I'll update them each day from the Market.'

'Great,' she said flatly. 'What are we going to have? The world's youngest Yuppie?'

'Yippie!' said Nicky, jumping up and down. 'We got bats.'

'BAT, Tiger, British American Tobacco.'

The floor, shelves and windowsill were strewn with toys, mostly cars and lorries. He was nuts about cars. A monkey holding a pair of cymbals was lying across the forecourt of a Lego garage, and a robot looked as if it was about to leap off the windowsill. Her husband tapped some more figures out on the keyboard, and Nicky watched intently.

Nicky.

Nicky sensed that something had gone bad between his Mummy and his Daddy, and with a child's intuition knew his Daddy was in some way responsible. It had seemed to make him even closer to Richard. If that was possible.

His father's son. He'd nearly killed her when he was born, but he'd never really be her son. Always his father's. They were close, so close. Cars. Planes. Lego. Games. Boating. Fishing. Guns. And now the computer they'd given him for Christmas. It was always Richard who taught him, Richard who understood his toys, Richard who knew how to play with them. Richard was his mate.

'American Express down two and a half.'

'Does that mean we've lost money?'

'Afraid so.'

'Aww.'

'Bathtime, Nicky.'

'Aww – just a few minutes more.'

'No, come on, you're late already. Start running it. Mummy's going to change.' Sam went out of the room and saw Nicky's nanny coming out of the kitchen. 'Hello Helen.'

'Good evening, Mrs Curtis,' Helen smiled nervously, unsure of herself as always.

'Everything OK?'

'Fine, thank you. He's had a nice day. He did well at school. They're very pleased with his arithmetic.'

'Good. Must have got that from his father – I'm hopeless at it.'

Sam went into their bedroom and felt the same coldness she had felt in the office; it seemed to be following her around. She stared at the bright, warm colours of the painting of the reclining nude on the wall, with her massive breasts and earthy clump of pubes and sly grin that she woke up and stared at every morning. Richard liked her. Insisted on having her there. She sat down on the four-postered bed, tugged off her shoes and leaned back for a moment. Her face stared back down from the mirrored panel on the top of the bed, her hair plastered down by the rain, her face white, much too white. Mirrors. Richard had a thing about mirrors.

She stared back at the painting of the nude. Was that what the tart in the office looked like? She wondered. The tart Richard had disappeared with off to a hotel in Torquay? Did she have big tits and a sly grin?

Bitch, she thought, anger and sadness mixing around inside her. It had all been all right. Fine. Great. A neat, ordered world. Happy times. Everything going well. Everything had been just fine.

Until she found out about that. It felt as if a plug had been pulled out from inside her and everything had drained away.

She sat on the edge of Nicky's tiny bed and flicked over the pages of *Fungus the Bogeyman* on his bedside table. 'Shall I read?'

'No.' He looked quite hurt. 'Tell me a story. You tell the best stories.'

She glanced around the room. 'You promised me you were going to tidy up. All those new things you got for Christmas are going to get broken.' She stood up and walked over to a cupboard door which was ajar and opened it further. A plastic airliner fell out, and the tail section snapped off and cartwheeled along the carpet. Nicky looked as if he was about to cry.

'That was silly. Who put that in there like that?' She knelt down.

Nicky said nothing.

'Was it you?'

Slowly, he pursed his lips.

'Maybe Daddy'll be able to fix it for you tomorrow.' She lifted the pieces off the floor and put them on a chair, then sat back beside him.

'It's my birthday on Sunday, isn't it, Mummy?'

'Yes, Tiger.'

'Am I going to get more presents?'

'Not if you don't tidy these up.'

'I will. I promise.'

'Anyway, you had lots of presents for Christmas.'

'Christmas was ages ago!'

'Four weeks, Tiger.'

His face fell. 'That's not fair.'

She was taken aback at how sad he looked, and stroked his cheek lightly with her hand. 'Yes, you're going to have more presents.'

Bribes. I'm buying his love. Buying my own child's love.

Shit.

'Yippee!' He pummelled the sides of his bed excitedly.

'Come on now, calm down. It's Wednesday. You've got four more days.'

'Three more.'

She laughed. 'OK. Three and a half.' Her headache was feeling a bit better.

Nicky puffed out his cheeks and contorted his face, deep in thought, counting on his fingers. 'Three and a quarter. Tell me a story now. Tell me a story about dragons.'

'You've had one about dragons. I told you last night.'

He sat back expectantly, blinking his large blue eyes. 'Go on, Mummy. Pretend it isn't finished. Pretend the dragon comes back to life and chases the man that killed him.'

'OK. Once upon a time in a land called Nicky-Not-Here-Land, there lived a horrible man.'

'Why was he horrible?'

'Because he was.'

'What did he look like?'

'Horrible.'

He lay back, and was asleep before she had finished. She stood up and he opened his eyes. She bent down and kissed him.

'Night, Tiger.'

'You didn't finish the story!'

Caught, she realised. Sharp. Kids were razor sharp. 'I'll finish tomorrow. All right?'

'All right,' he said sleepily.

'Night night.'

'Night night, Mummy.'

'Do you want the light on or off?'

He hesitated. 'On please.'

She blew him a kiss and closed the door quietly behind her.

Sam watched Harrison Ford dancing with Kelly Mc-Gillis in the headlights of his beat-up station waggon on the television screen. Her eyes smarted and she felt a surge of sadness for all that she – or they – had lost. For all that could never be the same again.

Richard slouched on the sofa in front of the television, whisky tumbler filled to its invariable four-finger measure beside him, and the bottle of Teacher's a few inches further away, almost empty. The gas log fire flickered in the grate the far side of him, and Sam shivered in the draught that blew in from the Thames through the plate-glass windows that stretched the entire width of the flat's living area.

The lighting in the room was low: just two table lamps were on, and there was a soft orange glow from the streetlighting across the river in Bermondsey. Sam turned her gaze away from the television and continued on around the oak refectory table, setting a red wine goblet at each place. 'How many glasses do you want out, Richard?'

'Uh?'

'Glasses. How many do you want out? I'm laying the table for tomorrow.'

'There's going to be eleven of us.'

'How many glasses each?' she said, slightly irritated.

'Three. We're having Chablis and claret. Folatières '83, Philippe Leclerc, then Calon Ségur '62. That's the last of my '62s. And a Sauternes – really good one – Coutet de Barsac, '71.' He picked up the tumbler and drained half of it, then lit a cigarette. 'Harrison Ford,' he said, blinking at the screen. 'Bloody good movie this.' He drained the glass, placed his four fingers carefully around the base, and poured the remainder of the whisky from the bottle. 'You'll like the Chablis.'

'Good,' she said.

'Archie's a real wine man, know what I mean? First growth, no shit. Three hundred quid a bottle touch for lunch – Lafites and all that stuff. Style! You'll like Archie. He's a good boy.'

'I think we should put one for Perrier as well. Everyone always wants it.' She looked at him, but he was engrossed again in the television. 'Are you serving port?'

'Yah.'

'I'll put port glasses out as well.'

'He's a big player, Archie.'

'Then you should have a nice game with him.'

'City, Sam. He's a big player in the City.'

'Perhaps he can teach Nicky something, too,' She

went over to the cabinet in the corner, and pulled out more glasses. The wind was howling outside, slapping the black water of the Thames against the piers below and shaking the rigging of the yachts. She could see the glints of light on the waves, the dark hulls of the lighters moored midstream. Bleak, she thought, turning away and carrying the tray to the table. 'Is this famous Andreas definitely coming?'

'Oh – er – yah.' Richard shifted about on the sofa and took a gulp of his whisky.

'So I'm finally going to meet him. What's his surname again?'

'Berensen.'

'Does he have a place in London?'

'No, he's just over on business.'

'From Switzerland? What exactly does he do? He's some sort of a banker, isn't he?'

Richard scratched the back of his head. 'Ah – yah – a banker.'

'A real gnome?'

'Yah.' Richard laughed, slightly uncomfortably. 'Actually he's quite tall.'

'Is he your biggest client now?'

'Yah. Sort of, I suppose.' He was sounding evasive, Sam thought, frowning. 'How's work?' he asked.

'Hectic. I should still be there now.'

'That guy Ken's making you work too hard. All this travelling you're doing is crazy. You're travelling too much, you know, Bugs.' He turned round.

His face, which had always looked fit and lean, had been sallow and lined lately, much older than his thirty-three years, and in the flickering light from the screen and the fire she suddenly caught a glimpse of what he would look like when he was old, when he no longer had the strength and energy that animated him and he started to shrivel and cave in, like a ghoul from a horror movie. It frightened her. Ageing frightened her.

'I have to travel.'

He drained two fingers of whisky and dragged hard on his cigarette again. The smell tantalised her, tempted her, and her refusal to weaken was making her irritated.

'I don't think you're spending enough time with Nicky,' he said.

'I spent three years with him, Richard. I quit my career for him.'

He leaned over and crushed his cigarette out. 'Dealer's choice, darling.'

'What do you mean?'

'It was your choice.'

'Our choice,' she said. 'I gave up three years. What did you give up? Why don't you give up three years?'

'Don't be ridiculous.'

'I'm not being ridiculous.'

'Bugs, I don't mind you working, but what you're doing is crazy. You're working all hours of the day and night, you bring your work home, half the time you spend roaring around Europe, jumping on and off aeroplanes. You're always off somewhere. France. Holland. Germany. Spain. Bulgaria. You went to Bulgaria about six times last year. I think you're ignoring Nicky. You're not being a good mother to him.'

The anger that was rising inside her went flat, as if it had been lanced, and she felt a sharp pang of guilt. She sat down on the dining chair, feeling limp, as something uncomfortable echoed from her own childhood.

She thought about her own childhood and how life had dumped on her then. She thought about her marriage and her happiness and the forgetting that had happened. Perhaps she had forgotten too much? Maybe it wasn't only children that could feel neglected and unwanted. Maybe adults could too. Maybe that's why it had happened.

3

'Something's wrong.'

'What's wrong?'

'Something.'

Sam heard the voices, low, murmuring, muted, like a snatch of conversation from across the room at a cocktail party, and stiffened. She turned around, craning her neck over the back of her seat, trying to see where they had come from, but the man and the woman behind her were asleep. She listened, but could hear only the sound of the aircraft's engines: a distant churning, like a dishwasher. Then the cycle changed, and she felt the plane begin to sink down into the cloud below.

Flying never normally bothered her, but suddenly she felt nervous. She stared uneasily at the trails of rain that streaked the window, and the swirling grey beyond. Landing. Her hands felt clammy with perspiration, and she realised she was shivering.

She wanted to put the clock back, not be on the plane at all. Stupid, unnecessary trip, she thought. Richard was right, she was jumping on and off too many planes. She wished she had not jumped on this one. Bucket seats; trying to save Ken money. Charter airlines took risks, someone told her. Calm down, Sam, she said to herself. Calm down.

There was a ping, and the 'No Smoking' sign lit up on the panel in front of her. Then another bell, higher pitched, faintly musical, like the gong of an elevator announcing its arrival. Beng-bong. The sound irritated her.

'This is Captain Walker.' His matey voice irritated her as well. There was a hum and a screech and a loud click. 'We've started our descent and expect to be on the apron in about twenty-five minutes. The weather in Sofia is cold – one degree Celsius and it's snowing. We hope you have enjoyed your flight with us and that you have a pleasant stay in Bulgaria. On behalf of us all, I'd like to thank you for flying Chartair, and hope you choose to fly with us again.' His voice was tired, clipped ex-RAF English. He was having to make the effort to sound friendly, and not as if it was just another charter flight, which it was; not as if he was tired and bored with dumping another load of cheap tourists in another cheap resort.

A little girl's head popped over the seat back in front of her. 'Hallo,' she said.

'Hallo,' Sam replied.

The girl's head disappeared and she heard giggling. 'I said hallo to the lady behind!'

Perspiration was trickling down Sam's face and she felt sick. She unbuckled her belt, slid across the empty seats beside her and walked unsteadily along the aisle which was sloping away from her, down towards the toilets, pushing against the seat backs to prevent herself from running forwards, waiting to be challenged by a stewardess, but they were busy stowing the duty frees and had not noticed her.

She reached the front of the aeroplane, still shaking, and was surprised to see the door to the flight deck was open. She stared through at the orange dials of the instruments and the captain and the first officer, in their white shirts, in their seats.

The first officer turned his head towards the captain, and she could hear him speak, clearly.

'Derek,' he said, 'there is definitely something wrong.'

The captain flicked a switch beside him, and spoke loudly and dearly. 'This is Chartair Six-Two-Four. Confirm we are on initial approach.'

A voice crackled back, sharp, tinny, with a precise, broken English accent. 'Chartair Six-Two-Four. This is Sofia tower. We confirm initial approach. Runway Two-One. We have visibility of only two hundred metres – check your landing minima.'

'Sofia tower. Chartair Six-Two-Four. Confirming runway Two-One.'

The captain leaned forward in his seat and adjusted a dial on the instrument panel. The first officer stared around. She could see the worry on his face, could feel his fear, as if it were a blanket of ice.

The microphone crackled again, and she heard the voice, more urgent. 'Chartair Six-Two-Four. We have you identified on radar. You are too low. I say again too low. Climb to seven thousand feet immediately.'

'We are at seven thousand feet,' said the captain calmly, a trace of weariness in his voice as if the man in the tower had become infected with the same irrational fear as the first officer.

'We have you identified on radar,' said the controller. 'You are at four thousand five hundred. Check your altimeter setting.' His voice rose in excitement and panic. 'Climb. Climb immediately! Discontinue your approach. I say again, discontinue your approach!'

'I have seven thousand reading on both altimeters. Please check your radar.' There was irritability creeping through the calm.

'Climb, Derek,' the first officer shouted. 'The mountains, for Chrissake. Fucking climb!'

'We're clear. The mountains are five thousand ceiling.'

There was a sharp click and the toilet door in front of her opened. A man stood there, in a black hood with slits for his eyes and mouth.

She reeled back, and he clamped a black leather-gloved hand over her mouth, cracking her head back hard against the bulkhead. She smelled the leather of the glove, new fresh leather, flung her head violently away, tried to scream, tried to back away, felt a lever behind her jamming into her back; then the black leather glove came over her face again and she ducked, heard a tremendous bang and the hissing of air, then suddenly she was out of the aircraft, spinning wildly in the turbulence, and the deafening howling of the freezing wind and the engines, spinning through a crazed icy vortex, falling, falling, falling through a blackness that seemed to go on for ever.

Then she was free of it, floating in the cold grey cloud as if it was water. She could push her arms and move through it. She went further away, swimming effortlessly, until she could see the silver Boeing in the distance, cloud swirling around it like tendrils of weed as it flew into the dark grey shape that loomed upwards in front of it, a shape that was barely discernible from the cloud.

At first there was silence. The aircraft seemed to go on for a long time into the solid wall of the mountain, and she wondered for a moment whether it was her imagination, or just a strangely shaped cloud. Then the tail section flew away and began to cartwheel downwards. It bounced up for an instant off a ridge, and something began to spray out of it, like champagne, and float down behind it. Luggage, she realised with a sickening feeling.

It bounced again, rose up, and did a half-turn in slow

26

motion. The stream of suitcases that followed bounced in the same place, deflecting in the same way, except some of them burst open leaving a wake of fluttering clothes.

A solitary passenger, strapped in his seat, flew up through the clothes, followed by another, then a third, their limbs shaking about like toys emptying from a child's cupboard as they plummeted back down.

There was a boom, and a ball of flame rose high up above. A fiercely blazing object joined the dance down the mountainside, showering sparks into the greyness all around it. An engine. It ploughed into the snow below her, hissing. Near it she could see the tail section, a stubby dark silhouette resting on the white snow, the top of the tail fin bent over at a right angle, the word 'Chartair' clearly visible, and part of the emblem of a prancing tiger and letters next to it G.Z.T.A.E.

And then there was a silence that frightened her. The cloud swirled around her, until she could no longer see the ground, until she could no longer tell whether she was lying face down or up. Panic began to grip her. She wanted to see Nicky, to hold him, squeeze him. She wanted to hug Richard, tell him she was sorry, tell him she forgave him, tell him she was sorry she had worked so damned hard. 'Where are you?' She turned her body over, then over again, trying to break away from the cold grey tendrils that were entwined around her. 'Let me go. Please let me go and see them. Just five minutes. Please. That's all. Five minutes.'

They tightened around her.

'Let me go!'

The air was getting warmer now, stifling; it was getting harder to breathe. 'Let me go!' she screamed, punching out with her fists, swirling, twisting.

She felt a cool breeze on her face.

'Bugs?'

Richard's voice, she thought, puzzled.

'Bugs?'

She saw a flat pool of light, and Richard standing near her in a striped shirt and paisley boxer shorts.

Different. The light was different. A dial blinked at her, orange like the dial of the aircraft, 0500. 0500. 0501.

'OK, Bugs?'

Richard was standing over her.

'OK Bugs?' he said again.

She nodded. 'Yes – I—'

He frowned, then struggled with the floppy arm of his shirt, and she heard the pop as the cufflink pierced the starch. Gold links with his initials on one side and his family crest on the other. Her wedding present to him. They'd come in a small wine-coloured box, and cost £216. Odd, the details you could remember. She stared at the reclining nude on the wall, at her face in the mirror above the bed, at the light streaming in from the bathroom door.

'A dream,' she said. 'I was having a dream.'

'You were making a horrible sound, really horrible.' He turned away toward the wall mirror, and knotted his tie. As he pulled it tight, she felt something pull tight around her own throat. Dread seeped through her, hung around her, filled the room. The black hood with the slits came out of the door at her and the black leather glove clamped over her mouth. She shivered.

Richard struggled into his trousers, disentangled his red braces and pulled on his silver armbands. She had loved to watch him dress when they had first started sleeping together. He was fastidious about his clothes. Shirts with double cuffs; trousers with buttons for braces. Proper trousers, he called them. She wanted to hold him suddenly, to hug him, feel him, to make sure he was real, still there; that her world was intact.

And then the revulsion as she remembered and she shrank back in the bed away from him, and shook with a sudden spasm of – fear?

'What were you dreaming about?'

'It – I – nothing. Just a nightmare.'

You're afraid to tell it, she thought.

Afraid that if you tell it—

'Must dash.' He leaned down to kiss her, and she smelled the coconut shampoo in his damp hair, his sweet Paco Rabanne aftershave and the strong trace of last night's garlic through the minty toothpaste on his breath. She felt a soft wet kiss on her cheek.

'Busy day?' she said, wanting him to stay just a moment longer.

'Japan. I reckon Tokyo's about to start going bonkers.'

'Don't be late. It would be nice if you could help me get things ready tonight.'

'Oh Christ, yah. Our dinner party.'

'It's for your clients, Richard.'

'I'll be back in good time.'

The front door opened, then slammed shut. She closed her eyes but opened them again, afraid of going back to sleep. She looked at the clock again. 0509. In a quarter of an hour he would be at his desk, chatting to Tokyo. Dealing. The Nikkei Dow. Gambling on equities, warrants, options, futures, currencies. So many variables. So many imponderables. He'd got angry with her once when she told him his job was like being a croupier in a high-tech casino.

The door opened and Nicky came padding sleepily in.

'Hallo, Tiger. You're up early.'

'I can't sleep.'

29

She put her hand out and tousled his hair. Soft, real. He shied away just a fraction, then put his head under her hand again for more.

'Give Mummy a kiss.'

Damp. It felt like a miniature version of Richard's. 'Why can't you sleep, Tiger?'

'I had a nightmare.'

'What was it about?'

'It was about a horrible man. A monster.'

She sat up and hugged him. 'That's because I told you a story about one, isn't it?'

He nodded solemnly. He was a serious child sometimes. Always thinking things through.

'He ate me.'

She stared at the forlorn expression on his face. 'I bet you tasted good.'

He stamped his foot on the carpet. 'Don't. That's not funny.'

'Mummy's got to get ready. Want to sleep in our bed?'

'No.' He wandered off, shuffling his slippers across the floor. As he went, she saw the aircraft sliding silently into the solid wall of the mountain. The tail section cartwheeling down. The luggage spewing out. The boom, and the ball of flame. She slipped unsteadily out of bed and walked to the bathroom, shivering, from the images, from the chill air, from the dark cloud of foreboding that hung over her.

A bad dream, that's all. Forget it.

She heard the thump of the engines of a launch going by, up river; deep, steady, rhythmic.

Then realised it wasn't a launch at all. It was her own heartbeat.

4

Sam sat in the reception of Urquhart Simeon Mcpherson, holding the Castaway story board on the sofa beside her, watching Ken pacing restlessly up and down, hands sunk into the pockets of his battered leather coat over his denim jacket and blue jeans, his black boots immaculately shiny: his uniform. Scruffy clothes, but always immaculate boots.

Two girls came in through the door chatting, nodded at the receptionist and went down a corridor. A helmeted despatch rider with 'Rand Riders' printed on his back waded in and thrust a package over the counter; he stood waiting for the signature, bandy-legged in his body-hugging leathers, like an insect from outer space.

Ken sat on the arm of the sofa, above her. 'You all right?'

'Fine,' she said.

'You look a bit tense.'

'I'm fine,' she repeated. 'Waiting like this always feels like being back at school. Waiting to see teacher.'

He pulled a pack of Marlboro from his jacket pocket, and shook out a cigarette. He clicked his battered Zippo and inhaled deeply, then ran a hand through his hair.

'Production meetings,' he said grimly.

Sam smiled. 'I know you don't like them.'

'That copywriter – Jake wozzizname – gives me the creeps.'

'He's all right,' Sam said.

'He gives you the creeps too?'

'No.'

'Something's given you the creeps.' He looked at her quizzically.

She felt her face redden, and turned away. 'Maybe I'm a bit tired. Early start.'

'What you doing this weekend?'

'Nicky's birthday party on Sunday.'

'Six?'

She nodded.

'Having a big one?'

'Nineteen of them. We're having Charlie Chaplin films and a Punch and Judy.'

'All his smart little friends?' He tilted back his head and peered down his nose, feigning an aristocratic accent. 'Rupert . . . Julian . . . Henrietta. Dominic, Hamish, Inigo and Charlotte?'

'And the Honourable Sarah Hamilton-Deeley.'

'Ay say. The Honourable Sarah Hamilton-Deeley. Sounds ripping good fun.' He dropped the accent and stroked his chin. 'Hope you think of me, down at the chip shop roughing it with the hoi polloi.'

Sam grinned, then saw something sad in his face. She wondered sometimes whether he liked his independence, or whether he would like to be married again, have kids. She realised how little she knew about him, about the private Ken Shepperd. Here in this environment, where part of him belonged, part of him was comfortable, yet another part of him seemed to yearn to be somewhere else, doing something else, away from the bullshit and the glitz; a man snared by his mistakes and his success.

'I'll save you a jelly,' she said.

'With a jelly baby in it?'

'Of course.'

He looked up at the ceiling, then the walls. 'It's a poxy room this. Do you know what their billings were last year?'

'Eighty-two million.'

'And they can't even get themselves a decent reception area.'

Sam stared down at the table sprinkled with magazines and newspapers. *Campaign. Marketing. Media Week. The Times.* The *Independent.* The *Financial Times.* The carpet had been specially woven with the agency's logo of concentric squares receding forever inside each other, like a television picture of a television picture of a television picture. A huge version of the logo dominated the rear wall, surrounded by framed ads, wrappers and packaging. A Ferrari gleamed in the shine of a patent leather shoe on a girl's foot. A man with a dazzling wholesome smile held up a toothbrush. A can of old-fashioned rice pudding was several feet high, Warhol-style.

'I think it's quite smart,' she said.

'Sorry to keep you.' Charlie Edmunds came into the room, tall, almost gangly, with a floppy mop of fair hair. He stood in his cavalry twills, Hush Puppies and Jermyn Street shirt like an overgrown schoolboy. God, people were starting to look so young, and they concentrated so hard on not being young. The young were all earnest, serious, like Charlie, trying to act like forty-year-olds. And the forty-year-olds desperately wanted to be in their early twenties. 'Sam, nice to see you. Ken. Looking well.'

They followed him up a flight of stairs, along a corridor and into a windowless room with blue fabric wallcovering, and a long blue table in Scandinavian wood with matching chairs. There was an open Filofax on the table, several coloured sketches and photographs. In the middle of the table were a cluster of Castaway bars in silver foil wrapping with lagoon-blue writing. The room had a fresh, woody smell, and there was a soft monotone hiss from a heating duct.

'The others'll be here in a moment,' said Charlie. 'Sorry to drag you over at such short notice, but this is an account we've pitched very hard for and they've decided to pull this particular product launch forwards, so we haven't a lot of time.' As if to underline this, he looked down at his slim Omega wristwatch.

Sam glanced at her own watch, then up at an abstract painting on the wall. It was no doubt deep and meaningful; everything inside the portals of Urquhart Simeon Mcpherson was deep and meaningful and done for a reason, but its immediate identity eluded her. The colours reminded her vaguely of a bedroom in a Holiday Inn. The door opened and two men came in. One, in his mid-twenties, was short, belligerent-looking and thin as a drainpipe. He wore a black unstructured jacket over a black collarless shirt and shiny black tapered trousers. His dark hair was cropped short at the front and hung in a long mane down the back, and his face was long and thin, as if it had been crushed between two elevator doors. His nose, also long and thin, appeared to be bolted to his face by his eyes which were much too close together. The other man, slightly older, was dressed in baggy white; the sides of his head were shorn to stubble and he had a thick clump of hair on top. He wore round granny glasses, and looked slightly better fed and better humoured.

Sam had met them several times. They always reminded her of a couple of beat poets who hadn't yet been discovered.

'Jake, Zurbrick – you know Sam and Ken,' said Charlie.

They nodded at each other. Zurbrick, the art director, smiled genially, shook their hands, adjusted his glasses and dug his hands in his pockets, and Jake, the copywriter, nodded once, curtly, exuding seriousness and a faint air of superiority.

They sat down and Sam put the story board on the table, opened her briefcase and pulled out her Filofax and her budget folder.

'Right,' said Charlie. 'You've – ah – you've both seen the story board—' He leaned forward and picked up a Castaway bar. 'And the – ah – product.' He seemed nervous in the company of the other two.

Sam picked up a pencil on the table in front of her and tapped it lightly on the Urquhart Simeon Mcpherson monogrammed memo pad which had also been provided.

'How's the budget looking, Sam?'

'It's a bit over.' She pulled it out of the folder and passed it across to him. He glanced down and turned to the total. 'Oh yah, that's OK. They'll live with that. There's going to be one suit going as well – have to budget that in, first class – and for the recce too.'

'Who's the suit?' said Ken.

'The marketing director of Grand Spey Foods. He's all right, Ken,' he said quickly. 'Won't give you any trouble.'

'All suits give trouble.'

'I think he's got a bit of crumpet out there.' Charlie smiled. 'You won't see much of him.'

Ken grunted noncommittally.

Sam saw the diminutive Jake sitting with his hands on the table as if he was waiting to be fed, eyeing Ken disdainfully. She knew what he was thinking. *You're an old fart*, he was thinking. *We should be using a younger director.*

'You've shot in the Seychelles before, Ken, haven't you?' said Charlie.

He nodded.

Charlie had warned her that Jake had been against Ken, that he wanted Tom Land, a twenty-four-year-old whizz-kid director.

'What's it like?'

Ken stared at Jake. 'Poisonous spiders. Snakes. Massive land crabs. Hostile natives.'

Jake blanched, and his face twitched. Charlie grinned.

'And gorgeous women,' said Zurbrick in his Brummy accent.

'We have to make a presentation at the client's headquarters in a fortnight. They've asked for the director and producer to be present.' Charlie looked at Ken, and he nodded.

'Where are they?'

'Just outside Leeds.'

The weather in Sofia is cold – one degree Celsius and it's snowing. We hope you have enjoyed your flight with us and that you have a pleasant stay in Bulgaria.

'All right with you, Sam?'

Charlie's voice was distant. She looked up with a start.

'All right with you, Sam?'

'I'm sorry?'

They were all looking at her oddly.

'Leeds? Presentation?'

'Fine,' she said. 'Yes, no problem.' She pulled herself up in her chair, smiled at Charlie, Zurbrick and then at Jake, who stared back like a bird interrupted from picking flesh off a carcass.

'The script and story board you have is still rough, of course,' said Zurbrick, 'but it's the pivot for the whole campaign. We're looking for great subtlety combined with high impact.'

Sam scanned the scenes on the story board.

'The big difference with this product – the unique selling point – is the health angle. It's not going to be perceived just as a sweet, it's going to be pitched as a Personal Nourishment System.'

'A *what*?' said Ken.

'A Personal Nourishment System.'

'I seem to remember when I was young, we used to call them chocolate bars,' Ken said.

Jake stared at Ken as if he was a relic in a museum. 'Chocolate bars,' he said, 'went out with the ark. We're talking concepts here. We're talking a breakthrough.' He was jigging up and down in his chair, then he jammed his elbow down on the table and leaned forward intently. 'This campaign is going to be in the text books in ten years' time.'

'This is different, Ken, very different, Ken,' said Zurbrick. 'It's got everything you need. The client believes it's the first confection to contain a totally self-sufficient diet. It's got a full daily vitamin programme. Protein. Glucose. Organic coconut. Coconut's high in nutrients. Roughage. It helps avoid wrinkles, senility, sunburn. Gives you energy. All you need with this is water.'

'Just water?'

He nodded.

'You could live on these?' said Ken.

'Absolutely.'

Ken shook his head. Sam shot him a warning glance.

'The big trick with this bar,' said Zurbrick, 'is that the biscuit part is on the outside. It's brilliant. You take it in the heat, and the chocolate can't melt, can't go sticky. It's eater-friendly. The wrapping's airtight, watertight. It's a real serious survival food. It isn't just a chocolate bar – it's a Nineteen Nineties High-Tech food. It's state-of-the-art nutrition.'

Ken looked at him as if he was mad.

'Two angles, Ken. One, the contents – they're amazing. Two, the image. Castaways are eaten by successful people.'

'We're talking energy,' said Jake. 'Energy and youth. Street cred,' he said, staring pointedly at Ken. 'We don't want this looking like some bloody Bounty ad from the Sixties, we don't want Robinson Crusoe's desert island. We're talking twenty-first century, y'know? This is a twenty-first century desert island. We don't want it looking like a bloody desert island at all, we want it to look like it's something from space. This is young high-aspirant food. Street cred food. We're pitching this at the people who don't have time for lunch. We're going to change society with this food. Remember Gordon Gekko? Michael Douglas? When he said 'lunch is for wimps'? Castaway is lunch. It's the *new* lunch.' He jabbed his finger forward, his eyes twitching as if they had come loose. 'This is what we're pitching. This is what the script is all about. This is the way I've written it.'

Sam glanced down at her memo pad. She had drawn a picture of an aeroplane.

'Eater-friendly. Shit. What a load of crap. What does eater-hostile food do? Bite you back?' Ken shook his head. 'They believe it, Sam, don't they? They really believe it!' He switched on the windscreen wipers.

Sam watched them, stubby, jerky, slightly clumsy; they more than anything betrayed the Bentley's age, she thought.

'Personal Nourishment Systems,' he said. 'The psychology's all wrong, that's what worries me. People need to eat together, need to sit around a table. What are we going to end up with? A world full of isolated morons wandering around with their Walkmans eating their Personal Nourishment Systems?'

She smiled. 'I thought it tasted quite nice.'

'Tasted like a Bounty with biscuit.'

The wiper in front of her smeared the water without wiping it away. Watching the road ahead was like staring through frosted glass. She saw ripples of movement, streaks of brake lights, traffic lights, distorted pedestrians like huge upright fish.

SALE. SALE. SALE. The signs flashed out at her from the windows of Kensington High Street. Ken leaned over and pulled a packet of chewing gum from the glove locker. 'Want some?'

'No, thanks.'

'Traffic's bad. We should have gone down the Cromwell Road.' He unwrapped a stick of Juicy Fruit and put it in his mouth.

She smelt the sweet smell for an instant, and then it was gone. She stared down the long, midnight blue bonnet. Brake lights, shop lights, traffic lights. Dark grey sky. Dismal. The last few bargains in the shops, then in a week or so they would be dressing the models with their summer clothes, stiff mannequins with silly gazes in bright bikinis and summer frocks. In February. Daft.

It was strange sitting so high up, in the deep wide seat, like an armchair. Her feet were buried in the soft lambswool carpet and she smelled the rich smell of the reupholstered leather. Her uncle had a car that was high off the ground and smelled of leather. A Rover. She always sat in the back, while her uncle and aunt sat without talking in the front. Sunday afternoons. The ritual drive in the country from their dull house in Croydon. Staring at fields like those in which once she had run free and played. Where once . . . but

39

that had been a long time ago and the memory was forgotten.

Leather. The smell of the leather glove in the dream. So clear. The black hood with the slits. A shiver rippled through her. The nerve was still there, raw, exposed. You could never really forget; only paper over the cracks.

When her parents had died, her aunt and uncle had inherited her without much grace, without much enthusiasm. They hadn't wanted her. She was an intrusion into their lives, into their flat childless tranquillity.

Her uncle was a morose man with a droopy moustache, irritated by everything: a noise, by lights left on, by the morning news. He shuffled interminably around the gloomy house tapping the barometer and muttering about the weather, although he never did anything that would have been affected by it. Sat in his armchair picking at his stamp collection with his tweezers, occasionally looking up. 'A Vancouver Island ten cents blue. Interesting.' Then he'd return to his silence.

Her aunt was a cold, humourless woman, who forever blamed God for her lot in life and went to church every Sunday to thank him for it. She was going through life amassing credits for the next life. She had one for marrying her husband. One for taking on Sam. One for having the vicar and his wife round for tea. One for joining the Samaritans – God knows what advice she dispensed – one for taking a purse she found in the street to the police. She had over three hundred credits written in a notebook Sam had once discovered. That had been twenty years ago. Sam wondered how many more she had added since.

The past was a strange place. Images changed with time. It tried to deceive you with its jerky black and white movies, with its faded photographs, its rust, wrinkles, its stubby wipers. Tried to pretend it had always been that way. Made it difficult to remember that everything was modern once; that everything around her now, in the street, in the shop windows, would be old one day, too.

The rain rattled hard for a second, then faded, as if a child had thrown a handful of pebbles. She turned and glanced out of the side window. The black print on the news vendor's billboard flashed at her like a single frame of a film and was gone.

'Stop, Ken!'

'Stop what?'

'Stop the car, for Christ's sake! Stop the car!' she yelled, groping for the door handle, pulling it, pushing open the door as he found a gap in front of a taxi and pulled into the kerb. There was the ring of a bicycle bell, and a cyclist swerved, scraping his wheel along the kerb, shouting angrily.

She fell out of the car, stumbled onto the pavement, and ran back to the news vendor. '*Standard*,' she said, grabbing the paper, pulling her purse out of her bag, fumbling, trying to open it, rattling the coins, spilling them around her. Then she stopped, oblivious to the stinging iciness of the rain, and stared down at the front page headline.

163 DEAD IN BULGARIA AIR DISASTER

Underneath was a photograph. The tail section of the aircraft, a dark silhouette resting on snow, the top of the tail-fin bent over at a right angle and part of the Chartair prancing tiger emblem clearly visible with letters next to it.

G.Z.T.A.E.

Chartair Six-Two-Four, she mouthed silently to herself, watching the newsprint darkening from the rain.

'Bulgaria has confirmed that a Boeing 727 belonging

to Chartair crashed this morning with the loss of all 155 passengers and eight crew. Full details have still not been released, but the plane is believed to have crashed into mountains whilst trying to land in poor visibility.'

She did not need to read any further. Turning, she walked slowly back to the waiting car.

She knew exactly what had happened.

'What is it?' dimly, she heard Ken's voice. 'Sam? . . . Hallo? . . . Anybody home?'

She pulled the Bentley's door closed, and stared again at the headlines and the photograph.

'What is it, Sam? What's the matter? Do you know someone on that plane?'

She looked ahead blankly, then pulled her handkerchief out of her bag and wiped the water away from her face. She felt more trickling down her cheeks and wiped that away too. Immediately they were wet again. She closed her eyes tightly, felt her chest heaving and sniffed hard, trying to stop the sobbing, but she could not.

She felt Ken's hand, tender, lightly on her wrist. 'Who was it?' he said. 'Who was on that plane?'

She sat in silence for a long while, listening to the rain and the sound of the traffic passing by.

'Me,' she said. 'I was on that plane.'

5

'Up their bottoms.'

'No!'

'It's true. They do.'

'I don't believe you.'

Richard picked up his wine glass, grinning drunkenly,

and swirled his wine around. 'They stick gerbils up their bottoms.'

'Honestly?'

Sam watched Sarah Rowntree's bright pampered face through the silver candelabra. The lights of a boat slipped past the window; she could hear the faint throbbing of its engine above the chatter.

'They put them in plastic bags then stick them up their bottoms.'

'I can't believe it!'

A draught of cold air, stronger than the others, bent the candle flames, and she watched the light dancing off the diamonds, the cutlery, the glistening cheeks. Friends. Dinner parties. She loved giving dinner parties.

Normally.

Her favourite way of entertaining. Cocktail parties were a hassle: small talk, good for prospecting business, that was all. Supper parties were as bad. You ended up perched on the end of an armchair, attempting to eat from a paper plate, with a dip on the side that didn't fit your wine glass, a paper plate that was always too small and bent when you tried to cut your ham and dumped your food on the floor if you were lucky and in your lap if you weren't.

Dinner parties were the civilised way. A few friends. Good food. Good conversation.

Normally.

Not tonight.

Tonight nothing fitted. Neither the food, nor the guests, nor her dress which was driving her nuts. The bouillabaisse starter had mostly disintegrated. Harriet O'Connell announced she had become allergic to fish, blaming pollution, and Guy Rowntree said he didn't eat garlic, so they'd split the one avocado she'd found in the fruit bowl.

43

The venison looked as if it had been cremated. The juniper berries in the casserole had fused into a thick, bitter sludge and the sauce had separated, drifting around on top like an oil slick.

And how the hell was she to know that juniper berries murdered claret?

It was Archie, on her right, who told her, informed her, lectured her. Archie Cruickshank – *You'll like Archie – he's a good boy . . . a big player – a real wine man, know what I mean?* – Archie with his wide blotchy face and his veins popping out, his fat belly and his pudgy fingers and his nose inside his wine glass like a pig sniffing for truffles. Archie had bored her and Bamford O'Connell, sitting on her left, rigid with vintages. ''78's much better than the '83.'

'Oh really?'

'Oh yes, absolutely. Shouldn't be drinking these '83s for at least another five years.'

'No?'

'The '82s are very underrated. Depends on the grower, of course.'

'Of course.'

He held his goblet up to the light and peered at it, keeping it at a distance as though it contained raw sewage. 'Pity about the claret. Assertive little wine, the '62. Should have been drunk a year or two ago, of course – but ruined by the juniper berries anyway. Give it such a metallic taste. Surprised Richard didn't warn you about that.'

'Yes, well, he's full of secrets.'

'Thought he was a bit of a connoisseur?'

She felt a breeze blow again, and sensed the huge medieval iron chandelier above them move a fraction. She looked up. It had light bulbs now, turned down low, in place of the thick candles it had once held. Then she looked along the table at the guests: at Andreas, down towards the far end, near Richard. Andreas Berensen, the Swiss banker who sat, hardly talking, watching, smiling silently to himself as if he was above all this. Tall, stiff, athletic-looking, in his late forties or early fifties, a cold, rather correct face with a high forehead, his fair hair neatly groomed each side of his head but thinned to a light fuzz on top. And a black leather glove on his right hand which he had not taken off. He picked up his wine glass and drank, caught Sam's eye, gave a smile that was almost a smirk and put his glass back down.

She felt the cold shiver again. The same cold shiver when he had come in the door and shaken her hand, shaken it with the black leather glove. Like the glove in the dream. Daft. Don't be daft.

Christ.

So much was churning through her mind. Guilt. Anger. I could have saved them she'd said to Ken, and he'd looked back at her gently and told her hundreds of people had dreams about air disasters and there was nothing she could have done; told her that if she'd rung the airline they'd have treated her the way they treated hundreds of cranks that called them every week.

But the anger raged on inside her. Anger and bewilderment.

Why? How? Did I really dream it?

The back of her dress was making her angry too; she couldn't get it comfortable, couldn't get it to sit right without pulling in one direction. She wriggled her shoulders, tried to ease the back up. She'd already gone out, once, to her bedroom, and ripped out the shoulder pads. Now she felt she wanted to go and put them back in. She wriggled her shoulders around again and felt the label scratching the base of her neck.

Archie shoved the rim of his Sauternes against his damp lips, tilted it and made a noise like a draining bathtub. A thin rivulet of wine dribbled down onto his tie. He had food all over him as well. She wondered if his wife dumped him in the washing machine when they got home. 'This is good,' he said condescendingly. 'Really quite good indeed. Gets mugged by the trifle, of course.'

She glanced at Bamford O'Connell, sitting on her left. One of Richard's oldest friends. With his raffish, centre-parted hair, his crimson velvet jacket and ancient yellow silk bow-tie, he looked more like an Edwardian dandy than a psychiatrist. His wife, Harriet, frumpily bohemian, who always looked as if she ought to be wearing sandals even when she wasn't, was sitting in the middle of the table, lecturing Peter Rawlings, a stockbroker, on ecological responsibility. Green Awareness.

'You see all we are is sponge, we're just sponges,' she informed him in her shrill, earnest, church bazaar voice. 'We absorb our environment like sponges.'

'There's a Futures market in sponges,' Peter Rawlings murmured.

It had been a mistake putting them next to each other. They had nothing in common and he was looking bored. She wished she had him on her right instead of Archie Cruickshank who was now slouched in his chair, staring thoughtfully at the ceiling and making an unpleasant slurping sound.

Archie. Every business had its share of ghastly people who had to be – teeth-clenchedly – tolerated, humoured, fawned over. She had her share too. Like Jake, the copywriter.

Sucking up, they called it at school. Nothing changed. You went through life sucking up. Then you arrived in heaven, clutching your notebook full of credits, like

46

Aunt Angela, for the Biggest Suck Up of all. Hey God, that was a great place you made. Only seven days? Wow. How did you do it? You made a few little booboos, but they're minor really they are, didn't matter – well, OK, it would have been nice if you hadn't taken my Mummy and Daddy and dumped me with two of the most miserable people you could find, it would have been nice if I hadn't had four miscarriages and then nearly been killed by my little Nicky, and if you hadn't nuked Hiroshima. It would have been nice if my husband hadn't bonked that little—

It would have been nice if that aeroplane hadn't crashed.

Her throat tightened and her stomach knotted with fear. It seemed suddenly that the volume control in her head had been switched off, and she could see everyone but not hear them.

She felt icily cold. Alone.

163 DEAD IN BULGARIA AIR DISASTER

Everyone in the room had stopped in freeze-frame. Then the movie started again. Her ears felt hot. Boiling. Archie began to eat his trifle. Other than lecturing her on wine he had asked her nothing about herself except to inquire how many children she had, three times so far. His wife, with peroxided hair and enormous boobs, was at the far end of the table trying to wrest Richard's attention away from Andreas. She looked more like a stripper than the wife of a banker.

'This is wonderful trifle, Sam,' Bamford O'Connell said in his rich Dublin brogue.

'Thank you.' She smiled, and nearly blurted out, 'Actually it's Marks and Sparks,' but just managed to stop herself. It had worked fine. She had taken it out of the container and bashed it about a bit.

A short, compact ball of energy, with a wildly

expressive bon-viveur face, O'Connell attacked another spoonful with gusto. He made life seem like a feast, whether it was eating, drinking, talking, or even sitting. Absorbed in studying others, he gave the appearance that life seemed a treat, an endless supply of pleasures. Catching her eye, he raised his glass. 'A little toast to you for all your efforts.'

She smiled again, and wondered if he could see her face reddening. He was quick, full of charm, and razor sharp beneath his mask of eccentricity. She could never forget that he was a psychiatrist, was always conscious of every movement, every gesture she made in his presence, wondering what it signalled to him, what inadequacies, what secret yearnings, what secret fears she was beaming out from the way she cut her food or held her glass or turned and touched a friend.

'Alive?' said a voice down the far end. 'Are they alive?'

She glared at Richard to change the subject, but he looked away, exchanged a poorly camouflaged grin with Andreas, then looked at the blonde. 'Yah, of course. Apparently when they wriggle around, it's very erotic – if you like that sort of thing.'

'I think it's disgusting,' said Sheila Rawlings.

'I bet you get worse things than that told to you by your patients, don't you, Bamford?' said Peter Rawlings, abandoning Harriet in a cloud of environmentally hostile cigarette smoke.

O'Connell smiled and caught Sam's eye, showing her he understood. He turned his glass around in his hands. 'I do. For sure I do.' He winked at Sam. 'That's why we put our patients on couches – so they can't see our faces when they tell us these things.'

'Who does this thing with gerbils?' said Archie's wife,

her eyes wide open, eyelids batting like beaks of hungry birds.

'Gays in America,' said Richard.

The phone rang.

Richard jumped up, walked across to his desk and picked it up. There was a silence for a moment as everyone watched him.

'Harry, gorgeous!' he said loudly. 'Fine, darling, it's a good line. No, I haven't – had to leave early . . . yah . . . it's definitely going to be a new ulcer drug. Unwind the hedge. Sell the warrant if you've got a natural buyer at a 10% premium to the ADR. What about Sony?'

'Richard,' Sam called across. 'Can't you ring him back?'

He covered the mouthpiece, and raised a finger.

Bamford O'Connell pushed his tumbling hair back away from his forehead. 'There's no peace for the wicked,' he said to Sam.

'Fifty-five and a half, did you say? What's the FX rate?' He tapped out a series of numbers on his calculator, then glanced at Andreas. 'Yah, okay, go for it. Buy me 150,000 shares' worth. Bye, darling. Talk to you tomorrow. Bye.' Richard hung up, switched on his Reuters terminal and tapped on the keyboard.

Sam glared at him furiously.

'Richard—' Peter Rawlings said. 'Where's IBM trading?'

'Hang on a sec.' Richard tapped the keyboard again. 'Shit, New York's going bananas.'

Archie looked round anxiously, then back at Sam, clearly tempted to go and see for himself but thinking better of it. Only Andreas showed no concern; he sat staring ahead, sipping his wine and smiling a cold, contented smile. Maybe Swiss bankers knew it all long before everyone else? Considered English money men to be their puppets?

'Bid 124 5/8. Offer 125 7/8,' Richard shouted out, then looked quizically at Andreas. Andreas gave him a brief nod of reassurance.

Sam got up from the table, conscious of the eyes on her, and walked over to Richard. 'Turn it off,' she hissed. 'At once.'

'I want to see if we're pushing the stock.'

'I don't care. I want it off. Now.'

She marched back to the table, all smiles, and started to clear away the pudding bowls.

'Can you get the cheese, please, Richard?' she said, carrying a stack out to the kitchen and putting it by the dishwasher. She switched the coffee percolator on. Richard followed her out with the rest. 'Brilliant bouillabaisse,' he said. 'That was seriously moreish.'

'It was dreadful. The venison was a complete disaster. Why's that man Andreas wearing a glove?'

'Always wears it.'

'It's creepy.'

'It's all right. I think he's had some accident – got an ugly scar on it, or something.' He put his hands on her shoulders. 'You're very uptight, Bugs. Relax.'

She shook herself free and tinned to face him. 'You're very drunk.'

'I'm all right.'

'You're behaving appallingly. Embarrassing everyone. We've had to put up with you wittering on about gerbils up bottoms, with your lecture on how Catherine the Great died being screwed by a horse, and with your going off and sitting down to work.'

'And you've been like a stuffed dummy all evening. You're not chatting; you're sitting at the end of the table staring into space. Don't you feel well?'

'I'm fine.'

'You look bloody awful. You've been looking white as a sheet all evening. I think you should see the quack.'

'I told you, I'm very spooked by that air disaster.'

'Oh come on, Bugs, you haven't turned into a fucking oracle.'

She glared back at him. Strangers. Two complete strangers. She could no more talk to him about anything important these days than talk to someone she met on a bus. It would be easier to talk to a stranger on a bus. She turned and went back into the room. Richard sat back in his place, and the blonde immediately oozed towards him. 'Have you ever tried it with a gerbil?' she said.

He lit a cigarette and inhaled loudly. 'No. Sam doesn't go in for kinky sex too much.' He saw Sam's face and looked away hastily. 'Actually, she's too busy dreaming these days.'

'Wildly erotic ones?'

'No – all about aeroplanes crashing. Reckons she dreamed about the one that went down in Bulgaria today.'

Sam caught Andreas's eye again; caught the cold, almost knowing smirk.

'I reckon she was dreaming of my penis. Hey, Bamford,' Richard shouted. 'Didn't Freud think aeroplanes were schlonkers?'

'Aren't you going to offer any port, Richard?' she said, trying to articulate clearly, hoping they couldn't hear the quavering in her voice.

Bamford O'Connell turned to her, and smiled a sympathetic smile that told her not to worry, not to be upset, that Richard was a fine chap really, and was just a bit sozzled.

'Port, ah, yes. Got some really good stuff. Warres '63. Archie?'

'Delicious cheese, this creamy one,' said the banker's wife in an equally creamy voice.

It comes from the breasts of fat blonde women she heard a voice in her head saying, and had to bite her lip to avoid blurting it out. 'Cambozola,' she said tartly, then remembered who she was, why she was here, and put on her forced smile again. 'Nice, isn't it?'

'How's the stately home coming along, Sam?' said O'Connell.

'It's hardly a stately home. It's just an old farmhouse.'

'I thought it was quite historic, with a ghost or something?'

She shook her head. 'I don't think so.'

'Moving, are you?' said Archie, his sudden interest startling her.

'We used to have a little weekend cottage and we bought something a bit bigger, but it got quite badly damaged in the hurricane.'

''Tis a good idea to get away from London,' said O'Connell. 'Have a break from the muggers.'

'The country's full of muggers, too,' said Richard. 'They drive around on tractors.'

Sam fetched the coffee and began pouring it out. O'Connell passed the cups down for her.

'Thanks,' she said, when he had finished.

'Are you all right, Sam?' he asked.

'Yes – I—' her voice trailed away.

'You're looking a bit peaky. Are you working hard?'

'No more than usual. I had a bit of a shock today, that's all.'

'What was that?'

'I—' She felt her face reddening. 'I . . . do you – do you know much about dreams, Bamford?'

'Dreams? Anyone who'd tell you they know a lot

about dreams would be lying. I probably know as much as anybody. Who do you ask?'

'Do you use them in your work?'

'Sure I do. They're very important – but there's still an awful lot we don't understand about them.'

'Adam's penis – the forbidden fruit,' Richard expounded. 'It's obvious. The serpent. Classic Freud. It was Adam's schlonker.'

'How clever,' cooed the blonde. 'I've never thought of that.'

Sam sipped her Perrier, then turned the glass around in her hands and looked at the psychiatrist. 'Do you think it's possible to – dream the future?' she said, feeling slightly self-conscious.

'Precognition?'

'Is that what it's called?'

'Do you mean dream events that actually happen?'

'Yes.'

He picked up his glass and sipped his port with such an expression of pleasure she wondered if she was missing out not having any. 'Fine stuff, this,' he said. 'Fine port. I'm going to have one hell of a headache tomorrow. Is that precognition?'

She tilted her head: 'I'm being serious, Bamford.'

He smiled, then frowned. 'Is this to do with the air disaster on the news this evening? What Richard was just talking about?'

She nodded.

He studied her. 'I have patients that see the future all the time.'

'Really?'

'They think so.'

'And do they?'

'I'd be a rich man, wouldn't I? I'd get them to tell me

53

the winners of horse races. I could sell investment tips to Richard. We'd clean up on the Market.'

There was a loud pop above her and Sam felt a sharp pain in her hand. She let out a shriek, and stared down. Slivers of glass littered the table all around her. A large shard stuck out of her Perrier water. A small stain of blood spread across her index finger. She looked around, disoriented. Everyone was staring up at the chandelier.

'How odd,' someone said.

'Must have been some paint on it; paint can do that,' said another voice.

'Must be one of those current surges,' someone else said. 'You know, in the commercial breaks everyone rushes to the loo. It overloads the electrical circuits.'

'But it's after midnight.'

Sam stared up at the chandelier. One of the bulbs had exploded; there was a solitary jagged shard left sticking out of the socket.

A cold prickle of fear swept through her. The pop echoed around her head, faded then came back louder, carrying with it a dim memory from the past that was fuzzy and unclear.

She frowned and looked down: at the grapes on the cheeseboard, at the tiny slivers of broken glass that glinted in the candlelight, at the knuckleduster jewels on the blonde's podgy fingers, at the dark empty silence of the flat beyond the table. The memory pricked through her mind like the pain of the prick in her finger. Then, once more, she caught Andreas's eye; he curled his gloved fingers around his glass and smiled at her.

6

Sam heard the sound of a tap and the vigorous brushing of teeth, and turned over in bed with the uncomfortable realisation that a new day had arrived without the previous one having departed. She opened her eyes slowly; they felt raw, bound with wire. A shaft of light spilled out of the bathroom door and was mopped up by the grey darkness, the lingering, theatrical darkness of early morning in winter. She could almost feel someone's hand on the dimmer lever, slowly moving it.

Cue daylight!

Enter Richard, stage right, from bathroom. He wears a navy towelling dressing gown from which his legs stick out, white and hairy. His blond hair is wet and slicked back, and there is a spot of blood on his chin where he has nicked a zit. He stretches back his lips to reveal shining white teeth.

Cut to product shot.

ZING! The toothpaste that more and more dentists are recommending.

ZING! The ecologically sound way to brush your teeth. Yes, folks! Because when you've finished the paste, you can eat the tube!

Yet another Personal Nourishment System brought to you by the manufacturers of Napalm. Plaque removed. Foliage decimated. Faces peeled away.

Sam jumped, shivering.

Someone walking over your grave, her aunt used to say grimly.

She tried to switch off the weird commercial that was playing in her mind in her twilight half-awake state. The hypnopompic state, she had read in an article once.

Hypnogogic and hypnopompic, when you saw weird things as you drifted off to sleep or woke up.

She relaxed for a moment, but then felt a sense of gloom creeping around her, enveloping her. Something bad. Like waking up after you got drunk and knowing you'd done something you regretted. Only it wasn't that. It was something worse, this time. She tried to think but it eluded her. Her index finger was hurting like hell. She freed it from under the sheet and peeled off the thin strip of Elastoplast bound around it. There was a crash which shook the room.

'Bugger.'

She looked up, blinking against the brightness of the bedside lamp which Richard had switched on, and saw him lying on his face on the floor, his legs pinioned together inside his trousers. He hauled himself up onto his hands and stared around the room, with a puzzled expression.

'Are you OK?' She glanced at the clock. 0544. He was late.

'Think I'm still a bit pissed.' He rolled over, sat on the floor, tugged his trousers off, then pulled them on again slowly, getting each foot down the correct leg this time.

'I'm not surprised, the way you and Bamford were carrying on.'

He rubbed his head and screwed up his eyes. 'We drank nearly two bottles of that port.'

'Why don't you have a lie-in?'

'Japan's going bananas.'

'It can probably go bananas without you.'

'Could be up four hundred points by now.' He sat down on the bed, screwed up his eyes and wiped his face with his hands. 'I've got a mega hangover,' he said. 'A serious wipe-out.'

He stumbled into his shoes, kissed her and she smelled the fumes on his breath.

'I wouldn't drive,' she said. Take a taxi.'

'I'll be all right. Fucking good evening,' he said. 'Great scoff.'

There was a click, and then the room went dark. She lay back and closed her eyes again. She heard the front door slam and the room was very silent, suddenly. So quiet you could hear a pin drop.

Or a light bulb explode.

She fell into a deep sleep.

She was woken by the roar of a bulldozer outside. A launch travelling fast up-river, crunching through the water. Someone was whistling 'Colonel Bogey'. She slipped her feet out onto the thick carpet and sat on the edge of the bed staring at them; the varnish on her toenails was chipped. A few traces of hairs showed on her calves; time for another waxing; she smelled the foul smell of the wax, and still had the small yellowy mark on the front of her shin where the idiot girl had burnt her last time.

There was the sound of a pneumatic drill, then a louder noise, from above: an aeroplane coming into the City Airport a few hundred yards up the river.

She caught a glimpse of herself in the mirror on the wall, and sat up straighter.

Deportment, young lady.

She ran her hands into her long brown hair and squeezed it tightly; she lifted it up and let it flop back down, giving herself a sideways glance in the mirror. Nice hair, rich, brown, chic.

Chic.

She could smile about it now, because it no longer mattered. But the sting had stayed with her for years.

That morning in London thirteen – fourteen – years

ago, when her aunt had taken her, under silent protest, to the Lucy Clayton modelling school.

'It'll do you good,' her aunt had said. 'Give you confidence.'

She could still see the withering scorn on the reedy interviewer's face. 'You're too small,' she had said. 'Much too small. Five-foot five, are you? We need five-foot seven here. At least five-foot seven, I'm afraid.' She had pushed Sam's face around as if she were a horse. 'Quite a nice face dear, very English Rose. You're really quite pretty, dear, quite chic.' The woman had said the word disdainfully, as if it were a deformity, not a compliment. 'Chic, but not *beautiful*.' Then the woman had turned to her aunt. 'Nice legs. Probably her best feature. Not long enough, of course, to be a leg model.'

Sam padded across the carpet and pulled the curtain open a fraction. It was a flat grey morning out there, a good hour yet from full light. She stared out at the brown water of the Thames, stretching out into the distance like a grubby tarpaulin. A grimy black and white police launch droned through it, rocking sharply, cutting it like a blunt knife. An empty lighter shifted about restlessly, moored to an enormous rusting black buoy. She heard the cry of a gull and saw the shadow of a bird, swooping low, slamming the surface of the water for an instant. The cold seeped through the glass and through her skin, and she hugged herself with her arms, rubbing her hands up and down them.

A duet of drills hammered in the building site below. A workman in a donkey jacket and orange hard hat walked slowly across the site, through the stark glare of the floodlighting, carefully picking his path, heading towards a fire burning in a black oil drum. Another workman somewhere out of sight was still whistling, this time ragged strains of 'Waltzing Matilda'.

At the edge of the site a bulldozer reversed, dug, swivelled, dumped, behind a hoarding with huge red letters. RIVERSIDE DEVELOPMENT. RIVERSIDE LIFESTYLES. The workman stopped, knelt down and pawed at the ground with his hand. He pulled something out, stared at it, rubbed it with his finger, then tossed it away over his shoulder.

Sam saw the ball of flame rising high into the sky, the engine showering sparks, bouncing, dancing.

The image froze for an instant in front of her and she could hear nothing. Silence.

Her finger was stinging as if there was a sliver of glass inside the skin and she put it in her mouth and sucked it hard. She saw the cold smile on Andreas Berensen's face. The fingers of his leather glove curling around the glass. Richard had been fawning over him: filling his glass first, asking his opinion first on each of the wines. Toadying. Sucking up. Richard never used to be like this. He used to be interested in her, used to be a proud man; Richard never used to suck up to anyone.

The cacophony outside started again, louder, deafeningly loud. Thought for the Day was beginning on the radio; she heard the cheery voice of Rabbi Blue, rich as treacle. 'I wonder,' he said, 'how many people remember their dreams? I wonder sometimes whether God has dreams?'

Clothes. Dressing. Image. What to wear today? She yawned, tried to concentrate, to focus on the day ahead. A first cut screening this morning, then lunch with Ken. She went into the shower, felt the fine spray, turned the temperature down cold. The needles of water drummed against her skin, hard, hurting. She came out and dried herself vigorously.

Better. Heavy dose of negative ions. One per cent better. What time had they gone to bed? Three? Four?

Port. Coffee. More port. More coffee. Andreas had left first, when Richard and Bamford started telling jokes. Harriet had lectured her on the state of the world. Harriet was worried about plastic; it gave out gases; you could get cancer just from sitting on a vinyl car seat.

She opened her wardrobe. First cuts: tense, tense, tense. Who was going to be at the screening? Hawksmuir. Horrible Hawksmuir. Jake yesterday and Hawksmuir today. Her two least favourite people. Dress to kill. It was a John Galliano and Cornelia James day, she decided.

She winced at the pain in her finger. From one tiny cut? Then she winced again from the sudden sharp pain she now felt in her head that went down her neck, deep into her stomach. She felt as if she had been slit open by a filleting knife. Weird. She felt weird. Seriously weird.

She put on a Galliano two piece. Battle dress. Fashion, she thought. Fashion was bewildering. As soon as you got the hang of it, it changed. She pulled out a stunning Cornelia James shawl and draped it around her shoulders.

Better. Great. Terrific.

She took a handkerchief out of a drawer, a small white handkerchief with French lace edging and her initials, S.C. embroidered in blue in one corner, and put it in her handbag. She tugged a comb through her hair, studied herself in the mirror then smiled, pleased with the effect. 'Zap!' she said. 'Kapow!' She clapped her hands together and walked out of the bedroom, wondering why those words had suddenly come into her head.

'No, you'll never get away with it,' said a voice with a deep American accent.

She heard Nicky giggle. There were several explosions.

60

'Not this time, Batman.'
KAPOW! SOCK! BIFF! BAM! ZAP!
'We'll see about that!'

Nicky and Helen were sitting at the table, watching the television. Nicky was holding his spoon in the air and milk was trickling down into his shirt cuff. Helen, spellbound, hadn't noticed, and Sam felt a flash of irritation. She grabbed the spoon and staunched the flow of milk with a kitchen towel.

Helen stood up. 'Sorry, Mrs Curtis – I—'

'OK,' Sam said, slightly coolly, giving Nicky back his spoon. Then she turned off the television.

'Aww!' said Nicky.

Helen sat down again, blushing.

'Nicky's watching too much television, Helen. He shouldn't be watching it while he's eating.' She smiled at Helen, realising she had sounded fierce, trying to reassure her.

'Sorry,' Helen said again.

Sam sat down at the table and poured out some orange juice. Nicky eyed her sulkily.

'What's happening at school today, Tiger?'

The Esso ads had worked on Nicky. When he was four he was a tiger. Ran around on all fours. Pounced. Hid in cupboards with a freebie tiger's tail sticking out. 'Tiger in here! Tiger in here!'

He stretched out his arm, seized the Sugar Puffs pack and poured a second helping sloppily into his bowl, spilling them all around. Without bothering to pour any milk, he shovelled cereal into his mouth.

'Grumpy, this morning?' Sam asked.

'I didn't sleep very well.'

'Mummy's tired today too.'

Mummy feels like shit.

'You were making noises,' he said.

61

'Did we keep you awake? I'm sorry.'

He shoved in more cereal, chewing with his mouth open.

'Thought you were a Tiger, not a camel.'

He closed his mouth and continued chewing, then stretched out and took a mouthful of juice. 'Batman,' he said. 'I want Batman.'

'Too much television is not good for you.'

'You make television.'

'Just the ads.'

'Ads are yucky. You made the ads for that new cereal. It's yuck. It tastes like dog's do.'

'And how do you know what dog's do tastes like?'

'It tastes of yuck.'

She caught Helen's eye. Helen looked at her with the uncertainty of a child looking at her teacher. Sam finished her juice and glanced at her watch. Eight-fifteen.

'Mummy's late. She's got to go.'

She went through into the living area to switch on the answering machine, and stared around the huge room with a faint feeling of dismay. The refectory dining table was still covered in coffee cups, half-empty glasses, overflowing ashtrays, butter dishes, and napkins strewn around like confetti. Two half-full bottles of Perrier water were missing their caps; she walked over and rummaged around for them. She found the stopper of the port decanter and put that on. A sliver of glass sparkled at her from an open salt cellar. She looked up warily at the iron chandelier. The one jagged shard of glass was still in the socket. The rest of the bulbs were fine, except that they were still on. She walked over to the wall and switched them off.

The room was filled with a grey light that hung heavily, thick with the smell of stale smoke and evaporating alcohol, a greyness that seeped into her skin like damp, that would make her clothes and her hair smell of cigar smoke if she stayed much longer. She glanced around at Richard's roll-top desk in the corner, his computer terminal beside it, at the grand piano with an antique opium-smoking kit on the lid, the two sofas down the far end by the television and the gas-log fire, the armorial shields on the bare brick walls, the swords, the medieval artefacts, the huge copper ladle for pouring gold that Richard had bought when the Royal Mint was being demolished. Richard's things, relics of his family's bloody past, portraits of dead ancestors, scrolls with thick red seals. Bare bricks and oak. A man's flat. It always had been and always would be. A helicopter roared past outside, a dark shadow passing the window.

'Bye, Tiger.' She stood by the front door, struggling into her coat.

Nicky came out of the kitchen. 'Bye,' he said flatly, walking towards his room.

'Hey! Tiger!'

He stopped and turned.

'Don't I get a kiss goodbye?'

He hesitated for a moment, then trotted over to her. 'All right,' he said. 'I'll forgive you. This time.'

'And if you're very good, I'll forgive you.'

'What for?'

'For being rude to your mummy.'

He pouted, then kissed her, and put his arms around her neck. 'I'm sorry, Mummy.' He kissed her again then turned and scampered off.

'Have a good day at school.'

'Friday! Yippee!'

Sam opened the front door and picked the *Daily Mail* off the mat. She turned to her horoscope. Pisces.

'Travel may bring surprises. Avoid arguments today,

however much a close colleague may irritate you. Both today and the weekend will be unsettling and may tax even your very strong inner resources.'

Thank you very much. Hope you have a nice day too. She put the paper inside her briefcase, closed the door behind her and walked down the dark hall, four floors up in the cold stone building that was still at the moment in the middle of nowhere. Another few years and there would be a thriving metropolis all around: colour, light, people, shops. Right now it was a mess; it was hard to tell what they were putting up from what they were pulling down.

She went out into the street, into the light that was a brighter shade of grey, into the smells of diesel oil and burning tar and the salty tang of the river. She felt the faintly gritty taste of dust in her mouth and heard the distant clatter of a train, the hissing of pneumatics, the rumble of a cement mixer.

Horoscopes. Who cared about horoscopes? Who cared about dreams? About light bulbs?

The grey E-Type was covered in a light coating of dust that had settled on it since yesterday, and their elderly Range Rover next to it had virtually changed colour under the stuff. She climbed into the Jaguar, pushed the key into the ignition and switched it on. The red warning light appeared and the fuel pump ticked furiously. She pushed up the choke lever and pressed the starter button.

The engine turned over several times, whining, snuffling, then fired with a sharp bang, and rumbled into life. The rev counter flickered wildly then settled down. She flipped down the screenwasher toggle, switched on the wipers, pushed the stubby gear lever into first, struggled with the handbrake, then gripped the thin wood-rimmed steering wheel and eased the car forward, listening to its engine sucking and grumbling like an old man woken from a comfortable sleep. The three small wipers smeared the salt and dust into a translucent film, and she gave the screen another squirt.

She heaved on the wheel, pulling out around a parked lorry into Wapping High Street, then released it, feeling it spin through her hands so fast she had to be careful not to let it burn them. Old things. Retro. Ken's idea. Heavily into retro. Run old cars as company cars. Smart image, good investment. She stopped at the main road, waiting for a gap in the traffic. A bus stopped in front of her, blocking her, and she glared at the driver who was looking fixedly ahead; like a carthorse in blinkers, she thought angrily.

Then she saw the poster on the side of the bus, staring her in the face as if it was taunting her, silver with an aeroplane and a blue prancing tiger, and the words boldly emblazoned.

'CHARTAIR – A GREAT LITTLE AIRLINE . . . NOW A GREAT BIG ONE!'

7

She parked and hurried across Covent Garden towards her club. There was just time for a quick swim. She tried to swim every morning before work, unless she had an early meeting or was travelling, and she wanted to swim badly today, to try to wake up some more, to clear the fuzziness out of her head.

She felt a bit better as she left the club, slightly more human but not much, walked down the narrow street and across the huge open square, past the old covered market building of Covent Garden, among the pigeons and the street cleaners who had the place to themselves for another hour yet. A gust of cold icy wind whiplashed her damp hair, and a piece of paper scudded along past her feet like a wounded bird.

DREAMS!

The word rippled through the glass of the shop window.

UNLOCK YOUR OWN SECRET WORLD!
DREAMS. DREAMS. DREAMS.

The window was filled with books on dreams.

DREAMS – YOUR MAGIC MIRROR.
THE POWER OF DREAMS.
THE A–Z OF DREAMS.

One of the small alternative bookshops she passed every day without noticing. She glanced at her watch, 9.20. She tried the door and was faintly surprised that it opened. She went in and the shop was filled with a crisp, pristine papery smell. New jackets, fresh print; it was a good smell. Books. She loved books.

A tall man in a black polo-neck glided noiselessly across the floor, his head swivelling from side to side like a robot. He stopped a few feet from Sam, inclined his head and raised his eyebrows. He looked clean, scrubbed, and smelt of organic soap.

'Dreams,' said Sam. 'I'm—' She felt flustered for a moment. He was making her nervous. He was the sort of man she should be asking for the complete works of Marcel Proust. 'I'm interested in something on dreams.'

'Mmm,' He rotated and glided across the floor, and made a wide, sweeping arc with his arm at a row of shelves, all labelled 'Dreams'. He turned around. 'Is it anything particular?' He spoke in a studied, hushed public-library whisper, and his breath smelt of peppermints. He ran his finger along the spines as if he were caressing a sleeping girl's back, then stopped and tapped one lightly. He pulled it out and held it in the air. 'This is a possibility. Are you a student?'

'No,' said Sam, feeling flattered. No, but I'd like to be. I'd like to look like one, and be as carefree as one. And be as young as one. An Oxford man, are you? Me? I was educated at the University of Life. Know it? Turn first left down the Bitter Vale Of Tears. Graduated to Thompson's. Never heard of it? J. Walter Thompson. Started as a secretary. Then became a production assistant. By the time I was twenty-six I had been made a junior producer (sounds the bizz, eh?). Then I gave it all up for a sprog. Oh, yes, working again now. Working and dreaming. Had a dream about an air disaster, actually – you probably read about it – that one in Bulgaria? I could have saved them all. Should have rung up the airline, shouldn't I? EVERYBODY OFF, BOYS, THIS ONE'S A GONER!

Would you have done?

Shit. I'm going nuts. 'No – I – I'm a layman. I'm just interested in – er – dream interpretation.'

He replaced it with a slingshot flick of his wrist, and arched his back a fraction. 'Ahh, hmm, let me see, I think, yes, this you'd probably get on with awfully well,' he said, as if he'd known her all his life. He pulled out a slim paperback with a picture of an eyeball and a fish on the front cover. 'Yes, this is the one. *What Your Dreams Really Say*.'

Sam glanced at the back cover. 'Dr Colin Hare, lecturer in Psychology at the University of Hull, has made Freud, Jung and other great interpreters of dreams accessible to the layman in this concise dictionary of dream symbolism.'

' "It lives beside my bed . . . essential waking reading." ' *The Times*.

She flipped through the index, then turned to the page headed 'Aeroplane', and scanned through.

'Flying: The longing to lift off, get out of a rut. Erection and sexual fantasies. Aeroplane = phallus. Can also = womb.'

She looked through some more pages.

'Swimming. Often means sex. The struggle with basic impulses or other problems. Can literally mean worry about keeping your head above water.'

She turned again to the review quotes on the back cover, reading them for reassurance. 'Fine,' she said. 'I'll take it.'

She left the shop, folded the paper bag around the book and put it into her handbag. She walked through the closed bric-a-brac stalls and crossed the street to the office, a narrow building sandwiched between a publisher and a shop that sold surgical appliances.

The ground floor windows had black Venetian blinds, with the blow-up of a strip of celluloid running across, and the words 'Ken Shepperd Productions' repeated between the frames. She pushed open the heavy chromium-framed Deco door, and went into the stark airiness of the reception atrium.

Sections of motor cars stuck out from the white walls, like strange modern sculptures. The front three feet of a red Alfa Romeo. The tail section of a Volkswagen Beetle. The seats in the waiting area were old leather car seats set into clear perspex pedestals, and the receptionist sat, looking slightly daft Sam always thought, behind the steering wheel of the sawn-off front end of a white convertible Cadillac Eldorado.

'Morning, Lucy.'

The receptionist stopped typing and looked up, a bleary-eyed confection of mohair sweater, blotched makeup and streaked wild hair, which she tried to shake away from her face, without success. 'Oh, yah, hi.' She paused. 'Yah, morning. Gosh.' She smiled sleepily. 'Someone called.'

'Anyone in particular?'

Sam watched Lucy scrabbling through a pile of message slips. She looked as though she'd had even less sleep than herself. 'Ah, somewhere here – yah. Rob Kempson, from Praiseworthy – wants you to come in for a brief – either—' She peered at the note. 'Yah, Monday or Tuesday morning. Could you call him as soon as poss? Yah – gosh – no others so far.'

Sam took the slip and blinked, her eyes feeling slightly gritty, stinging from the chlorine in the pool and from tiredness. She walked past the life-size waxwork of Ken slouched in a wicker chair behind Lucy, presiding over his emporium from behind the copy of the *Daily Mail* that was changed every day, and glanced down warily, as she always did, to check that he wasn't playing a macabre joke by sitting there in person, as he had done once. The waxwork sculptor had captured the details well: the denim shirt and the curling hair, black turning to grey, and the slightly ragged, slightly dented I'm-going-to-one-day-change-the-world-before-it-changes-me-face. Everything except the eyes which stared blankly, lifelessly, unlike his real sharp blue eyes.

Windows of the soul. Strange things, eyes.

The waxy sheen of his skin wasn't like him either. The waxy sheen that did not smell of tobacco and talc and hairs and clothes and booze; the sculpture smelt of nothing and was cold to touch, shiny and hard.

This is what he would look like when he was dead.

She climbed the elegant staircase, past more sections of cars: the rear of an old London taxi recessed into the wall, with the door removed so you could sit in it if you wanted, the slatted, cobalt blue bonnet of a Bugatti, held to the wall by leather straps.

The building was on three storeys, with a basement. Ken's office was at the top, in the eaves, and his snooker room was in the basement which was also their viewing room. Sam's office was on the first floor, and there was a tiny office further along occupied by Drummond, their gofer.

She walked down the landing and into the stark black and white of the office she shared with their PA, who was sitting at her desk in a thick sweet fug of cigarette smoke.

'Morning, Claire.'

Claire had a maddening habit of never saying 'good morning'. Some days she did not even look up, and if Sam was in the office first, Claire would come in silently and sit down. Today she swept her short layered hair back from her round, pug-like face, and smiled. It was her favourite bad-news-coming smile. 'Can you guess what?'

Sam looked down at her and raised her eyebrows. She seemed to get a kick out of announcing problems.

'Giraffes! He wants four giraffes!'

The smoke was making Sam's eyes even sorer, and her finger was hurting like hell. 'Who wants four giraffes?'

'Ken.'

'Is he starting a zoo?'

'I don't know.' She shook her head. 'I give up. I really give up. Where on earth can I get four giraffes from?'

'Harrods,' said Sam, taking advantage of the stunned silence her remark brought to get past Claire's desk to her own safe haven by the window. And air, fresh air, however cold it might be. She pushed the window open and stared out.

'Harrods?' said Claire.

'Yes. They sell everything.' Sam watched a mummer dressed in black sitting on the kerb, drinking coffee from a thermos, then turned round and sat down at her desk. 'Try some of the animal companies in the Knowledge,' she said, picking up the phone and shuffling through her mail with her free hand.

'There's another problem. This one's a real disaster. It's the Polar night.'

'Bears?' said Sam, punching the dial buttons.

'No! Darkness. The Polar night. Didn't anyone realise?'

'Realise what?'

'The quote we've done for the fish fingers shoot – you know, JWT – the Superfingers – the trawler going past an iceberg? In the Arctic?'

Sam nodded, listening to the voice at the other end of her phone. 'Can I speak to Rob Kempson, please?'

'It's the Polar night, Darkness! No one's thought of that.'

'Could you tell him I returned his call, please. I'll be here for another half-hour, then back this afternoon.' She looked up at Claire. 'Studio, Claire. It'll be a studio shoot.'

'It's got to be location. The client specifically wants the Arctic.' She lit a new cigarette and flapped the smoke away with her hand. 'I don't know. I give up. I really give up.'

The door opened and Drummond shuffled in, tall, thin, hunched and dopey, like a sleepwalking anglepoise. 'New showreel,' he said, and sniffed, staring around the room as if he had just arrived in outer space. He held up a hard grey plastic box. 'Where do you want it?'

'It's got the BMW in, hasn't it, Drummond?' Sam said.

He nodded and sniffed again. 'And the Bacardi.'

'Leave it here, I want to see it. Ken and I both need to check it.'

'Do you know anything about giraffes?' asked Claire.

'Giraffes?'

'Yes, giraffes.'

Drummond gazed at her blankly, a drip running from his coke-addled nose. 'They don't dream much.'

'Dream?' Claire said.

'They only dream about half an hour a night. Shows they're not very smart.'

'Are you an expert on dreams, Drummond?' said Sam.

'Me?' He looked around the room, as if to check that he was the Drummond she was addressing. 'Weird things, dreams. Heavy duty. Inner Space.' He frowned, put the U-matic cassette on Sam's desk, then wandered out of the room.

'Mrs Wolf said this was going to be a bad month,' said Claire.

'Wolf?' said Sam dimly. 'Wolves. Giraffes. There seem to be a lot of animals around this morning.'

'My clairvoyant. Mrs Wolf.' Claire picked up the phone and started dialling.

Sam went out down the corridor to the coffee machine and poured herself a cup. She blew away the steam, took a couple of sips, then went back to her office and buzzed Ken on the intercom. 'We ought to leave in five minutes. We're due at the cutting room at 10.30.'

'I thought we were screening here.'

'Hawksmuir always wants to see the first cut on the cutting table. Do you want to walk or shall I call a taxi?'

'We'll leg it. Pick you up on the way down.'

Sam looked at Claire. 'Is she accurate, your clairvoyant?'

'Yes, she's very good. She told me Roger and I would split up.'

'Does she ever give you good news?'

'Sometimes.' Claire smiled, and stared up at the ceiling, her eyes shrinking back into their fleshy sockets and glazing over, almost as if she was going into a trance. 'Sometimes she gives me very good news.'

They stood in the small windowless cutting room, surrounded by racks of film cans, loose strips of celluloid and sticky labels, millions of them, attached to everything in sight and written all over with marker pens, and stared down at the small screen of the Steenbeck editing table.

Tony Riley, their editor, killed the overhead light, and the machine rolled with faint hum and a click of sprockets. The cream bonnet of a car appeared on the screen, long, stylish, vintage. A hand came into view and turned up the volume on the dashboard radio.

I'm in paradise . . . I'm in paradise . . . I'm in paradise. Sam mentally sang the words of the song that hadn't yet been recorded, the hard beat that would play over this. The camera pulled back to reveal a young, trendy man driving a large Fifties convertible Mercedes through the night. He was drumming the steering wheel with his hands in time to the beat of the music, and driving very slowly, no more than crawling speed. The camera showed a close-up of his face, slick, cocky, hedonistic, then cut to the view ahead. A long, narrow street, full of elegant houses with open doorways down both sides.

Leaning out of each doorway was a girl, dressed

erotically. As he drove slowly though, eyeing them, they came forward, seductively brushing the car with their hands, their feet, with the fronds of a whip, raising their gowns a fraction, showing their stockings, their garters. He turned from side to side in his seat, humming the tune.

I'm in paradise . . . I'm in paradise . . . I'm in paradise . . .

There was a cut to a hospital bed, with a man lying in it, being wheeled along the street by two orderlies in white. The girls recoiled in horror as the bed passed through, and stood in frozen silence, watching as it was brought to a halt in front of the Mercedes. The camera zoomed in on a gaunt, desperately ill young man. He was just recognisable as the same man who had been driving the Mercedes.

'Heaven or hell—' The words ran through her head automatically. 'Don't leave the choice to someone else. Use a condom.' The camera tracked past the bed and showed the Mercedes again, abandoned at the side of the road, burning fiercely. Ahead down the street, more cars were on fire and flames were leaping from the houses.

The machine clicked off and the overhead light clicked on.

Silence. Always a bloody silence.

Director's first cut.

The script according to Ken Shepperd. International award-winning director. Twenty grand's worth of fee.

The silence got longer.

We came in on budget, Sam thought. My contribution. Iron rod rule over Ken who would cheerfully have blown it, blown the profit.

To get it even righter than right.

Tom Hawksmuir, tall, sour copywriter, with a crop of blond hair twenty years too young for his booze-lined

74

face, Euan Driver and Bentley Hewes. The agency Creative Team.

Hawksmuir punted the first missile. 'Looks like he's driving the Merc out of a fucking showroom.'

'The girl with the boa feather – didn't you shoot a close-up, Ken, when she climbs on the bonnet and tries to straddle the star?' said Bentley Hewes.

'Wouldn't get that through the IBA in a million years,' Ken said.

Cigarettes lit up. Ken. Tom. Tony Riley. Three out of six smoking. She wanted one too. So badly. The smoke irritated her nose and she sneezed. She opened her handbag and rummaged for her handkerchief; it wasn't there. Strange, she thought, rummaging again, unzipping the inside pockets and checking those too. She remembered clearly taking out the handkerchief, the one with her initials embroidered on; could have sworn she'd put it in her bag.

'The girls,' said Hawksmuir, 'they simply don't look like tarts. They look like sweet little girls from next door in fancy dress.'

'I thought that's the point,' Ken said, slowly, tersely.

'The script said tarts. Hookers, prostitutes. Not little girls dressed up in their mother's finery for a laugh.' Hawksmuir stared penetratingly at Sam. 'What do you think of the girls, Sam? Do you think they're sexy?' He gave her a leering smile. 'What do women find sexy in other women?'

'I thought the point of the commercial was to hit teenagers, Tom,' she said, finding she too was having to make an effort to stay calm. 'I don't think many teenagers go to prostitutes. They sleep with the girls next door, and they think that that's safe. We've tried to use girls that we felt teenagers, male and female, would relate to.'

'Let's go back to that girl in the boa.'

'Let's have another run through.'

'Let's get pissed, said Ken, as they walked back down Wardour Street. It had turned into a fine, clear day, cold in the blustery wind; crisp. They ducked into the trattoria. It was early. Clean pink tablecloths and shiny cutlery, bread rolls and grissini sticks in their packets, neat, undisturbed.

Sam still felt unsteady when she left the office shortly after six, the stale, caraway taste of the kümmel they had drunk with the coffee lingering in her mouth. She tried to work out how much they had had: two bottles of wine, maybe three, then the liqueur, two glasses, at least. 'Clear your head,' Ken had said.

Clear it? Christ. She screwed up her eyes and blinked, and the lights of the early London evening all shifted to the left. There was a dull ache in her stomach, a sharp cheese-knife pain down the centre of her forehead and she was shaking slightly from too many cups of coffee.

She stumbled over a paving stone. The sharp cold air was making her worse, she realised, as she walked unsteadily towards the car park. She wondered for a moment whether she was all right to drive, stopped, and decided she definitely was not. She saw a 'Hire' sign bearing down out of the dark, and tripped forward with her arm raised.

'Wapping High Street,' she said to the driver. 'Sixty-four.' She wondered if she was slurring her words. The rear seat seemed to rise up to meet her before she had got to it, and she sat down with a sharp thump. Oblivion. For a time in the restaurant, there had been oblivion, and it had felt good, felt marvellous, felt as if she was standing on the top of the world.

Ken hadn't mocked her dream. He was interested, wanted to hear all she could remember, helped her compare it to the events that had been reported in the news, on the television, on the radio. He didn't have an explanation, but he believed her. Coincidence, he had said finally, trying to reassure her. It was nice just to be believed.

Now the oblivion had mostly faded and she was remembering again.

She stared out at the news-vendor's hoarding, dimly lit by the street lamp above it, and listened to the rattle of the taxi's engine as it waited to pull out into the Strand.

AIR DISASTER – PILOT ERROR!

Yes. Now they knew too. They should have rung her and she could have told them. All the grisly details.

Me? Sure, what you want to know? I was there. Eye witness account!

This is Sam Curtis. News At Ten. In Bulgaria.

She sat back and peered out at the lights, the lights that passed, blinked, dazzled and were gone; lights that lit up the mannequins in the shops and threw shadows across the pavement through which people hurried against the cold, against the drizzle, against the clock. Did they all dream too? she wondered, feeling a sudden wave of nausea. She swallowed hard and held her breath, and the wave passed. She closed her eyes and drifted into a jumbled morass of thought.

Then she noticed the taxi had stopped.

'Sixty-four?' said a voice.

She opened her eyes, confused, blinking in the darkness. She felt an enormous weight of tiredness, too tired almost to get out of the taxi. She glanced at the red digits of the meter. £3.75. She pulled a banknote out of her handbag and pushed it through the glass. 'Make it four pounds fifty.'

He took it and sat in silence for a moment, then turned around and thrust something back through the partition window at her. 'I'd rather have money.'

She felt a thin, stiff piece of card. 'What's this?' she asked.

'It's what you gave me.'

'I gave you a—' She paused, and blinked again as the interior light came on and stared down at what she was holding.

An orange and white airline boarding card, with the word CHARTAIR printed on it and the number, slightly crooked, that had been stuck on afterwards. 35A.

'I didn't – this . . . I didn't give you this – I' She looked up baffled, trying to see the taxi driver's face in the darkness of his cab. Then his own interior light came on, and she could see clearly.

She felt the shock ripple through her, picking her up from her seat like a surging wave and dumping her hard on the floor. She lay there, humiliated, still not wanting to believe, looked again at the boarding card, confused, trembling with fear, then back up at the hooded face that was staring at her, the mouth and one eye grinning malevolently through the slits, the other eye nothing but a livid red socket with the lashes bent inwards.

8

Time froze.

She saw the smile, the hatred; the determination.

Oh Christ, somebody out there help me. Please.

She shot a brief glance through the taxi's window at the darkness, wondering if she could out-run him. The street was quiet and there were alleyways and hoardings and empty buildings. If he caught her he could take her to any of a hundred places where she would not be found for days.

He was chuckling, enjoying his own private joke, watching her, grinning at her. Taunting her.

She stared at the boarding card, then up again, trying to understand, trying to get her brain to work properly, to make sense. She was in a taxi. She must be safe. Surely.

She shot out her hand and tugged hard on the door handle.

But it would not move.

She threw all her weight onto it. Still nothing. She stared up at him angrily, and he was roaring with laughter. She crawled to her knees and tried to pull down the window, and the metal flap sheared away, cutting her finger. She dived across the other side, and tried that door handle too. But she knew, even before she reached it, that it would not move. She scrambled back, grabbed the other door handle again and shook it wildly.

'Help! Let me out! Let me out!'

'Lady?'

'Help me!'

'Lady?'

She shook the handle again.

'Lady? Are you all right lady?'

The voice cut through the darkness, puzzled, gentle.

'Lady?'

She stared, blinking at the pool of orange light. Street lamp, she thought.

'Are you all right, lady?'

She heard the rattle of the taxi's engine, and a man with a kind face, in a peaked cap and moustache, was staring down at her worriedly from the driver's seat.

She suddenly realised she was lying on the floor, felt it shaking, could smell the rubber matting. She was clutching the door handle. 'I—' Her head swam with confusion and she thought for a moment she was going to pass out. She closed her eyes tightly, then opened them again. 'I'm sorry,' she said. 'I . . . had – I—'

He came round and opened the door for her, then helped her to her feet and out of the cab. 'I thought you was having a funny turn in there for a moment.'

'I'm sorry,' she said again, beginning to feel foolish as she became more conscious. 'I fell asleep . . . I was having a – dream. How much do I owe?'

'Three seventy-five,' he said. 'Do you want an 'and to your doorstep?'

Three seventy-five, she thought vaguely. Same as in the dream. 'No, fine. I'll be fine, thank you.' She handed him a fiver. Make it four-fifty—' She hesitated. 'I've been a nuisance. Keep the change, please.'

She turned and hurried away up the steps into the porch, heard the dick as she broke the beam and the automatic light came on, silently and obediently. She tapped out the combination code and turned around. She saw, through the darkness, the face of the driver as he reset his meter then switched off his interior light.

She stood and waited for him to drive off, shaking, her mind blurred with fear.

9

The woman's shadow fell across the gravestone, blocking the dim glow of light from the distant church window. The wind shook the trees, rattling the branches like bones, and carried faint strains of hymns from the choir practice; the woman was panting.

Tall, heavy boned, in her early seventies, she was unused to running, and it took her a while to catch her breath and for the pain in her chest to subside, took her a while for the excitement that bubbled like a cauldron inside her to calm enough so she could speak.

Her shadow bobbed over the words, revealing them for a moment, then blotting them out again.

'BILLY WOLF. 1938–1964.'

She knelt, as was her custom, closed her eyes tightly and murmured a rapid sequence of inaudible prayers. She rocked backwards and forwards, murmuring faster and faster until the words became a single high-pitched keening, and thick tears brimmed in her eyes, blinding her. Then she remained in silence, with her eyes tightly shut, until she could no longer contain her excitement. She opened her eyes and stood up.

'I've brought you a present, Billy,' she said in a guttural mid-European accent. 'You're going to be very pleased with me. So pleased! I know you are. Look, Billy!' She pulled the handkerchief from her old beaten-up handbag and held it out to the gravestone.

'It's hers, Billy! This'll do, won't it?' She beamed. 'I know you're pleased. It's taken so long to find her. The uncle and aunt adopted her, you see. They changed her name, took her a long way away. But we've found her again now. Little bitch. We're all right, now, Billy.' She held the handkerchief up once more, smiled at it, then folded it and put it carefully away in her bag. 'We've got everything, Billy.

'We're going to get her now.'

10

'Hey look at that! Ferrari – wow! Go faster, race it Mummy! Aww!'

The tail of the red sports car disappeared into the distance.

'Why are you driving so slowly, Mummy?'

'We're doing eighty, Tiger.'

'That's not very fast.'

'It's ten over the speed limit.'

'Was that man breaking the law then?'

'Yes.'

'Daddy breaks the law. He did one hundred and thirty-five last Saturday. Hey! Here's Daddy. Ohh.'

Sam glanced at Nicky in the rear-view mirror of the Range Rover, his face pressed against the window.

'It's not Daddy. It's just like Daddy's. Except Daddy's is a faster one. Why are we turning off?'

'We have to go shopping.'

'Oh noo! Do you like shopping, Helen?'

Helen looked round. 'Depends what I'm buying, Nicky.'

'How can anybody like shopping?'

'And now coming up before the news is the weekend weather report for Sussex and the South Downs. And it's going to be dry and windy with a possibility of gales . . . so hold onto your hats and your wigs and let's take you back to the summer of '67. The Kinks. "Sunny Afternoon".'

She drove into the parking lot of Safeways, the song stirring some vague pleasant memory inside her. They each took a trolley and marched in. Nicky sideswiped a display of alcohol-free lager, then crashed head-on with another trolley and got them so firmly locked together they both had to be abandoned. He swung on a barrier, trod in someone's basket and climbed a mountain of Heinz Baked Beans – 4p OFF! – which disintegrated under him.

She drove out with a feeling of relief.

'Are we having burgers?'

'Yes.'

'And sausages?'

'Yes.'

'Goodee!'

She braked hard and the tyres squealed as the Range Rover slewed to a halt throwing Helen forward against her seat belt.

'Sorry,' Sam said, staring up at the red traffic light. She turned around to Nicky, strapped into the rear seat. 'Okay, Tiger?'

He nodded, intently studying the cars crossing the intersection. 'Ford, Ford, Datsun, Rover, Toyota, Ford, Citroën, Porsche! Is Daddy going to be there, Mummy?'

'He'll be there tonight. He's gone shooting.'

'I want to go shooting. He promised to take me shooting.'

'Perhaps he'll take you tomorrow.' Shooting. She screwed up her nose, wishing Richard wouldn't encourage him. She wanted Nicky to be brought up in the country, and cultivated friends in London who had places in the country, as well as trying hard to make friends locally. The only thing she did not like about the country was shooting. She accepted it, but always uneasily. She turned back around and looked up at the road signs. LEWES BRIGHTON EASTBOURNE TUNBRIDGE WELLS. The light changed, she pushed the gear lever forward and let out the clutch.

'Vauxhall, Austin, Volkswagen, Jaguar, Ford, Honda, Volkswagen, Fiat . . .'

'Hey! Give us a break, Tiger.' Car names. He knew every single one.

'Is the goose going to be there, Mummy?'

'On the farm? I expect so.'

'Would a goose peck you?'

'Yes.'

'Would it kill you?'

She smiled. 'No.'

'Would it eat you if it did kill you?'

The black hood with the knife slits stared out through the taxi driver's partition.

'It wouldn't kill you.'

The raw livid eye socket.

Nothing. They were nothing. Old images from old dreams. They meant nothing; forget them. The mind playing tricks. Been upset over Richard's affair – probably triggering it off.

And the dream of the air disaster?

Coincidence. Ken was right. Coincidence, Leaving it behind her now. Leaving it all like a vanishing speck in the rear-view mirror. The country was the place she loved. Great to get away from London. The whole weekend. Nicky's party. Hard work but fun. The weekend was going to be great, would heal the wounds.

She turned off the main road into a narrow lane with a tall hedgerow on each side. A pheasant scurried along like a lame old woman. It was difficult to get used to the lane being much brighter now, since the hurricane last October. The trees that had made it dark had mostly gone. Everywhere you looked in the countryside you saw broken trees, uprooted trees, as if a giant had clumped through kicking things over for fun.

'I know where we are now! I know where we are now!'

She drove in through a narrow broken-down gateway, across a cattle grid, past a sign marked FARM LANE, OLD MANOR FARM, LANE HOUSE, and forked onto a ribbon of crumbling concrete like a causeway across the ploughed field. The Range Rover lurched through a pothole, dipped again, the suspension crashing, the steering wheel kicking hard in her hands. A faint smell of mud, manure and damp straw permeated through the closed windows.

'This is a silly road,' said Nicky.

She turned left again on the far side of the field, past the front of the farm with its cluster of outhouses, barns and silos, and down a steep hill. The rooftop of the house came into view first then disappeared behind some fir trees. They wound down past a tumbledown barn, which always made something creep inside her, round to the front of the house.

The house had been fine when they'd bought it and they could have lived in it as it was, but Richard didn't think it was grand enough. He had had it gutted, rooms knocked through, new mouldings on the walls and ceilings, a swimming pool dug out, a hard tennis court laid. Money pouring out like water; money she didn't know they had. Money that Andreas seemed to magically provide through deals she did not understand. Andreas, the Swiss banker whom Richard had befriended, had become obsessed with, talked to on the phone constantly when he was at home, fawned over when he had come to dinner. She wondered whether Richard had begun to change when the money started to roll; or was it when he had started going with the tart in the office? Or was it Andreas? Andreas whom she had finally met two nights ago. With his black leather glove.

They'd lost part of the roof in the hurricane and it was still being fixed now. Rusty scaffolding clung to the wall at one end, a sheet of bright blue tarpaulin flapping from it in the wind. Something about the scaffolding did not look right to her – it seemed to have come loose, seemed to be swaying.

The house was a Victorian farmhouse. The farmer lost both his legs in an accident, and had gassed himself in the tumbledown barn with the exhaust fumes of his car. His widow had sold off the farm and moved away; they'd only heard the story after they'd bought the house and she wondered if she would have tried to dissuade Richard had she known. Since she had heard the history, she always felt the house had a slightly melancholic feeling to it. It was the inside she liked most: the large, elegant rooms, some which they had made even larger, large enough to entertain in style, but not so large the place wouldn't feel like a home.

She swung the steering wheel to avoid a crater in the crumbling driveway. 'That's a job you can have, Tiger,' she said, more brightly than she felt. 'You can fill in the holes.'

'No.'

'Why not, Nicky?' said Helen.

'Umm. Coz there might be fish in them.'

The gravel of the circular drive rattled against the underside of the Range Rover, thick wall-to-wall gravel that the wheels sank into up to their hubs. She pulled on the handbrake and switched off the engine. Silence. Peace. She felt a gust of wind rock the car. Nicky tugged excitedly at his door handle. 'Birthday tomorrow! Yeah!'

'You're looking forward to it, aren't you?' said Helen.

'Yeah!'

' "Yes", darling, "yes", not "yeah". Okay?'

He hesitated, then grinned impudently at his mother. 'Yeah!' he said. 'Yeah! Yeah!' He jumped down and ran across the drive.

Sam looked at Helen, shaking her head and smiling. Helen blushed. 'I'm sorry,' she said. 'I'm trying to get him out of it. He's very strong willed.'

'Like his father,' Sam said, opening her door and stepping down. The wind tugged her hair, pulling her backwards, and a piece of grit blew into her right eye making it smart. She blinked hard, dabbing it with her handkerchief, then opened the tailgate.

She paused for a moment and stared at the view. Straight down over the fields down to the banks of the River Ouse, the open fields beyond, and the South Downs in the distance beyond that. To the right, the spires and walls of Lewes, the chalk bluffs and the ruined castle perched on the hill. Even on a bleak, blustery January morning, with the flattened trees with their roots in the air, it was stunning. Exhilarating. She wished she could put her wellies on and walk off into it right now, as she turned and hefted the first box of groceries towards the house, glancing up at the scaffolding again and the blue sheeting that flapped and cracked like a backing sail.

She opened the door and the smell of fresh paint engulfed her. She sniffed it, and it felt good. Helen followed her in, holding a bulging brown bag.

'God it's cold!' Sam carried the box through and dumped it on the kitchen table. She stared proudly at her brand new navy Aga, and switched it on, listening to the tick of its oil pump, then the whoof of its flame. She opened the cupboard and switched on the central heating. There was a clunk, a rattle, a tick, another whoof, and the slatted door began to vibrate.

She went back outside, crossing with Helen who was bringing in a case of Cokes. Nicky was following her, struggling under the weight of a carrier bag. She smiled.

'Can you manage, Tiger?'

He nodded a grim determined nod, and she took another box and followed him in, her feet scrunching on the gravel, watching him tenderly as he put his carrier down, then picked it up again. Such a tiny chap, but he hadn't seemed so tiny when he was born.

Caesarian. The idiot gynaecologist hadn't realised her cervix was too small for him.

No, Jesusgoddamn no! Oh my Christ!

A great job you did, Mr brilliant gynaecologist. Mr Framm. Mr smooth-talking great bedside manners Framm. Brilliant bit of surgery on me. What did you use? A shovel?

No more children? Won't be able to? Great. Triff. Thanks very much.

You could sue him someone had said, but what was the point? It wouldn't bring her another child.

Sue. Everyone sues everyone. Join the lepers with their begging bowls outside the Halls of Justice. Sue. Sue. Sue. You leave people alone these days; you don't dare touch; don't dare lift them bleeding to death out of the wrecks of cars in case they sue you for doing it wrong.

Nicky put the carrier down on the kitchen floor. 'I'm going to check my base now, make sure that's all right. I've got work to do in it.'

The barn was where he had his secret base; at least he wasn't scared of barns, she thought, watching him scamper off. He'd have asked Richard to come and check it out with him, but not her. She was all right for the odd game, the odd bit of amusement when he was bored, for putting him to bed and telling him stories, but it was Richard that he really liked to be with. Richard, who took him fishing, played with his cars, taught him to swim and use a computer and sail a boat. Some things you couldn't change no matter what you did. It was good that they loved each other so much. Except sometimes she felt left out. Sometimes she felt as lonely as when she had been a child unwanted by her aunt and uncle.

She went back outside, heaved another box of groceries out of the tailgate and carried it through the fresh blustery air. It could all be so good here. Was all just beginning to feel so good. And then. Richard. Oh you stupid sod!

She lugged her suitcase inside and tramped up the filthy dust sheet that covered the staircase. 'I thought they were going to finish painting the stairs. They are blighters, these builders.'

There was so much to be done. So much potential. So much you could do – if you had the enthusiasm. ENTHUSIASM. It had been there when they'd bought the place. Yes-yes-yes. The estate agent had given them the key and let them go back for the second viewing alone and they'd made love on the bare dusty floor.

Yes, please. Can we really afford this?

Sure we can, Bugs.

Yes, please.

Last June.

She walked past the dust sheets stretching away down the dark corridor, the ladders, the tins of paint, the rolls of lining paper, into the bedroom and put the case down on the floor. Mirrors. On all the walls. On the doors of the massive mahogany wardrobe they'd acquired with the house. There was one on order to go up on the ceiling. What did he like looking at so much? His own hairy bum?

She walked over and gazed out of the window at the thickening cloud and the swirling leaves. She watched the wind blowing, in the grass, in the trees, in the ripples on the distant river.

Slider.

The black hood stared out at her through the glass partition.

The orange and white boarding card.

Seat 35A.

She heard a click behind her, a gentle click like a door closing, and she felt a sudden fear clam around her like a cold mist. She stared on out through the window, at nothing but a blur. Someone or something had come into the room and was standing right behind her. So close, she could almost feel breathing down her neck.

She shook her head, trembling, and gripped the radiator beneath the sill tightly, so tightly she could feel the ribbing cutting into her hands. She wanted to turn, now, turn and face whoever it was. But she could not.

'Yes?' she said, instead.

There was silence.

'What do you want?' she articulated clearly, loudly.

Still there was silence.

She spun round, filled for an instant with a mad boldness. But there was nothing. Nothing except her reflection.

She sat down shakily on the white candlewick bedspread and took the page from Friday's *Daily Mail* out of her handbag. She looked at the large photograph of the tailplane in the snow, and the smaller inset photograph of a Boeing 727, with the tiny caption underneath: 'Similar to the one that crashed.'

She turned the page, staring at the photographs of the pilot and co-pilot, one smiling, one stem. Neither the names nor the faces registered anything with her. She looked down the column until she found what she wanted: the emergency phone numbers.

She picked up the telephone and dialled. The number rang for a long time before it was answered.

'Is that Chartair?' she said, feeling foolish.

'Yes it is,' said a woman's voice.

'I wonder if you could give me some information about the . . . crash?'

'Is it about a relative, madam?'

'Er – not—' Sam felt flushed, afraid what the woman might think. That she was a crank with a ghoulish interest. 'I think perhaps I had a relative on the plane,' she said, knowing that her lie did not sound convincing.

'Could you let me have the person's name?' said the woman, her voice becoming impatient.

'I have the seat number. 35A.'

'35A? Your relative was travelling in 35A?'

Sam wanted to hang up. The tone of the woman's voice was flattening her. 'Yes,' she said. 'I think so.'

'Wouldn't have been on this plane. There were only thirty-two rows.'

'I'm sorry,' said Sam. 'So sorry – I must have . . .'

'Do you have a name?'

'Name?'

'Of your relative.'

'I'm sorry,' Sam said. 'I've made a mistake. I don't think they . . . he . . . were . . . was on that plane at all.' She hung up feeling hot, flustered, watching her reflection in the mirror putting the phone back on the bedside table.

35A.

She tossed the numbers around in her head, added them together, subtracted them, said them over to herself, trying to find some clue. She pulled the book she had bought out of her handbag and shook it out of its crumpled paper bag.

What Your Dreams Really Say.

She stared at the eyeball and the fish on the cover, then glanced at the biography of the author inside.

'Dr Colin Hare Ph.D., D.Sc. A Fellow of the British Psychological Society. Winner of the University of London Carpenter Medal for "great innovative work". Considered Britain's leading authority on dreams, he lectures extensively throughout the world.'

She flicked through a few pages, then turned to the index. Hood. Hood. '*Hood*, see Mask.'

'To dream of yourself or others wearing a hood or a mask can be a warning of deception by someone you trust.

'It may alternatively indicate an aspect of your personality.'

That was all. She looked up 'Numbers' and turned to the page.

'Three: The male genitals. Father, mother, child. The Trinity.

'Five: The flesh. The body. Life.

'Any letters of the alphabet indicate pleasant news on the way.'

'Mumbo jumbo,' she muttered. Some people could do *The Times* crossword in four minutes. Not her; never. Riddles. Puzzles. She'd never been any good at them. Thicko Sam.

She heard the rattle of water inside the radiator, and felt a sharp cold draught down the back of her neck. She was frightened again, felt goosepimples on her shoulders, her arms, on her thighs. The door of the room swung open a fraction with a click, half closed then opened again, click, click.

There was a louder click from her right and the mirrored door of the wardrobe swung slowly open. Her heart crashed around inside her chest as she stared, paralysed for a moment, into its dark interior. The metal coat hangers clanged together, gently, chiming.

There was a splitting crack of wood above her, then

another, as if someone was walking over the joists. The whole room seemed to be coming alive around her.

She went out onto the landing, hurried along it and halfway down the stairs, then stopped, and stared back up, trying to compose herself. She could still hear the coat hangers chiming as if they were being played like musical triangles.

11

'Seventeen, eighteen, nineteen.' She looked quizzically at Helen.

'Yes. I make it nineteen.'

The long trestle table in the dining room was covered with a bright tablecloth, nineteen paper plates, pink and yellow napkins, red and blue striped paper cups. The walls were festooned with balloons and ribbons, and there was a large banner along one saying 'Happy Birthday Nicky.'

'Looks wonderful, doesn't it?' Helen's voice tingled with excitement, and Sam smiled, pleased for her. Pleased that she could be so thrilled at something so simple, and hoping the feeling would rub onto Nicky. Nice, old-fashioned, simple.

'Great,' she said absently, watching Helen rub her hands together gleefully, like a child. She was a child, really. Nineteen. Her funny spiky hair, and her thick North Country accent, and her superstitions. Seeing omens in everything. Don't look at a new moon through glass. Turn money over in your pocket. Say 'grey hares' on the last night of the month and 'white rabbits' in the morning. She frowned uncertainly, hoping Helen wasn't going to riddle Nicky with fears and guilt and make him cranky.

Like people who dreamed of air disasters.

She felt a breeze on her face, and heard the wind again rattling the windows. The house seemed to let in draughts as a leaky boat took in water. She walked through the hallway, and stared at the bare floorboards of the staircase, wondering if it had looked better with the dust sheets on, and smelled the wood smoke from the newly lit fire that was roaring and spitting in the drawing room.

With the fire lit and Richard back the house seemed OK, fine; it had been the wind that had scared her, the wind and the central heating starting up; the house had been empty for five years, it was all damp, it was bound to creak and crack and make strange sounds when the heating came on and the wood dried out. Richard had explained to her before. It all made sense; sure. It was fine. It had been her imagination in the bedroom, the wind and her imagination and the drying out house.

She opened the kitchen door and saw him sitting at the table, his shotgun spread out in bits. Nicky, standing beside him, his face streaked in gun oil, was polishing the stock. Richard rammed the cleaning rod down through one barrel, then the other.

'Honestly, Richard! Not on the table!'

He closed one eye, and squinted at her through each barrel in turn. 'Going to have to have these re-ground. Pitting. Can't understand it.' He poured some oil onto a rag, then began to wipe the barrels.

'Didn't you hear me? I don't want that on the table. We have to eat on that.'

'It's all right.' He studied the triggers for a moment, then inserted the can between them. 'Only a bit of oil.'

She heard the clunk as he squeezed the can and bit her lip, feeling guilty suddenly.

Domestic bliss. The family all together. Something

she'd never had; one of the few things you could give to a child that mattered. She pulled a couple of newspapers out of a cupboard, and smiled down at him. 'Slip these underneath.'

He glanced at them. 'I've read them.'

'Richard,' she said reproachfully.

'Look, Mummy!' Nicky held up the shining stock.

'That looks wonderful, Tiger. Time for your bath now.'

'Daddy said we can go shooting tomorrow, coz it's my birthday.'

'If you've got time. You're going to have a busy day tomorrow.'

Nicky's face fell, and he turned to his father. 'We will have time, Daddy, won't we?'

Richard smiled. ''Course we will. Let's have a kiss goodnight.'

Sam watched him hug his father, arms around his neck, the simple, total, uncomplicated love of a child. Crazy with love. She'd been crazy with love for Richard too. Loved him, admired him, respected him. For ten years. Until.

'Will you tell me the story you told me the other night, Mummy? About the man who killed the dragon, and the dragon came back to life?'

'You want that one again?'

'Tell it again. Do! Please!'

The man who killed the dragon and lived happily ever after.

Happily ever after, Childhood's greatest myth.

'Go and run your bath, Tiger, and Mummy'll be up.'

Nicky scampered off.

'He's exhausting,' Sam said.

''Night, Tiger.' Richard put the gun barrels down and refilled his whisky glass, wrapping his hand around it, getting the level exactly to the top of his fourth finger. He took the glass to the tap and ran in some water. 'You look nice, Bugs,' he said tenderly. 'Like that jumper on you.'

She glanced down, to check what she was wearing. 'Thanks.'

'I—' He hesitated, then dug his hand into his corduroy pocket and pulled out a small package. 'I—' He blushed – 'got you a little present.'

'For me?'

He held it out to her; it had classy foil giftwrap, but clumsily done, and crumpled, with far too much sellotape which she picked away carefully with her nail. Inside there was a small slim leather box that looked old. She looked at Richard uncertainly, and he nodded at her. She lifted the lid and saw an elderly looking Rolex watch, with a slim rectangular face and twin dials.

'It's – er – genuine – antique. Thirties. I thought – your retro stuff – go with the image—'

'It's the bizz,' she said, lifting it out. 'Very trendy. It's – beautiful.' She kissed him. 'it's lovely.' She removed her own watch, put it on the table and strapped on the Rolex.

'You have to wind it, of course.'

'Yes. Funny, two dials – so you can tell the time in different parts of the world? For early jetsetters?'

'One's for the hour hand, the other's minutes.'

She smiled. 'Ah.'

'Should improve your street cred.'

'Should do.'

'Like it?'

'Yes. It's wonderful – it—'

He sat back down at the table. His eyes were watering. He was crying. 'I'm sorry, Bugs. I've made such a hash. I – I've really—' He bowed his head slightly and rested it in his hands. 'I love you, you know, I really love you. I don't want to lose you.'

She went to him, put her arms round him and held him tight for a moment, cradling his head, and blinking away her own tears of sadness. Sadness for what had happened, for how he felt; sadness that even in her arms part of him felt like a stranger. She stroked his face. 'It's a lovely watch. It must have cost a fortune.'

'I wanted to get you something very special.'

'You're spending a lot of money these days.'

He sniffed. ''S all right. Into some good deals. Andreas reckons we'll be fine as long as nothing happens to the Japanese market.'

'Is it likely to?'

He drew away from her and took a hard pull on his whisky. She stared at him, and thought she could see a faint trace of worry in his face. 'Is it likely to?' she repeated gently.

He sniffed again. 'No.' But she sensed an element of his usual confidence missing. 'How long have you been dealing with Andreas?'

He shrugged. ''Bout eight or nine months.'

'He seems to have helped you make a lot of money.'

'Yah's a good bloke.' He flushed slightly.

'Do you trust him?'

'Straight as a die.'

'Is he?'

He nodded.

'Doesn't sail close to the wind?'

'No – he's—' He hesitated – 'actually, he's – ah – quite cautious. He's a director of a bank. Quite a substantial outfit.' He scratched the back of his head awkwardly. 'Why are you—?'

'I just thought he was a bit odd, that's all.'

'The Swiss tend to be a bit cold.'

'How was the shoot?' she asked.

'Good bag.' He looked relieved that she had changed the subject. 'Hundred and eighty pheasants. Brought some back. Think I'm going to build a proper game larder.'

She began to turn the winder of her watch carefully, backwards and forwards; it had been years since she'd wound a watch, she realised.

'You've got the Punch and Judy organized, haven't you, Bugs?'

'Yes.'

'What time's kick-off?'

'Three o'clock. You'd better get the projector set up. You won't have much time tomorrow, since you've got to fetch your mother.'

'The old goat.' He took another large pull on his drink. 'She's getting past her sell-by date.'

'Nicky might say that about you and I one day.'

'Probably will.'

'Doesn't that bother you?'

He shrugged. 'No.'

She kissed him again on his cheek. 'I'll go and tell Nicky his story.' She went out of the room and closed the door, blew her nose and wiped her own tears away. She climbed the stairs slowly, turning her mind back to the story of the man who killed the dragon and the dragon came back to life, except this time it turned into two dragons, and the man killed both of them and then it turned into four and he killed them too. Killed them dead.

12

'Oobie, joobie, joobie! Who's a naughty girl, then?'

Sam stared at the candy-striped stand; Punch swivelled around in his pointed hat, with his great hooked nose, rapped his baton down hard on his tiny stage and screeched:

'Naughty, naughty, naughty, naughty. Who's been a naughty girl, then?'

One of the children shouted out, 'Nicky's mummy has!'

Punch swaggered up and down along the stage, repeating to himself, 'Nicky's mummy's been naughty, has she? Nicky's mummy's been naughty, has she? We'll have to see about that, won't we?'

'Yeah!' came the chorus.

'Ooobie, joobie, joobie, who's been a naughty girl, then?' He swivelled and stared directly at Sam, leaning forward over the stage and curling and uncurling his index finger at her; it was a long finger, out of proportion with the size of the puppet, and the action unsettled her.

'Oobie, joobie, joobie,' he repeated over and over, curling and uncurling, leaning closer; the children were silent now, sensing an atmosphere. 'I think she ought to be punished, don't you, children?'

'Yeah!'

Punch stood upright and rapped the stage with his baton again. 'Who thought she was on an aeroplane?' He cackled with laughter.

Sam smarted with anger, with bafflement.

'Naughty! Naughty! Naughty!'

The baton came down. Whack, whack, whack. Harder, this time with real menace.

'Who's going to have to be punished then?'

'Nicky's mummy!' came the chorus.

Stop this. I want to stop this. Get him out of there. He's mad.

'We could beat her with a stick!' he screeched, then ducked down out of sight. 'Or we could . . .'

He reappeared.

But now he was wearing a black hood with slits cut into it.

Sam tried to back away, tried pushing herself on the carpet, but she was wedged against something, something hard, soft; the sofa, she realised.

She could see his lips smiling through the hood, then he winked, and his left eyeball shot out, hit the floor and rolled across the carpet, rattled onto the bare floorboards, bouncing against the skirting board and carrying on rolling, rattling like a cannonball.

The children shrieked with laughter.

He lifted something shiny, metallic up over the floor of the stage.

She shivered.

Shotgun.

He raised it up swiftly and aimed at her.

'*No!*' she screamed.

She saw the spurts of flame from the barrel and felt a sharp sting on her cheek.

The lights went out, and for a moment she was covered in darkness, sticky, cloying blackness that pressed against her eyes, her ears, forced its way into her mouth. Then a row of red digits appeared above her, and she blinked, startled by their brightness.

0415.

The darkness was becoming tinged with red, as if the light was bleeding into it. She heard a sharp snort beside her, a gurgling sound and several more snorts. Then Richard's voice.

'Wassermarrer?'

She felt a chill breeze. Dream, she thought. Dream.

0416.

Light poured out of the clock like blood into a bath. She heard Richard's voice again. 'What the fuck was that?' Heard the sound of his arm sliding through the bedclothes, a loud clank, the sound of water spilling, 'Shit', then the click of the light, which blinded her for a moment.

'Jesus,' he said.

He was staring up at the ceiling. Cracks ran out in all directions across it, like veins in an old woman's hand.

Like glass that had been hit by a bullet. She shivered.

Right above her head, a small chunk of plaster was missing completely. Her cheek was hurting like hell, she realised. Gingerly, she put her finger to her face, and felt the hard, flaky plaster crumble between her fingers as she touched it.

Richard leapt out of bed, horrified. 'It's fucking coming down. Get out of here!' He struggled into his dressing gown and she climbed out of bed too, and pulled her own dressing gown on. The ceiling seemed to be moving, breathing, sagging, cracking more as she looked at it. It looked like eggshell now, like a hard-boiled egg that had been dropped and the shell had cracked all around it.

'It's the water that got in after the fucking hurricane,' Richard said as she followed him out into the corridor. 'The survey said the roof had been leaking and the loft above our room had damp. The central heating's drying it out and the joists are warping.'

They ran down the corridor and checked Nicky's room, and then Helen's room, snapping their lights on, saying 'It's OK, it's OK,' then snapping the lights off again and closing the doors.

'Are their rooms safe, Richard?'

'They look fine. The roof was badly holed above our room – ours is probably the worst.'

There were no beds in the spare rooms yet, so they lugged sheets and blankets downstairs and made makeshift beds up on the two sofas in the drawing room. Richard stoked up the fire, got it going and piled logs onto it, and she lay on the sofa, snugly wrapped up now, her heart not thumping quite so badly, and watched the leaping flickering flames. Watched them as they slowly faded and died and dawn began to break outside.

13

The frost scrunched under her feet, and she rubbed her hands together against the icy air. The sun hung low in the sky over the Downs, pale, weak, as if it had been left on all night. The river slid past below her, dark brown, silent, like the fear that was sliding through her.

She touched the graze on her cheek gingerly and looked down at the mark on her finger which had now almost gone. There was a muffled pop, like the bursting of a paper bag, then another; she turned and saw Nicky running flat out across the lawn towards a small grey ball of fluff that was rolling about, flapping.

'It's not dead, Daddy! It's not dead!'

She saw him poke a hand forward nervously, then jump back, watched Richard striding over, gun crooked under his arm. Teaching him to shoot, already. Promised him a gun for his ninth birthday. Guns. Killing things. Hunting. Would the world ever change if children were taught to follow old instincts? Or was it foolish to ignore them, to try to pretend they no longer existed? Choices. So many choices to make in bringing up a child. So many decisions that could change or forever affect them. Decisions. Who the hell was equipped to make them?

She glanced at her Rolex. It was five past one. 'Richard,' she called out, 'we'd better have lunch.' She sighed. Her few moments of respite were over. The five minutes she had managed to grab for herself in the midst of the preparations. The rest of the day was going to be chaos. She yawned. Her back ached slightly, but nothing much. It had been OK on the sofa. It would have been even more OK if she could have had another twelve hours of sleep.

Oobie, joobie, joobie.

The weird taunt echoed in her head, and Punch's finger curled out towards her, curled, uncurled.

Oobie joobie joobie. The taunt seemed to hang in the air around her, then dissolve.

The whole damned ceiling could have come down.

Did that trigger the dream? she wondered. In that split second that the plaster struck? Was that how dreams worked? Did they all happen in a fraction of a second?

'Mummy! We shot a pigeon.'

'Very clever, darling.' She glanced down at the litter of wrapping paper on the kitchen floor, at the remote controlled car, already with a bit broken off. The BMX was in the garden, lying on its side. 'Don't you like your bike?'

His eyes lit up. 'Yeah!'

'It's not going to do it much good lying out in the garden. The grass is wet.'

'I'm going to use it again this afternoon. I am.'

'You shouldn't let it stay wet.'

'I'll dry it, I promise.'

'You won't.'

'I will. I promise I will.'

'Promises are important, Tiger. Never make a promise you can't keep. OK?'

He looked away. 'Yes,' he mouthed silently. 'Richard!' she called. 'Come on, lunch!' She could hear him on the telephone.

'Yah!' he shouted. 'Just a sec.'

She dug the ladle into the stew, and tipped a small portion onto Nicky's plate.

Richard came in.

'Who were you talking to?'

'Oh. Andreas. Just a—' He picked up the wine bottle which Sam had already uncorked. 'Are you having some wine, Mummy?' Richard hovered over his mother with the bottle.

Sam stared at her mother-in-law's thin wrinkled face, with her make-up too thick and her hair elegantly coiffed, too black. She always dressed well in expensive clothes that were now slightly frayed, not because she could not afford new ones, or to have them mended, but because she simply wasn't aware. It always seemed strange, his calling her Mummy. She wondered if Nicky would still be calling her Mummy when she was old like that.

'Wine, Mummy? Would you like some wine?' Richard repeated, louder.

'Coffee, I think,' she said. 'Do you do espresso?'

'We're going to have lunch first,' said Richard patiently, more patiently than usual.

His mother turned towards him. 'Your father'll have some wine, I expect. He's late.' She opened her handbag and scrabbled about in it, slowly, deliberately, warily, like a dog scratching away the earth over a hidden bone.

She pulled out a compact, clicked it open, and examined her lips. She took out a lipstick, and twisted the stem.

Sam and Richard exchanged a glance. His father had been dead for eight years.

'Would you like some stew, Mummy?'

'I'll have a cigarette now, I think, darling.'

'We're going to eat first, Joan,' Sam said, kindly but firmly.

Her mother-in-law frowned, puzzled.

'Have you thanked Granny for your present?' asked Sam.

Nicky looked forlornly at her. 'I only got handkerchiefs.'

'Handkerchiefs are jolly useful,' said Helen.

'Granny,' said Nicky, turning to her. 'We shot a pigeon.'

She rolled her tongue over her lips, then carefully put the lipstick back into the bag. She pulled out her cigarettes, and extricated one from the pack.

'Mummy, we're still eating,' said Richard, irritated.

'When's his birthday?' she said. 'Sometime soon, isn't it?'

'Today,' Sam said. 'It's today.'

Her mother-in-law frowned again and looked at her watch. 'Usually home by now.' She looked up at Richard. 'Probably in a meeting.'

'I'm sure he won't mind if you start without him,' said Sam. 'Why don't you have some stew?'

'Pigeons are naughty. Daddy's going to give me a gun when I'm – er – when I'm nine.'

'Elbows off, Tiger.' She turned to Richard. 'Do you think we should call the Punch and Judy man? He should have been here by now. Said he'd be here by one.'

'Looking forward to your party, Nicky?' asked Helen.

'Umm,' he said thoughtfully. 'Yes.'

They heard the sound of a car and Sam looked out of the window. A small, elderly Ford pulled up. 'Thank God,' she said, hurrying out of the room, as if she was afraid he might change his mind and go away.

He stood apologetically on the front doorstep, an unassuming little man in a drab suit and a thick mackintosh, with two huge suitcases.

'I'm so sorry I'm late,' he said. 'So terribly sorry.' He smiled, exposing a row of crooked rotting teeth, yellow and brown, and his breath was foul, as if he had been smoking a pipe. 'My wife's not well, I had to wait for the doctor.' He looked afraid. There was fear in his eyes.

'I'm sorry,' she said.

'Thank you. It's one of those—' He paused. 'I'm sorry,' he said. 'I'm here to be cheerful, to make the party go.' He smiled again and she could see he had been crying.

She felt a tug on her pullover and saw Nicky standing there.

'This is the Punch and Judy man, Tiger.'

'Hallo, young man. Happy birthday.'

Nicky looked suspiciously up at him.

'Say hallo, Tiger.' But Nicky said nothing. The man was thin and pale, with a slightly translucent skin; his head was almost bald on top, with a few strands pulled over and plastered down. He looked like a forgotten toy. 'Do you want a hand with your bags?'

'No, no, oh no, no, I can manage, thank you.' He picked up the two enormous cases and staggered forward, breathing hard. Sam saw tiny beads of sweat on his forehead, and she shivered suddenly. He made her feel uncomfortable. This little man who could make children laugh and scream and cry, this little man with his sick wife and his suitcases full of puppets.

What a life, she thought, what a life, to turn up every day on strangers' doorsteps. Did he love children? Or was he weird? As she stared at him she felt afraid, as if the man was carrying death into her house, carrying it in his two big heavy suitcases.

Nicky was looking at her anxiously. He stretched up towards her and spoke in a quiet, conspiratorial voice. 'Mummy, he doesn't look like Punch and Judy.'

'I'm sorry we're a bit early.'

'No, that's fine, really.' Sam smiled, staring at the woman, trying to think of her name. The wife of a City friend of Richard's. They owned a stately pile somewhere near here.

'It was very nice of you to invite Edgar.'

Sam looked down dubiously at the scowling child. A brat. It was stamped all over his face. 'Delighted,' she said.

'I trod in cow shit this morning,' Edgar said.

'Darling!' said his mother. 'I don't think Mrs Curtis wants to know about that.'

'I'll just get Nicky.' Sam looked around. 'Tiger! Come and meet your first guest!'

Helen appeared, holding Nicky gently by the arm, coaxing him along.

'This is Edgar,' said Sam.

'Give him his present.'

Edgar thrust out a small package. 'I trod in cow shit this morning.'

'Edgar!' said his mother.

'What do you say, Nicky?'

Nicky went bright red. 'Umm. Thank you very much. We shot a pigeon this morning,' he added.

'Shall we open that later, Nicky?' said Helen, lifting the package. 'We'll put them all together so we don't get in a muddle.'

'Why don't you show Edgar your presents, Tiger?' said Sam. She smiled at his mother. 'Would you like to come in?'

'Thanks, no. Have to dash. Be back at six?'

'OK. Bye.' Sam closed the door.

'I want to shoot a pigeon,' Edgar said.

'We're having a party now, Edgar,' she said. 'You can come back one day and go shooting with Nicky and his father if you like.'

'I want to shoot one now.'

'Nicky has got a radio controlled car. Would you like to see that?'

The child stamped his foot. 'Pigeon,' he said. 'Eeeeee, urrrrr, grrrmmmm.' He sprinted off across the hall, then stopped and glared through the kitchen doorway. He marched in and across to Richard, who was reading a paper. 'Urr.' He said. 'Grrremmmm.'

Richard carried on reading.

'Urrrr. Grrremmmmm.'

Richard glanced over the top of his paper. 'Sod off,' he said.

'Urrrr,' said the child, screwing up his face. 'Urrrr, urrrr. I want to shoot a pigeon.'

'Ask her, she'll take you.' Richard nodded at his mother, who was studying her face in her compact through a stream of cigarette smoke, and carried on reading.

Edgar put up his hand and tugged the paper down sharply, ripping it. 'I want to shoot a pigeon.' He stamped his foot.

Richard shot out his hand and grabbed the boy's ear.

'Ow!'

Shoving the paper aside, he stood up, twisting his ear harder, and marched him out of the kitchen.

'Owwwww! Arrrrrrr!'

He gave one final tweak for good measure.

'Richard, what are you doing?'

'Little bastard,' he said.

Edgar stood in the hallway, bawling, as Richard walked back into the kitchen. Sam stormed in after him. 'What have you done to that child?'

'Little bastard tore my paper.'

'Did you hit him?'

'No, but I will do next time.'

The doorbell rang.

'Oh God,' she said. 'Three o'clock, it's meant to start. Why are they all coming early? Can you shove the sausages in the oven? The bottom right-hand.'

'I'll put that little bastard in if he comes in here.'

'Shall I get the door, Mrs Curtis?'

'Thank you, Helen.' She looked back at Richard. 'Have you put the gun away?'

'Yes.'

'What's your mother doing?'

'She wants to know when we're having lunch. Bloody daft bringing her here.'

'It is her grandson's birthday.'

'You'd better remind her.'

'She's not completely gaga. She did buy him a present, and a nice card.'

'I wanna go home,' Edgar bawled.

'Hi Sam!' a voice called. Sam went back into the hall.

'Vicki!' She dashed over. 'Come in.'

'I've got to collect Peter from sailing.'

'Hallo, Willie.' Sam looked down at the slightly lost-looking child.

'Thank you very much,' she heard Nicky whisper, holding another brightly coloured package.

'Rowie!' Nicky's godmother.

'Sam! Mmmn!' Their cheeks collided and they each blew kisses out into the air.

'How are you, darling?'

'Fine. Great.' Sam tousled the hair of Rowie's stern little boy.

'Hallo, Justin.'

'Hallo, Auntie Sam.'

'This is daft, Sam. We live a mile away from each other in London, almost in the next-door village down here, and the only time we see each other is at kids' parties! How about lunch this week – Tuesday any good?'

'Sure. Why don't we have lunch at the club? A swim and a sauna? They have a good salad bar now.'

Another car was pulling up. Chaos; she felt bewildered for a moment. Then she saw the Punch and Judy man come down the stairs and walk through into the drawing room, quietly, meekly, gliding. Like a ghost, she thought.

14

'Sausage, Celia?'

The little girl raised her pig-tailed head. 'I don't eat sausages. My mummy says they're common.'

Sam stared at her, flummoxed for a moment, then moved on down the table with the heavy tray, listening to the babble. 'Sausage, Willie?'

'Yes, please.'

'I always have prawns at my parties,' said Celia loudly, to no one in particular.

Richard followed, with a tray of hot quiche.

'I don't eat quiche,' she heard Celia say.

'You'll get spots if you don't eat quiche,' he said.

She puffed up haughtily in her pink frock. 'My mummy says I'm going to be very beautiful. I'm going to be a model.'

'Are we having a film? Are we having a film?' said an excited voice Sam did not recognise. She stared at Nicky at the head of the table, in an orange paper crown, fists sunk into a half-eaten burger, ketchup, and relish oozing out the sides of it, his face and new jumper streaked in the stuff, like a Jackson Pollock painting.

'What film? What film?'

She looked at her watch. Just past four.

Babble. A child blew a plastic bugle. Another blew a low-pitched whistle, from which a strip of coloured paper uncurled. A little girl ran excitedly into the room, sat down and began whispering to her friend, who then rushed out. Sam saw the Punch and Judy man standing in the doorway, and she nodded at him.

'OK, everyone! Punch and Judy time!'

There were excited squeals, and a couple of groans.

'Can we all go next door, please.'

She herded them through into the drawing room and tried to get them seated on the floor in front of the candy-striped Punch and Judy stand. It was wobbling a bit and she could see the side move every few moments as the man shuffled around inside, sorting his things out. She watched it warily for a moment, traces of last night's dream echoing around her head as she listened to the babble. Helen wandered through the kids, dishing out lollipops.

'There's a real man inside there.'

"Course there isn't.'

'How do you know?'

'I looked.'

'How could you look? You're not tall enough.'

'I bet I am.'

'I bet you're not.'

One small girl sat on her own, slightly away from the rest, with her hands over her eyes.

Sam went out into the kitchen. Her mother-in-law was staring into her compact mirror, caking more make-up onto her nose, a thin thread of smoke rising from a mound of lipstick-covered butts in the ashtray beside her.

'Joan,' Sam said, 'the Punch and Judy's about to start. Would you like to see it?'

'Punch and Judy, dear?' She frowned. 'No, I think I'd prefer to stay in here. My lipstick's a bit smudged.'

'It looks very nice. I'm sure Nicky would like it if you came in.'

Her mother-in-law began to rummage in her bag again, the dog scratching through the earth for its bone.

There was a ripple of laughter from the drawing room. 'See you in a minute.' She walked across the hall, and paused in the doorway of the drawing room. The Art Deco clock on the mantelpiece caught her eye. Coming up to four-fifteen.

The time seemed familiar for some reason.

'Oobie, joobie, joobie! Who's a naughty boy, then?'

'Oh no I'm not!' squawked Punch, his soft pointed hat and hooked nose appearing over the top of the tiny stage.

'Oobie, joobie, joobie! Naughty, naughty, naughty!'

The words sent a prickle of anxiety through her.

'Oh no I'm not!'

'Oh yes you are!' shrieked Mrs Punch, dancing up and down in her gaudy frock.

'Oh no I'm not!'

'Oh yes you are!'

'Come on children, I'm not naughty am I?'

'Oh yes he is!'

Sam looked over the sea of faces, some grinning, some with lollipop sticks poking out of their lips. The girls in their party frocks, the boys in their shirts, mostly grubby already, and short trousers slightly dishevelled from the games. What sort of people would they become when they grew up? You could tell the meek and the assertive, the bullies and thinkers. Christ, they all had a long way to go before – before what? Before they could begin to understand? Look at me – I'm a grown up – thirty-two – and I don't even begin to understand. Maybe life wasn't about understanding at all? Maybe there was something else. We all charged through, looking in the wrong cupboards and missed the point. Would these children one day become old and baffled and still be opening and shutting cupboards? Rummaging through handbags for – cigarettes? For – the key to life? Like Richard's mother in the kitchen? No, not any more. We're entering the Age of Aquarius. It'll all make SENSE. The new UNDERSTANDING.

''Ere, children, help me. If you think I'm not naughty, shout out with me, all right? OH NO I'M NOT!'

'Oh no you're not!' There was a faltering chorus, uncertain, slightly embarrassed.

'Don't listen to him!' shrieked Mrs Punch. 'Say, "OH YES YOU ARE!"'

She stared at Nicky, sitting there, rapt. He was a nice chap, she thought; he cared, even now; he'd grow up to be a caring person.

'OH YES YOU ARE!'

She was vaguely conscious of the door opening at the far end of the room.

'That wasn't very loud!'

'OH YES YOU ARE!'

Something wasn't right.

Something was making her feel very frightened.

'Come on, louder!'

'OH YES YOU ARE!'

She saw the smile on his face first, forty feet across the room, the smile of a demon, not a small child. In an instant it was gone, and instead there was a laughing boy, a greedy little boy who has got his way and is happy, for a fleeting moment, until he becomes bored again. He was laughing, laughing to himself, laughing while the blood stopped flowing inside her and was turning to ice.

'Edgar,' she said, mouthing the word. 'Edgar!' she shouted against the sea of voices that were rooting for Mrs Punch.

'Edgar!' she shouted again, against the sea of voices that were now rooting for Mr Punch. 'Put it down! For God's sake put it down!'

It couldn't be loaded. Impossible. Richard was careful. He couldn't be that foolish.

'Edgar!'

He stood by the door, staggering under the weight of the shotgun like a drunken miniature gunfighter.

The finger.

Curling in the night.

4.15.

The clock. In the bedroom. When she had woken up.

4.15.

The clock on the mantelpiece.

4.15.

The finger on the trigger.

Oobie, joobie, joobie.

'*Edgar!*' She took a step forward.

The gun swept wildly across the backs of the children, up at her, up at the ceiling, then down at the children again.

'I'm going to shoot pigeons now.' She heard the words clearly, across the room, through all the noise, as clearly as if he was standing next to her.

The barrel was swinging up towards her.

'*Edgar, be careful! Put it down!*'

Pointing straight at her.

'OH NO I'M NOT!'

'OH YES YOU ARE!'

'EDGAR PUT IT DOWN.'

She could see straight into them, straight down both barrels, even from here.

'OH NO I'M NOT!'

Shut up. For God's sake shut up, you fool. Can't you see? Haven't you got peep holes in your damned box?

'Whack whack, ouch!'

'You hit me and I'll hit you.'

'DOWN, EDGAR, DOWN, PUT IT DOWN.'

'Oh no you won't.'

'Oh yes I will!'

She heard a solitary giggle.

His finger closed around the trigger.

'EDGAR!'

She stared down desperately at Nicky, tried to walk towards him, to get Nicky out of the way, to stop Edgar.

Whack.

'Ouch.'

'Where's he gone? Where's he gone?'

'HE'S BEHIND YOU!'

Mrs Punch spun round. 'Oh no he isn't!'

'OH YES HE IS!'

She spun round again. 'Oh no he isn't!'

'OH YES HE IS!'

Sam saw the spurt of flame from the barrel, and dived for the floor. Saw Edgar catapult backwards; the puzzled look on his face. Saw the gun in slow motion float upwards then drop silently to the ground, slowly, fluttering like a huge feather.

She spun around and saw what looked like snow suspended in the air all around the striped stand. Something hurtled along the floor, rattling loudly, bounced off the skirting board and stopped by her feet. Punch's head. It lay, grinning at her imbecilically, with one eye and part of its cheek missing.

Then the bang reached her, rippled through her like a shock wave, throwing her sideways, deafening her, like hands clapped over her ears so all she could hear was a faint ringing.

She saw the laughter fall from the faces, like masks that had dropped off. She scanned the room frantically. Nicky sat with his mouth open, holding his lollipop in his hand. She scrambled to her feet and stepped through the motionless children that were frozen like ornaments, and knelt down, flinging her arms around Nicky, hugging him. 'OK, Tiger! You OK?'

She looked around wildly as he nodded. 'Richard,' she said. 'Richard!' Conscious of saying the word, but unable to hear it. But he was already there, wading across the room as if someone had pushed the slow button on a video.

She could smell the acrid cordite now. Her ears cleared, and she heard a child sobbing. Nicky was still staring up at the stage, with its ripped-open canopy and the shreds of cloth that were floating down from it, as if he was waiting for Punch to pop back up and grin.

The candy-striped box shook once, then again, then moved several inches to the left. Then it moved again, drunkenly.

Oh God no, she thought.

Then it stopped moving and the Punch and Judy man came out, bewildered, his face sheet white, and staggered around the room with his arms outstretched in front of him. 'Police,' he said. 'Please fetch the police.' Then he staggered out into the hall.

Richard marched grimly across the room, holding his shotgun in his hand. Another child began to cry, then another.

Sam stood up and rushed out after the Punch and Judy man. 'Are you all right?' she asked.

'Police,' he said. 'Police! Fetch the police! The police!' He windmilled his arms.

'Are you all right?'

He stamped his foot like a child. 'I want the police!'

'I'll – I'll call them,' Sam said, backing away slowly. She felt Richard's cautioning hand on her arm, and he nodded for her to go back into the room.

'Shall we – play a game – everyone?' she heard Helen say, as she walked into the sea of shocked faces and the babble of tears, and through to the rear of the room. Edgar was sitting on the floor in the doorway, screaming, and she knelt down.

'Are you all right?' she said.

He carried on screaming.

She waited until he subsided. 'Are you all right?'

'My arm hurts.' Then he screamed again. 'It hurts!'

'Let me have a look at it.'

He shook his head and she grabbed his arm, furious. 'Let me see it.'

He looked up at her startled, and stopped screaming.

Sullenly he held it out. She tested it carefully. 'It's fine. You've just bashed it, that's all. Maybe that'll teach you not to play with guns.'

He stayed on the floor and glowered at her, as she walked back into the drawing room, looking down at the children, then again at the ripped canopy. There was a nasty peppered area on the new wallpaper, and she saw the edge of one curtain had also been damaged. She gazed around the rest of the room, at the clock on the mantelpiece. Twenty past four.

Oobie, joobie, joobie.

The pink curling finger.

She closed her eyes for a moment, hoping this too was a dream and that she could wake up and nothing had happened.

'Musical bumps!' said Helen. 'We'll play musical bumps!'

She opened her eyes. Helen was trying, trying so hard. 'Musical bumps,' Sam echoed. 'Good idea!' Trying to smile, trying to beam and look cheerful, staring down into the blank numbness and suspicion and fear, and she knew even without the cold silence that greeted her that you couldn't fool children with a cheery smile. Dragons did not die and people did not live happily ever after. But you had to try, because perhaps, sometimes, life was about trying.

Good idea!' she repeated. 'We'll play musical bumps!'

15

'Hi – Vivien, isn't it? Sorry, Virginia – of course! Look, I'm terribly sorry – Simon's a bit upset. We've had a bit of an . . . nobody's hurt, it's all right . . . accident with a – one of the children got hold of my husband's – but it's fine. Really—' Simon's mother's face had gone sea-sick white. 'Fine, really. He's OK – fine—'

Simon shuffled out of the house, his hair limp like his face, holding a silver foil balloon with the words 'THANKS FOR COMING TO NICKY'S PARTY!' printed on it in mauve letters, which bobbed above his head as he walked.

I had a dream about it, you know; yes! This is the second time actually. Last time was a little worse – 163 people snuffed it.

Stop looking like that, you snotty cow. I'm not loopy. I'm not a crank.

So I dreamed it? What did you want me to do? Cancel the party? Sorry Tiger, no more parties. Mummy has nasty dreams?

Anyhow, I didn't think it was a premonition – pre-cognition – what d'you call it? Seeing-the-future dream because a chunk of plaster came down and hit me on the face. So that's what I thought had caused the dream. I thought that after the aircraft dream, then Slider in the taxi, I was all spooked up. I just thought – hell – that was a weird dream. The dream book tells you that guns are phalluses – yup, schlonkers, and shooting is sexual aggression.

So I worked it all out . . . you see Richard and I aren't exactly what you'd call—

Thoughts shovelled through her mind as she walked across Covent Garden. It was a fine, sharp, cold Monday morning, and the fresh air was waking her up. She'd felt too tired to go for her early swim and was regretting it now. Her head was muzzy, sore with tossing in bed through the night watching an endless movie of threatening images: of Punch and guns and Slider grinning and people coming out of doorways and popping out of lift hatches, all wearing black hoods, and eggshell cracks rippling across ceilings, and roofs coming down, smothering her, burying her in a dark void, burying her and Slider together, him on top of her, with the eyeless socket staring at her, laughing at her.

She pushed open the Art Deco door and went into the office. She felt disoriented. There were girls all around, on the sofas, on the chairs, and others standing. They had shoulder bags and clutch bags and big leatherette portfolios, and were dressed in battered macs or flak jackets or great puffy coats like eiderdowns wrapped around them over the tops of their jeans and boots; smoking, chewing, hair-tossing girls who looked hopefully at her as if she was a magician that had come to free them from the wicked witch.

Shit. Casting session.

Need that this morning like a hole in the head.

Midnight Sun.

Kapow!

For-hair-that-comes-alive-after-dark.

Boom!

Midnight Sun.

For-people-who-come-alive-after-dark.

Zap! Biff! Klap-klap-klap!

Midnight Sun.

Very-special-shampoo-for-very-special-hair.

Midnight Sun.

Very special shampoo.

For very special people.

'Morning Lucy. Ken in?'

'Gosh – ah – yah.'

'Anyone from the agency here yet?'

'Gosh – ah – no.'

Lucy looked as though she had been to a children's tea party, too, and had got ketchup and relish over her face and in her hair, except it was dye in her hair and make-up on her face, blodged, smudged and much too much.

'Good weekend?'

Lucy yawned. 'Yah, Bit heavy.'

Sam glanced around at some of the girls, walked past Ken's waxwork with its fresh *Daily Mail* and went up the three flights of stairs to his office. She rapped on the door and went in.

It was more like a lair than an office. Clients did not come up here; they were seen down in the basement with the snooker table and screening theatre and the full up-front image. The office under the steeply sloping caves was plain, simple. A comfortable sofa, two easy chairs, the walls covered in framed photographs of awards, of location shots: Ken in action, waving his arms, stabbing a finger, sitting in a chair, reflecting in the shadow of a crane dolly, Ken shaking hands with or issuing orders to a plethora of personalities, mostly minor familiar faces from the commercials on the box, and a few more famous ones, like Orson Welles, Robert Morley, Frank Bruno, John Cleese. The right-hand wall was dominated by a movie poster, a gaudy yellow and green high-tech mish-mash.

'ADLANTIS! THE LOST WORLD OF THE 20TH CENTURY!' proclaimed the title.

Ken had nearly lost his house because of that movie. Three years ago, when she'd first joined him, it had been touch and go. Cash flows, projections, interminable meetings with his bank manager that he reported to her, quite openly, afterwards. He'd been bust. Seriously bust. Over two million in the hole. He'd spent it on his dream, on his burning ambition, on his big break into the movie business. He'd put all the money he had and all the money he could borrow, hocked everything, the house and all, for his big break.

ADLANTIS! THE LOST WORLD OF THE 20TH CENTURY!

Five thousand years after civilisation is wiped off the face of the earth by thermo-nuclear war, primitive life starts up again on the planet earth . . . Centuries later, Ignav Flotum IIIrd, a Borodovian monk on an archaeological dig, discovers an old tin can . . . Convinced this is a time capsule deliberately left behind by another age it is opened in grand ceremony . . . to reveal . . . a television commercial director's showreel. From this reel a picture of late twentieth-century society is gradually pieced together. They conclude that since most of the movies only run for thirty seconds and the longest for only one minute, the concentration span of twentieth-century man must have been extremely low, thus contributing to his downfall, in spite of the clear socio-economic messages portrayed by these movies.

The movie had never been completed, and Ken had always been slightly evasive about the reasons. Sometimes it was because the leading actor had been a raving egomaniac. Sometimes the weather had been to blame. Sometimes the pressure of the executives from the studio that had partnered him but had never come up with all the dough they had promised. But mostly, she felt, it had never been finished because he had lost heart in it long before the money had ever run out. He promised to show her what there was of it, one day, but she wondered if he ever really would.

At least his house had been saved, his huge Victorian house on the edge of Clapham Common filled with weird objects, things he had collected, suits of armour, bizarre pictures, a tumbledown miniature Roman temple folly in the garden. He loved the house, had put years of thought and effort into making it something stunning, wild, with a Byzantine bathroom and medieval dining room and Baroque drawing room with a minstrel's gallery. Crazy, nuts – but stunning. The house had the space to take it without the styles clashing. The furniture was beautiful. It was a fun place. He lived in it on his own, from choice. His divorce had been a long time ago and the wounds had been deep. There were girls around, sure, always someone in tow, some bright young hopeful, more intelligent than the average but kept at a distance, kept at bay, kept out of his heart which was a strictly private place.

He was sitting behind his desk reading a letter, looking as if he had just got in, his denim jacket still on and a scarf hanging around his neck. He glanced up and smiled. 'Got my jelly baby?'

'Jelly baby?'

'From Nicky's party. You promised.'

'Oh – shit – I—'

'What time's the casting session meant to start?'

'Nine-thirty.'

'Anyone here yet?'

'Some of the talent. No one from Saatchi's.'

He looked at her. 'Christ, you look terrible. Are you OK?'

She nodded and swallowed hard.

'How did the party go?'

She turned away, wishing she hadn't come up here now, not wanting him to see the tears. She gazed at a photograph of Ken on his hands and knees, trying to show a sheepdog how to eat its food. She heard his intercom buzz sharply, then again. It gave a longer more insistent buzz and then was silent. She heard it buzz in another office, somewhere else in the building, and then she felt a hand lightly on her shoulder.

'What happened, Sam? Is it the air crash? Is the shock hitting you?'

She felt the tears running freely down her cheeks, and squeezed her eyes tighter, fighting. 'It's horrible, Ken. Oh Christ, it's horrible.'

'What's horrible?' he asked gently.

'It's happened again.'

'What's happened?'

She shook her head. 'Another dream. I had another dream.'

The intercom buzzed again and Ken answered it. 'OK,' he said, and put the phone back down. 'Everyone's here – we'll have to get down. Want to tell me later? We'll have a drink? This afternoon – after it's over?'

She sniffed. 'Thanks. I'll be down in a minute. Just have to make a quick phone call.'

She opened the door.

'Sam, don't worry. Everything'll be OK.'

She nodded, unconvinced.

'You haven't really had a break for a long time – you even came in over the Christmas hols. Why don't you take a few days off? Go away with Richard somewhere?'

'I'm OK. Thanks.'

'You need a holiday, Sam. Everyone does. Go skiing or something – have a break. Hey, I nearly forgot, I read this in a magazine and cut it out for you. It's about dreams.'

'Thanks.' She took it and put it in her handbag. 'I'm sorry I forgot your jelly baby,' she said, then went out and down the stairs.

Drummond was walking along the corridor, studying the label on a box he was carrying.

'Hallo.' He paused, as if trying to remember her name. 'Sam,' he added as if it was an afterthought.

'Hallo, Drummond.'

'Good weekend?'

'Fine.' She smiled wearily.

'How're the dreams?'

'Dreams?'

'Giraffes. You were dreaming about giraffes, or something.' He frowned and stared at the label again, mystified.

'I thought you'd said they don't dream much.'

'They don't.'

'I'd like to be a giraffe,' she said, opening the door and going into her office.

Smoke swirled around her, blue, thick Monday morning smoke, like mist. Claire seemed to need twice as many cigarettes on a Monday. 'Morning, Claire.'

Claire was concentrating on a script she was reading. Sam thought she detected the briefest nod, but wasn't sure. She opened the window sharply to release the fumes, to release her irritation at Claire, then changed the paper in the blotter on her desk.

'Good weekend?' said Sam, trying to force some conversation.

Claire glanced up for a second. 'All right.' Then read again.

She wondered what Claire did in the evenings, at weekends. All she knew was that she'd had a boyfriend called Roger with whom she'd split up, and that she lived in West London. Getting her to talk about her private life was like trying to pry open a superglued clam. She glanced down at her thick pile of post. It would have to wait.

'I've put the hotel details on your desk, Sam,' Claire said suddenly.

'Hotel?'

'Leeds. The Castaway presentation. You're doing it Friday week at nine in the morning. You asked me to book a hotel for the Thursday night.'

'Oh yes, thanks.' She quickly sifted through the post, the memos, costings to be done, the calls to be returned, checking for anything urgent, feeling tired and tensed up, wishing she had gone for her morning swim. Everyone talked about shrinks these days, about new stress ailments, yuppie flu: yuppie syndrome, she'd read somewhere. Maybe she had yuppie syndrome, whatever that was.

She saw the plane flying into the mountain. The finger curling in the night. Edgar coming into the room with the gun. Something cold trickled slowly through her, like a finger tracing its way down a frosted window. She shuddered, and pulled out a phone directory.

She found the number of Bamford O'Connell's Harley Street practice, and dialled it. A brisk pleasant woman answered.

'Is it possible to speak to Dr O'Connell?'

'May I ask who's calling please?'

'It's Mrs Curtis. I'm – we're – friends of his.'

He came on the line only seconds later, surprising her. 'Sam?' His thick Irish brogue was full of warmth.

'I'm sorry to call you at work, Bamford. I wondered if it was possible to see you – professionally.'

'That was a great evening last week.'

'Thanks.'

'You'd like to have a chat about something?'

'Please. I – it's about what we were discussing at dinner.'

'What was that?'

She looked at Claire, then down at her desk. 'Dreams. I've had another. I—'

'Would you like to come round to the flat this evening?'

Claire stopped reading and listened, without looking up.

'Is it possible to see you privately?' Sam felt herself getting flustered.

'Sure, come here, see me here. Is it very urgent?'

Yes, it's urgent as hell. 'No, I—'

'If it's urgent, I could try and make a few minutes today. Otherwise, Thursday morning, twelve o'clock. I'd have a bit more time then.'

'Thursday would be fine. Thanks, Bamford,' she said. 'I really appreciate it.'

As she went out of the office and closed the door, Claire turned around and smiled.

Sam went down the stairs slowly, thinking. The entrance atrium was packed with girls now, there was a babble of chatter, a haze of smoke and perfume, a small dog yapped excitedly and the switchboard was warbling while Lucy ignored it, phone to her ear, deep in some personal conversation. The front door opened and a man came in, fast, determined, pushing his way through the throng of girls, staring straight at Sam, walking towards her, striding; a great bully of a man dressed in black with a hood over his face, his eyes barely visible through the two thin slits.

She felt her legs buckling and a cold flushing sensation in her stomach; her head spun. She crashed against Ken's waxwork, saw the newspaper crumple and thought dimly, Damn, he'll be annoyed, as she stumbled, grabbing the cold, icy cold hand for support, felt something give, felt the whole arm tear away at the shoulder, and she staggered forward holding the hand as if it was a child she was taking across a road, staggered forward holding the hand with the severed arm attached to it, through the horrified faces and the screams of the girls, bounced off the wall, off Lucy's white Cadillac door, as she tried to stop, to back away, to turn and run from the man with the black hood and the eye slits, but she kept stumbling forwards, through the girls that were backing away open-mouthed . . . smart, pretty, beautiful girls staring at the arm, wide-eyed with horror, then her feet ran into each other and she fell forwards, making a slight whinnying sound.

Help me. Get me away from him. Oh Christ stop staring, don't you understand?

He was standing over her, in baggy black trousers and a grimy jacket and a black balaclava against the cold. He was holding a crash helmet in one gauntleted hand and a jiffy bag in the other, which he dropped as he knelt down to help her to her feet.

'Orl right, doll?' he asked. He smelled of leather and tobacco and a faint hint of hot engine oil.

'Fine, thanks – I . . .' She stood swaying, staring blankly around at the silent faces that stared back, listening to the yapping of the dog.

'Ssh, Bonzo! Quiet!'

'Sam! – Gosh, Sam. You OK?'

'Yes, I—'

'Ken Shepperd Productions?' said the man in the balaclava, holding out the jiffy bag. 'Need a signature.'

Sam stared down at the severed arm on the floor, at the sea of faces, at the crumpled newspaper. She picked up the arm and carried it back to the waxwork. 'Lucy, if you've got a moment . . .' She was conscious she was talking slowly, almost as if she was sitting on the ceiling, looking down at herself speaking. 'Perhaps you could nip out . . . and get a new *Daily Mail*.' She peered inside

128

the shirt-sleeve and saw the jagged hole below his shoulder. She put the arm limply in his lap, then turned and went down the stairs to the basement.

16

The water hissed and spat; she felt the rush of heat in her nostrils, and rivulets of sweat running down her face and her body. She glanced at the thermometer, which was still rising, leaned back on her towel on the hard wooden slats and breathed in the scorching steam that was thick with the smell of pine.

'Any more?' Rowie stood, holding the small wooden bucket, naked and running with sweat too, her ginger hair matted to her head, her breasts hanging down, a hint of sag, of droop. She would have to be careful, Sam thought, she could easily run to fat. Was beginning to show signs already: her freckled skin was looking creamy, slightly puffy, around her neck, her arms, her thighs, and the great ugly stretch marks that seemed to be getting more noticeable.

Rowie. Partner in crime through five years of school. Sam had been chief bridesmaid at Rowie's wedding; she'd been flung the bouquet and caught it, and the superstition had come good. She'd met Richard and they got married eight months later.

Rowie. Life had come easy for her. Boyfriends, marriage, children, four of them, no effort. Everything progressed for her, straight, easy, linear; took life as it came and it had always come good.

'I feel guilty,' she once confided to Sam. 'I don't know why I have such a nice life.'

There was always a storm somewhere, or a disaster or a tragedy, waiting to happen, but so far it never had.

The only glitch had been discovering her third child was dyslexic, and that was being sorted out.

Sam looked at Rowie's body again. You are running to fat. Good. Hooray. Great. You're going to be plump and waddly in a few years' time.

Christ.

She felt a wave of shock at the malevolence of her thoughts. Did she wish fatness on her? Disaster? Was she really fond of her or jealous as hell? She stared down at her own body, good firm breasts, just right. They wouldn't get limp and saggy. She looked at her thighs and her legs, firm, skinny almost, like her wrists.

It must be like fucking a skeleton.

Richard had said that once about an anorexic-looking model who had walked past them on a beach. Did he think that of her too? Christ, it was hard to get the balance right.

A great fat shapeless hulk of a woman in a bathing hat came into the sauna, gave a surly nod and studied the thermometer.

Don't you dare put any more water on, Sam thought, watching her. Great tree-trunk thighs, a Mr Bibendum stomach and breasts like empty sacks. She had no bum at all, just the huge flab of her back which ran into her thighs; shapeless, as if God had dumped her on earth without having finished making her.

I don't ever want to look like that. No thanks. Skinny lib.

They plunged and shrieked and showered and the Big Hulk followed them, dampening their chat to nothing in particular. Sam showed Rowie where her leg had got burned from the careless waxing, and Rowie told her they'd taken the kids skiing over Christmas and she'd got a bruise on her bum that had only just gone. Then they dressed and went and helped themselves to gazpacho and tuna salads filled with beanshoots and pulses and nuts and seeds and other strange things neither of them recognised which would probably make their stomachs fizz and rumble all afternoon, sat down in a quiet corner, free now from the Big Hulk, and clinked their glasses of organic apple juice together.

'Cheers!'

They each smiled.

'Gosh, it's been ages,' Rowie said.

'Since before Christmas, actually. Not since September.'

'September? That long?'

'Before the hurricane. I'm certain.'

'Time. I don't know what happens to it. New watch? It's wonderful.'

'Richard gave it to me – to improve my street cred.'

'It's gorgeous. God, you know what Suzy said to me last Saturday? She said, "Don't come shopping with me, Mum, you ruin my street cred." Eleven. She's only eleven!'

Sam grinned. 'You can blame it all on commercials.'

Then there was a silence. A long flat silence in which all her thoughts began to pile up and cut away her elation at seeing Rowie again, and crush her down. Rowie split open her granary roll and dabbed a piece in her gazpacho, like a nurse swabbing a wound, thought Sam suddenly, and shivered.

'How's Richard?'

'Oh, he's . . . you know. Fine. Busy, I—' She shook her head, staring into Rowie's face the way she might have stared into a mirror.

'Oh God,' said Rowie, as she saw the trickle from Sam's eye, and heard Sam make short jerking sounds, her face contorted as if someone was pulling a wire tight around her neck.

They sat in silence while Sam tried to compose herself. She split open her roll as well, dunked a piece in the soup and felt the fierce taste of onions and tomato and garlic in her mouth.

'What's happened?'

Sam picked up her spoon and poked around in the soup bowl. She hadn't talked about it; not to anyone. Because . . . because it made her feel such a fool. Maybe Rowie knew anyway and was just being nice? Everyone else did; the Pearces and the Garforth-Westwards and the Pickerings and the . . . shit, oh shit, oh shit. She looked up.

'The boys – Roddy and Guy and that lot – have a shoot in Scotland the first week in January, every year. Richard always goes with them. He went off this year as usual, except two days after he'd gone, at six o'clock on a Sunday evening, I got a call from the police. I thought they were phoning to tell me he was dead or had an accident. It was horrible. They gave me the registration number of his BMW and asked who owned it.' She stared intently at Rowie's puzzled face, then jammed her elbows on the table and leaned forward, feeling better now she was actually talking about it. 'His car had been parked on a double yellow line outside a hotel in Torquay since Friday evening. They'd towed it away and it hadn't been claimed, so they'd been worried it had been stolen.' She gazed quizzically at Rowie.

'Naturally.' Rowie stared back, and realisation dawned slowly across her face. 'Oh God – you mean?'

Sam nodded. 'Yes. With a girl from his office – some hot-shot little Eurobond dealer.' She gazed down at her soup and rolled the spoon over. 'Unfortunately, I didn't immediately twig. I assumed his car had been stolen and dumped, so I rang the boys – I got their number in Scotland from Juliet – to speak to him.' She shook her head. 'Can you imagine what a fool I felt? How small I felt? His friends – our friends – they knew. They were trying to cover up for him like a bunch of school kids.'

'Christ. You poor thing, Sam. You must have felt an absolute—'

'I did.'

'What did Richard say?'

'Not a lot.'

'And he hadn't noticed his car was missing from Friday night to Sunday afternoon? What on earth was he—' Rowie stopped in mid-sentence. 'Oh, Sam, I'm sorry.'

Sam sighed. 'I thought our marriage was – you know – something very special, that we – that it was all going—' She grimaced and stared down at the table-cloth. 'I thought at least we respected each other. It's just . . . I don't know, the way he did it – the timing – I think Christmas is a special time. Am I being ridiculous?'

Rowie smiled and shook her head.

'All this thing about Aids. That's been bothering me too. I mean God knows where she's been.' She shook her head. 'But it's our friends – that's what's really got me. Christ, I saw some of them over Christmas. They knew then that he wasn't going shooting with them and I bet the girls knew too. I haven't heard a dicky from any of them since.'

Rowie sipped her juice, and spoke over the top of her glass.

'These things happen, Sam.'

'You always think they happen to other people.'

'It doesn't necessarily mean much. To Richard. It doesn't mean that he doesn't still love you very much, not necessarily; a lot of people have affairs just for sex.'

'I know. Part of me says it's daft to get so angry – that

all men have affairs, and it's part of married life, and another part feels that I don't want to touch him ever again. We haven't made love since. The thought of it makes me feel ill.' She stared at Rowie. 'Is that normal?'

'I don't know, Sam. All marriages are different. I always thought you had a good marriage.'

'Yes. I did too.' Sam shrugged. 'Richard just seems to have changed recently.'

'In what way?'

'It's hard to describe, exactly. He's started to make a lot of money – big money – the last eight or nine months. He's become very pally with a Swiss banker chap who I think's very weird, but that may just be me. He really fawns over him; rings him all the time to consult him on things. Speaks to him more than he speaks to me.' She swallowed some soup. 'The gun at the party . . . he would never have left his gun lying around before. He used to be quite a patient man, but he's become very snappy. He was quite brutal to Edgar before the party started.'

'Maybe he's worried. Everyone in the City's been very twitchy since the Crash. Did he lose much?'

'He said Andreas warned him it was going to happen, so he was OK.'

'Andreas?'

'The Swiss guy.'

'Have you ever been tempted to have an affair?' Rowie asked.

'No. You get gropers at parties, but they just turn me off. Have you?'

Rowie smirked and ate more bread. 'It's been going on for years,' she said.

Sam felt as if someone had pulled a plug out inside her. The whole established order of the world seemed to be turning on its head. 'Who with?'

'A black guy.'

'*What?*'

'My aerobics teacher.'

'You're kidding.'

'It's – strictly sex only,' Rowie said. 'You know, I didn't think women were meant to feel that way, but we have this great thing.' She smiled apologetically, and looked sheepish, as if wondering whether she should have told her after all.

'I thought you had a good marriage,' Sam said. 'Special, like ours.'

'Other pastures always look greener. Yup. Our marriage is fine. But James works all the time, and I just started getting . . . I don't know—' She smiled again. 'I'm not in a very good position to pass moral judgements, am I?'

'Is anybody?' Sam pushed her soup bowl aside and picked at her salad. 'How's Justin? Was he very upset after the party?'

'No,' Rowie said. 'He thinks it was all very exciting, that it was all part of the Punch and Judy show. How about Nicky?'

'I think he's very shocked still. Richard keeps going on about how resilient kids are, but I'm not so sure.'

Richard had paid the Punch and Judy man five hundred pounds to keep him from calling the police.

'*I don't want you to teach Nicky to shoot any more.*'

'*It wasn't his fault.*'

'*I keep thinking what might have happened. Just a few inches lower and he would have killed that man – or Nicky – or any of the children.*'

'*It was mother's bloody fault.*'

'*Don't be ridiculous.*'

'*It was. Leaving a cigarette burning on the hall table. Christ, if I hadn't seen that the bloody house would*' *have gone up. I was so angry, I just forgot about the gun, I suppose. That's what I must have done . . . I still can't believe it. I always lock it away, and put the cartridges on top of the wardrobe. I was sure I had done that. Certain.'*

She'd tried to tell him she had dreamed it and he'd told her not to be ridiculous.

'I'm not sure how resilient adults are either,' Rowie said.

They stayed and talked until it was past three, about men and life and kids and people they used to know and didn't any more but bumped into or heard of from time to time. Sam tried to ease the subject of dreams in, wanted to talk to her, wanted to say 'I dreamed it would happen' but the chance didn't come and there wasn't a break in the conversation where she could bring it in without feeling foolish.

Rowie suggested Sam took the afternoon off and they went shopping. Hell, how many afternoons had Sam taken off in the past three years, and surely everything could wait until tomorrow? So they went shopping. They tramped Covent Garden, then went across to South Molton Street and each bought stuff the other admired, and thought would look great, and Sam wondered why she was bothering to look great for Richard, and why Rowie was bothering to look great for James, and when Rowie bought a really zany track-suit number she knew that was not for James's benefit at all.

Then suddenly Sam found the chance and told Rowie, and instead of making her feel a fool Rowie said she could understand; that *she* could tell when things were going to happen herself, she told Sam; she got FEELINGS. She had an aunt who was very psychic, who always had the same dream the night before there was going to be a death in the family: she'd see a stranger in the distance walk on a beach at low tide and go into the sea and disappear, and the next day a member of the family would die, but she could never tell who.

They had drinks in a wine bar they stumbled across in Hanover Square, and then more drinks, a bottle or so of Chardonnay. It was good. Sam wondered if Archie at her dinner party would have approved of it. They got pissed, really, seriously, pissed, until they were clinking glasses and giggling like schoolgirls, and Rowie told her not to worry, everyone had FEELINGS about things from time to time and some people had stronger FEEL-INGS than others, but Sam was fine, she wasn't going nuts, and a hooded man from the past wasn't coming to get her. She was probably shaken up by Richard's affair and it was triggering off all sorts of unpleasant things in her mind.

That was all.

So go home.

Relax!

OK?

Sam grinned and started walking to clear her head, feeling vaguely guilty, but not that guilty, that it was late and she hadn't rung Richard and she'd missed Nicky's bedtime. She hadn't made up her mind whether to collect her car or take a taxi, and knew she shouldn't try to drive because she was smashed, but somehow she found herself in Covent Garden when the rain started to come down as if a tray of water had been tipped out of the sky, and there wasn't a taxi in sight, so she sprinted for the car park.

17

The rain seemed to stop as abruptly as it started, leaving the London night in a shiny black lacquer on which spangles of light danced, winked, glinted. She glanced out of her side window and could see the reflection of the Jaguar on the black tarmac as clear as if she was driving beside a lake.

A Belisha beacon winked at her and she stopped. A man hurried over the crossing holding a broken umbrella.

THE NORTH. M1

She frowned. North. She was going north. Christ, she was sloshed. What was the time? What the hell was the time? London seemed quiet, too quiet. She stared at the clock, and could hear it ticking loudly, suddenly, like a grandfather clock.

Quarter to ten.

It felt like 4 a.m.

Quarter to ten. Christ. Had she and Rowie been drinking all this time?

She came into Swiss Cottage, and a car hooted angrily on her inside.

'Oh sod off,' she shouted into the dark, swinging the steering wheel, then heard the angry horn of a taxi right beside her. She braked cautiously and blinked, the lights blurring together. Slow down. Got to slow down. Wrong direction. Got to head for the City.

But she turned further away, going up Fitzjohn's Avenue towards Hampstead. A white Ford Capri, sitting up on huge wheels, drew alongside her and a yobbo gave her the thumbs up. She turned away contemptuously, then dropped down into second gear and floored the accelerator. She felt the tail of the Jaguar snake as the rear wheels spun, then eased off, felt the tyres bite, heard the roar of the engine, felt the surge of power as she accelerated forwards. She pulled right across, overtaking in the oncoming lane, saw headlights coming down the hill towards her, closer. The engine was screaming, she changed into third and missed the gear. There was an angry grating and the car began to slow down, the headlights almost on top of her now. She was still stabbing the gear lever, trying to find the gate, and jerked the wheel hard to the left. The lorry passed her, inches away, shaking her with its vibration and its slipstream.

Shit.

Then she saw the police car coming down the hill, slowing, as if it was looking for somewhere to turn and come after her.

Stop.

Stop, she thought. Got to stop.

Don't be stupid. Get away!

She swung right, without indicating, into a side road and accelerated down it. It came out into a busy street, brightly lit, with shops, restaurants, cafés, pubs. Hampstead High Street.

Shit.

She turned left, then saw another side street on her right, and turned into it. It had trees, cars parked down both sides and large terraced houses. She looked at her mirror for signs of a car following. Nothing. She slowed right down, crawling along, until she found a gap, and pulled into it. She switched off the ignition, then the lights, and breathed out. Quiet. So quiet, she thought.

She climbed out of the car into the strange translucent light and looked up, hazily, at the full moon that was burning down between the branches of the trees. Bright, she thought, brighter than the sun. She walked along the road then stepped onto the kerb to avoid a car which came thundering down, far too fast, as if it had been deliberately trying to hit her, and she stood for a moment, watching its tail lights disappear.

She glared up at the brilliant moon again, then walked on down the road, afraid of the shadows of the trees, like dark pools of blood. Afraid of the trees themselves that seemed to be watching her, and afraid of the brilliant light of the moon in the open that lit her up, exposing her like a startled rabbit caught in a car's headlamps.

She breathed a sigh of relief as she came out into Hampstead High Street. Cars. People. Noise. The glare of the moon was diffused by the streetlights, by the lights from the shop windows. She felt safe now and looked around for a taxi. Two passed in succession, both carrying passengers. A greasy-looking man in a Japanese sports car slowed down, peering at her. She turned away and noticed a red, circular tube sign a short distance away. She glanced once more up and down for a taxi, then walked up the street and into the station.

It was grimy, draughty, and seemed to be empty, apart from the woman in the ticket office, who stared at Sam through the Plexiglass window. A severe, elderly woman with her hair raked sharply back, her face caked in make-up and her lips a brilliant ruby red. Something about her reminded Sam of her aunt.

'Wapping,' Sam said. 'I'd like a ticket to Wapping.'

'Return?' said the woman sternly, as if it was a reprimand.

'No, I just . . . I just want to go there.' She was conscious that she was still drunk, slurring her words, stumbling over them, and her mind raced, trying to find the word she wanted, but it ducked away elusively, like a child dodging behind dark trees. 'I don't want to come back.'

'We don't do one-way from this station,' the woman said, her head not moving as she spoke. 'No singles.'

Single. That was the word. Single. Why had it been so difficult? she wondered.

'I'll have a double then,' said Sam and, almost immediately, the make-up on the woman's face began to crack, and her lips parted and widened. For an instant, Sam was frightened as the woman's expression changed and her mouth widened even more, then her shoulders began to shake up and down and her eyes sparkled. She was laughing. Sam realised; she was roaring with laughter. At her joke.

'Have a double!' said the woman. 'Have a double.' She roared again, and Sam grinned happily, feeling warm, warm deep inside.

'Funny. That was so funny.' She winked at Sam and jerked her head. 'Go on, that was so funny I couldn't give you a ticket after that.' She jerked her head, 'Go on. If the inspector catches you, tell 'im Beryl said it was all right.'

'I ought to pay you,' said Sam.

'Nah.' She jerked her head again, and Sam walked off past her and through the empty barrier.

She found herself facing a bank of lifts, with large steel doors, more like goods lifts than passenger lifts.

She pushed the button for the lift and waited. Faintly, behind her, she heard a peal of cackling laughter from the woman in the ticket office, and smiled to herself. The woman laughed again and the tone changed slightly, as if she was laughing at her rather than with her. Then she saw the sign in front of her, red letters on white board, huge. So huge, she wondered how she could have missed it: OUT OF ORDER.

She walked to the staircase, and then began to descend the stone steps that spiralled down, around a steel-cased shaft, listening to the clacking echo of her footsteps. WARNING. DEEPEST STATION IN LONDON. 300 STEPS. USE ONLY IN EMERGENCY. Somewhere in the distance she heard a clank and a rattle, and the sound of voices. The wall stayed relentlessly constant, unrelieved even by graffiti. Grimy drab tiles.

Christ. Like going down into a public lavatory.

The sign was right, the stairs seemed as if they would go on for ever, and she wondered how far down she was now. It felt deep, very deep, but there were no markers, no clues, just the same monotonous downward spiral, around the shaft. She passed a cigarette butt that looked as if it had been recently stamped out. It was getting darker, she realised. Further away from the moon. The colour seemed to be going from the tiles, and the temperature was getting colder.

Then she felt the jerk of a hand around her neck.

For a split second she was furious, then fear surged through her, paralysing her.

No. Not me. Please not me.

She was pulled backwards so sharply she thought her spine was going to snap, and she cried out in pain. She felt something in her neck, pushing in, crushing the bone and pushing out the air, choking her. She felt the hand, hard, rough, over her mouth, crushing her lips against her teeth, and tasted blood. She tried wildly to bite the hand, felt it jammed up against her nose. It smelled of onions.

Like Slider.

Please God it's Slider. Please God this is a dream and I can wake up.

She heard a door open, and felt herself being dragged

through. She tried to kick, to break her mouth free and shout, then she was pulled again and her feet slid away completely from under her, and she was arched backwards, violently, her scream of pain trapped in her throat.

The light faded completely, and she heard the clang of a door closing.

She was in pitch darkness. Herself and her attacker.

She heard his breathing, hoarse, panting. Malevolent.

Help me. Please. Don't let this be happening.

She felt a hand, rough, calloused, sliding up her thigh. She struggled wildly, but could not move. The fingers reached the top of her tights, and she felt them rummage harshly through her pubic hairs for an instant, then thrust up deep inside her, his fingernails cutting her like a knife, and she wanted to scream, but still the hand was over her face.

Oh God, no you bastard, let me go. No, *no*.

Then she felt her panties tugged down, and heard them ripping.

She tried to bite again, tried to wriggle, but his grip was like a vice, and every movement was agony. She stared, wide-eyed, into the darkness. There was a click then a whirring sound somewhere in the room. Think. Think, for Christ's sake. Self defence. Hurt him. Fingers in his eyes. His eyes. Which way was he facing?

She could hear him breathing heavily, grunting, like a pig. She felt a cold draught of wind up between her legs, then the fingers thrust in even further, so hard they were going to split her apart, heard the pop of a button, then the sound of a zipper. Her assailant was moving, slowly, cautiously, preparing himself.

No. God no. Please God no.

'Kiss me. Tell me you love me,' he said in a bland North London accent, and she felt his mouth nuzzling her ear. 'Tell me you love me,' he repeated, in a seductive French accent this time, nuzzling her ear again, and she jerked away, from the wetness of his mouth, from the stench of cigarettes and beer and onions on his breath. The fingers slipped out, probed gently through her pubic hair, caressing. 'Tell me you love me,' he said again, harshly. Then there was silence as she stared around the dark, her heart crashing, her brain racing, thinking, thinking, listening to his panting, which was getting louder, faster.

Outside she heard footsteps, and she felt her assailant grow tense, the hand over her mouth tighten.

Help me. Please help me.

The footsteps passed by, two or three people. She heard someone call out, someone laugh, someone shout something back. They faded away. There was a deep rumble, and the floor trembled slightly for a moment.

'Tell me you love me,' he said. 'Tell me you love me.'

She felt the hand lift away a fraction, enough to let her speak, and she lunged out with her mouth, as wide open as she could stretch it, and bit, hard, tried to bite a chunk out of his hand.

'You bitch!'

As his grip released, she sprang away from him, kicking out, smashing with her fist, then kicked again, felt something soft, heard a groan, then her head smashed into the wall and she bounced off, dazed.

'You cunt bitch!'

She kicked out again, as hard as she could, scrabbling with her hand to find the door, then kicked again, hit air, could not see his shadow in the darkness. She felt a hand grab her hair and lunged forward with her finger, felt something soft, gelatinous, and he screamed. She thrust forward, kicking out wildly again, pushing with her finger and again he screamed. The grip on her hair slackened.

Door handle. It was in her hand. She pulled, and the door opened and she fell out onto the stone staircase. 'Help!' she tried to scream, but it only came out as a whisper. 'Help me. Oh God help me!' She scrambled up the steps. Christ, run, for God's sake. Run. She tried, but she couldn't even raise her leg to the next step up. She heard the door opening behind her. Run, run! She pushed forward against the air that was like a wall. Help! She tried to scream again, but nothing would come out.

She grabbed the hand rail, trying to pull herself up the staircase, but it was steep, too steep. She pulled again, feeling her arm muscles tearing against the strain, against the force that was preventing her.

'Cunt bitch.'

She tried again, but still she could not move.

The hand closed around her neck, and she was jerked violently back.

She lashed out with her elbows, but her arms were being held tightly and she could scarcely move them. 'No!' she screamed. 'No! No! No!'

She jammed her feet down onto the steps, trying to get a purchase, but it was no use. She was being dragged back down, back to the dark room.

'No! No! No!'

'Bugs?'

'No!'

'Bugs?'

'No!'

'Sam?'

The voice had changed, was gentle now. A different voice.

'Bugs, are you OK?'

She felt a cold draught blow across her face.

'Bugs, darling?'

She felt the sweat pouring down her face.

'Bugs?'

Her whole body was drenched, and she shivered.

'Bugs?'

She heard the rustle of sheets, the clank of a bed spring, then a click and there was brilliant white light that dazzled her, brighter even than the moon.

'You OK, Bugs?'

Richard's face, close, so close she could not focus.

'Horrible. It was horrible.'

'You were screaming,' he said.

'Sorry. I'm sorry.' She eased herself up in the bed, and sat, her heart pounding.

'Probably the booze,' he said.

'The booze?' She was aware of a sharp ache in her head.

Jumbled memories jostled in her mind. Christ, how much had she drunk? How had she got home? She tried to remember, panicking. There was just a blur.

'You were pissed as a fart.'

'I'm sorry,' she said blankly.

'It was bloody funny. The way you kept telling Julian not to worry.'

'Julian?'

'Holland.'

Holland, she thought. Julian Holland. Edgar's father. She remembered now. He had been in the flat when she had arrived home. 'I felt sorry for him.'

'I think he thought you'd flipped. You virtually sat on him, and kept telling him it was all your fault, because you'd ignored your dream.'

Dream. She shivered. 'He looked so – so unhappy. So guilty.'

'Can hardly expect him to be jumping up and down for joy.'

'It was nice of him to come round.'

'I played squash with him. He wanted some exercise.'

'Did I thank him for the flowers?'

'About a hundred times.'

She stared at the curtains, flapping gently in the draught. 'They're grubby,' she said.

'Grubby? The flowers?'

'The curtains. We'll have to get them cleaned soon. We've never had them cleaned.' Her head ached and her mouth was parched. She smelled onions again. Hot warm onions and booze and stale smoke. 'Have you been eating onions?'

'Yah. Pickled. We had fish and chips and pickled onions. They were seriously good. From that place – that little parade of shops.'

'You played squash and then had fish and chips?'

'Yah.'

'I thought you were trying to lose weight.' She sipped her water, then closed her eyes tightly against the light and felt herself back, suddenly, in the dark room. She shuddered and sat up, afraid to go to sleep.

'OK?'

'Fine,' she said. 'I'm fine. I think I'll just – read – for a while.'

18

Bamford O'Connell's waiting room smelled of furniture polish and musty fabric, like every medical waiting room Sam had ever been in. *Tatler*, *The Field*, *Country Life*, *Yachts & Yachting* and *Homes & Gardens* had been laid out neatly. Too neatly, fanatically neatly. She wondered if they had been laid out by the patient who was closeted with O'Connell now, behind the closed door.

I've got this thing about tidiness, Doctor. I've just tidied up your waiting room. If there's someone out there untidying the magazines, I'm going to chop their head off with a machete. You will understand?

Of course. If that's what you feel you must do. It's important not to repress your feelings.

It would be a good thing if I did chop her head off, wouldn't it? Stop her dreaming.

Yes it would.

I could take her head home in a plastic bag and stick it on a spike in the garden. And every morning I could say to her 'Naughty, naughty, naughty, who had another bad dream last night?'

Someone with a ballpoint pen had added tiny round glasses and a goatee beard to the model on the front of *Vogue*, making her look like a rather sinister Sigmund Freud.

The door behind her opened, startling her, and she heard Bamford O'Connell's voice, slightly softer than usual, with less of an Irish accent. 'Sam, hallo. Come in.'

The psychiatrist was wearing a sober Prince of Wales check suit and serious tortoiseshell glasses. The eccentrically dressed bon viveur of the dinner table had changed into a studious man of authority. Only the centre parting and the hair that was too long remained of the private Bamford she knew. She found the change to this new persona oddly reassuring, as if it put a distance between her and Bamford the friend.

He closed the heavy, panelled, privacy-assured door with a firm click, and the sudden silence of his consulting room startled her. She wondered if it was soundproofed. Like eyes adjusting to light, her ears slowly adjusted to the stillness that was only faintly disturbed by the hissing of car tyres from the rain-soaked Harley Street three floors down, and from the gentle, more constant hissing of the wall-mounted gas fire.

The room was neat, elegant, sparse, with a mahogany desk, an oak bookcase, two comfortable reproduction Victorian armchairs, a chaise longue, and a large painting on the wall that looked like rhubarb in a thunderstorm.

'Sit yourself down, Sam.' He pointed to one of the armchairs. 'Great evening that was, last week. Wonderful fun.'

'Good. It was nice seeing you both. Harriet's looking well.'

He sat down behind his desk, the window framing him in a landscape of rooftops, grey sky and falling rain; heavy, steady rain, the sort of wet Sunday afternoon rain you saw falling in movies and through French windows on theatre sets. He tugged his jacket sleeves up a fraction to reveal a smart watch with a crocodile skin strap, and neat sapphire cufflinks. 'So, to what do I owe this great honour?'

'I need some help – advice. It's professional, this visit. I want to pay you for it.'

'You'll do no such thing.'

'Please, Bamford, I want to.'

'I won't hear of it. Anyhow, I shouldn't be seeing you without a referral from your doctor.' He winked. 'Tell me.'

She looked down at the carpet, expensive, pure wool, mushroom coloured, then up again. 'We were talking at dinner – about dreams . . . premonitions.'

'That air disaster in Bulgaria,' he said. 'You'd dreamed about it.'

'Yes.' She paused, glanced up at the light bulb

hanging from the ceiling and felt a cold chill. 'I – I had another dream.' She stared at the bulb again. 'Over the weekend . . . which came true.'

He tilted his head slightly and interlocked his fingers. 'Tell me about both the dreams.'

She told him of the air disaster dream, and the Punch and Judy dream, and Punch appearing with a black hood and the shotgun, and what happened subsequently. He sat in silence staring at her so intently he was beginning to make her squirm. He seemed to be reading her face like someone reading the small print on a policy.

'This black hood that was in both dreams – do you have any associations with it?'

She sat still for a moment, then nodded.

'What are they?'

She looked down at her fingers. 'It's . . . something from childhood. I – It's a long story.'

He smiled encouragingly. 'We've got plenty of time.'

'There was a boy in our village,' Sam began. 'I suppose you could call him the village idiot, except he wasn't comical. He was nasty . . . malevolent, evil. He lived with his mother in a farmhouse just outside the village. It was a creepy place – quite big, isolated. There were always rumours of weird things going on there.'

'What sort of things?'

'I don't know. Black magic, that sort of thing. His mother was sort of . . . a witch, I suppose. She was foreign. My aunt and uncle used to talk about her occasionally, and the rumour was that she was the wife or the mistress of a German warlock who was into ritual killing, and that Slider was his son, but—' She shrugged – 'that was village gossip, probably. She was certainly very weird. Reclusive. There were a lot of strange goings on at the farm. A friend who lived in the village told me

150

years later that the woman had had an incestuous relationship with her son, but I don't know how she knew that.' Sam smiled, 'You get a lot of strange gossip coming out of a small community. She – the woman – got pregnant, had a daughter, but no one ever saw her. I don't know whether it was by her son. There were rumours of ritual orgies and God knows what else. All the children were always told to keep well away. The house had a very creepy feel. I can still remember it very clearly. People's pets used to disappear – dogs and things – and they always said that Slider had got them.'

'Slider?'

'That was his nickname. He had a glass eye which he used to slide in and out. He'd walk down the High Street and when he saw anyone he'd slide it out and wave it at them. It was all red, livid, behind, and his eyelashes used to bend in the wrong way.' She looked up at O'Connell, but he showed no reaction. 'Sometimes he put a small onion in his eye instead. He'd take it out, wave it at someone, chew it, then spit it out.'

O'Connell frowned slightly.

'No one knew how he'd lost it. The rumour was that a cat he was torturing had scratched it out, through I think he'd been in a car accident and had lost it then. There were rumours that he used to torture animals – the pets that he'd taken. After he died and his mother moved away the garden was dug up. Apparently it was like an ossuary.'

'How old was he?'

'Early twenties, I suppose. He also had another deformity. On one hand he only had one finger and a thumb; it was withered – horrible – almost like pincers.'

'Was that from an accident?'

'I don't know. I think it was something he was born with.'

'How did he die?'

Years, she thought. I haven't talked about this for years. Not to anyone. The fear had been so strong that she'd never even told Richard. In case . . . in case just telling it brought it all back. She felt something moving towards her, a shadow like a cloud, or a wave that was piling up behind her; she shivered, and stared at O'Connell again, for courage, for reassurance.

'I killed him.'

There was a long silence. 'You killed him?' he said finally.

Sam nodded and bit her lower lip. Talking about this . . . weird. She thought it had all faded away; thought that if she forgot it all for long enough, it might be as if it never had happened. Thought that after twenty-five years she was safe, finally. Safe from Slider.

'You murdered him?'

'No . . . I – I was playing out in the fields, and I heard this scream coming from a barn. It was quite isolated, almost derelict – hardly ever used. I ran over to it and heard noises up in the hayloft – horrible strangling noises – so I climbed up the ladder and saw him – Slider – wearing this black hood . . . strangling – he'd just raped and strangled a girl.

'He chased me across the loft, then got on top of me. I didn't know who he was at that moment, because of the hood, but I knew he was going to kill me. I bit him, and kicked and somehow I gouged him in the eye and his eyeball flew out. He got even madder, then . . . I don't remember exactly what happened but part of the loft was rotten, and he fell through and got impaled on an old machine on the ground.' She was shaking now, shaking so hard that even when she clenched her hands together she could not keep them still. 'There was a metal bit – a sort of spar – that had gone right through his neck. I could see him staring up at me; there was blood all around him. It was dark in the loft, because the light bulb had broken – it had got broken in the struggle. There was myself and the girl that was dead. I knew she was dead – I don't know why, but I knew – but I didn't know if Slider was dead or OK. He still had the hood on, and all I could see was the one eye looking out of the slit at me. I didn't know if he was going to climb up off the machine suddenly and come and kill me . . . And I didn't dare go down because—'

'What happened?'

'I stayed up there. I'd worked out that somehow I could stop him from climbing the ladder – I would throw bales of straw on him if he tried – but he still didn't move. Then it got pitch dark and I couldn't see him any more, and that got even more frightening. Then, later, I heard voices, saw torches, and I heard my father. I just screamed and screamed.'

'And Slider was dead?'

'Yes.'

'Who was the other girl?'

'Someone from the village. I didn't really know her. She was older than me – in her teens.'

'How old were you?'

'Seven.'

'That's quite a memory to carry from childhood, Sam.'

'There's more,' she said. She looked down at her wrist and began to toy with her watch strap. 'After this happened, I started dreaming of Slider.'

'One would have expected you to,' said O'Connell.

'I used to have the same recurring dream. That I heard the scream and went to the barn and climbed up into the loft, and Slider would come out of the darkness at me.

Except he didn't die in the dream. He was always about to get me – lying on top of me, with his one eye missing and just this red socket coming closer – then I'd wake up, and something bad would happen.'

'Such as what?'

'It started small. The first time I had the dream, my hamster died the next day. Then, each time, it seemed to get worse. I'd get sick, or my mother was having a baby and lost it. Then last time I had the dream I woke up and . . . my parents had been killed in a car crash.'

'That was all when you were seven?'

'Yes.'

'And you didn't have the dream again after that?'

'No . . . it was almost as if he'd got what he wanted, I suppose – got his revenge.'

'Could you tell at all from your dreams what sort of bad things were going to happen?'

'No.'

'And now you're getting the image of this Slider with these two dreams?'

'There have actually been three dreams with him in.' She told him of her dream in the taxi. 'I had a very weird dream the night before also,' she smiled. 'You probably think I'm cracking up.'

'Tell me it.'

She told him about her dream of Hampstead underground. When she finished, it was still impossible to read his reaction.

'This hooded man – Slider – was this the man in your dream down the underground?'

'I don't know – I didn't think so. I couldn't see his face, but there didn't seem to be a mask – except—' She tailed off. 'He smelled of onions.'

'You look very tired Sam. Are you on any medication?'

'No.'

'Not sleeping pills? Tranquillisers?'

'No. Nothing.'

'Does Richard know you're here?'

She hesitated. 'No . . . I'd be grateful if you didn't—'

'Of course.'

She stared into his expressionless eyes then away at the expanse of polished wood on the top of his desk, with nothing on it except a gold pen, lying flat. Then she glanced down at her fingers. Biting her nails, she thought, looking at her thumb, with part of the skin bitten away as well. Ugly.

'I wondered if there were any pills you could give me that would stop me from dreaming.' She was picking at it, picking, picking. Stop. She tried, then began to pick again.

He pushed out his lower lip, then tapped his gold pen with his fingers. 'There are inhibitor drugs, but they have a lot of side effects. They'll cut down your dreaming at night but you'll start having day dreams, hallucinations, instead. Tell me, Sam, if you're seeing the future, what are you really frightened of? Isn't it helpful? Can't you use this information?'

'It's not like that. It's as if . . . as if I'm making these things happen by dreaming about them.'

'You caused the plane to crash?'

She nodded.

'And it wouldn't have crashed if you hadn't dreamed it?'

She felt her face redden slightly, and shrugged.

'These dreams you had as a child after this hooded man was killed – how soon after the dreams did things happen?'

She racked her brains back in time. Hazy. Childhood was just a mass of images. Like dents in an old desk they became smoothed over the years, part of a familiar landscape, and you couldn't remember the order in which they came, no matter how hard you tried. 'It varied, I suppose.'

'A day? A week? Several months?'

She heard the cry of her own voice.

'*Mummy!*' Hugging. Crying.

'*It's all right, darling.*'

'It was always soon. The next day, or a few days.'

'Did you ever have anything bad happen when you hadn't had dreams?'

'I – I suppose so, yes.'

Silence.

I see what you're saying.

She picked again, tore away a piece of skin and it hurt.

'There's an air disaster in the news every few weeks, Sam. If you dream of an air disaster, it's almost bound to come true.'

'Not with all the details in my dream, surely?'

'Did you write them down? Before you heard of the disaster?'

'No.'

'I know you're an intelligent girl, Sam, but you're very tense at the moment. Do you think there's any chance at all you might be crediting your dream with more detail than was in it? That you might be making the dream fit the facts?'

'No.'

'Look at the other dreams for the moment – your hooded fellow in the taxi who gave you a boarding card. That doesn't seem to me to be anything prophetic. You found out that there was no such seat number on the plane, didn't you?'

'Yes, I did.'

'35A, wasn't it? Those numbers might have some other significance. Do they mean anything to you?'

'No.'

'They'll be in your dream for a reason. Everything in our dreams is there for a reason, but you can only get to understand them if you go through analysis.' He smiled. 'Don't look so worried.'

'Do you think I should go to an analyst?'

'If you feel your dreams are disturbing you to the point where they're affecting the quality of your life, then it's something you could consider.'

'What would an analyst do?'

'He would try to uncover the anxieties that are causing these dreams. Try to find the root of them. Bring them to the surface. Help you to understand why you are having them.'

She picked at a different nail. 'I still think that I've – that these things have been premonitions, Bamford.'

He pulled open a drawer on the right of the desk then pushed it back in again, without appearing to take anything out. Then he did the same with the left-hand drawer. Like an organist setting his stops, she thought. 'Let's have a look at the Punch and Judy dream: Punch disappears, reappears in a black hood and fires a shotgun at you. You wake up and a chunk of plaster has fallen on you from the wall. Is that right?'

'From the ceiling.'

'The next day a kid gets hold of your husband's gun and fires it during the Punch and Judy show.' He picked up his gold pen and rolled it between his neatly manicured fingers. 'Well, there are connections, for sure, but I don't think you could have foretold what was going to happen from that dream. I don't think anybody could. Let's turn it around a bit, Sam. How did a boy of six get hold of a loaded gun?'

'Richard—' She hesitated. 'We're not sure. Richard thinks he must have left it out. He normally keeps it upstairs, with the cartridges on top of a wardrobe so it's out of Nicky's reach.'

He nodded. 'So he might have put it away?'

'It's possible, but unlikely. The boy said he found it against a wall.'

O'Connell leaned forward. 'You see, Sam, it could well be that dream was telling you something, but not in the way you think. Consider this as an alternative: you gave up your career for Nicky, and because his birth was difficult you couldn't have any more children. Maybe you feel anger at him. Maybe deep in your subconscious you feel that if you didn't have him around—?'

Sam stared, flabbergasted for a moment, anger building up inside her. 'Are you saying it was me? That I gave him the gun?'

'I'm not saying for a moment you do feel that way, but I want to show you the possible alternatives, areas that an analyst would probe, trying to find the real reason for that dream. Your dreams indicate to me you have problems that you've got to get to grips with. By dismissing them as premonitions, you are ignoring their real meanings, brushing them away under the carpet. It's much easier to put them down as premonitions than to face their real truths.'

'Don't you think you're trying to dismiss everything with a cosy Freudian explanation?' she said coldly.

'I'm not trying to dismiss anything. But you need to understand what dreams are really about, Sam.' He put the gold pen neatly down on the desk and steadied it to prevent it from rolling. 'Our lives are a constant balance between sanity and madness. Most of us get by all right. We keep our emotions under control when we're awake, but they all come pouring out in our dreams when we're asleep: jealousies, pain, thwartings, grief, anger, desires, and the past. Most importantly, the past.' He realised the pen was distracting her, and put it away in a drawer. 'Daddy's having it off with my mummy and I'd like to do that, but if he catches me, he'll cut my goolies off . . . Or in your case, Daddy's got a huge donger and I've only got a tiny clitoris, so I'm inferior . . . you know? The primal scene and all that stuff?'

She smiled weakly.

'The dream you had about going down the underground . . . you've told it very well. You've made it sound like a narrative. I could follow the story easily.' He raised his hands. 'But I don't understand a thing about it. You see, it's probably full of symbols that are personal to you.' He paused and looked awkward suddenly. He shifted about in his chair, then leaned forward, put his elbows on his desk and rested his chin on his hands.

'Sam,' he said softly. 'Do you mind if I ask you something very personal? If you don't want to answer that's perfectly all right.'

'No – of course.'

'I couldn't help noticing at dinner that things seemed very strained between you and Richard.'

Her face reddened.

'Are things all right between you?'

Penis starvation. Of course. That's unhinged me. That's why I have these nutty dreams. Of course!

He leaned back, without taking his eyes off her. 'I think you would find it much easier to talk to a stranger. Would you like to see a member of my unit at Guy's who without harassing you in any way would help you to sort it out?'

'I don't know.'

'If your dreams are bothering you to the point where you feel they're affecting the quality of your life, then you should consider it. Equally, they might all just go away.'

'They're not going to go away,' she said.

'Why do you think that?'

'I don't know. It's just a feeling.'

'Would you like me to recommend someone?'

'I wish I could believe you, Bamford. I wish I could believe all that analysis stuff. But I know I'm having premonitions. I could have saved the lives of those people.'

'Forget premonitions, Sam. They're nothing more than lucky guesses. That's all. Don't get caught up down that alleyway.'

She felt a flash of anger. 'Why not? Nicky could have been shot – any of those children could have been. I might have been able to prevent it.'

He shook his head gently, and it inflamed her anger even more. 'Whatever you decided, Sam, let me give you one piece of advice. Stay away from the hokum guys.' He tapped his head. 'It's all in here. It doesn't matter what anyone else says. I know. The medical profession knows.'

'God you're a smug bastard,' she said.

He did not react at all. There was a long silence, in which he continued to stare at her, and she felt her face getting hotter and redder, sorry she had said that, guilty that she'd taken so much of his time and had spat it back in his face.

'Sam,' he said, 'you've come to me for help, for advice. I've given it to you. What do you want me to do? Tell you to go and see a clairvoyant? A medium? Send you off to a dream group? To a parapsychologist? I want to help you, not make things worse.'

'If you want to help me, Bamford, you've first got to believe me.'

He pushed each of the sleeves of his jacket up in turn, scratched his nose, then put his elbows back on the desk.

'I'll tell you what I believe. I believe that *you* genuinely believe you are having premonitions.'

'And you think they're just delusions?' She stared at him, the anger flaring again. 'Do you want someone else to die? Will that prove it?'

He sat back in his chair and rested his hands on the arms. 'Hooded men,' he said. 'Your hooded fellow – Slider?'

She nodded sullenly.

'Sam, you're a grown woman. You're a mother and a successful businesswoman. And you're still dreaming of your childhood bogeyman. There's no living person I know of who can foretell the future consistently. There never has been. There are lucky guesses and intelligent guesses, and sometimes the brain whirrs away during our sleep and presents probabilities to us. That's all. Your big ugly hooded fellow who stinks of onions is frightening the hell out of you, and you think you're being haunted by the ghost of someone who died twenty-five years ago. Some creature that comes to you in your dreams and is trying to destroy you. If he wants to destroy you, then why does he keep tipping you off? Giving you warnings?'

She felt cold again, cold and empty and all twisted up. She stared up at the light bulb then out through the window at the rooftops and the leaden sky. 'Maybe it's some game he's playing. Some macabre game to sort of . . . torment me . . . You know? Just playing with me – until he's ready.'

'We're all haunted by ghosts, Sam; but they're not

spirits, or demons that have come back from the grave. They are our own personal fears, anxieties.' He tapped his head again. 'We need to get inside there, Sam, and pluck him out. That's what an analyst would do.'

She stared at him then shook her head. 'I wish you were right, Bamford.' She screwed up her eyes tightly.

Christ I wish you were right.

19

Sam sat in front of her dressing table, putting on her make-up. She was wearing the black lace bra, panties and suspenders that Richard had given her for Christmas the year before. She wondered if he would remember, and she wondered why she was wearing them now. A signal? An olive branch?

She eyed herself, then leaned closer to the mirror examining the crow's-feet around her eyes; they were getting more pronounced all the time. This is it, girl, all downhill from here. Be a Wrinkly soon; then a Crumbly. Then . . . nothing at all. The void. Godless black nothingness. She touched the lines lightly, stretched the skin, making them disappear for an instant, then stared again at the photograph of Richard and herself on a yacht in Greece; the year after their wedding; nine years ago. They looked so young and carefree then. How much softer her face was, how much fresher. Now a new line seemed to appear every day. She frowned into the mirror and a row of wrinkles popped out along her skin that she had never seen before.

Maybe it was the photograph that was changing, not her face? Maybe her face had always been like that and the photograph was receding into the past? Showing a woman who was getting younger and younger. So young sometimes she seemed like a total stranger. She unscrewed her lipstick.

Bamford O'Connell. Was he right? Maybe. Maybe. She shrugged at herself, and pushed her hair back away from her face. No grey hairs yet, but they'd be along soon.

Do you think there's any chance at all you might be crediting your dream with more detail than was in it? That you might be making the dream fit the facts?

No. No way, absolutely not. Surely not?

Oh shit. You're screwing up my head, Bamford. I had it all there, in sequence. Don't mix it up for me, just because I don't fit into any of your neat boxes.

'Where are you going, Mummy?'

She saw Nicky in the mirror, standing in the doorway, and turned around, smiling. 'We're going out to a dinner party.'

'Whose party?'

'The Howorths'. Do you remember them?'

'Are we going to the country?'

Sam carefully traced the lipstick across her lips. 'Uh huh.'

'Is it the weekend tomorrow?'

'Tomorrow's Friday. Come and give Mummy a kiss.'

Nicky trotted over, and she stroked his hair.

'Top of your class in arithmetic again today?'

'Yes, I was.'

'That's very clever. Mummy used to come bottom in arithmetic.'

He looked around suddenly, at the sound of the front door, then sprinted out of the room. 'Daddy! Daddy! Daddy!'

'Hi, Tiger!' she heard Richard say out in the hallway.

'Daddy! Can we set the Scalectrix up? We haven't had that set up since Christmas. Can we do it tonight?'

'Stop bloody whining at me.'

'Please, Daddy, can we set it up?'

'Jesus, Tiger! Bloody leave off, will you?'

Richard stormed into the bedroom and kicked the door shut behind him. 'Fucking whingeing on and on at me. What the hell are you wearing that for? You look like a whore.'

'You gave it to me.'

'Been fucking Ken in it?'

She stood up, livid. 'Are you drunk?'

'No, I'm not fucking drunk, but I'm going to get fucking drunk.' He charged out of the room, and Sam stared, bewildered, after him. The rage. She'd never seen him in a rage like this. He came back into the room with a whisky tumbler in his hand and slammed the door again.

'What's the matter with you?' she asked.

'Get those fucking whore clothes off and put something decent on.'

The menace in his voice frightened her. He was like a madman.

'I thought you liked—'

He marched over, grabbed the bra and ripped it away, so hard it tore, burning her flesh in the process. She shrieked in pain, then slapped him hard, really hard, on the face. 'You bastard.'

He blinked, and stared at her, and for a moment she thought he was going to come at her, going to come at her and kill her. But instead he blinked again, as if half waking from a trance, backed away and sat down on the bed. He drank some of his whisky then bent down and untied his laces. He kicked off his shoes, swallowed more whisky and lay back, closing his eyes. 'What time are we due there?'

'Eight,' she said.

She pulled the rest of the bra away, eyeing him warily and took a new one out of a drawer. 'Don't you think you'd better have some coffee rather than whisky?'

He said nothing.

She removed her lace panties, screwed them up and dropped them in the waste bin, and put on some fresh ones which matched the bra. She put on her dress, in silence, took her evening handbag out of the cupboard, and looked in her daytime bag. She noticed an envelope in amongst all the junk, and took it out. There was a magazine cutting inside it, which she unfolded and glanced at, puzzled.

'DREAMS – BEHIND CLOSED EYES THE FUTURE OPENS UP.'

Ken. Ken had given it to her on Monday and she'd forgotten about it. She went out of the bedroom, holding the article, and closed the door. She heard Nicky's bath running, and went into his bedroom. He was sitting sulkily on his bed. She went over and sat down beside him. 'Daddy's had a bad day, Tiger.'

'He promised we could play Scalectrix tonight.'

'We have to go out tonight.'

'He shouted at me. I didn't do anything wrong.' He began to cry and she held him tight. 'I'll play Scalectrix with you until Daddy's ready.'

'No,' he sobbed. 'Got to set it up. Only Daddy knows how to set it up.'

Helen came in, 'Bath's ready, Nicky.'

'Have your bath, Tiger, and I'll tell you a quick story before we go.'

He stood up, his face long and wet and walked slowly over to the door. Sam followed him out, then went down the corridor through into the living area and sat down on a sofa in front of the television. She was quivering with the pent-up anger and confusion inside her. This was a new Richard, something completely different; something she did not know how to handle. Maybe it was he that needed to see Bamford O'Connell, not her? Maybe the Market had been bad today. He was grumpy sometimes when the Market was bad. But never like this. She looked down at the article and began to read.

Dreams should be taken far more seriously than they are, claims David Abner, a clinical psychologist at Guy's Hospital who believes that not only are dreams a rich source of creativity, but they also offer valuable insight into personal and psychological problems, as well as, on occasions, a glimpse into the future.

Perhaps the most famous of all 'premonition' dreams was that of the Biblical Pharaoh, whose dream of seven fat cows being swallowed by seven thin cows enabled Egypt to conserve food over seven good years and stave off potential famine over seven poor succeeding harvests.

More recent figures, too, have been profoundly affected by their dreams. Hitler was saved by one of his, when as corporal in the First World War, his nightmare of being engulfed by debris caused him to wake up and dash outside, only for a shell to land on his bunker seconds later and kill all the sleeping occupants.

Dreams have inspired great inventors. Elias Howe invented the sewing machine after he dreamed of natives throwing spears with eye-shaped holes at their tips, and thus solved the problem of where to put the hole in the needle.

And in religion, leaders have taken the view that God speaks to his prophets through dreams. 'Many people still believe that today, and I'm sure to some degree it is still true, whatever God is, that dreams can be seen as messages from the universe,' says Abner. 'It seems that some people are receiving stations. Jung called it 'Collective Unconscious'. Whatever the explanation, whether it is ultimately scientific or spiritual, there is no question that in dreams some people seem to tune into a field of insight not open to the waking, conscious mind.'

In the next few months, Abner and a fellow group of dream therapists are planning to set up a phone-in 'dreamline', where people can both instantly have premonitions registered, and discuss their dreams with therapists working through the night.

In the meantime, people interested in learning more about their dreams can join in a series of dream groups being set up under his auspices. Phone 01–435–0702 for details.

Sod you, Bamford. Sam picked up the phone. Sod you and your stay away from the hokum guys. Sod you and your damned arrogance, she thought, as she heard the phone ring and a man's voice answer, a soft, laid-back American accent.

'Dave Abner.'

'I, er—' She felt foolish and looked around, making sure no one had come into the room. 'I read an article in – er – about your—'

There was a silence, followed by a distant 'Uh-huh', then a pause, 'Which article was that?'

'Someone cut it out. I'm not sure where from – about your dream groups.'

'Oh yeah, I remember.' He sounded bored. 'This number's wrong. They shouldn't have put this number. They should have put Tanya's.'

'Tanya?'

'Tanya Jacobson. She's doing the dream group right now. I'll give you her number.'

She dialled the new number, and a husky woman's voice answered, harassed, somewhat breathless. 'Hallo?'

'Could I speak to Tanya Jacobson, please?'

'Yes, speaking,' the reply came, somewhat irritable, and for a moment Sam was tempted to drop the receiver back down.

'David Abner gave me your number,' said Sam nervously. 'I read an article about your dream groups, and I wondered—'

'You'd like to join our group?' The woman's voice had changed, become friendlier. 'You've called at just the right time. This is an amazing coincidence! We're looking for one woman to complete the group. Listen, we're starting a new group next Monday night. Is that too soon?'

'No,' Sam said.

'Wow! Wonderful! You sound wonderful. I get feelings, you know, vibes. You get them too?'

'Yes,' said Sam hesitantly, dubiously. Feelings, Feelings. Everyone seemed to have feelings these days.

'OK, what's your name?'

'Mrs Curtis.'

'So formal. Wow. What's your Christian name?'

'Sam.'

'Sam, that's nice. You're going to fit in wonderfully. We start at seven-thirty. If you come a little early, you can have coffee, meet everyone. I'll give you the address. Do you know Hampstead?'

'Hampstead?'

'We're very near the tube.'

A chill went through her.

'Tube?' Sam felt herself shaking. She wanted to hang up, now, hang up and forget it.

Hampstead.

The tube.

'Hallo, Sam? You still there?'

Hampstead. Near the tube. The words banged around inside her head. *Hampstead. Near the tube.*

'Willoughby Road. Do you know Willoughby Road?'

'I can find it,' she heard her own voice say, as if spoken by a stranger.

'Off the High Street. You come out of the tube, turn left, and just walk down.'

'I'll drive,' said Sam. 'I'll be coming by car.'

She hung up. The room seemed cold, suddenly, and the wind rattled the windows. Rattled them like an angry stranger who was trying to get in. A stranger. Like Richard. Christ, what the hell was wrong with him? She heard the thump of the engines of a large ship heading upstream, then another gust of wind shrieked through the rigging of the moored yachts, rattling the halyards that were loose, and strumming the ones that were tight, tight as guitar strings.

Tight as her own nerves.

20

The rain which had been falling hard all day finally stopped just as she left the office, and in the darkness the roads were streaky kaleidoscopes of reflections of brake lights, indicators, street lamps. Puddles of glinting black water butted up against the gutters, as if left behind by a falling tide, and cars sluiced through them, throwing the water up like bow spray. A Belisha beacon flashed on-off-on-off, its beam sneaking across the road towards her, and she stopped. A man hurried over the crossing holding a broken umbrella.

Exactly as she had seen in her dream.

She felt her stomach tensing. Everything. The rain, the darkness, the reflections were exactly as she had seen in her dream. It was unfolding like a replay. She wanted to stop, turn around; go home. Instead she drove on up Avenue Road, biting her lip, drawn by some force she could not stop. Drawn as if the dream insisted on replaying itself to her; as if it had a mind of its own.

As if it was challenging her.

She blinked hard, wondering for a moment whether she was awake now.

Ten past seven.

She glanced anxiously at the clock and wished she had left more time, but she had sat in her office, reluctant to leave, waiting until the last moment when she had to make the decision to go or forget it. She had to find the place yet, and park. *If you come a little early, you can have coffee, meet everyone.*

THE NORTH. M1.

She drove into the Swiss Cottage one-way system, and a car hooted angrily on her inside. 'Sod you.' She swung the Jaguar's steering wheel, then heard the angry horn of a taxi right beside her. She braked cautiously and blinked, as water splashed onto her windscreen. She switched on the wipers, and everything blurred for a moment. She pulled over into the right-hand lane, and headed up Fitzjohn's Avenue towards Hampstead. A white Ford Capri sitting up on huge wheels drew up on her inside and a yobbo gave her the thumbs up.

She shivered. No, she thought. It wasn't possible. It could not be happening.

The same white Ford Capri as she had seen in her dream. The same yobbo. Making the same gesture.

Don't be ridiculous, she told herself. Coincidence. That's all. She turned away contemptuously, then dropped down into second gear and floored the accelerator.

She heard the roar of the engine, felt the tail of the Jaguar snake as the rear wheels spun, then eased off, felt the tyres bite and the surge of power as she accelerated forwards.

There was a car moving slowly in front, and she pulled right across, overtaking in the oncoming lane. Headlights were coming down the hill towards her and ice-cold fear swept through her.

No. Please God, no.

The lorry from the dream. Bearing down.

She heard her own engine screaming, slammed the gear lever forward and there was a fierce clacking and the stick kicked violently in her hand. The car began to slow down, the headlights almost on top of her now. She stabbed the gear lever forward again, and jerked the wheel hard to the left. The lorry passed her, inches away, shaking her with its vibration and slipstream.

Shit.

She saw the police car coming down the hill, slowing, as if it was looking for somewhere to turn and come after her, and she felt a cold hand around her forehead, tightening like a vice.

The dream. It was the dream. Exactly, everything. She wanted to stop, turn around, go back. She turned right, drove down the street that could have been the one she had driven down in her dream, but might not have been, and then left into Hampstead High Street. On her right, almost immediately, she saw the same tree-lined street from her dream, no doubting this one, and found herself turning automatically, as if it was drawing her into it.

Willoughby Road.

It was the street she wanted.

She stared, disbelieving, at the sign, then heard the toot of a horn behind her and drove forward, peering through the side window, trying to read the numbers.

There was a gap in the line of parked cars halfway down the street; exactly where she had parked in her dream. She stopped the Jaguar and reversed into it, then got out and looked around. A droplet of water hit her on the forehead, and she put up her hand in surprise. The dark evening had a stillness to it that she found eerie, as if all was not quite right, as if something was about to happen and the night was waiting.

Don't be ridiculous, she told herself as she looked at the doorways, trying to read the numbers. Then she smiled wryly as if she had discovered some private joke: she was parked right outside the address she had been, given. Number 56.

She went in through the open gateway and down the faded mosaic steps to the basement. At the bottom were a couple of dustbins, several empty cardboard packing boxes, and a cluster of empty milk bottles. There was a small plastic push-button with an illuminated plastic panel beside it which read 'Dream Studies Centre.'

She stared at the button, unable to push it. She wanted to turn and run back to the car and drive away. Something had drawn her here that did not feel good. Something that was making her tremble and feel sick and scared. She shuddered. Her stomach felt as if it was being wound through a mangle.

What would Bamford say? Perhaps it was all to do with fear of the dream group. The similarities in the drive here had been coincidence, and her fear of going down the tube steps was really her fear of coming down these steps, into the unknown.

She raised her finger and pushed the button gently, so gently she hoped it might not ring. It rasped back at her, inches from her face, piercing, shrill, as if it was angry it had been disturbed.

'Hi. You must be Sam.'

'Yes.'

'You found us?'

'Yes. Fine. It was easy.'

'Terrific. Wow! Wonderful. I'm Tanya Jacobson.' A small plump bundle of energy in a shapeless brown smock and black woollen leggings, with a wild frizz of hair and a scrubbed, earnest-looking face that was definitely a make-up free zone. A lump of crystal hung from a cord around her neck and her pudgy fingers were covered in chunky rings with large, gaudy stones. She gave Sam's hand a short friendly shake. 'Come in.'

Sam followed her down a dingy corridor and into a small room with battered chairs lined around the walls and a bare pine coffee table in the middle.

'Have a seat, Sam. I just want to have a quick talk before we go in.' The woman sat down, tucked her feet under her chair and rested her head on her hands, fixing her gaze on Sam.

'Nice face, Sam. I should think you're a really kind person. Am I right?'

Sam blushed. 'I don't know.'

'Have you been in a dream group before?'

'No.'

Tanya Jacobson nodded her head up and down in a straight line. 'Are you married?'

'Yes.'

'Does your husband know you're here?'

'No.'

Tanya Jacobson looked mildly surprised. 'OK. Fine. That's fine.' She raised her head off her chin then lowered it back down again. 'What do you do, Sam?'

'I work for a company that makes television commercials.'

The woman smiled. 'Right. Wow. So you're the one that's to blame?'

Sam smiled back, thinly.

'Tell me, why do you want to join a dream group?'

She shrugged. 'I don't know much about it. I've been having some very strange dreams which seem to keep coming true. I read the article and I thought I'd give you a call.'

'You think you're having premonitions?'

'Yes.'

The woman sat up eagerly, like a puppy wanting to please, thought Sam. 'Good! You can tell the group. Now tonight you can see how you feel, how you resonate with everyone. If you feel good then we hope you'll join us permanently.'

'Permanently?'

'For the life of the group. Normally about two years. We meet every Monday, and it's—' She looked embarrassed – 'nine pounds a session. Do you think you can live with that?'

'Two years seems a long time.'

'Dreams take a long time to work through, Sam. We have to get the dynamics going. You'll understand. I think you're really going to be good.' She patted Sam's hand. 'You have a slight disadvantage, because the rest of the group has been together for some weeks, and they're resonating nicely. It's going to take you time to resonate.'

'Does . . . does everyone here have premonitions?' Sam asked.

'Well, we're a group, Sam. I'm a psychotherapist, OK? A psychologist. What we do is work our dreams through. Premonitions, precognitions . . . that's all a little bit—' She tilted her head from side to side – 'a little bit fringe, OK? We're trying here to really connect with our dreams, go with them, free associate, get some good dynamics going. OK? Shall we go through?'

Sam followed her out down the short corridor. She did not like the answer she had been given, the string of heavy jargon. The paper had said they were studying premonitions, but this woman, Tanya Jacobson, seemed to be dismissing them.

They went into a large square room that smelled of stale cigarette smoke and old furniture, except there was hardly any furniture in the room. A bare light bulb hung from the ceiling. There were no chairs, but old, battered cushions, bean bags and poufs were spread around the floor in a large circle. Several people were lying sprawled out on them, leaning against the walls, their feet stretched out across the threadbare carpet. She felt hostility at her presence. She wanted to turn and walk out.

'OK, this is Sam, everyone. We'll go round in turn. This is Barry – he leads the group with me. Barry, this is Sam.'

A lanky man lay stretched out in a shiny black karate suit, his feet bare, his limp, shiny black hair brushed forward in a Beatle fringe over his eyebrows. His eyes were closed and he was muttering intently to himself. He raised an arm like an Indian chieftain, without opening his eyes. 'Good to meet you, Sam,' he mumbled, then continued with his private muttering.

'And this is Anthea.'

A woman in her fifties was coiled up in a corner, staring at her, blinking slowly like a basking snake. She was wearing a homemade jumper and grimy jeans, and had long red hair that hung down to her waist, and which covered her arms and her chest like a rug. The woman gave her the faintest acknowledgement, then gazed up at the ceiling with a puzzled look, as if she had just felt a drop of rainwater.

'Hi, I'm Gail.' A pretty blonde-haired girl introduced

herself in a New England accent. She looked smart and elegant, and rich in her white silk blouse, velvet headband and Cartier wristwatch.

'Hallo.'

She smiled gently, sympathetically at Sam. 'It's pretty difficult, huh, the first time?'

Sam smiled and nodded.

A voice in a flat northern accent said 'Clive,' and an aggressive-looking man in his late thirties, with short, tousled, prematurely greying hair stood up and shook her hand grimly, as if it was a duty to be got over with like having an injection, then sat down again and hunched up inside his baggy jumper.

'Find yourself some space that feels good, Sam. Would you like some tea? We have camomile or dandelion, or there's coffee – Hag or Nescafé.'

'Nescafé, please.' said Sam.

'Do you take milk, sugar?'

'Milk please. No sugar.'

The basking snake uncoiled a little, and the man in the baggy jumper leaned back and stretched his arms. *Keep away*, they were saying, *Keep out!*

Sam sat down well away from them on an empty stretch of cushions near the door. 'We're just waiting for one more – Sadie – then we'll be complete for tonight,' Tanya called out. 'Roger's rung to say he has flu, so he won't be making it. I told him we'd be keeping mental space for him.'

Sam looked around the room. There was a frosted glass curtainless window high off the ground, a wall-mounted convector heater, a small table with a telephone on top of an answering machine, and a pine dresser that was being used as a bookcase and dumping ground for coffee mugs and full ashtrays.

The walls were painted in faded white Artex, and

there was a closed off serving hatch with a dusty red Buddha, that looked like a half-melted candle, on the ledge in front. There was one solitary picture on the walls, a framed print of a languid eighteenth-century boy reclining on a bed and gazing at an ornament he was holding.

Tanya Jacobson came back into the room, and handed Sam a scalding mug.

'Keeping your distance, are you, Sam? Keeping your space?'

Sam was uncertain whether she had done something wrong or given away some important clue about her personality. She felt awkward, uncomfortable; and unwanted. She heard the clatter of an electric heater, and the click of the door closing.

'Sadie's late again,' said Tanya. 'I think she has a problem with her timekeeping. She has a lot of dreams about clocks.'

'And sex,' said the man in the baggy sweater. 'She seems to have a lot of dreams about sex.'

'I think she has a bit of a problem about sex,' said the American girl.

Tanya nodded her head noncommittally, with the faintest trace of a sympathetic smile. 'We all have problems. That's what the group is for. Now Sam, the way we introduce someone new to the group is to get them to tell a dream. Did you bring one with you?'

'One with me? I haven't written any down – no.'

Tanya tapped her head. 'In there, Sam. Is there a dream you can remember that you'd like to tell the group?'

Sam shrugged. 'I—' She looked around. The basking snake in the corner appeared to have gone to sleep. The man in the baggy jumper was staring fixedly at the wall ahead, and she wondered if he was sulking because he hadn't been asked to tell a dream. The American girl smiled intently at her and gave her a nod of encouragement.

The door opened and in came a tiny woman with a figure like a rugger ball and a prim face that was heavily caked in make-up, only partially visible behind a curtain of limp brown hair. She mouthed a silent apology, checked her bright red lipstick with her tongue, then sat down primly on a pouf and opened her handbag with a loud click. She rummaged in it, pulled out a pack of cigarettes, a lighter and a small tin, from which she removed the lid, and set it down on the floor beside her. She looked like a goblin perched on the pouf, Sam thought, and wondered what she was going to do with the tin.

'Sadie, we have a new member in our group tonight. Sam, this is Sadie. Sam's going to tell us a dream. It doesn't matter if it's an old dream, Sam.'

Sadie smiled at Sam, a long, lingering smile that Sam first mistook for warmth, but then realised, as it continued, was a warning shot across her bows.

She turned away, confused, and heard the click of the woman's cigarette lighter, and her sharp, smug, intake of smoke.

'Did you remember a dream you had last night, Sam?' said Tanya Jacobson.

She felt her face reddening. 'No – I – I don't think I dreamed last night. At least I—' She stared helplessly around the room. It was wrong. All wrong. She saw the American girl, nodding encouragingly, willing her on.

You poor deluded sod, she thought.

What do you want me to do? Tell you to go and see a clairvoyant? A medium? Send you off to a dream group? I want to help you, not make things worse.

She saw Sadie squatting on her pouf and caught the

slight narrowing of her eyes. *Don't take up much time*, she was saying. *I have important dreams to tell.*

'Last week, er—' Sam faltered. 'Last Tuesday night, I had a dream that . . . that seems to be coming true. At least, some of it.'

'Would you like to tell us about it?'

Sam told them her dream of Hampstead tube station, feeling foolish, talking at their blank faces, at the blank wall, talking whilst Tanya Jacobson sat on her cushion, rocking backwards and forwards with her eyes closed, and whilst Sadie squatted on her pouf, puffing on her cigarette and tapping the ash into the tin she had brought. She wondered whether anyone was taking in a word she said.

When she had finished the silence continued. The American girl leaned back and gazed at the ceiling, and the man in the baggy jumper stared at the wall ahead.

Tanya Jacobson appeared to take several deep breaths, then opened her eyes. 'Okay, Sam, the first thing I want you to do is to free associate.'

'Pardon?' said Sam.

'I want you to tell me anything that comes into your mind about the dream.'

'Replay.' Sam said.

'Replay?'

'Yes. The journey here – it was exactly as I dreamed it. Coming here was like a replay of the dream.'

Tanya stared at her with a faintly disinterested look on her face. 'Don't get too stuck on that for a moment. There's a lot going on in that dream. Is there another reason why you dreamed Hampstead? Did you ever live here? Or know anyone that lived here?'

'No.'

'It was very filmic,' the American girl said suddenly. 'There was a very Buñuel feel to the first part. Then,

179

when you went down those steps, it was like a tunnel, it gave me the feeling of – you know? The Harry Lime movie. *The Third Man*.'

Anthea uncoiled a fraction in the corner, and raised her head. 'Sewers,' she said slowly, articulating very precisely, as if she were teaching a foreigner to speak English.

'Sewers?' echoed Tanya Jacobson.

'Sewers,' she repeated. 'Gail's got it wrong. It wasn't tunnels, it was sewers.'

'I'm not connecting with you, Anthea,' said Tanya.

'Oh for God's sake.' Her voice was getting louder, deeper, more haughty. 'In the film. *The Third Man*. It was sewers they went down, not tunnels.' She lowered her head and began to coil back up again.

'That was a good movie.' Barry spoke without opening his eyes. He scratched the side of his left leg with the toes of his right foot. 'Orson Welles.'

'And Joseph Cotten,' said the American girl.

'Vagina,' said the man in the baggy jumper gruffly. 'I'm getting a vagina.' He sat upright and clasped his hands together, staring at Sam. He had a face that might once have been kindly, but now had a hardened, slightly embittered look. 'You're going down inside this vagina and you're finding something horrible there. There's this man that grabs you, takes you into this dark room where there's no light, and he's trying to strangle you, rape you. I'm getting this very strong feeling that you hate men.'

'Don't you think it could be pre-existence, Clive?' said Tanya Jacobson.

He frowned, then sat back and dug his hands into his pockets. 'Pre-existence,' he said. 'Hmm.'

Tanya Jacobson threw her head back, then tilted it forwards again. 'You know what's coming through to me? We've got several different dreams here. The journey. The buying the ticket. The travelling down the steps. Now the travelling down, I'm connecting very strongly with pre-existence, you know. Like birth reversal.'

Sam tried to make sense of the jargon. She stared at the print on the wall of the man looking at the ornament. He looked puzzled too.

'You mean she's going back into her mother's womb?' said the American girl.

Tanya gave three sharp nods of her head as if she was trying to shake water out of her hair. 'She's going down into this sort of tunnel, then suddenly she gets pulled into this dark room. In birth it would be the opposite.' Tanya stared at Sam. 'In birth, you start inside the womb, then you move down the tunnel, then the doctor or whoever delivers you pulls you out.' She patted her chest. 'I'm getting strong feelings that you're dreaming about going back to the womb. It's a nice safe place in there, you don't have to do anything. It's nice and warm and snug. It would be a good place to escape to. No traumas in there. No premonitions. Are you connecting, Sam?'

'I'm not sure,' she said hesitantly.

'What sort of birth did you have, Sam? Traumatic? Caesarian or something like that, or was it normal?'

She shrugged. 'I don't know. I never—' She trailed off and Tanya smiled, reassuringly.

'It's a big shock, being born,' Tanya said. 'It never leaves us. Keeps coming back in our dreams.'

Wide. So wide of the mark, Sam thought.

'Is that connecting with you, Sam?'

'No,' she said apologetically.

'Do you know this man?' said Barry, his eyes still shut.

Do I? Slider? Was he Slider? Onions? Christ, do I want to get into all that? That's why you're here. I know. But.

'No.'

'He could be your animus,' said the American girl.

'Do you know about animus and anima?' asked Tanya.

'No,' said Sam.

'Jung said we have an opposite self which appears sometimes in our dreams. If you're a man, you see a strange woman who is your dream self, and if you're a woman, then a strange man. He could be your animus. Do you feel violent towards anyone? Towards yourself?'

She shook her head.

There was a long silence. Tanya Jacobson sat back with her eyes closed. Then she opened them again. 'Let's try and free associate a bit more. This person was trying to rape you in the dream. Think about rape. Free associate. Just say anything that comes into your mind.'

Sam looked around the room, then at the picture once more. Her heart felt heavy. The heater continued to rattle, and somewhere above she heard the muted shrill of a doorbell.

'Slider,' she said.

The man in the baggy jumper turned his head towards her, studying her thoughtfully, and the American girl smiled.

'Who is Slider, Sam?' said Tanya Jacobson. 'Do you want to tell us about Slider?'

She told them the full story of how she had discovered Slider, and how he had died, and how she had kept on dreaming until her parents had died.

When she had finished, there was a silence that seemed to go on for ever.

'That's awful,' the American girl said. 'That's really awful. It's made me feel all creepy.'

There was another long silence.

'How did you feel about it, Sam?' said Tanya Jacobson.

The words were like a distant echo, and she looked around, baffled, wondering if they were really addressed to her. She saw Sadie, on the pouf, and for a moment she thought she was perched on a mountain ledge.

'I can't remember, really. Numb, I suppose for a long time. I felt that he had done it, that he had killed them. I didn't dream of him again for a long time.'

'Why do you think that was?' Tanya said.

'I suppose my parents dying was the worst possible thing. There wasn't anything worse that he could do.'

Tanya nodded. 'Who brought you up after this, Sam?' she said.

'An uncle and aunt.'

'Were they nice?'

'No. They resented me. They were very cold people.'

'Did you ever tell them about Slider?'

'No.'

'Have you ever told anyone, Sam?' said Tanya.

'No.' She hesitated, remembering she had told Bamford O'Connell.

'What about your husband?'

'No.'

'What happened when you dreamed of him again?' Gail asked. 'How long after was it?'

Sam stared at her. 'Twenty-five years after. It was two weeks ago.'

'Wow,' Tanya Jacobson said. 'You're holding a lot inside you, aren't you? All bottled up. Can't tell your uncle and aunt. Can't tell your husband. But it's going to come out in your dreams, Sam, it always does.' She leaned forwards. 'You see, Sam, it doesn't matter what we try and hide from the world – we can't hide things from ourselves. It all comes out in our dreams, and it keeps on coming out until we face them, deal with them. But it's good, Sam. It's good that it's come to the surface, because you can deal with it now. You're going to have to face it, talk about it more, then he'll go away.' Tanya clasped her hands together dramatically. 'You have to meet your monster, Sam. We all have our personal monsters that come to us in our dreams. One of the things we try to do here is to meet them, and understand them. Then they go away.'

Sam stared back at her, then glanced at her watch. Were the others getting impatient? She wondered. She could see Sadie glaring down at her own watch then back at her, puffing angrily on her cigarette. 'Would someone else like to have a go – I've had rather a lot of time.'

'Don't worry about the others for a moment, Sam. This is your dream. Let's worry about you. I don't think we're ready to move on yet. OK?'

Sam suddenly felt very emotional, on the verge of weeping. She looked around and saw friends looking back. Even some of the hostility of Sadie's gaze seemed to have softened. Safe. She was safe here.

'Do you have any other associations?'

Sam closed her eyes, wondering if she dared. She opened them and looked around. It was beginning to seem easy to talk. 'Yes . . . my husband.' She felt her face reddening. 'The man in the dream smelled of onions. When I woke up, I could smell onions on my husband's breath.'

'And you associated him with the rapist?' said Tanya.

Sam bit her lip. 'He's been having an affair.'

'Wow!' Tanya clapped her hands together. 'I think

you're really beginning to connect!' She rocked backwards and forwards. 'We've got a whole bag, here, haven't we? This hooded man – Slider – you know, he's really strange for me. I'm connecting with the hood – like a mask. I think that part of what you are seeing in him is some dark side of yourself. You know? You can't let your real self show, can't let your feelings show, you keep them all safely hidden behind the mask. I think he represents so many things for you. Part of him is nasty adult, your cold uncle and aunt, they're a threat to you, taken away your nice, kind, warm parents and given you this cold resentment, this total lovelessness.' She shook her head, then stared hard back at Sam. 'Think of your description of him, Sam. The hood, the one eye – what else does that remind you of? You know? What does that make you think of?'

Sam tried to think, but could not concentrate.

'The old one-eyed trouser snake? It makes me think of a penis, Sam. A giant penis.'

Sam's heart sank. Did all analysis end up down the same road, at the same place? Did everything end up with a penis?

'You've been violated, Sam, haven't you? Your childhood was violated by this man, now your adulthood is being violated again by your husband. Does this resonate?'

Sam felt irritated suddenly. Crap. This was all crap. 'I'm sure it all fits very neatly, but I think that's a side issue. The point is that I had a premonition – about the Bulgaria air disaster. I dreamed it the night before it happened. There was someone in the dream with Slider's hood on his head. The next day, I dreamed of him again, in a taxi. It's as if he's linked with each of the premonitions. I don't know – like a sort of a harbinger. I feel that more bad things are going to happen. I had a second premonition a few days later, and he appeared again.'

Tanya raised her eyebrows. 'Sam, dismissing a dream as a premonition is the easy route. I think you're using that as an excuse not to face the real meaning of the dreams. I'm not saying that you don't have premonitions, or what you think are premonitions, but I'm not connecting with them. I don't think they matter.'

'They matter to me.'

'OK! They matter to you.' Tanya glanced at her watch. 'There's one other thing I want you to think about which could be important: this man chasing you. You were trying to run up the stairs from him and you couldn't move. Being chased by the opposite sex can mean that you fancy someone, but feel guilty about it – that you don't dare respond to the overtures. Am I touching any nerves?'

'I – I don't know. I don't think so.'

'Are you happy if we leave it there for a moment?'

Sam shrugged.

'OK, there's plenty for you to think about there,' Tanya said. 'Has anyone else brought a dream?'

'Yes,' Sadie said, almost bursting.

'Would you like to tell us, Sadie?'

'It's another of my sex dreams.'

Sam detected a faintly irritable sigh from the man in the baggy sweater, and tried to remember his name. Ian? Colin?

Sadie dipped into her handbag and pulled out a thick notebook. She leaved through pages of handwriting, then stopped. 'This was last Monday night, after the group. I was in this big old room, up in an attic – it was like my parents' house, but it was much bigger, and there was this little old lady in the corner, all wrinkled, sort of watching me. She was doing tapestry, but she was trying to embroider this sheet of metal with a drill.

'Anyhow, I was lying naked on this bed, and I was manacled, and I realised that she was the one who had manacled me, and the metal sheet turned into a score-board, and she was going to be scoring.' She looked smugly around the room and took a cigarette out of her pack. 'Clive came in the room. I didn't recognise him at first, then I realised he had on that baggy sweater he always wears.'

Sam looked at him, and saw him almost fuming with rage. Clive, that was his name.

'He started making love to me, but he wasn't satis-fying me, so I told him he'd have to go to the back of the queue and try again later. Then this young boy from the office came in, and told me he'd been fancying me like mad for months and he really wanted to be my toyboy.'

The dream seemed to go on interminably. The young boy from her office. Robert Redford. Prince Philip. Jack Nicholson. John McEnroe. Paul Hogan, Richard Gere. All, it seemed, had desired her secretly for much of their lives. All had been unable to satisfy her.

Finally, everyone was standing up. The two hours had passed. Sam had resonated well, she was told. 'Do you think you're more in touch with your feelings?' Tanya asked her.

'Yes, I think so,' she said dubiously.

Everyone was embarrassed about handing over their money, and it changed hands quickly, silently, almost shadily, like contraband, as if acknowledgement would somehow debase what they were going through.

'So you're going to come next week, Sam?' Tanya asked.

Barry still lay on the floor in his black karate suit,

with his eyes closed. He raised his right arm. 'Bye. Good meeting you.'

She wondered if he had ever once opened his eyes to look at her, and whether he would recognise her again.

'Yes,' Sam said.

'You keep a lot inside you, don't you?'

'I suppose so.'

'We'll have to get it out,' Tanya said. 'It's going to take a long time. Just don't get sidetracked into those pre-monitions, Sam. We don't dream the future—' She tapped her head through her frizz of hair. 'But we make connections. We meet our monsters. Forget the manifest, Sam. You've got to connect with your deep psyche.'

'I'd like to believe you,' Sam said.

'You will, you'll believe me.'

She walked out and up the basement steps, with her thoughts a churning vortex. Reassurance. It felt good to be reassured, to be told the answers. Schoolteachers told you the answers, too. They knew the answers to many things.

But not always the ones that mattered.

You have to meet your monster, Sam.

Kill the dragon. Kill him dead.

She went outside into the dark night.

Went out to her monster.

21

The night seemed mild, more like summer than early February, and the group dispersed silently into it, with scarcely a 'good bye'. She looked up at the sky, as she climbed into the Jaguar. The branches of the trees were like cardboard cut-out silhouettes against the brightness of the full moon.

She turned the ignition key, listened to the tick of the fuel pump, then pushed the starter. The engine turned over, then died. She pushed the choke lever up and tried again, keeping the starter button pushed hard in, listening to the churning of the engine, the hiss of the air intakes, the whine of the starter motor.

She took her hand off the button, and the noise faded away. There was the clicking of a ratchet, then silence. She slid the choke down to halfway, then tried again. Still nothing. She looked at the clock.

Quarter to ten.

She switched the ignition off, switched it back on and tried again. Again the engine turned over lifelessly.

'Come on, don't do this to me. I've got an early start.'

She sat, and blinked hard. She felt completely drained and a little foolish. Christ, what had she said? What had made her blurt all that out? To total strangers. To a bunch of loonies. What had they thought of her? Who cared? Probably more than they had thought of Sadie and her drivelling fantasies.

She tried again and kept on trying until she heard the battery beginning to die, and then she stopped, and looked at the clock again. If she phoned the RAC how long would they take? she wondered. An hour at least. Possibly two or three. She had a breakfast meeting at quarter to eight in the morning, and did not want to arrive shattered. The car was OK here, safe. She could send Drummond up to sort it out in the morning.

She shivered, and did not know why.

She locked the car and as she did so she heard the squeal of tyres and the roar of an engine. She looked up and saw a car hurtling down the street, its lights on full beam, making straight towards her.

Like in the dream, she thought, panicking, running

around the back of the Jaguar onto the kerb, watching the car thunder past.

Like in the bloody dream.

She shivered again.

We don't dream the future . . . but we make connections. We meet our monsters. Forget the manifest, Sam. You've got to connect with your deep psyche.

She walked down the street, feeling nervous of the shadows of the trees, like dark pools of blood, and afraid of the brilliant light of the moon in the open that lit her up, exposing her like a startled rabbit caught in a car's headlamps.

The dream. It was all like the dream.

As she crossed the next pool of light, it faded suddenly, as if it had been extinguished. There was a patter, like tiny feet, then a splodge of cold water hit her forehead.

Rain. She felt relieved. It had not rained in this part of the dream.

The downpour followed quickly, within seconds, and she wondered whether to run back to the car and get her umbrella. But she was only a short distance from the High Street, and saw a taxi cross in front of her.

'Taxi!' she shouted and ran, but it had gone by the time she got there. She stood there as the rain became even heavier, drenching her, staring at the blurring headlights, tail lights, searching for a yellow 'For Hire' sign.

Another taxi rattled past, its tyres sluicing, shadows of people huddled in the back, then another, also taken. She felt her hair plastering down on her forehead and her coat becoming heavy from the water. Some way up the hill she saw the tube sign. For a moment she hesitated, gazed down the street and then up at the lines of lights. No taxis.

It wasn't raining in the dream.

You'll be OK.

No, Sam. No.

Oh shit.

You have to meet your monster.

Dream. It was just a dream.

It's much easier to put them down as premonitions than to face their real truths.

Vagina. I'm getting a vagina.

You mean she's going back into her mother's womb?

Of course. Didn't everybody?

Maybe they did.

She ran towards the tube station, then stopped. Don't be so bloody stupid.

Scaredy cat! Scaredy cat! Scaredy cat!

Me?

Scaredy cat! Scaredy cat! Scaredy cat!

Actually, I don't take tubes any more – well – you know, muggers and all that. Richard doesn't like it.

Scaredy cat!

She ran on again, towards the sign.

You're not going to go down there, Sam!

Oh yes I am.

Oh no you're not!

Oh yes I am.

Oh no you're not!

Oh piss off.

She ran inside, past several people huddling in the entrance, into the chill dry smell of dust and staleness, and stared around at the ticket machines.

Out of order. Out of order. The third one seemed to be working and she opened her bag, pulled out her purse, then hesitated, trying to find Wapping on the list of stations, but could not.

She walked over to the ticket office, trembling, wondering if the same woman from her dream was going to be sitting there. She felt relieved when she saw a young man, with a heavy beard.

'Single to Wapping, please.'

'The lifts aren't working,' he said, raising his eyebrows.

'I'm sorry?'

'The lifts. We've got a problem with the power.'

'I can walk.'

He frowned. 'Have you been here before?'

'No.'

'It's a long way down.'

She felt a prickle of anxiety. 'I—' She paused. 'I don't mind.'

He shrugged. 'Ninety pence. Turn right.' He pointed with his hand.

She took the ticket, and walked through the unattended barrier. There was a sign at the head of the stairs.

THE LIFT SHAFT AT THIS STATION IS THE DEEPEST IN LONDON. 300 STEPS. USE ONLY IN EMERGENCY.

The grimy tiled walls were familiar, like the walls of a public lavatory; like the walls in the dream. She stared at the steel-cased shaft in the middle of the staircase exactly as she had seen it in her dream.

Christ, how the hell did I dream this so accurately?

Maybe I've been here before? A long time ago?

Must have been.

She was shaking.

Relax! This is a tube station. Everyone uses the tube.

She listened, hoping some more people would come so they could walk down together. There were brisk footsteps, and two men, deep in conversation started down the staircase. She heard more footsteps behind and the chatter of foreign students. A huge crowd of them, Italian, stylish careless, chattering excitedly, laughing, energy, enthusiasm. Life. She started walking down with them, hurrying, to stay in their midst, not to be left behind on her own.

They were halfway down when she felt something snap, and her handbag fell to the ground. It bounced and rolled over down several steps; her Filofax fell out, and burst open, scattering paper all around.

Shit.

She knelt down, as the students stepped carefully through everything, without the pitch of their chatter altering. She crammed the sheaves of paper back untidily, hurrying, feeling foolish, then looked at the broken strap of her handbag. A rivet had sheared. Then she became aware of the silence. She was shivering from her soaking clothes, from the draught, and from fear, she realised, stuffing the Filofax back into her bag. The chatter of the students had already faded, and she was alone. Turn around, she thought, turn around and go back up.

She looked up and then down. Each was as dark and silent and menacing as the other.

You have to meet your monster.

Was this what Tanya Jacobson meant?

Here?

She stood and listened and the chatter of the Italians was gone completely.

Calm, Sam. Calm. Just go on down. You'll be fine.

She tucked her bag under her arm, took one step down, then another and heard the sharp echo of the shuffle of her feet.

It wasn't raining in the dream.

The ticket collector was a woman in the dream.

Dream. Just a dream. That's all.

She began, slowly, to walk down further, until she had completed one spiral and then another. Deep below her she heard the faint rumble of a train.

In the dream there hadn't been any other people. There were plenty of people around tonight, surely there were? She walked down further, tiptoeing, trying to walk silently so there was no echo, so that no one could hear, so that if he was there waiting then – Christ, she thought, her coat was rustling, her handbag rubbing against it. She stopped again and listened. There was another faint rumble, then silence. How many steps now? How far had she come? She felt the back of her neck prickle. Someone had crept down after her. Someone was standing behind her.

She spun round.

No one.

She felt her heart beating, beating so loudly she could almost hear it. Come on, Sam. Meet your monster. Meet your monster.

And what the hell did you do when you met him?

Hit him with your bag and try to out-run him? Out-run him to where? To an empty platform?

She stood and stared fearfully back up the steps, then continued on down, slowly, trying to be silent, and knowing she wasn't.

I must be nearly at the bottom, she thought. How many steps? Three hundred. She walked down some more, counting. Five. Six. Seven. God it was a long process. She could not even be halfway down yet, she calculated.

Then she froze.

Right beneath her, only yards away, she heard the shuffle of a foot.

She listened again, motionless.

Someone was standing below her, breathing heavily, panting.

She heard the scrape of a foot again.

Yards away.

Then she saw the shadow on the wall.

Stationary. Moving very slightly.

Someone standing very still, trying not to be seen.

Someone waiting for her.

The grimy walls seemed to be closing in around her. She felt ice cold water running through her.

Then the shadow began to rise up the stairs towards her, swiftly, determined. It grew larger, darker.

She heard footsteps, like drum beats. And a man grunting.

Grunting like a pig.

She turned and ran, tripping.

No. Help me. For Christ's sake help me.

She stumbled and fell, bashed her knee, picked herself up, threw herself up more steps, grabbed the handrail, pulled herself on up.

She bounced off the wall on her right, then stumbled across, her shoulder crashing painfully into the rail on her left. Her lungs were searing, but she ran on, hearing breathing behind her, footsteps behind her, the grunting, the shadow chasing her own, touching it then falling back.

Then she was at the top and running, out through the barrier, through the people sheltering in the entrance and out into the pelting rain and the lights of the street.

She leaned against the wall, gasping for breath, swallowing deep gulps of air, feeling her heart crashing inside her chest. She doubled up in agony as a stitch gripped her stomach, and stayed there shaking as the rain washed the perspiration from her face.

She pulled off her gloves, and let the rain cool her hands, staring up at it thankfully.

She stayed a long time, until she had become little more than part of the furniture of the street; invisible; just a huddled thing, another of the derelicts of any big city you stepped past a bit faster and made sure you did not look at. She limped down the street, her ankle hurting like hell, towards a telephone booth she could see in the distance.

She thumbed through the book, and found the number of the RAC.

'May I have your membership number?' the girl said tartly.

'My card's in the car. We have a company membership. Ken Shepperd Productions.'

She hung on for a long time before the girl came back. When she did she sounded surly, disbelieving, reluctant. 'If you wait with your car, we'll get someone there when we can.'

'How long will that be?'

'At least an hour. We have a lot of call-outs at the moment.'

She climbed wearily back into the Jaguar, locked the doors, and sat gazing blankly ahead. She closed her eyes, her brain churning, wondering whether she had imagined it. She saw the shadow moving, heard the shuffle of feet, the breathing, the grunting, the shadow following her up the steps. She shuddered and stared fearfully out of the window, at the dark, and switched on the radio.

She snapped it off again almost immediately, afraid suddenly of not being able to hear the sounds outside, and sat and waited in silence, thinking about the dream group and about Bamford and about the shadow that had come up the steps towards her.

And if Bamford was right? And Tanya Jacobson?

If the shadow had been in her own mind?

If. If. They probably were right.

Damn them.

Nutty as a fruitcake, old boy.

My wife?

196

Sam?

Got a brick missing from the load, I'm afraid.

The rattle of an engine startled her; she felt the beam of a spotlight, and saw the breakdown truck pulled up alongside her. The driver waved, and she raised her hand in acknowledgement. She unlocked the door, with a stiff, frozen hand, and climbed out. The rain had stopped, but the air felt cold.

'Won't start?' said the man. Young, chirpy.

'No.'

'Nice car. Ought to be in a museum.'

'It's been very reliable.'

'It's the electrics in these old Jags. They ought to be rewired – complete new loom – that's usually the problem.' He slipped into the driver's seat, turned the ignition and pushed the starter motor.

The engine fired immediately. He revved it several times whilst she stood, in numb disbelief in a cloud of thick, oily exhaust. He revved it again, hard, too hard, she thought, but beyond caring, then he stuck his head out. 'You probably flooded it. Sounds fine. Very sweet.'

She shook her head slowly. 'No. I didn't flood it.'

He shrugged.

'There's another reason,' she said.

'Loose connection?'

She shook her head. 'No.'

The RAC man frowned. 'Temperamental, is she?'

'Temperamental,' she echoed, looking away. Somewhere in a room above them she heard a faint tinkle of laughter, then a man's voice, raucous, and another tinkle of laughter. She heard the clicking of a bicycle, and the creak of brakes, and saw an elegantly dressed woman dismount, and carry the bicycle up the steps of number 54.

'Can I have your card, and I'll just get your signature.'

'I'm sorry,' she said. 'I'm sorry you've been bothered.'

He ducked into his cab and pulled out a clipboard. 'Probably flooded. Happens all the time. What's this got? Triple SUs?'

'Pardon?'

'SU carbs?'

'I don't know.'

'Flooded, most likely.'

She pulled the card out of the glove locker and handed it to him. It would have been easy to have agreed with him. Yes, I flooded it. How silly of me. But it hadn't been that. Nor a loose connection.

It hadn't been anything that a mechanic could have dealt with.

22

It was after midnight when she arrived home, and the hall was in darkness. She closed the front door quietly and took off her soaking wet coat. She could see a dim pool of light through in the living area, and walked down the corridor.

Richard was hunched over his desk, in front of his Reuters screen, whisky tumbler and bottle of Teacher's beside him. He turned his head.

'Look wet,' he slurred.

And you looked smashed out of your brains. 'It's pelting.' She walked over and kissed his cheek. 'Still working?'

'Andreas said there was going to be some action tonight. Reckoned there could be some big movements.'

He blearily rubbed his nose, poured out another four fingers, then tapped his keyboard and leaned forward as if trying to focus on the screen. He frowned at the changing figures. 'Where've been?'

'Oh – we've got a problem over a shoot. Fish fingers – Superfingers – the client wants it done on location in the Arctic, and we're trying to persuade them to do it here in a studio.' She was glad he wasn't looking at her; she had never been good at lying. 'Then the car wouldn't start.'

'Bloody ridiculous car to poddle round London in. I tell you, that bloke Ken's got a serious ego problem.'

'It's nothing to do with ego. He likes old cars; they're a good investment and a good image.'

'Especially when they break down in the middle of the night.' He frowned again at the screen.

She stared out of the window, watching the rain sheeting down onto the dark silhouettes of the restless lighters and the black water of the river. At least the aggression had gone, that strange violent temper he'd arrived home with when he'd ripped her bra. Her slap seemed to have done something and he'd been calm since; testy, but calm.

'Jon Goff rang. They've got some theatre tickets for Thursday, to see some new Ayckbourn thing.'

'Damn, I want to see that. Can't, Thursday. That's the night I have to go to Leeds. We've got a presentation on Friday morning.'

He squinted at some figures, then checked something on a pad on his desk. 'Jesus!' he shouted at the screen, his voice an agonised roar. 'You can't fucking do that! How can you?' He crashed his fist down on his desk. 'How can you fucking do that?'

'Ssh,' Sam said. 'You don't have to shout like that. Nicky—'

'Fuck Nicky. Jesus Christ. What's the Market fucking doing? Andreas never gets it wrong! What do they think they're playing at? Tokyo told me they thought New York looked cheap.' He glared belligerently at the screen cluttered with endless rows of figures and the strange names and symbols. Jargon. Language. A language that was as alien to her as the language of the dream group would have been to him.

She stayed, standing silently behind him for several minutes, watching as he drank more, tapped in more commands, cursed some more. He seemed to have forgotten she was there, seemed oblivious to anything outside of the small screen with its green symbols.

She left him and went to undress, and lay in bed for a long time, with the light on, thinking. Thinking about Richard and what was troubling him and wishing they could talk more openly, wishing she could tell him about her dreams without him sneering and wishing he could tell her what was wrong. She thought about Bamford O'Connell, about the dream group. She churned through the air disaster, the shooting, going down the steps of Hampstead tube station. She looked at the clock. 0215. Richard still had not come to bed.

Bamford O'Connell and Tanya Jacobson had now both said the same thing.

In my mind.

What had been coming up the tube station stairs? Her own imagination?

She heard the click of the shower door, then the sound of running water. Odd, she thought dimly. Odd Richard having a shower before he came to bed. She thought again of the steps and the shadow, thought about it for the hundred millionth time.

Nothing. There was nothing. Why the hell didn't I go on down?

Meet your monster.

Not me. I'm scared.

Scaredy cat, scaredy cat!

'Bye, Bugs.'

She smelt the minty toothpaste, and felt his kiss. She sat up with a start. 'What's the time?'

'Twenty-five past six. I'm late.'

'It's morning?'

Richard's eyes were bloodshot, and his face was pasty white. Hers probably was too.

'I'm playing squash tonight.'

'Will you want supper?'

'Yah – be in about nine.'

'OK.'

The door closed.

Morning. She hadn't dreamed. Had she slept? She slid out of bed feeling strangely alert, fresh. Must be a good biorhythm day. I feel great. Terrific. I'm resonating.

It's going to take you time to resonate, Sam.

Wow, Sam, you really resonated well.

I did?

Resonate, she thought as the hard droplets of water of the shower stung her face, and the soap stung her eyes. Resonate! She smiled. She felt light, carefree, as if a weight had been lifted from her. Watch out, Slider, I'm resonating. I'm going to get you, you horrible slit-eyed creep.

She dressed and went into the hallway. Helen came out of her room in her dressing gown. 'Good morning, Mrs Curtis. You're off early today.'

'Yes, I've got a breakfast meeting. What's Nicky got on at school?'

'An outing. They're going to London Zoo.'

Sam walked through into Nicky's room. He was just beginning to wake up, and she kissed him lightly on the forehead. 'See you this evening, Tiger.'

He looked up at her dozily, a sad expression on his face. 'Why are you going now, Mummy?'

'Mummy has to go in early today.' She felt a twinge of guilt. What was he feeling? she wondered. Unwanted? A nuisance? Someone in the way of her career? Bamford O'Connell's words flashed at her.

You gave up your career for Nicky . . . Maybe you feel anger at him. Maybe deep in your subconscious you feel that if you didn't have him around—?

She stared down at Nicky, reluctant to leave him, wanting to hug him, wanting to take him to the zoo herself, to show him the giraffes and love him. Wanting him never to feel for one instant the way she had felt throughout most of her childhood. 'See you this evening,' she said, turning reluctantly.

'Will you be late tonight, Mummy?'

'No.'

'Promise?'

She laughed. 'I promise.'

'You didn't tell me a story last night.'

'Mummy was a little late last night.'

'Will you tell me one tonight?'

'Yes.'

'About the dragon? Will you tell me that one again?'

She smiled and nodded, stroked his hair, kissed him again, then went out and down the hallway and put on her coat, which was damp.

It was still fairly dark outside, made worse by a swirling mist that was thick with drizzle. A glum paperboy in a sou'wester was standing in front of the mail boxes, sifting through the papers.

'Flat Eleven,' Sam said. 'Have you got them?'

The lenses of his glasses were running with water. He peered helplessly through them.

'Don't worry,' she said, and hurried to her car.

Her energy faded fast, and by the time she got to the office after her meeting she felt tired and sticky; grungy. The hotel dining room had been hot, stuffy. Everyone had sat drinking too much coffee, crunching toast, bleary-eyed, surrounded by the smells of aftershave, fried eggs and kippers. What the hell had the meeting been about? Nothing, that was what it had been about. The suits at Mcphersons wanted Ken to understand the importance of this commercial, the significance of being invited to Leeds to make the presentation. Earnest, serious hellos. Positive handshakes. This wasn't going to be no ordinary commercial. No, sir. The coming of Christ was an insignificant blot in the annals of time compared to the new Coming. The Dawning of A Great New Era. CASTAWAY. The first Personal Nourishment System. The Twenty-first Century Food. Food that Resonates.

The ashtray was filled with fresh, lipsticky butts, and the smoke haze was thick. Claire was hammering on her typewriter, head bent low in concentration.

'Morning, Claire.'

Claire lifted her hand a few inches in acknowledgement and carried on her frenetic typing.

'What are you typing?'

'I'm just doing this for Ken,' she said, almost furtively.

'What is it?' said Sam, getting increasingly infuriated.

'They don't want the giraffes.'

'What?' Sam opened the window and breathed in a lungful of wet Covent Garden mist.

'They're cancelling.'

'The whole shoot?' Sam said, alarmed.

'No. They've decided to use pantomime giraffes. They're worried about the animal rights people.'

'Booze, cigarettes, animal rights, exploiting women . . . for God's sake, we're not going to be able to make commercials about anything.' Sam sat down at her desk and slit open the top letter. It was informing her of an increase in lab charges.

Claire shook a cigarette out of the pack and looked slyly at Sam. 'Horrible, that thing on the news. Did you hear it?'

'What thing?' said Sam absently, concentrating on the letter.

'That poor woman.'

'Woman?'

'Last night. The one who was murdered.'

She read the first paragraph again, irritated by Claire's chatter, trying to calculate the true cost of the increase.

'It was on the radio this morning. Hampstead tube station.'

Sam looked up with a start. 'What, Claire? What are you talking about?'

'Last night. A woman was raped and murdered at Hampstead tube station. It was on the news this morning. Makes you wonder where you're safe, doesn't it?'

The room seemed to be dissolving around her. She felt her legs shaking and a sharp acidic sensation in her throat.

Claire began typing again.

'Hampstead, did you say? Hampstead tube?'

Claire did not seem to hear her.

'Jesus.' She looked at her watch. It was twenty past eleven. She went outside, across to the news vendor and stood by his stand in the driving rain with no coat on as the first edition of the *Standard* was dumped by the delivery van, and the vendor untied the string, slowly, agonisingly slowly.

She read the headlines again, then again, stared at each word of the bold black type in turn, as if she was afraid to read on, as if by reading on it might all suddenly come true and she would find she was the girl who had been—

RAPED AND MURDERED ON THE UNDER-GROUND.

Oh Christ.

Oh sweet Jesus, no.

She was only dimly aware of the world that was continuing around her. A taxi dropped someone off. Two people hurried past under an umbrella. A van was unloading parcels.

Then she saw the photograph underneath.

Saw the woman's face smiling out at her, as if she was smiling at her and no one else. As if there was a secret understanding in that smile.

She reeled sideways, crashed into the vendor who smelled like a damp sack, apologised, held onto the news stand and stared again, numb with shock, at the photograph.

Please, no. Please let this be a dream.

She walked back slowly, crying with misery, help-lessness, shame, guilt. Guilt. Guilt. Scaredy cat, scaredy cat, could have saved her! Could have saved her! Could have saved her!

Her.

She'd been talking to her only minutes before.

It wasn't true. It couldn't be. It had to be a—

She blundered in through the office door and knocked Drummond, who was coming out, flying. The box he was carrying fell to the ground with a sharp crack and rolled into the gutter. 'Sorry,' she said. 'Sorry. Sorry.'

She walked past Ken's waxwork – the arm had been glued back on although the angle looked odd – and up to her office. She sat back at her desk and put the wet and soggy paper down and stared again at the photograph, then the words, then the photograph again.

A thirty-seven-year-old mother of a young child was brutally raped and murdered at Hampstead Underground Station last night.

Tanya Jacobson, a psychotherapist, was found dead in a boiler room halfway down the notoriously deep stairwell shortly after ten o'clock by a maintenance electrician. Ticket clerk, John Barker, had warned Mrs Jacobson earlier that the lifts were out of service and that the steps went very deep.

Premonitions, precognition . . . that's all a little bit – fringe, OK? We're trying here to really connect with our dreams, go with them, free associate, get some good dynamics going.

She looked up and saw Claire watching her. 'I know her,' Sam said bleakly. 'I was with her just – before – she was . . . I went to this—'

The dark room. Knickers being ripped down. Hands around the neck. The stench of onions.

Tell me you love me.

Cunt bitch.

No. Please, no. Don't kill me. Please don't kill me – I have a child – please—

Sam felt an icy coldness torrenting through her, deep inside. She closed her eyes then opened them again. 'It must have been minutes—' She paused. 'I could have prevented it,' she said.

Claire looked up at her, and frowned.

Sam thought again of the grunting, and the dark shadow that came up the stairs towards her. 'I ought to call the police,' she said. 'Tell them I was there.'

'Did you see anything?'

'Yes – I . . . I don't know,' she sighed.

She stood up abruptly and wandered around the office, clenching her hands. She walked over to the window and stared out at the sheeting rain, at puddles, at awnings, at black umbrellas and at an old man who was sifting through the contents of a litter bin.

Dead.

Terrific. Wow! Wonderful. I'm Tanya Jacobson.

Tanya Jacobson. Sam felt the coldness of the draught on her hands, and water from her wet hair running down her face.

Just don't get sidetracked into those premonitions, Sam. We don't dream the future – but we make connections. We meet our monsters.

'I dreamed it,' she said.

Sam, dismissing a dream as a premonition is the easy route. I think you're using that as an excuse not to face the real meaning of the dreams.

Maybe it was the other way around? Were they using the psychology route to avoid facing up to premonitions?

Christ. There must be someone who—?

She felt the heat from the radiator rise up through the cold draught, as she continued to stare out through the window. 'That clairvoyant you go to, Claire. Why do you go to her?'

'Mrs Wolf?'

'Yes.' Sam turned around. 'What do you go to her for?'

'I go to her for guidance.'

'Is she accurate?'

Claire swept her hair back with her hands and looked sharply up at the ceiling, as if the answer was written there. 'Yes, she's – very accurate. She's very accurate indeed.'

'Does she help you to understand things?'

'She's very good at . . . helping people to understand things.'

'Would she see me, do you think?'

'Oh yes, I'm sure she would. You can just go along. You don't even need an appointment, although it's best to make one. Wednesdays. She's always there Wednesdays.'

23

The shop was in a narrow street in Bloomsbury. She could see the sign halfway along on the other side. 'THE WHOLE MIND AND BODY CENTRE.' It was painted blue, and she sensed weird vibes coming out from it even from this distance. She glanced at her watch. Fifteen minutes early.

There was a smaller sign in the window of the shop, a stand-up card which she read when she got closer.

EVA WOLF, CLAIRVOYANT
SITTING TODAY.

Another on top of a neat stack of pyramids proclaimed THE WONDER OF PYRAMIDS! There was also a row of rock crystals, several packs of Tarot cards, an assortment of books – *Realise Your Full Psychic Potential* said one, *Understand Magik*, said another – and a silver four-leafed clover charm bracelet wrapped around a sign which said THE PERFECT VALENTINE GIFT!

The interior of the shop was, like the sign, blue, with blue-tinted fluorescent lights throwing down harsh light across the shelves and the open floor. Designer occult, she thought. She went inside and the feeling of hostility almost overwhelmed her. She wanted to turn and run – from the heat of the blue fluorescents and the smell of joss sticks and the glare of a woman who looked up at her from behind a half-dismantled cash register.

Was she Mrs Wolf?

Her red hair was pulled back tight across her scalp, her skin tight over her face, as if she'd been affected by some freak pull of the moon. She wore a black polo neck sweater which showed her nipples clearly, like two black spikes.

Sam turned away and looked around. There were several crystal balls on a shelf in front of her. A rack of meditation cassettes, more pyramids, astrological charts, shelves stacked with candles, some of them black, a pouch with several small stones laid on it, a display of herbal sleep tinctures, and all the time the smell . . . the joss sticks, yes, but something else, something weird. Seriously weird, she thought, the fluorescent lights burning down on her scalp like sun-ray lamps.

The woman was bent over the cash register, picking at it with a screwdriver like someone trying to get the meat out of a lobster.

'Excuse me?'

The woman looked up. 'Yes?' It seemed to come out without her mouth moving, almost without a sound, almost as if she had imagined it. She felt strangely disoriented.

'I have an appointment with Mrs Wolf.'

The woman skewered the cash register again. 'Through the books. Downstairs.' Without looking up this time; again the mouth had not moved.

Sam walked through to the back of the shop, past a stack of pocket books and hesitated at the top of the stairs.

Cut and run.

Don't be silly.

Claire comes here. It's fine. Maybe that woman just had a row with her boyfriend or something? Or her girlfriend? She went down a steep, narrow staircase into the basement, which was an extension of the books section. A man with a pigtail, dressed in black, was restocking the shelves. There were books all around, piled on tables, on shelves, in dumpbins. Past them on the far wall she saw an arrow pointing down a short corridor to a door.

'Eva Wolf, Clairvoyant', was handwritten in large script and underneath in smaller writing it said:

CLAIRVOYANT SITTINGS. 30 Mins.	£12
PALM READINGS	£10
AURA READINGS	£10
TAROT	£12
PRIVATE SEANCES BY ARRANGEMENT	

The door was slightly ajar and a guttural mid-European voice called out from behind it. 'Is that Mrs Peterson? You are rather late. I have another appointment.'

'No, I'm Mrs Curtis.'

There was a silence. 'I don't think Mrs Peterson is coming today. Come in, please. Come in.'

Sam pushed open the door and went into a room that wasn't much bigger than a toilet cubicle. The bare brick walls were painted the same blue as everywhere else and a single blue light bulb hung overhead. The room smelt faintly of joss sticks and strongly of a noxiously sweet perfume. Mrs Wolf was seated behind a tiny round table, which she dwarfed, wearing a dark polo neck sweater and an unfastened afghan waistcoat. She sat bolt upright, a tall, heavy-boned woman in her early-seventies, her stiff face daubed with gaudy make-up, and poker-straight wiry grey hair that hung down around it and over her forehead in a fringe. Her eyes stared at Sam from their shadowy sockets, like wary creatures of the deep.

'Please shut the door behind you. Put your coat on the hook.'

Sam did so and sat down. The woman took her hand quickly, snatchily, like a bird taking food, and held it firmly in her own large hand; it was hard, calloused, as if she spent her spare time digging potatoes, and her nails were unvarnished and had dirt underneath them. There was an old Bible on the table, wrapped in cracked cellophane, and a coffee cup with lipstick on the rim.

The woman stared at her, as if she had been expecting something quite different and Sam felt awkward, too close, as if her personal space was being invaded.

'It was a sitting you wanted?'

'What I really want is – just to talk. I want some advice . . . I'll pay for your time.'

The woman did not react. 'You've half an hour. You may make what use of it you like.'

They sat in silence for a moment and Sam felt increasingly uncomfortable. She heard footsteps upstairs and the faint sound of an extractor fan; she looked at the woman's stiff, serious face and saw she had two warts, and a mole with a hair growing out of it. The face seemed to stiffen even more and slowly, almost imperceptibly, she began to quiver; Sam felt her hand trembling.

'I've been having what I suppose are premonitions . . . in my dreams. It started a couple of weeks ago. I—' She heard her own voice tailing away. What did she want to hear? she thought suddenly. Why had she come here at all? She felt a rising surge of fear inside her.

Stay away from the hokum guys.

'I was hoping you might help me to understand why these are happening.'

Mrs Wolf was giving her the distinct impression that she wasn't really interested. 'That would be the spirits telling you things.'

'Spirits?'

'It all comes from the spirits.'

'Ah.'

'It's all part of God's love for us.'

'Ah.'

Mrs Wolf's expression mellowed; she leaned forward and patted the Bible tenderly, affectionately, as if it was a baby she had just been suckling. 'The Good Lord is always watching over us; He doesn't mind if you are Christian or Jewish, because there is room for everyone in the Kingdom of God.' She smiled a distant, private smile. 'He still understands and He tells me to tell you that He's keeping room for you. Any time you want to enter into Him He will receive you.'

Very reasonable of Him.

'Kindness. He's so full of kindness. Kindness and love.'

'That's why he killed my parents.'

'He's asking us to say a prayer together. A little prayer for protection and understanding and then we'll say the Lord's Prayer.'

The clairvoyant closed her eyes and held Sam's hand a little tighter. Too tight; she was crushing it.

'Gracious Spirit, as we join together here, we ask for blessing upon all of those who come from Spirit to be with us and we ask a blessing, please, for Mrs Curtis. Now, Father, we ask for protection and we know that when we come to Thee, as we stand in Thy grace, we are indeed protected from all of earth's conditions. If we could come to You more often, we would find that peace and tranquillity that exists only in Your presence . . .' There was no feeling of sincerity in the woman's words; she could have been reading from a telephone directory. It was almost as if she was . . . mocking?

Claire believed this woman? Swore by this woman?

Give her a chance.

'Amen.' The clairvoyant stared hard at Sam.

'Amen,' Sam said, half under her breath.

The woman's hand was cold. Uncomfortably cold; how could she be that cold?

'I'm getting a connection with advertising. Would you understand that?'

You know that. I told you when I made the appointment that Claire had recommended me. 'Yes,' Sam said.

'I'm being shown two people in Spirit – could be your grandparents. No, they're younger. Could they be your parents?'

Sam frowned.

'Died when you were quite young, did they?'

Had Claire told her this?

'I'm being told there was a break in your career – a young child involved – but that was in the past?'

Sam nodded, reluctantly.

'I see difficulties with a man at the moment. This is a very ambitious man, and I'm shown his heart being torn. Pulled in two directions. I don't know if it's between you and work, or between you and another woman. Does that mean anything?'

Sam nodded again.

She tightened her icy grip on Sam's hand even more, so much that Sam winced, but the woman ignored her, closed her eyes tightly and started breathing in hard, short bursts. Sam stared, her hand in agony, and to her horror saw sweat beginning to pour down the woman's face. She wondered if this was a trance.

RAPED AND MURDERED ON THE UNDER-GROUND.

Last night she had lain in bed reading until she was too tired even to turn the pages any more. She had felt herself going down the dark steps, waiting for the shadow, and when she finally saw it and had turned to run, she had not been able to move, and had stood and screamed. Then Richard had grunted and asked her if she was OK.

No, damn you. I am not O.K. And you don't believe me, do you? You don't believe that I was down there, down the tube station, minutes before it happened.

Had a lucky escape didn't you, Bugs?

That was all he'd said. Big grin on his face.

He thought it was funny?

Mrs Wolf's eyes opened and they were filled with a strange, uncomprehending fear. They closed again and she was still drawing short, almost desperate, breaths. She spoke slowly, almost as if she was sleeptalking. 'Do – you – know – a – man – with – only – one—' Then the panting started again, and the woman began shaking her head from side to side and whimpering, 'No – no – no – no—'

The room was becoming icily cold. Sam could see steam from the woman's breath, thick vapour that hung in the air. She felt goose-pimples running down her arms, down her back and a churning feeling in her stomach.

There was a strange rumbling sound, like a distant tube train, except it seemed to be coming from above them, not below. As she listened to it, she felt the coldness in the room seeping through her, turning everything inside her to ice.

There was a sharp ping above them.

The light went out.

Sam snapped her neck back, staring up, trying to see the bulb, then looked around wildly in the sudden pitch-black darkness.

The clairvoyant continued to pant and whimper. Then her grip began to slacken, and Sam felt the temperature in the room warming.

'I think we'd better stop,' Mrs Wolf said. 'I think we'd better stop.' She was still breathing heavily.

'Please tell me . . . please tell me what's going on,' Sam whispered.

'There's . . . I—' She heard the rustle of the woman's clothes in the darkness. 'They won't show me anything. Nothing.'

'Why? I don't understand.'

'It's better if you don't.'

'I want to know.'

'There'll be no charge. I can't give it to you. I can't give you what you want.' The woman's chair scraped back.

'Why not? Please explain—'

'You want to know what's going on? The future? I can't see. I can't show you.'

'Why can't you?'

'I can't. Open the door. We must open the door!'

'Why can't you?' Sam's voice was rising.

'Because there's nothing there,' the woman said.

'What do you mean?'

'There's nothing there.'

'You mean you can't see anything?'

'Nothing.'

'What . . . what does that mean?'

The clairvoyant's voice was trembling. 'No more future. It means – that you don't have any future.'

Sam felt her hand released; heard the woman move; the sound of the door opening and dim light from the corridor filled the room.

'There's no charge,' said the woman. 'Just go. Get out!'

'Please—' Sam said. 'Please just explain. Tell me—'

'Out, get out! Get out!' the woman cried. 'Get out! No charge, just get out!' She was screaming now. 'What have you brought with you? Take it away. We don't want it here. Take it, get out, get out!'

Sam stared up at the bulb. It was intact, but blackened. She stood up, stunned, her mind numbed.

'Get out of here!' the woman hissed again. 'Take it away. Take it with you.'

Sam backed away out of the room and down the corridor, past the man with the pigtail who glared malevolently. She climbed the stairs and saw the woman with the pulled-back red hair still skewering the cash register, glance up and follow her with her eyes.

Sam stumbled through the shop and out into the street, her brain a vortex of confusion. It was a cold, sharp afternoon, the sky a watery blue, with the sun already setting. Four o'clock. A waiter came out of a Greek restaurant across the road and locked the door behind him. Two men strode past chatting, one rubbing his hands against the cold.

She began to walk as fast as she could away from the shop, from Mrs Wolf, away from the woman with the pulled-back face, blinded by the raging confusion in her mind. She kept bumping into people, then saw an object in front blocking her path and stepped around it, off the pavement, onto the road.

There was a howl of brakes and she looked up, startled, at the taxi that was stopped inches from her.

The driver's head came out of his window, a cloth cap

with clumps of hair either side. 'Woz wiv you then? Woz your fuckin' game? Trying to get yourself bloody killed?'

'Sorry,' she said. 'Sorry.'

Through the blur of her tears she saw a small park across the road; she went into it and sat down on a bench.

She lowered her head into her arms, and thought for a moment she was going to be sick. She could feel the world turning like a huge fairground wheel, accelerating, spinning her round, making her giddy, then rising up and trying to tip her onto the grass. She held onto the seat, held on tightly; held on because she knew she was tilted so far over now that if she let go she would fall out into space.

No more future . . . you don't have any future.

OK. I want to wake up now. Dream over.

Two barristers walked down the path in front of her, in their gowns and wigs; she watched them, hoping they might turn into frogs or giraffes, or take their clothes off and leap in the air so she would know it was a dream for sure, but they simply carried on walking, talking.

She stared up at an advertising hoarding on the side of a high-rise office. Huge bold letters, already illuminated for the falling darkness. Huge bold letters that beamed at her as if they were taunting her.

SAFEGUARD YOUR FUTURE WITH THE GUARDIAN ROYAL.

24

The heavy traffic streaming north was gradually thinning the further away they got from London. They could have been on another planet or travelling through space, Sam thought, staring out through the windscreen. Just blackness peppered with drifting red lights and occasional orange blinking lights and the rushing of wind, and bridges that passed overhead and seemed to suspend time for a fraction of a second, and signs that came out of the dark then flipped away again past the windscreen.

NORTHAMPTON. COVENTRY. LEICESTER. LOUGHBOROUGH 10. SERVICES 15.

Lightning forked across the sky and a few blobs of water hit the windscreen. The interior of the Bentley was dark, just the weak glow of the dials on the dashboard and the radio which was on but was turned down too low to hear. Ken had been quiet, uncharacteristically quiet; they had both been quiet.

'It was Claire who suggested her?' he asked suddenly.

'Yes.'

'She's been to her?'

'I think she goes quite often; she swears by her.'

'Did you tell Claire what she said?'

'No. I don't find her very easy to talk to.'

'You don't like her very much, do you?'

'I think she's a bit weird.'

'She's quite efficient.'

'How much do you know about Claire, Ken?'

'Not a lot. Lives in Ealing. Used to live in South Africa. Worked for a small commercials company there for eight years.'

'Do you know what she was doing for them?'

'Same as what she's doing now.'

'I don't think she knows very much about the business.'

'She had good references.'

'Did you check them?'

'No. She said the company had gone bust. It was at

the same time she split up with a boyfriend, which is why she decided to come back to England. You don't think the references are false, surely?'

'No, I'm sure they're fine. I think I'm just very . . . I guess freaked out by everything that's been happening.'

'You need to get away, Sam. Can't you and Richard go off somewhere for a few days?'

'He doesn't seem to like going away these days.'

'I'd like to go round there and give that cow a bloody thrashing. The Whole Mind and Body Centre,' he said contemptuously. 'Load of sodding con artists, that's all. Loonies. Dream groups, clairvoyants, shrinks—' He glanced in his mirror and moved across into the nearside lane. 'Perhaps we ought to try to find a witch doctor. Maybe they've got one in Leeds.'

She smiled.

'What are we going to do with you, Sam?'

'You needn't worry. I don't have any future.'

'Of course you have a sodding future.' He took his hand off the wheel and touched her arm lightly. 'I want you to have a future. It's crap, Sam. Look, none of us has any future. In the long run we'll all be dead – so what's she saying? You're going to be dead in a hundred years? Was she any more specific than that?'

'Why do you think she said what she did? I thought these people – if they saw something bad – weren't supposed to tell you.'

He shrugged. 'There are some very weird people in the world, Sam. Maybe she just didn't like you . . . was envious that you are young and pretty and thought she'd scare the hell out of you for fun.'

She saw another fork of lightning streak through the sky, then vanish. Like a light bulb going out.

Pop.

Ping.

Light bulbs.

Light bulbs went all the time, didn't they? If you had something sticky on them, like paint, then they could explode. Couldn't they?

The woman with the pulled-back face.

Mrs Wolf.

Weirdos. Ken was right. They conned Claire. But they hadn't conned her. Oh no. Great trick that, the light bulb trick. Works a treat, hey? Every one a winner.

Another sign drifted out of the darkness towards them.

LEEDS

Another sign followed it, black and white this time.

163 DEAD IN BULGARIA AIR DISASTER.

Then another swirled out of the darkness, bending, curling, like a sheet of newsprint.

RAPED AND MURDERED ON THE UNDER-GROUND.

It was coming straight at them, hit the windscreen and flattened out like the wing of a giant insect. Ken switched the wipers on and the blades smoothed it out like a poster on a billboard, so that she could see it clearly, read it clearly, see Tanya Jacobson's face staring through the glass at her, smiling, winking.

Are you resonating, Sam?

Sam shrieked.

'Sam? You OK?'

Ken's voice. She blinked hard and stared ahead. Nothing. No newspaper. Just the blackness and the tail lights and the wipers clearing the spots of rain, and a new light now, a tiny winking light on the dash. They were turning off.

'Fine,' she said. 'I'm sorry. I was dozing.'

The hotel was only a short distance from the motorway, and there was a battery of signs so no one could miss it.

TROPICANA GOLF & COUNTRY CLUB.
TROPICANA INDOOR POOL AND GRILL
   BAR – OPEN TO NON RESIDENTS.
PARADISE ISLAND CREOLE RESTAURANT.
PARADISE DISCO.

The palm tree emblem was emblazoned on the two entrance columns and bedecked in fairy lights shining out through the rain, which was falling harder now. It was emblazoned again, forty foot high, on the wall above the entrance porch. Country club, Sam thought. You'd never get permission to build a twenty-storey hotel in the middle of the countryside, but a country club: that was a different matter. Image. Packaging. Labels. You could do anything you wanted if you knew the right label to stick on it.

RESIDENTIAL GUESTS ENTRANCE.
GOLF CLUB.
PARKING.

They followed the arrows that were in the shape of palm fronds down an avenue lined with trees and bushes to the main entrance. As they pulled up outside the door, Sam stared around uneasily at the darkness, feeling a sudden frisson of fear.

'Looks a bit naff,' Ken said.

She gazed at the copper palm tree above the porch, then around again at the darkness.

'What's the matter?'

'Nothing.' She smiled. 'It's fine.'

The entrance lobby was festooned with tropical plants, bright lights, rattan furniture, and painted a lush tropical green. A girl in a matching tropical green dress, with a small gold palm tree engraved with the name 'Mandy' pinned to her chest, tilted a mouthful of gleaming white teeth at them.

'Good evening, Madam, good evening, Sir. Do you have a reservation?'

'Yes, we're in the Grand Spey Foods party.'

'Ah.' She looked down and rummaged through a sheaf of paper. 'Mr and Mrs—?'

'Mr Shepperd and Mrs Curtis.'

'There's a message for you from a Mr Edmunds. They have been delayed in London and won't be here until late. If they don't see you tonight, they'll meet you in the foyer at eight-fifteen in the morning.'

'Thanks,' said Ken. He turned to Sam. 'Let's dump our stuff in our rooms then have some dinner.'

A cocky teenage porter with bum-fluff on his upper lip, and 'Bill' pinned to his chest, showed Sam to her room first and Ken went with them. Sam was on the nineteenth floor. 'Get a lovely view of the motorway,' Bill snickered, unlocking the door.

It was a small fresh bedroom with bamboo furniture and bright green drapes and bedspread, a carpet with a rush matting pattern and on the wall was a print of a Gauguin painting she vaguely recognised of a black man and beautiful black woman sitting on the floor of an art gallery.

'Quarter of an hour?' said Ken.

'Fine.'

They went out and closed the door, and she pushed the brass buttons on her suitcase; the locks opened with sharp clicks.

Shit. Did she really bring all this stuff? For one night? She untied the straps and sifted through the layers of flattened clothing. Thick sweater. Had she really packed that? And another? Three different outfits? Nuts, nuts, nuts. It was hot and stuffy in the room. She went over to the window, pulled back the curtain and saw a balcony. She unlocked the door and stepped out onto it.

She felt the cool air, refreshing, could hear the rain falling through the darkness, and see the motorway stretching away into the distance like a never-ending neon sign. She looked down and saw the roof of the swimming pool directly beneath her, a huge octagonal-shaped glass dome over a pool set in a brightly lit indoor tropical garden. There was a thin haze of condensation on the glass making everything slightly fuzzy. She watched a fair-haired woman with a fine figure slowly stretch out on a deck chair under a sun lamp, and toss her hair back. To the side of the pool was a wooden bar with a coconut matting roof, where several people sat wearing nothing but swimming costumes. She wondered what the temperature was in there.

She leaned against the balcony rail trying to get a better view and it seemed to move a fraction under her weight. She stepped back nervously, stretched out her hand and tested it. It was fine, rigid. Standing at arm's length, she pushed harder against it. It was still fine. Had she imagined it? Come on, Sam, pull yourself together. Nervous of everything. Relax. She went back to the rail and put her full weight on it, defiantly. She even gave it a shove with her bum, just to see.

25

'Island In The Sun' came round for the third time on the Paradise Island Restaurant muzak. It was suffocatingly hot, as if the hotel was determined to spare no detail in maintaining the illusion of the Indian Ocean on this damp green strip of countryside sandwiched between the motorways.

The walls were uneven and painted white, with bits of fishermen's netting hanging from them. A model wooden schooner sat on a high shelf. Sam's mouth was feeling hot and blasted from a Creole fish curry, and she sipped some mineral water. Ken lit a cigarette. There were blotches of sweat on his denim shirt, around his chest and on his brow.

'You're looking a bit more cheerful,' he said, picking up his glass. 'Cheers.'

'Cheers,' she said. 'I must remember to keep on smiling. I keep forgetting.'

'Yeah, well – it's not a bad thing. It's very dangerous to be too cheerful.'

'Oh yes?'

'I think sometimes we ought to put people in hospital for feeling cheerful. We'd have a far safer world if everyone was miserable, depressed; cheerful people are dangerous – blinkered optimists all bloody bashing on regardless. Don't worry, old boy, it's all going to be fine, eh what?'

She grinned. 'You're probably right.'

'Want any pud?' he asked, looking around for a waiter.

'No, thanks.'

'In a year or two's time, they won't have to bother with menus in restaurants – they'll just be serving everyone Castaway bars. How would you like it served, Madam? In its wrapper? On a plate? Would you like us to cut it for you? To eat it for you?' He dabbed his forehead with his napkin. 'I'm sweltering. They ought to warn you to bring tropical clothes when you come here. Fancy a quick walk? Get some air?'

They went out of a side entrance. The lightning and the rain had stopped and there was a mild breeze which felt good. They walked down a path towards the golf course, and it got increasingly dark as the lights from the hotel windows faded behind them. Then the path stopped and they walked on the soft wet grass of the golf course itself, treading carefully, in now almost pitch darkness.

Ken took her hand and held it firmly, comfortably, protectively. Safe. She felt safe with him. He squeezed her hand, and she felt a good warm feeling inside.

Two silhouettes came out of the darkness towards them. Sam saw the glow of a cigarette, heard a whisper and a giggle, then they passed.

'Do you believe in the supernatural, Ken?'

He was silent for a long time. 'I'd never rule anything out, Sam,' he said finally. 'Half the scientists who've ever lived have ended up being proved wrong. Scientists, doctors, they can be arrogant buggers. Who knows? Who knows anything? When electricity was invented, scientists ran around screaming that it was impossible, that it did not exist, that it was all an illusion, the work of the devil – whilst businessmen went out and made lamps.'

She smiled.

'I don't know about seeing the future. The way you're seeing things . . . it's weird. I don't know if it's supernatural, or whether you're seeing through some time warp. Or is it just odd coincidences? Know what the Indonesians used to do?'

'No.'

'They used to read the future in the entrails of chickens. I saw it on TV. It looked disgusting.'

She giggled, suddenly feeling light-headed. 'Did it work?'

'It seemed to work for them. How would Richard feel if you started doing that?'

'He'd—' She shivered, suddenly feeling cold. 'Let's turn back.'

'Actually, my father – he didn't exactly have

premonitions, but he used to get . . . feelings about things. The Blacks, he used to call them. 'I've got the Blacks coming, boy. A big Black.'

'What did he do when he had them?'

'He got quite nervous. He was a superstitious man, and he used to be doubly careful. Sometimes something bad happened and sometimes it didn't.'

They walked around towards the front of the hotel, past the outside of the swimming pool, and Sam glanced up at the towering hulk of the building, up towards her room, then around again at the darkness. It felt almost as if someone else was out there in the darkness with them, someone who they could not see but who was listening to them, watching them.

'What did your father do for a living?'

'Spent his life out on strike, mostly. Silly bugger. Print worker on a newspaper in Nottingham. Red Harry, they called him. He was going to lead the revolution. He was going to be the Russians' number one in England. "Won't be long now, boy!" he used to shout at me across the breakfast table. "They'll be 'ere any day now, boy!"'

'What happened to him?' Sam asked.

'Eventually got kicked out of his job. The lads supported him for a few weeks, then they drifted back to work. He got very bitter about it. He got bitter that the Russians never came, as well. He died bitter as hell. I remember my aunt coming up to me at the funeral. "'Ee was a luvly man, your Dah. A luvly man. 'Ee never did anyone any 'aarrm."' He squeezed her hand again. 'What a bloody epitaph, eh? She hadn't the guts to say he was a stupid fart who pissed his life away.'

'Is that how you remember him?'

'No. I'd left home before he got the boot. When I knew him, he still had his fire and his enthusiasm. Used

226

to read me bedtime stories about the Russian Revolution. He couldn't understand it when I went into advertising. Wouldn't speak to me for years.'

'Sad.'

'Still, I don't expect my epitaph'll be much better.'

'Why not?'

'I used to be a bit like my dad. I thought I could change the world. I wasn't an agitator, but I thought I could change it through being creative, through movies. Instead, all I do is feed the system. Feed it with ads for chocolate bars and Japanese cars and wholemeal bread. That's what's going to be on my epitaph. "Here lies Ken Shepperd. He made more wholemeal bread commercials than anyone else. Tough and gritty with nowt taken out. The man who gave the world *wholemeal dreams*."'

She laughed, and they reached the hotel door.

'Let's have a drink,' Ken said and they went through to the Paradise Bar and Disco and sat in a dark corner table. A group of salesmen were at a nearby table. One was telling a joke and the others were tittering, and a woman, too old for her long blonde hair and the mini skirt she was wearing, sat on her own at the bar. Ken glanced at her, caught Sam's eye and winked. 'Shall we buy Jake a present? Have her waiting in his room?' He signalled the waiter over and ordered a bottle of Krug. 'Courtesy of Grand Spey,' he said. 'Want to dance?'

She looked at him, surprised. 'Sure.'

He took both her wrists and led her onto the dance floor, pulling her gently towards him. She felt a tingle of excitement in her throat, and it ran down her neck into her stomach.

'When A Man Loves A Woman' was playing, and he stared at her, quizzically, and moved a fraction closer.

No, Sam.

Big danger.

Her arms were throbbing, and she felt a trickle of perspiration run down the back of her neck. He tilted his head forward and their lips touched gently dusting each other. She jerked back as if she had had an electric shock, then gave him a brief peck and put her cheek firmly against his. She felt the roughness of his stubble, smelled his cologne and his hair shampoo and the clean earthy smell of his sweat through his denim shirt.

They danced, their cheeks together, and she glanced around warily for a moment in case Charlie Edmunds or either of the others or anyone else she knew might be in the room, but there was no one other than the group of salesmen roaring at another joke and the hooker at the bar smoking a cigarette.

She felt Ken's hands stroking her back, firmly, suggestively, and she remembered suddenly another time that she thought she had forgotten for ever. The cold, sharp night. The rich smell of leather from the car's seats. The light sensuous touch of the boy's hand just above her stocking on her goosepimpled thigh, and the car's radio playing hot steamy midnight passion music, 'Je T'Aime, Je T'Aime'. The windows were steamed up, and she remembered thinking that there might be a Peeping Tom lurking out there in the dark. She remembered vividly the sound of tearing paper, the oily rubbery smell of the Durex, the rustling of clothes and the awkward grunts. Then lying back, moments later, with a deadweight on top of her, saying to her 'How was it? Was it good? God it was great!' It was? She wasn't even sure whether anything had happened, whether he had come, or whether he'd had whatever it was called – premature something or other?

Sandy. She could remember his name, but his face was gone. Fair hair, that was all. The rest was a blur.

The music stopped and she pulled her face away. Their eyes met. 'I find you very attractive, Ken. Don't tempt me.'

'Me? I'm just dancing,' he said, but his eyes stayed locked on hers. 'I'd like to sleep with you.'

She shook her head. 'We've got a great relationship, Ken. Let's not—' She shrugged. 'I have to be strong right now, I have to be strong and keep my head clear – somehow.' She hugged him tight, 'I'm sure that making love with you would be the most wonderful thing in the world, but I can't, OK?' She nipped the tip of his ear gently with her teeth, then pulled away. 'Let's sit down and have a drink.'

The champagne was on the table, and he poured some out. They clinked glasses and drank, and Ken lit another cigarette.

'I thought that things between you and Richard—' he began.

'They're not that great,' she said. 'I don't know what's the matter with him. He's changed so much in the past few months.'

'How do you mean?'

'He's a different person. I don't know whether it's—' She stared down into the bubbles. 'There's a rather weird man he's become terribly pally with. I don't know if this chap's got some hold over him . . . like a Svengali.'

Ken frowned sceptically.

'I mean it, Ken. He's always on the phone to him. He used to back his own judgement – always seemed to do all right – then this guy, Andreas Berensen, gave him some advice or tips last year which came good and Richard made a lot of dough, and now he virtually won't go to the loo without asking his permission.'

'Who is this Andreas Berensen?'

'He's a director of one of those Swiss banks.' She shrugged and drank some more. 'Maybe I'm just being neurotic about him. Maybe it's not him at all – maybe it's me. Maybe Richard just doesn't find me attractive any more. He's drinking a hell of a lot. I sometimes wonder if he's having a nervous breakdown.' She smiled sadly. 'I – I feel it's important that I've just got to be around. I've got to be strong.'

'Richard's a lucky guy.'

'Having a loony for a wife?'

'You're not a loony, Sam. You're a great, terrific, wonderful girl. OK?'

'Yes, boss.'

Ken grinned and Sam glanced around the room again.

'You look nervous about something, Sam.'

'No. Just seeing if the others—'

'Seeing if teacher's arrived to send us all to bed? Nothing really changes in life, does it?'

'Don't you think so?'

'No.'

'Don't you think we—' She tilted her head back to look at him from further away – 'we get harder?'

' "She thought love was nothing more than the contact between two skins – but she still cried when I left." '

'Françoise Sagan?'

'You read her too?'

'I used to be into glib philosophy.'

'And what are you into now? Reality?'

'No,' she said. 'I'm beginning to think I've had enough reality. I've had reality all my life. I think I deserve a bit of fantasy.'

Ken grinned again. 'I'm sorry. I should have worn my Superman costume.'

She touched his shoulder lightly. 'How did the ad go? "You only had to look at the label"?'

He stared back hard at her. 'What the hell are we going to do with you? There must be some experts in premonitions – there's experts in bloody everything – there must be people who aren't cranks and aren't sceptics. Some organisation, maybe, or at some university. Your shrink friend you went to sounds like a conceited berk. Have you rung him and told him about Hampstead?'

'No. I still don't think he'd believe me.'

'What did you tell the fuzz? Didn't they come round and interview you?'

'They just wanted a statement – what time I was down there, who I saw. They told me I was sensible not going on down those stairs.'

'Did you tell them about your dream?'

'I didn't think that—'

'I can imagine him reading it out in court.' He put on a thick North London accent. 'The – er – witness, yer honour, saw it all in a dream, you see. She reckons it were done by this geyser wot wears a black 'ood and died twenty-five years ago.'

She laughed, uneasily. 'Did your father do anything about his premonitions? Did he ever see anyone about them?'

'No, never. He just accepted it. His family came from a mining background – they're a superstitious lot, miners – they just accept things, without questioning them too much.' He stood up and took her wrist. 'Let's have one more dance.'

He held her tightly on the dance floor. 'Sure you don't want to change your mind?'

'I'm an old woman, Ken. An old woman who's losing her marbles. I thought you only went for young glammy models?'

He kissed her cheek tenderly. 'Really old, aren't you,

Sam? Can hear your joints creaking and your bones rattling.'

She punched his stomach playfully with her fist.

'It's me,' he said. 'I'm the one that's getting old. Past forty and it's all downhill.'

'Does it worry you, age?'

'I keep noticing things. Tiny physiological changes. My skin getting saggy; hairs sprouting in odd places. My memory going. I talk to people sometimes and forget who it is I'm talking to. They'll probably find me one day asleep under a railway arch, wrapped up in newspapers. "Silly old bugger, don't remember who he is, keeps prattlin' on about wholemeal bread and chocolate bars. Yeah? Well maybe he's hungry. Don't look as if he's eaten in days."'

She giggled. 'Come on, it's bedtime.'

'Alone?'

'Alone,' she said firmly.

26

A single sharp rasping sound woke her.

Doorbell.

She opened her eyes and it rang again.

Doorbell.

The room was filled with strange yellowy light. Like sepia.

It rang again.

Coming, I'm coming. Christ, Richard why don't you answer?

She put out her hand and felt him lying there, on the wrong side. What on earth?

Oh Christ.

The door bell rang again, but it wasn't the doorbell, it

was the rasping snore of the man asleep on the wrong side of the bed.

Ken.

Oh Christ. No, surely not? Surely she hadn't?

He was still there. It would have been easier if he'd slunk away in the darkness and they could have met at the breakfast table and pretended it hadn't happened.

Maybe.

He was still there and he was snoring and it was early morning. Daylight. Her mouth tasted foul. Her stomach churned over, rumbled, tensed up. She lay still not daring to make any more movement, not wanting to wake him, not until she had had time to think. It was all there in the morning light, everything that you could hide from and curl up from in the darkness. Darkness. Darkness was a place where you could pretend that nothing was real. She wondered how she was going to face Ken, and she felt a feeling of sadness and stupidity as if everything she had worked so hard for, the past three years, she had thrown away in one night. She stared numbly at the ceiling, wishing she could push the clock back a few hours, to last night.

What was it going to be like? What were they going to say to each other? Was he going to tell her this morning that it would be silly for her to go on working for him? Or would he let it ride, let it come to its own conclusions? Long stony silences in the office. Biting remarks. Casting sessions when she would study his reaction to each model, the pangs of jealousy eating her insides. And finally clearing out her desk. Was that what the future held in store?

Just his head was visible under the rumpled sheet, his hair tousled, the brown stubble on his jaw, mouth slightly open and the rasping snore. She wondered if he was dreaming now; what did other people dream? She listened to the heater clattering, ticking and blowing, and stared at the Gauguin print on the wall, at the woman with the one bared breast, firm, pointed, and she looked down at her own breasts and they seemed small and sagging in comparison.

Must brush my teeth before he wakes. She slipped quietly out of the bed and felt a flutter of anxiety as he stirred, but he settled down again and continued snoring. She walked silently across the carpet, opened the balcony doors and slipped through the curtains into the first weak rays of the dawn sun. The sky was a mixture of greys and yellows, and the air smelled fresh, moist, strangely warm, you could almost believe you were in the Indian Ocean, she thought. Even the motorway seemed further away, empty, silent, like a canal. A low mist hung over the ground, and through it she could see some of the contours of the golf course, the grass shimmering with water.

The sun seemed to be getting brighter as she stood there, and she felt the thin warmth of its rays now on her naked body. It gave her a curious sense of freedom, and she was surprised that she was not feeling self-conscious about being naked.

I have a lover.

The feelings inside her were weird. She felt light, almost lighter than air for a moment, then slow and ponderous, heavy as lead. Something had changed inside her; something that had happened in the night had changed for ever in a way she knew she was going to understand, but did not yet.

She stared down at her breasts, and at her dark pubic hairs, the ends tinged a gingery gold by the sunlight. Her whole body became bathed in a gingery blonde glow, as if she was standing under a huge lamp.

She leaned against the wet balcony rail, and looked

down. The lights inside the glass dome were on; a workman, who looked tiny from here, was vacuuming the pool which also looked tiny, like a tear drop. A waiter ambled towards the poolside bar carrying a crate of beer bottles which clinked together noisily, and she was surprised how clearly she could hear them through the glass and nineteen storeys up.

The fair-haired woman whom she recognised from yesterday strode into the pool area, holding a towel and a book. She stretched the towel out on one of the recliners under a sun lamp, and settled herself down into it. Sam leaned further forward, to see what was directly beneath, and the balcony seemed to wobble.

Loose, it was loose.

No it's not, it's your imagination. Go on, try it again.

She stepped back nervously.

Scaredy cat! Scaredy cat! Scaredy cat!

The rail is loose.

Scaredy cat!

They slap these junk hotels up. What do they care about safety? The rail is loose.

Scaredy cat!

She went slowly, cautiously, back over to it, and peered over the edge. Christ. The drop down.

Vertigo.

She took a pace back, her head spinning.

Scaredy cat!

I am not afraid. Damn it, I am not afraid. I'm not some crank who's scared of balcony rails. She marched forward, gripped the rail firmly with both hands and looked downwards.

There was a sharp, rending crack and the entire balcony tilted forwards, throwing her against the rail.

No. Oh Christ, no.

The rail was holding the entire weight of her body.

'Ken! Help! Help!'

There was another crack and it tilted some more.

She turned her head. The balcony door was above her now, several feet above her.

'Ken!'

She was whimpering.

Oh God help me. 'Ken! Ken!'

There was another crack and she lurched further forwards, almost overbalancing. Don't look down. Don't look down. Don't move. Gently. Gently. She tried to turn, to climb back up on the sheer slippery floor, but the angle was too steep and each time she moved she felt the balcony lurch further downwards.

Help me, someone.

The woman below was stretched out under the sun lamp, directly beneath her.

I'm going to fall on you. Get out of the way!

The waiter carried another crate of beer towards the bar.

Look up. Please look up.

'Help!'

A tight rasping whisper.

'Ken! Help me.'

She was swaying now. The rail was making splintering cracking sounds. She could feel it giving beneath her. She tried to push away, but it just sagged further.

She looked desperately back up at the door. 'Ken!' she called. 'Ken!'

Then she saw him coming, and her heart leapt. OK, it was going to be OK, he'd know what to do. The balcony lurched again and she screamed.

'I can't hang on.'

He came through the door, Ken, stark naked, except he had a hood over his face, a black hood with knife slits.

'Ken? Are you mad? No games, Ken. No – no – no—.'

There was a deafening rending, tearing sound.

Ken stood there, watching her.

Smiling. His lips smiling through the slit.

There was one more lurch, a ferocious snap, then she was falling, plummeting, hurtling down.

She felt her stomach crash up inside her throat. Clutching the rail still. The glass dome got bigger, bigger, the air screamed at her. The woman, she thought. The woman. I'm going to kill the woman.

'No. No!'

She heard a buzzing sound, sharp, insistent.

Darkness. Darkness all around. Filled with the buzzing.

She was cold, drenched with – water from the pool?

The buzzing again.

A strange clattering sound above her. Heating duct?

The darkness. The void.

The buzzing sound.

Telephone?

She put out her hand. Nothing.

It buzzed again.

She tried the other side, felt something hard, heard a sharp clatter, felt the unfamiliar receiver in her hand.

'Your early morning call, Madam.'

'Wasser? Thank – thank you – I—' But the operator had hung up.

Christ.

The terror began to subside and her head swirled in confusion. She groped with her hand for the light switch, found it, pressed it and the light beside her bed lit up, dazzling her for a moment. She spun round and looked at the right-handed side of the bed, then sighed with relief: it was undisturbed; the pillows were fresh, undented. She closed her eyes, gulping in air,

237

feeling the cold, plunge pool cold, of the sweat on her body.

Thank God. She was conscious she was mouthing the words. She slipped out of bed, went over to the window and opened the curtains. It was still dark outside, dark and raining. She walked across the room and into the bathroom, turned on the tap and stared at her frightened face in the mirror.

It was another one, she knew. The same feeling, the same vividness.

The same as the other dreams that had come true.

27

She stared out of the Bentley's window, through the weak reflection of her own face at the blackness beyond. The void. Nothingness.

Hell was the void where you could scream for ever and no one could hear you. A void where it was always cold and where you never grew any older and never died and never escaped. For ever.

Charlie Edmunds and Jake and Zurbrick from Urquhart Simeon Mcpherson had all been having breakfast when she'd gone down in the morning, and she had not been able to tell Ken about the balcony dream until now that they were on their way back to London. She left out that he'd been in bed with her.

The day had gone well. Grand Spey Foods had liked the Castaway commercials, and had liked Ken. They would recce in April and shoot in May, three commercials, back to back; the budget had been approved at over six hundred thousand pounds.

She told Ken how she had gone out on the balcony when she'd first arrived and thought it was loose then, but had checked it and it seemed all right, and he'd told her she shouldn't be spooked by the dream, that maybe there had been a tiny bit of looseness and it was her survival instincts warning her. Maybe the same instincts that had warned her about the gun being left around and the rapist in Hampstead.

'It could be that you've got sharp antennae, like rabbits' ears. Like Bugs Bunny.'

'Richard calls me Bugs.'

'Maybe that's why.'

'He says that sometimes when I'm thinking I stick my front teeth out, like a rabbit.'

'I hadn't noticed.'

'Maybe you never see me thinking!'

'I suppose "Bugs" is better than "Jaws".'

'Thanks a lot!'

Ken drove for some minutes in silence, then lit a cigarette. 'I don't know about the air disaster – maybe that's coincidence – but the other two . . . maybe someone up there likes you.'

'My fairy godmother?'

He smiled. 'I favour the sharp antennae.'

'You're beginning to sound like Bamford.'

'Bamford?'

'Our shrink friend.'

Ken said nothing. He inhaled on his cigarette and tapped the rim of the steering wheel.

'Do you ever think about death?' she asked.

'Sometimes.'

'Are you afraid of it?'

'I'm much more afraid of life.'

'What do you mean?'

He tilted his head back. 'Afraid of going to my grave, I suppose, without having put anything back.' He wound his window down a fraction and flicked some ash out. 'I feel that when we live, we're constantly taking things – burning up petrol, polluting the atmosphere, decimating forests, you know. Always taking. I think we all need to put something back into the world in return. That we ought to try and leave it a better place than when we arrived. I don't feel I've done that yet.'

'You're funny.' She smiled, and felt his hand on hers, squeezing gently. 'Nice funny. You think a lot, don't you?'

'Maybe I think too much. What are you doing over the weekend?'

'Going to the country. Richard's shooting tomorrow and we're going to a dinner party tomorrow night. Then on Sunday – nothing, I hope. What about you?'

'I'm off to Spain in the morning. The Jerez shoot.'

'Yes, of course. How long are you away for?'

'Back Wednesday, if we stick to schedule.'

'What are Spanish crews like?'

'They're OK. You've got quite a few quotes to do.'

'It's going to be a busy year.' She laid her head against the soft leather, closed her eyes and listened to the faint swooshing of the tyres and the sounds of the traffic on the motorway all around them. Her toes were warm, roasting warm from the heater, and she felt very tired now; she dozed.

She woke up with a start as the Bentley bumped along Wapping High Street.

'You've had a good kip,' Ken said.

'I'm sorry, I wasn't much company.' Then she saw the two police cars parked in the street outside the warehouse; she glanced at Ken and their eyes met and she saw him frown, but he said nothing. She looked at the cars again, one with the City of London Police crest emblazoned on the door, the other unmarked, apart from two discreet aerials.

Ken helped her in with her suitcase and stood watching as the elevator door closed, and nodded, without saying, that he would wait a few minutes, in case.

Christ.

She knew.

She was absolutely certain as she stood in the gloomy light of the lift, listening to it shuffle and clank slowly upwards. It stopped with its usual sharp jerk, and her suitcase fell over with a bang. She lugged it down the corridor, then stood outside the door to the flat, rummaging through her handbag for her keys. There was a stillness about the whole building, a quiet uneasy calm as if neighbours all around were waiting silently, watching through their spyholes.

When she opened the door, Nicky came hurtling down the hall like a missile. 'Mummy!'

Not his normal gleeful greeting, but an angry, confused cry for help.

'Tiger! What is it Tiger?'

He was close to tears. 'They cut open Teddy.'

She felt a strange feeling of unreality, as if she wasn't really here, but was imagining it. Dreaming it. 'Teddy? Cut open? Who cut—?' Then she saw a policeman come out of Nicky's room.

Helen followed in his wake, walking slowly.

'What's happened, Helen?' Sam asked. 'Have we been burgled?'

Helen shook her head slowly. She was in shock.

Sam felt a sharp twist of fear in her stomach. Was this real? Was she really here? The door frame seemed to slide towards her, and struck her hard on the arm. She stumbled into the hallway, putting her hand out to steady herself, and held onto the edge of the coat stand. 'Helen? What is it?'

'They pulled all his tummy out,' Nicky started crying, and his face swirled in front of her.

'Burgled? Have we been burgled? Where's my husband?'

The policeman walked down the corridor towards her and stared at her, embarrassed. He was young, about twenty, she thought, tall and gangly. 'Mrs Curtis?'

'Yes.'

'I think – er – the Inspector . . . perhaps you'd better have a word with him. Or your husband.' He pointed down towards the living area, then backed away and walked towards her bedroom.

'Why are you going in there?'

'The Inspector,' he said. 'He'll explain.'

'I don't want you going in there.' She rested her hands on Nicky's shoulders.

The policeman went bright red. 'I'm afraid we have a warrant, Mrs Curtis.'

'A what?'

'A search warrant.'

'What are you—'

Christ.

Was this another dream? Another nightmare? Was Slider going to come down the corridor?

A search warrant.

'What are you looking for?' she asked.

'I think it would be best if you spoke to the Inspector, Madam.'

'I want to see it.'

'The Inspector—'

'You're not going in there until I've seen it.' She turned to Helen. 'Don't let him in there.' She knelt down and kissed Nicky. 'One second, darling. Wait here, and don't let that man go in my bedroom.'

'He cut open my teddy, he did,' Nicky sobbed.

242

'I'll cut him open,' Sam said, glaring at the policeman and sounding as if she meant it. She stormed down the corridor, then stopped as she saw another policeman on his knees in the kitchen, peering underneath the dishwasher with a torch. Pots, pans, plates, dishes had all been pulled out of the cupboards and stacked on the work surfaces, and something snapped inside her.

'Get out!' she screamed. 'Get out of my kitchen!' She grabbed a drawer, any drawer, and yanked it out; it was full of knives and spatulas and whisks and wooden spoons and she hurled it at him. It flew across the room, showering its contents out, hit the wall above him and fell down onto his head with a hard crack, hurting him. From the way he groaned, hurting him a lot.

'Sam.'

Richard grabbed her arm. 'You've got to let them.' He turned to the constable on the floor who was rubbing his head and staring at his finger. 'Are you OK?'

The constable screwed up his eyes. 'Could you get her out of here, please?'

Richard led her through the living area.

There were two men in the room. One was standing by the refectory table, in a brown suit with bell-bottom trousers and a sixties Beatle-cut hairstyle, tying up bundles of documents with red ribbon. The other was kneeling down in front of Richard's desk, pulling more documents out of a drawer, mustard socks and white hairless legs sticking out of his grey suit trousers. He glanced over his shoulder and then stood up, a burly man who might have been a bit of a boxer ten years before, with a greedy face and eyes that bulged out slightly, giving him the expression of a well-fed frog. His suit was too small, and crumpled, and his shirt collar was loosened, his tie halfway down his chest. He gazed at Sam in a faintly patronising way, as if he did not have to bother with her, as if she too was a child whose teddy bear he could order to be ripped open. 'This the missus?'

Richard nodded, eyeing Sam like a cornered animal. Then he stiffened, tried to smile a reassuring everything's-fine smile but it flashed across his face like a nervous twitch. 'Bugs, this is Inspector – er?'

'Milton. Like the poet. Detective Inspector Milton.'

'Good evening,' she said.'

'Company Fraud Department, City of London Police.' He jerked a thumb at the man in the brown suit. 'Detective Sergeant Wheeler.' Wheeler carried on binding the documents without looking round.

Fraud Department.

Sam stared, baffled for a moment.

Images flashed at her. Richard's behaviour. His strange late hours bent over his computer screen. The money for the new house. The Rolex. The booze.

Something trickled through her, cold, unpleasant.

Detective Inspector Milton looked at her contemptuously. I could eat you for breakfast and fart you out into the pond, lady, so don't mess with me.

'Nice flat, Mrs Curtis,' he said, in a snide, nasal voice. 'I was brought up round here. My parents used to live around the corner. Couldn't afford the rents now, of course, could they? Still, I suppose that's progress.'

'I want to see your ID and your warrant.'

He fished his wallet out of his pocket and opened it one-handedly in a well-worn movement, holding it up so the lady could see it clearly, read it clearly, let the lady have all the time she needs, just like the rule book says.

By the book, lady, know what I mean? Doing all this by the book. Know your types. Smart bastards. Well

244

we're smarter these days, Feet may still be big, but now our brains are big too. It's our hearts that have got smaller.

The photo showed a younger, thinner version of his face, with a startled expression and his eyes bulging even more. Then he snapped the wallet shut, put it back into his inside pocket and with the same hand, pulled out a sheet of paper which he handed to her. There was a crest on the top, several rows of formal type, their address and a signature at the bottom. R. Fenner. Magistrate. He folded it up and put it back in his pocket.

'Perhaps you could tell me why you're here?'

He scratched his nose with his finger. 'I expect your husband'll tell you later, if you ask him nicely.' He fingered the top of Richard's desk. 'Beautiful furniture. Cost a few bob that desk, eh? You people make me sick, Mrs Curtis. Yuppies. You ought to be on the stage, you should. You'd be good playing the indignant wife, you know that? Bet you like spending your husband's money for him, but your hands wouldn't be dirty, would they? Bet your nose is clean as a whistle. Bet if I looked up your nostrils there wouldn't be a bogey in sight. Be like looking up the barrels of a brand new Purdey.'

'Have you rung Bob Storer?' Sam asked Richard.

'He's on his way over.' He shook a cigarette out. 'Nothing we can do, Bugs. Just got to let them get on with it.'

She glared back at the Inspector. 'I don't care what bits of paper you've got with you. You don't ever speak to me like that again.' She turned to Richard. 'Can we have a word in private?' She walked out of the room.

Helen was standing in the hallway. 'It's Nicky's bath-time. Do you think it'll be all right if I bath him?'

'You'd better let them check down the plughole first.'

Helen nodded, uncertain whether Sam was being funny or serious.

Sam went outside into the passageway, waited until Richard had joined her, then closed the front door. 'What's going on, Richard? What on earth is this all about?'

There was a clang behind her and she spun round. Ken was standing in the elevator door. 'OK, Sam? Is everything—'

'It's fine. Thanks. Fine. I – I'll see you – er—'

'Thursday.'

She smiled thinly, watched the door slide shut and heard the clunk and whine of the elevator descending, then looked back at Richard. 'What is it, Richard?'

'It's nothing,' he said. 'Really.'

'Nothing? The Fraud Squad crawling all over our flat? You can tell me, for Christ's sake.'

'It's OK, Bugs.' He tapped some ash onto the floor. 'They're just sniffing around, that's all.'

'Sniffing around?' She stared at him. 'What have you done?'

'Nothing.'

'The police don't rip open teddy bears unless they think there's something inside them.'

He shrugged. 'Bit of aggro from the Surveillance Department of the Securities Association. The aftermath of Guinness, I suppose. All that insider dealing stuff. They're still trawling their nets.' He looked away evasively.

'Are you mixed up in all that?'

'No. Of course not.' He took a deep drag on his cigarette. 'Everyone's jittery about insider dealing. I've put a few clients into a deal which happened to hit the big time and the Securities boys can't believe it was luck.'

'There's more, isn't there, Richard?' she said. 'There's more to it than that.'

'No. Not really.'

'Are you going to be arrested?'

'No.' His face went bright red. His cigarette was almost down to the filter. He held it between his fingertips like a workman, dragged hard again and inhaled deeply. 'Not yet, anyway.'

28

Sunday morning. She lay in bed watching Richard dress, with Nicky, warm, curled up beside her. Nicky who kept waking the last two nights and running into their room, terrified the nasty man with his big knife was going to come back. He'd slept between them, and she'd lain awake mostly, listening to his breathing and his occasional funny little whimpers, and it made her feel safe having him there.

Bastards.

Inspector Milton. Milton, like the poet. Come to take your paradise away, lady. Oh yes, I'm one smart bastard, you see. One smart bastard with a great big chip.

Wisest men
Have erred, and by bad women been deceived;
And shall again, pretend they ne'er so wise.

She glanced at the clock. 7.45.

Did you ever read him, your namesake, you great frog-eyed bastard? You smug creep who left a little boy terrified. Happy? Happy that my son's met a real live bogeyman? Who ripped his teddy bear open with a knife? Brave. Oh so brave.

247

Smug. Jesus, so smug. Walking out with your cardboard boxes filled with papers, all neatly tied in red ribbon by your gawky friend in his time-warp suit.

Nicky was awake now; blinking, his eyelids making little scratching sounds against the bedclothes.

'Bye, Bugs.'

She looked at Richard and felt his anguish. She lifted up her hand and touched his face. 'Drive safely. When will you be back?'

''Bout midday,' he said in a voice so heavy he could scarcely lift it out of his mouth. 'Bye, Tiger.' He ran a hand across Nicky's head.

'Are you going shooting, Daddy?'

'No, Tiger.'

'You said I could come with you today. You said we could go shooting today.'

'We will do. This afternoon, OK?'

'Where are you going now?'

'I have to do some business.'

'Can't I come with you? Where are you going?'

London Airport. To meet Andreas. To sign some documents.

She heard the bedroom door open and close, then the front door, the scrunch of gravel, the roar of the BMW's engine. She looked up at the ceiling, freshly plastered and painted; the builders had got that done fast enough, at least in the bedroom. They'd found rot in all the ceilings and there were ladders, planks, gaping holes, and more scaffolding up outside because they'd had to agree that the roof couldn't be bodged any more. There'd have to be a new roof and Richard had said the money was fine, all fine. Until Milton (like the poet) had turned up on Friday.

Nicky was sleeping again and she dozed. A while later

Nicky stirred then got out of bed, but she scarcely noticed because now she was slipping into deep, tired sleep and stayed asleep until nearly ten.

When she opened her eyes and saw full daylight through a chink in the curtains she stared at it blankly, flatly, feeling limp like an old busted tyre that had run flat too long and had finally come off the rim. No energy. Wiped.

She went down to the kitchen and made some coffee. Helen came in.

'Morning, Mrs Curtis.'

Sam smiled. 'Sleep well?'

'Yes. So quiet here. It's like home.'

'Where's Nicky?'

'He went outside a while ago.'

She went over to the fridge and poured out some orange juice. She sipped it and it hit her stomach harshly, acidicly, made it twinge.

'Mummy!'

The scream sounded like the wail of a siren.

'*Mum-mee!*'

They flung themselves out of the kitchen through the side door.

'MUM-MEE!'

They stared around, up, down, across the fields, down towards the river.

The river?

Sam started sprinting down towards it.

'MUM-MEE. MUM-MEE. MUM-MEE!'

She stopped dead and spun round. Above her. Up. On top of the scaffold.

A dreadful creaking sound.

Tearing, rending.

Oh my God Jesus, no. Christ, no. No. No.

Arms around the new scaffold as if he was hugging it

because he loved it and not because he knew that if he let go he would be dead.

It had come loose from the wall of the house and was swaying like a broken crane, tilting, shrieking and creaking, one way then the other, it bashed against the wall, nearly throwing him free, then swung away again, so far this time she was certain it would topple over, but instead it swung back and smashed against the wall again, harder this time, chipping chunks of brickwork away, clanging, the sound echoing down through the pipes.

Sam sprinted over to the base, tried to hold it with her hands, Helen stood beside her and tried too but they had no chance of holding it. It tilted even more over, and some of the base lifted up from the ground right beside her, then it righted again for a moment, smashing and clanging back against the wall.

Sam ran around the side, to the old scaffold that was still attached, and began to climb.

Her hand numbing on the ice cold rusted metal, she hauled herself up, ignoring the ladder up the inside of it, felt the wind blowing as she climbed and the structure vibrating.

'*MummyMummyMummy!*

I'm coming. Coming. Coming.

She felt a muscle pull in her thigh, and her hand cut on something sharp. A slipper fell away from her foot. She heard the creaking, clanging, behind her, turned, saw Nicky now only feet away, then his face was in front of hers, so close she could touch it, then he swung away out of reach. Oh Christ, no, please no . . . so far surely it was going to topple this time, then he swung back towards her.

'Darling, give me your hand . . . here, take it, mine, that's right, that's right!'

She clenched her hand over his, clenched it so hard she was never going to let go again. He started pulling away from her, and she pulled harder, could feel his arm stretching. 'Hold on, Tiger, just hold on!'

Stretching more. The pain was unbearable. He was coming loose – careful – be careful – pulling him off it.

Then she felt herself moving.

No.

There was a sharp crack.

No.

A splintering sound.

The scaffolding was bouncing, like a spring.

Let go, let go, let go.

Falling.

She let go his hand in terror, in disbelief.

The wall was moving away. Nicky moving away, staring at her, his face frozen. Sideways, going over sideways.

No.

It was her that was going over.

The ground was rushing towards her.

Falling.

She spun, desperately trying to push back, but it was too late, far too late.

She felt the inside of her head rotating, then the ground hurtled at her, slammed into her, smashed her stomach up into her spine. She felt a tremendous windedness, heard a click from her jaw, smelt wet grass, mud. There was a strange muffled clanging sound all around her. Like church bells.

'Bugs?'

The ground was soft.

It moved underneath her as if it was sprung.

Bedclothes.

A dream. It had been a – Richard staring at her, the light was odd, different.

'How are you feeling, Bugs?'

She frowned. Her head ached like hell. She moved and her arm ached too. Her tongue was stinging; she could taste blood in her mouth.

'Nicky,' she said. 'Where's Nicky?'

'Nicky's fine. He's just a bit bruised.'

Nicky peered down at her, wide open eyes, serious. God he looked so serious sometimes. She put an arm up to stroke him. The movement hurt, and she winced.

'How are you feeling, Mrs Curtis?'

A stranger's voice, a man, pleasant, standing over the bed in a white smock with a stethoscope curling out of the pocket, looking intently at her.

'I—' The room seemed to spin around.

'You've got concussion.' He glanced at his watch. 'You've been unconscious for over three hours.'

Three hours? No, he'd got it wrong. There must have – it had just . . . 'Where am I?'

'You're in the Sussex County Hospital, in Brighton.'

'Hospital?'

'Yes, I'm afraid you had a very nasty fall. We've X-rayed you and given you a scan. You're fine. No bones broken, but I think you're going to feel a bit jarred and sore.' He smiled, a pleasant reassuring good-bedside-manners smile. He was young. Younger than her. 'You've been very lucky, I think, the height you fell from. Fortunate we've had so much rain, it must have made the ground very soft.' He smiled again. 'I'll come back and see you in a little while.'

'Thank you,' she mouthed, but nothing came out. She felt disoriented. Sunlight was shining into the room, weak winter sunlight and she could see the sky. She had no idea of the time; it felt like afternoon.

The door closed, then there was a clanking sound. She felt the bed sinking.

'Tiger, don't do that,' Richard said. 'You're winding Mummy down.'

She heard footsteps, then Nicky's voice, excited. 'I can see the sea!'

She stared at the white ceiling and the light bulb above her head. She pushed her tongue around inside her mouth. It was sore along the top; she tasted the blood again.

Scaffold.

I was on scaffold.

She looked back at Richard, watched him with damp frightened eyes. He sat down beside her and held her hand.

'I'll sue those fucking builders.'

She shook her head, slowly, carefully. 'It wasn't – not their fault—'

'It was coming away from the wall. Could have crashed down on anyone. Could have killed anyone underneath it.'

'Nicky shouldn't have—'

'Scaffolding's meant for climbing up. That's what it's for.' He sniffed. 'How are you feeling?'

'My head hurts.'

'They thought you'd fractured your skull.'

'How did your meeting—?'

'Fine. All going to be fine.'

She squeezed his hand.

''S a good hospital,' he said. 'They want to keep you in overnight. The doctor said you can leave in the morning.'

'It's Sunday, isn't it?'

'Yes.'

'I've got a meeting in the morning.'

'I'll call Ken. The doctor doesn't want you to go back to work for a day or so.'

'Ken's away. Could you call Claire? Tell her – or Lucy.'

'Sure.'

'What's out here, Daddy?'

'The corridor, Tiger. That's where we came in.'

Nicky leaned over the bed. 'I'm sorry, Mummy.'

She smiled at him. His eyes were red from crying.

'Give Mummy a kiss.'

He leaned over and gave her a nervous peck as if he shouldn't give her a long one in case it hurt. 'I only went up to see if there was a nest.'

'Did you find one?'

'No. Are you coming home now?'

'Tomorrow.'

'Oh. Can we stay with you?'

'You stay with Daddy tonight.'

He slid away from the bed. 'I'm going exploring.'

'Don't go out there, Tiger,' Richard said.

'I won't go very far.'

She heard the door open and shut, and felt Richard stroking her hand. He bent towards her a fraction and spoke quietly, as if he did not want to be overheard. 'I have to go to Switzerland, Bugs, on business – Montreux. I thought maybe you'd like to come. We could go on to Zermatt, have a few days' skiing.'

Zermatt. They went to Zermatt the first Christmas they were married.

'I have to go in the next week or so. I thought maybe next weekend.'

She stared into his anxious eyes. 'What have you got to do?'

He glanced around nervously. 'I've got a bit of dosh stashed away in a bank over there. I want to make sure that it's safe if the going gets rough . . . make sure we can keep paying the mortgage, and Nicky's school fees.'

'I've got my job, if anything—'

'Yes, I know, but there's no point in—'

'Don't do anything illegal in Switzerland, will you, Richard?'

'No, it's fine. Andreas has sorted everything out. I just have to move a bit snappily before—'

'Before?'

He shrugged. 'I don't know. No one really knows. It'll take the police a while to sift through everything. They're raiding people all over the shop. They've done Archie as well. It might be several months, but it could only be a couple of weeks.'

'How much trouble are you really in?'

He got up from the bed and walked over to the window. ''S not serious. Get a fine or something,' he said evasively.

'That inspector – Milton – kept saying you wouldn't have such a nice view from a prison cell.'

'Frighteners, that's all. Talking big. He was all mouth.'

'He was horrible.'

He came back over and sat down. She felt fully awake now, though her head was aching badly, fully awake and churned as hell. She was sorry for him, really sorry for the first time since she'd arrived back and found the police. Sorry for him and torn up and twisted inside. Christ, it had all been so fine until – the tart? The dream of the aeroplane? Now it all seemed to be collapsing around her.

Like scaffold.

'Think you could get away?' he asked.

'I'll have to check my Filofax. At home.'

'Be nice if you came.'

Richard and Nicky stayed until she'd had supper and the nurse came in to give her a pill to help her sleep.

'I'm whacked,' she said. 'I'm not going to need any help sleeping.' But she took the pill anyway, and it made her feel better, gave her a strange surge of excitement.

Hope.

Answers. There were answers. There were answers to why it was all happening. You just had to look in the right place, that was all, find the secret button or maybe some magic code word. Go away, Slider, I command thee. Into thy dungeon, Oh foul beast. Slink away in disgrace and ne'er darken my doorstep again. You foul cursed creature of darkness.

Out, out, vile jelly.

What the hell was in the pill? She felt smashed, euphoric. Then a great wave of tiredness picked her up, and she floated along with it until it gently lowered her back down.

She slept.

30

They kept her in hospital until late Monday afternoon, when Richard collected her and drove her to London. She arrived at the office on Tuesday with a dull headache, and Claire looked up as she came in. That was

something, she thought, Claire actually looking up;
progress.

'How are you?'

'OK,' she said.

She wished Ken was in, that he wasn't away filming in
Spain, that she could go up and tell him, tell him about
her antennae, sharp, so sharp. Too damned sharp. She
picked up the top letter on the pile on her desk.

It was a brief but courteous note from the secretary of
the Royal Yacht Squadron. 'The committee regrets that
it cannot permit its premises to be depicted in advertise-
ments, regardless of the singular merits of your particular project.'

Damn.

It was a great script. The crusty old buffer sitting
outside the clubhouse pulling out his spectacles and a
packet of condoms falling out of his pocket with them.

*You can't teach an old sea dog new tricks. But you
can kill him with a new disease. Wear a condom. It's an
admiral thing to do.*

She picked up the next letter, then put it down again.
Her hands trembling, her eyes damp. Fear. It seeped
through her, deep inside her, cold as melting ice. She
opened her handbag and pulled out *What Your Dreams
Really Say*, and glanced again at the brief biography of
the author, then picked up the phone and dialled Directory Enquiries.

'I'd like the number for Hull University, please.' Sam
covered the mouthpiece. 'I dreamed it. I dreamed I fell –
from a balcony.'

Claire gazed back at her without replying for a moment . . . almost – almost, it struck Sam, as if she
thought it was amusing.

The operator gave her the number and she wrote it
down.

'How did you like Mrs Wolf?' Claire asked.

'I thought she was weird.'

'She's very accurate, I find. Didn't you?'

'I hope not,' Sam said, staring down at the number, and dialling it.

'Hull University,' said the voice that answered the phone.

'I'd like to speak to Dr Colin Hare in the Psychology Department, please.'

'Putting you through.'

'Psychology,' said a man's voice, abrupt, slightly irritable.

'Could I speak to Dr Hare?'

'May I ask who's calling?'

'Yes, my name is—' Sam saw Claire watching her, and felt uncomfortable – 'Mrs Curtis.'

'Can I tell him what it is about?'

'Yes, she said, 'It's about his work on dreams. I just wondered if it was possible to have a word?'

'He's on a call at the moment.'

'May I hold?'

'Yes. You can hold.'

'Thank you.' She looked at Claire. 'I've got a splitting headache. Would you mind nipping down to the chemist on the Strand and getting me some Disprin?'

'Sure, I'll just finish this—'

'Now,' Sam said, more snappily than she had meant.

Claire stood up slowly. Sam handed her a fiver, and Claire walked out of the room.

'Yes, hello?' A gentle, slightly nervous voice.

'Is that Dr Hare?'

'Speaking.'

'I'm sorry to – er – bother you . . . I'm calling you because I'm desperate. I need help.' Her voice was faltering, breaking up and tears were coming in and choking the words in her throat.

'Tell me,' he said patiently, as if he had all the time in the world to listen. 'Do tell me.'

'I'm – things are happening. My dreams . . . I'm having—'

Calm down, Sam, for God's sake! Take it gently. *Don't sound like a fruitcake.*

'I keep having dreams which come true, but I can't read them. They're slightly different . . . I think I might even be making the future happen. Does that sound daft?'

'Well, I – could you give me a bit more detail?'

'Would it be possible to come and see you? Nobody believes me. I really need to talk to someone who knows about dreams. If I could just have half an hour of your time?' She felt a bit calmer. 'I don't think I can really explain it that well over the phone, but I think my life is in danger. And my family, and other people. I just need someone who can maybe explain a few things about dreams to me. If you don't have the time yourself, perhaps you could suggest someone?'

'I'd be happy to have a chat. Precognitory dreams are something we are studying here at the moment, so you've called at a good time . . . Unfortunately it'll have to be in April or May, as I'm off to the States on Friday for about two months, lecturing. Perhaps I could contact you when I get back?'

She clutched the phone hard in her hand. 'I must see you before you go. Please. I can't – I – I could be dead by then.'

Idiot.

Stupid thing to say.

'Oh dear,' he said. There was a silence. 'That does sound very drastic.'

'I'm sorry,' she said, 'I don't want to sound dramatic
– but it's true.'

'I could see you late tomorrow afternoon. Is that any
good?'

'Yes, I—'

'Where are you phoning from?'

'London.'

'It's a bit of a journey.'

'I don't mind.'

'How old are you?'

'Old?'

'Yes.'

'Thirty-two – well – almost thirty-three.'

'Ah, good, yes – we are studying subjects in exactly
your age group. Ah – if you came up, would you – ah –
be prepared – ah – to spend a night in our sleep laboratory – it's very pleasant – at the university – it's just like
a hotel bedroom – apart from the wiring of course. It
would help us – and it might help you?'

'I'd try anything.'

'I know that we have a – ah – vacancy in the laboratory tomorrow. That would tie in rather well.' He had
begun to sound quite enthusiastic. 'I'm going to be – yes
– I – I'm at my flat tomorrow afternoon – just opposite
the university – perhaps – if you come there – we can
have a quiet chat – first?'

He gave her the directions and she repeated them
carefully, writing them down, thanking him again and
hung up, then looked at her Filofax for any meetings she
would have to cancel. She felt a surge of excitement, of
hope. Maybe a simple answer. Or would he just say the
same too? Sharp antennae and coincidences?

She picked up the next letter on the pile, and opened
it.

On the floor below, the front door swung shut behind

Claire as she walked out into the street, and crossed over towards the chemist.

31

She stared out of the window of the train, at the Humber river seeping through the drab countryside like ink spilt across a school desk, and at a cluster of brick chimney stacks on the horizon, like tent poles supporting the dark canopy of sky.

A man walking down the corridor, stopped and peered in at her, stared for some moments and moved on, then the train went into a tunnel and she felt scared, scared that the door might slide open and he would come into the compartment in a dark hood. The tunnel roared around them, echoing, thundering, then they came back into the light, past a level crossing with a line of traffic waiting for them.

Wednesday afternoon. Had the dream group met again on Monday? Led by Barry, the silent man in the black karate suit? Had they met and discussed her dream? What the hell did they all think? That she was some kind of a witch? Or had it not occurred to any of them to connect the dream? Were they all too busy resonating?

The man walked back, peered into her compartment again and she glared at him venomously. Go away. Go away Slider or whoever the hell you are. Leave me alone. Piss off. He hesitated, turned around, and walked off.

It could be that you've got sharp antennae, like rabbits' ears. Like Bugs Bunny.

Sure, of course, Ken. Doesn't everyone who dreams of a balcony collapsing know what that really means?

Surely Freud knew? And Jung? It said in *What Your Dreams Really Say* that balcony was a mother's breast. Of course. Mother died. I lost her breast. Simple. And of course Freud knew that balcony = scaffold. Plain as daylight, old boy.

It's much easier to put them down as premonitions than to face their real truths.

Of course.

Richard thought she was nuts coming up here. Told her that concussion did strange things to the mind and she needed rest, peace and quiet, told her to take it easy for a few days so she'd feel fit and strong for Switzerland. Told her Switzerland would make her feel better. Sure. It would stop her premonitions, and make his business better and mend their marriage. Switzerland was full of magical properties.

The problem was that when you tried to tell people about your premonitions, after they had come true, they thought you were a little batty. Poor old Sam. Fell off a scaffold onto her head. Never been the same since. Of course, she was already slightly unhinged by her husband's affair . . .

Real truths?

In the distance she saw a stream of lorries crossing a suspension bridge. They passed a bunkering station, a lightship in the middle of the estuary, a row of cranes hunched against the sky like old men with fishing rods, then the train slowed, and the word HULL flashed past the window.

The real truth was that children could have been shot, and it was lucky that they had not been. That she could have been raped and murdered and had escaped because she had dreamed it. That she was damned nearly killed on the scaffold because – because . . . because she'd failed to recognise something from the dream of the balcony?

The real truth was that 163 people on the aircraft might still be alive. That Tanya Jacobson might still be alive. Whilst Bamford talked about Freud, about jealousies, pains, thwartings, about penis envy, about cosy things that he was comfortable with. Cosy things that explained everything. And nothing. Cosiness. Dream groups. Steps down into the tube station. The vagina. That was all. It didn't matter that you got raped and murdered, as long as you understood the dream. As long as it resonated.

The taxi dropped her outside a row of 1930s semi-detached houses opposite the main gates of Hull University. 'Bell not working. Please come up to first floor and shout,' said the handwritten note on the door.

She hefted her small overnight case up the narrow staircase and onto a dark, gloomy landing. A door opened behind her.

'Mrs Curtis?'

She turned around and saw a short, bearded man in his forties. He was wearing crumpled corduroy trousers and an Arran sweater and had straggly, untidy hair, which he was making worse by rummaging a finger through, as though he was searching for something he had left in there. He had a piece of sticking plaster above his right eye.

'Dr Hare?'

'Ah!' He had the embarrassed, faintly disorientated air of a man who has walked into a ladies' washroom by mistake. 'Yes. Ah – Colin, please.'

She smiled. 'Sam.'

'Sam, right.' He windmilled his arms and looked up at the ceiling as if worried it was about to collapse on him. 'Bulb's gone again, I'm afraid.'

Sam felt a fleeting chill. Another one.

Come on girl, don't be daft. Can't get spooked up every time a light bulb goes.

Hare clapped his hands together and rubbed them. 'Good. Your train – I thought you'd be here a bit earlier. Late, was it?'

'Yes, I'm afraid so.'

'Well – er – come in. I'm afraid it's a bit of a – rather embarrassing, actually – probably as well. I was just starting to tidy up—'

She followed him into a large bedsitting room, and recoiled in shock.

It seemed as if a hurricane had just passed through.

Clothes were strewn everywhere, books lay on the floor, some opened, their covers bent back. There was a spidery coffee stain in the centre of one wall, and following it down she saw a broken cup lying against the skirting board. A smashed compact disc player was tangled with the wreckage of a standard lamp. A radio was on the floor, its casing shattered and its wiring and batteries spewed out; above it, a chunk of plaster was missing from the wall. An elderly Olivetti typewriter lay upside down on the floor near a broken wooden table, and sheets of manuscript littered the place like confetti. The window looking out onto a dull neat garden had a crack right across it.

He raised his arms helplessly in the air. 'I apologise. Terrible mess, I'm afraid. My—' He hunched his shoulders. 'My wife and I, we just had a bit of a fight. Divorce, you see.' He rummaged in his hair again, then lightly tested the plaster above his eye, staring around with a bewildered expression. 'I'm not quite sure how I'm going to explain all this to my landlady.' He checked his beard carefully with his fingers, then closed the door behind him and locked it. 'Just in case she comes back. She's rather possessive, you see. I'm sorry.'

'Can I give you a hand clearing up?' Sam asked. What on earth could they have had a such a fight about in this crummy room? Had he walked out on her? Shacked up here with a mistress? Was he a little raver underneath his ramshackle academic exterior? Her eye caught a colour photograph on the mantelpiece above an electric fire of two little girls in school uniform. The glass on that was cracked too.

He transferred a pile of books and junk from one side of an ancient sofa to the other, then took her coat, and hung it over his arm. He hovered, tugged at his pullover, scratched his beard and checked both flaps of his shirt collar.

'I really appreciate your seeing me at such short notice,' she said.

He took the coat off his arm, held it up in the air and stared at it, like a conjurer who has got his tricks confused. I'll just hang it up. I'll be all right in a minute. I'm, a bit flustered, you see. Would you like tea?'

'Thank you.'

'There's coffee if you'd rather.'

'I'd prefer coffee.'

'Yes. Good. I'll just – if you want to use the – it's down the corridor.' He walked across the room to the kitchenette, almost on tiptoe, as if trying to compensate for the noise he must have made earlier.

She listened to him foraging through the crockery, heard the sound of a fridge door, then the shriek of a kettle, as she looked around at the hopeless mess. Maybe this is what you were supposed to do when you discovered your husband was having an affair? Smash everything up?

He came back into the room carrying a tray with two steaming mugs, and a plate scattered with biscuits.

Something crunched under his feet, and he looked down lamely at a smashed cassette.

'Coffee, you said?'

'Thanks.' She took the mug, raised it to her lips, and blew on it to cool it. It did not smell like coffee. She sniffed again, trying not to let him notice. It was tea.

'I'll put these biscuits here. You must be hungry. It's a long trip.' He sat down opposite her, perching on the edge of his chair.

'I thought your book was very good.'

His eyes widened, and he smiled. 'Ah. *What Your Dreams Really Say*?'

'It's very interesting.'

'You found it helpful?'

'Yes, I did. Well, some of it.'

'It's all right, as far as it goes. They edited an awful lot out. Just stuck to the classic interpretations. I didn't have any space for premonitions. That'll be in the next one.' He stirred his tea and glanced nervously towards the door. Sam wondered whether his wife would come bursting through at any moment wielding an axe; and how she would cope with the demented woman if she did.

He looked at his watch. 'Have to keep an eye on the time – Laszlo likes people to get settled in early.' He saw her frown. 'The dream laboratory. We'll go over there in about half an hour. I've arranged for you to have supper in the canteen.'

'Everyone seems to ridicule the idea of premonitions,' she said.

'Of course they do, it makes them feel safe. If they rubbish a thing in their own minds, then it can't pose any threat to them.' He put his teaspoon down. 'They think parapsychologists are cranks. I'm a scientist, that's all. I'm a scientist who won't be blinkered.' He looked at his watch again. 'Let's talk about you. You told me on the phone that you feel your life is in danger.'

'Yes.'

'Do you mind if I tape our conversation?'

She shook her head, and he ducked an arm into the debris and pulled out a small recorder. He switched it on, put it on the table in front of her and tested it with a hint of triumph in his face, as if he had scored a point over his wife by finding something she had not destroyed. He crossed his arms and leaned back in the chair. 'Why don't you start by telling me everything you think I should hear, then we'll go to the laboratory and monitor your sleep and dream patterns, see if we spot anything unusual. We could have a discussion tomorrow. I have a meeting in the morning, but lunch is free. Could you stay until then?'

'Yes. Thank you.'

'Good. Well—' He waved at her to start.

She told him the full story, while he sat nodding his head, grunting from time to time, and continually crossing and uncrossing his arms as if he was practising a new form of semaphore.

'What a shame that these weren't all logged in advance,' he said. 'They sound very interesting examples. Two of them seem very clearly precognitive: the air disaster – I know several people who saw that one – and the murder of that poor woman in Hampstead. By precognitive I mean that you clearly saw into the future. The others seem rather more premonitory – warning dreams, but not—' He wrung his hands together – 'not quite so specific. Good examples, though, very good examples.' He raised a finger, leaned forward and switched off the tape. 'Tell me. This hooded man – Slider – he's linked in some way with each dream?'

'Yes.' She smiled at him uncertainly, almost disbelievingly. She had been expecting him to mock, pull them apart. But he didn't.

He believed her.

And she realised now she wished he didn't.

'I don't think you should be frightened, Sam. You obviously have a remarkable gift.'

'I don't want it. I want to get rid of it. I just want to lead a normal life.'

He smiled, as if it were a private joke. 'A normal life. Have you ever considered the possibility that life without premonitions is an abnormal life? Dreams and premonitions have helped shape the world. Calpurnia saw Caesar's death in a dream. She could have saved his life – if only he hadn't ridiculed her. Even the Bible says that all events are foreshadowed.'

He picked a careful path over towards the windows. There was a sickening crunch under his foot. 'Bloody woman,' he muttered. He reached the window and looked out. 'Sam, sixth sense – psychic awareness, whatever you like to call it – is a part of normal life. It's as much a part as eating, drinking, breathing, thinking. We suppress it because society thinks it doesn't need it, that it's smarter to teach a child to use the phone than to transmit a message by telepathy.'

'Why would someone suddenly become psychic?'

'I don't believe anyone does *suddenly* become psychic. We are all born with these powers but they fade out very quickly in most of us, because we don't use them. Our society actively discourages us from using them, as you've been discovering from the people you've been to for help.' He turned round. 'Most people are afraid of being ridiculed, so they leave it at that, don't give their psychic abilities any chance to develop. But these powers don't go away; we still have them. Some of us have the ability to use them instinctively; some of us need a clonk on the head to re-activate them.' He shrugged. 'They're there. We are all born with them, as much as we are born with arms and legs.'

'I don't remember having a clonk on the head.'

'You don't have to be dropped on your head. A trauma can do it just as well. Look at yourself – someone tried to rape and kill you when you were a little girl, a ghastly man in a black hood . . . you lost both your parents together. Pretty big traumas.'

'But these dreams stopped after my parents died. Stopped for twenty-five years. What's started them again?'

'Well, that's what we have to try to discover. There's some trigger – something obviously linked with this hooded one-eyed man. Perhaps we'll learn something from the laboratory.' He looked at his watch again, as if he was anxious to get out of the room.

Anxious in case his wife came back?

'I think we'd better get across now. We can continue talking.' He stood up, fetched her coat, helped her into it, then insisted on carrying her overnight bag.

It was dark outside and beginning to snow. They stopped at the kerb, waiting for a gap in the thundering traffic, the howling, blattering heavy rush hour traffic, cars heading home and trucks heading to the docks, wipers clacking, lights glaring, gears grinding, and he shouted at her, above the roar, 'If you tried to walk across this road with your eyes shut, you'd be knocked down and killed. Yet most of us travel through life with our minds shut.'

The slipstream of a lorry buffeted her sideways and her lungs filled with foul diesel exhaust. Another dark shape loomed down the road, blasting the night with its exhaust, its tyres churning the white flecks of snow to pulp and flinging slush up at them. They sprinted across and walked in through the gates of the university.

She felt envious of the students they passed in the harsh glare of the campus lights, thinking she'd like to be a student now, that she'd like to be young and starting it all again. A boy and girl passed them, talking earnestly, clumping along in their Doc Martens. Street fashion. Street cred. She would look ridiculous in Doc Martens, she thought. She would *feel* ridiculous in them.

Students. Target market. Future As, Bs, Cs. Consumers. Future yuppies. Come autumn, you'll all be eating Castaways.

They went across the quadrangle, in through a door and up two flights of stone stairs.

'I'm afraid it's not much, but it's quite comfortable,' Colin Hare said as they walked across the second floor landing. He pushed open a door and turned on the light, then stepped aside.

It was a neat, small bedroom, with a wide single bed that looked as if it was fresh out of a furniture store, and an unmarked beige carpet. There was a wardrobe, chest of drawers, television and a wash basin. The room smelt new. The curtains were drawn, and the navy-blue counterpane on the bed had been turned down. It could have been a hotel bedroom anywhere in the world, except for the cluster of wires dangling from a pod on the wall above the bed.

It scared her.

Something about it wasn't right, and she did not know what. It was like a show bedroom with fake walls on the furniture floor of a department store. It wasn't real. It would be like undressing and going to bed in a shop window. Only it wasn't that either.

Something else. She shivered. Tell him 'no thanks'. Tell him you have to go now.

Why? He's trying to help.

That's what you think.

'It's quite different to what I had imagined,' she said. 'It's very ordinary looking. Nice. Much nicer than half the hotel rooms I've stayed in.'

'We need it to feel normal for people.'

'I thought I was going to be in a glass booth.'

'No, we don't need to watch you whilst you're asleep. We get all the information we need from the printout. I'll show you the monitoring room.'

As they came out of the door, a studious-looking girl holding a bundle of papers walked past. 'Good evening, Dr Hare,' she said in a Scottish accent.

'Ah, good evening, Jane. This is Mrs Curtis – a new subject.'

Subject. Like a laboratory frog in formaldehyde?

'Good evening,' said the girl politely, before disappearing down the stairs.

'She's one of our researchers, doing a post-grad at the moment. I'll show you my office,' Hare said. 'I prefer to see people out of the office. It's quieter.' They went across the hallway, and he pushed open the door to a chaotic room littered with papers, computer terminals and overstuffed filing trays; it wasn't much tidier than his bed-sitting room.

They went further down the hallway and into a small brightly lit room with a battery of electrical equipment, computer screens, and two massive graph plotters. A young man in his late twenties was poring over sheets of graph paper. He had dark, Slavic features with heavy black rings around his eyes. He shovelled a handful of jet black hair off his forehead and studied something intently. His hair tumbled forward again and he shovelled it back again, mildly irritated.

'Laszlo, can I introduce you?'

The man looked round at them and rubbed his eyes blearily, as if he was grumpy at being interrupted. 'Mrs Curtis?' he said, in an abrupt, disinterested voice. Sam wondered if he had been the person who answered the phone yesterday.

She smiled. 'Yes.'

'Good,' he grunted, then yawned.

She frowned. There was a silence.

'Er – Laszlo calls this place the Hull Hilton,' said Hare, sensing the awkwardness.

'Ah,' she said.

Laszlo turned back to his graph, and began studying it again. 'Have you ever been in a sleep laboratory before, Mrs Curtis?' he said, without looking up.

'No,' she said.

'No problem.' He made a mark on the graph with a pen, pursing his lips in concentration. 'You don't have to do anything. Just sleep.' He giggled, an unexpected, high-pitched, boyish giggle. 'Just sleep. Have dreams. You have the fun, we do the work. That's right, Dr Hare?' He addressed the professor by his surname as if it was a joke.

Hare turned to Sam. 'People don't realise quite how boring dream research is,' he said. 'One of us has to sit in here all night, watching the graph. It's pretty intrusive on the private life of the investigator.'

Sam wondered if that was why he had got divorced. 'Can't you leave me sleeping, then read through it in the morning?'

'No. We have to keep an eye on the plotter. Pens run out, the paper has to be replaced.' He picked up a sheet of graph paper, on which she could see eight rows of blue lines, some zig-zagging, some squiggling. 'Each of these is just twenty seconds of sleep. We get through two and a half thousand sheets in a night's sleep. We need to interact with the sleeper. If we see some unusual activity, we want to wake them up right away, find out what was going on. And the other thing we do is this—' He smiled proudly, and tapped a small control panel with a row of gauges and switches on it. 'Lucid dreams,' he said. 'Do you ever have lucid dreams?'

'What are those?' she asked.

'When you become aware in a dream that you are dreaming?'

'I've had one,' she said. 'A long time ago.'

'Yes? And were you able to do anything about it?'

'What do you mean?'

'Were you able to control the dream? Manipulate it?'

'No. I just knew that I was dreaming.'

'Do you know much about sleep? About dreaming?'

Sam shrugged. 'Not really, I suppose.'

'How often do you dream?'

'Normally?'

'Yes.'

'I don't know – once or twice a week.'

'No. You dream every night. All human beings do. In eight hours of sleep, you'll have between three to five dream periods, starting from ten to fifteen minutes long and increasing to about thirty to forty minutes. But you probably won't remember any of them. You'll only remember them if you wake up either in the middle of a dream or immediately after.' He showed her a wodge of printout sheets. 'You're looking sceptical. It's all here. If you stayed long enough, I could prove it to you.'

She watched the jagged lines, as he ran his finger along each one in turn. 'That's low-voltage flat stuff from the front of the brain – not much activity during sleep. That spidery one is the Rapid Eye Movement Scan, REMS. Your eyes blink very fast when you are dreaming. These are other regions of the brain: respiration, cardiovascular

273

activity, body temperature.' He scratched his head. 'You see, when you remember a dream, fine, great, we can analyse it, log it, see if any parts come true. But what about all those dreams you don't remember? Those five periods every night? Two or three hours a night, of which you maybe remember a few seconds once a week? What's happening then? We know you're dreaming, but what are you doing? What's happening to you?' He tapped his head. 'What's going on in there? Are you having premonitions that we're missing because you don't remember the dreams? Are you out of your body, out on the astral? Travelling in time? If you could become aware that you are having a dream, then you might be able to remember it. You could wake up at the end and tell it. We have a microphone in the bedroom and a voice-activated tape recorder.'

'You can really do that?'

'There's a big bonus. If you can be aware that you are dreaming, then you can control your dream.'

'How do you make someone aware they are dreaming?'

He pointed to the grey control box. 'This sends out an extremely low voltage electrical signal. We wire it to the subject's median nerve, and when we see that they've entered the dream state, we fire the signal. What it does is let that person be aware he or she is dreaming – without waking up. Then they can take charge of their dream.'

'And if they were on a plane that was crashing, could they save it?'

Hare dug his hands into his pockets. 'It may help to identify the difference between a precognitive dream and a dream that is simply a nightmare.'

'If you stop the plane crashing, then it's just a nightmare?'

'We don't know, but that's the sort of area we're researching. You might be an excellent subject for that. When I get back from America—'

'It's good for your fantasies,' said Laszlo, without looking up from his work. 'You're having some dull old dream, then you get the buzz that you're dreaming. You can have anything in the world that you want. You want to shack up with Tom Cruise, you just imagine him, and away you go!' He looked up. 'You begin to wonder what's so smart about being awake.'

'I've been wondering that for some time,' Sam said.

32

Sam ate supper in the canteen on a formica-topped table, amid the chatter and bustle of the students and the smell of chips and batter and tinned oxtail soup of the day. Then she went to bed just the way she would have in any hotel room, except the bathroom was not en suite, but across the corridor, which was awkward.

Hare and Laszlo came in and wired her up, wished her sweet dreams, then went out and closed the door.

She sat up in the bed and turned the pages of *Vogue*. Smart women stared back at her, cold arrogance on their chiselled faces, preening at her in their finery as if she was a mirror. Elegance. She wondered how elegant she looked now, with the wires taped all over head. A girl in a negligee sat on the shiny black bonnet of a Porsche. Two male models looked disdainfully at her, a father and son pose, the old man in tweeds, on a shooting stick, the son in a sharply cut suit.

'Old Men Dream Dreams, Young Men See Visions,' said the caption beneath.

She put the magazine down on the bedside table, had

a sip of water, then turned out the bedside light. She settled down slowly, carefully, making sure she did not dislodge any wires. Her head hurt where the wires were pulling her hair, but she did not dare touch them. The bed was comfortable, soft, more comfy than her own. There was a chill draught from the window which she had left open a fraction, and she heard footsteps in the quadrangle below.

'Ouch. Keith, you bastard!'

'No!' a girl screamed, giggled, then screamed again. 'No, I didn't mean it, no, not down my neck! Oh, you bastard!'

They were clearing away in the canteen somewhere near by. Clattering trays, cutlery. Taps were running. A record played faintly in the distance, Buddy Holly's 'Every Day'. Christ, it was going to be hard getting to sleep tonight. Strange noises. The greasy smell of chips from the canteen. The painful tugging of her hair.

Premonitions.

Hare believed her. But. There was something odd about Hare. Something not quite right. And about Laszlo.

Were they both sitting in the lab now, in front of the plotter, watching her brainwaves? What had Hare talked about whilst they were wiring her up? Five stages of sleep. Stage one, the hypnagogic state. Hypnagogic.

When you're just beginning to drift away. You often see strange faces, weird faces, scary images.

Then there was stage two – deeper sleep; stage three – when the body was shut down; stage four – deep sleep, the mind a blank; and then stage five – REM sleep. Dreaming.

She hadn't even gone into stage one sleep yet.

She turned over again restlessly, fumbled for the control panel above the headboard, and pushed a switch. The television came on. She wondered how her brainwaves were going to look now, as she blinked at the sudden brightness of the screen and watched a commercial she did not recognise.

A long shot of a mountain, covered in snow, the sun bursting over the peak. In the distance was a tiny speck, coming towards them; then a sign flashed across the screen.

'AROLEID.'

The sign vanished and the speck got closer, and the sign flashed again.

'AROLEID.'

It strobed on and off, intercut with the speck that was getting bigger all the time, until it filled the screen.

'AROLEID,' said a voice she vaguely recognised, in a whisper followed by a laugh. 'AROLEID.'

She frowned. Aroleid? What on earth was Aroleid? She switched off the television and stared up at the ceiling, and saw the blades of a large fan revolving slowly, like a propeller. Strange, she thought, she had not noticed it before. It was cold in the room, cold in the bed. She wondered why the fan had been switched on.

The door of her room opened, then closed quietly. She heard someone breathing, the clink of a key, and the distinct click of a lock sliding home.

Someone locking it from the inside.

She stared, trembling, into the darkness. 'Who's there?' she said. Who the hell was it? Dr Hare? Laszlo? Why had they locked the door? 'Who is it? Who's that?'

Silence.

She could see someone standing by the door, a dark shadow, almost motionless, but not quite. A dark shadow that she could hear breathing.

'Dr Hare?'

Her voice was sounding strange, constricted. Christ.

Who was here, in this building? How loudly would she have to shout to be heard? What was showing on the plotter now?

Surely they would see it?

Unless.

Laszlo?

Christ, no.

The shape began to move towards her.

'We'll see how this looks on the graph,' said a voice she knew. The same voice on the commercial on the television a few moments ago. Not Dr Hare's. Nor Laszlo's.

She felt pressure on the sheet under her chin, then the bedclothes were ripped away. She screamed, a short, gargled scream, and felt a gloved hand over her mouth.

'Calm down, you silly bitch. I'm just going to fuck you, that's all. You'll like it. You'll love it.'

She stared up at the dark shape. There was a click and the bedside light came on and she blinked at Slider standing over the bed in a metallic green jump suit, like a motorcycle racing suit, thick black gauntlets, and goggles over the eye slits of his black hood.

She shrank back, and saw his mouth grinning through its slit.

He held something out towards her, offering it to her, something orange and white: an airline boarding card. He waved it over her eyes so that she could read it, clearly.

CHARTAIR 35A.

'You'll be needing this. Very soon. You shouldn't leave it lying around in the back of taxis. That's careless, so very careless.' He let go of it and she watched it flutter down onto her chest. 'Oh look, it's fallen!' He leered at her. 'You're slow, aren't you, bitch? So slow. The fall. From the balcony? Good, wasn't it?'

He grinned again, showing all his filthy broken teeth. 'There's more to come. So much more. So much further to fall. You've got the really big fall to come.'

She watched him, as he strutted over to the wash basin and picked up her toothpaste. He unscrewed the cap, held the tube up. 'Like games, do you? Puzzles? Riddles? See what you think of this!' He began to squeeze out the toothpaste. It fell in long streams onto the carpet as he rolled up the tube until it was empty, and then dropped it onto the floor. 'Messy stuff, toothpaste. Don't bother with it myself.'

This is a dream, she thought; surely this is a dream? A lucid dream?

'What have you got all those wires on your head for?' he asked. 'Trying to beat me with high tech? Stupid little bitch, aren't you? It's time you had a lesson. I think I'm going to give you one.'

Lucid dream. I'm having a lucid dream.

If you can be aware that you are dreaming, you can control your dream.

'No,' she said, surprised at how firm she sounded. 'I don't want a lesson. I'm going to give you something. I'm going to give you a Castaway bar.'

He looked puzzled.

Concentrate. Castaway bar. Castaway bar!

One appeared in her hand.

I can have anything in the world that I want, she thought suddenly. She thrust it out to him. 'Eat it,' she said.

He walked over and took it, and she sat up in bed, watching him unwrap it and bite a piece off.

'What do you think of it?'

'It's all right,' he said. 'It tastes a bit like a Bounty with biscuit.'

'That's what Ken said.'

'He said the same?'

'Yes.'

He smiled.

She felt a surge of confidence. 'I want you to tell me why you keep coming back to me, Slider. What do you want? Why don't you leave me alone?'

He licked his fingers. 'It was good, that bar.'

'Like another?'

'No.'

'It's no problem to get you another. I can fill the whole room with them if you want.'

'You could fill the room with Castaway bars?'

'Yes. And I could make you disappear if I wanted. But I don't want to do that. Not yet. I want to know what you want. I want to know why I'm having these dreams.'

He raised his arms, and looked surprised. 'I'm your friend, Sam.' He sat down beside her. 'I'm your friend, that's why! You're having them to protect you. I'm showing you the future to warn you of danger. You've got to learn to trust me.' He put an arm around her and squeezed her gently. 'I'm your friend. See? Happy?'

'Great.'

He smiled. 'Great! This is great. You thought I wasn't your friend?'

'Yes.'

He chuckled. 'Ridiculous. That's crazy.'

She felt him heaving up and down as he began to laugh, and she laughed with him. They sat together, laughing almost helplessly for a long while. Then they sat in silence, peaceful silence.

'Listen, Sam, you mustn't worry about the future. It's all taken care of. All the details.' He squeezed her again, then jumped up from the bed, went over to the door and opened it.

'Don't go,' she said.

'I'm not going. I want to see if the papers have come.' He opened the door and stooped down, then turned around, holding up *The Times*. 'It's a good place this, isn't it?'

'Yes,' she said. 'Wonderful.'

He pushed his goggles up onto his forehead, opened *The Times* and scanned through it, then he folded the pages back, came over to the bed and sat down again. 'I told you I'd taken care of all the details. Look!' He held the pages in front of her.

ANNOUNCEMENTS AND PERSONAL.

She looked up at him, at the eyes through the slits, the eyes which suddenly looked so cold and hard she could not tell which was the glass one.

'Come on,' he said, becoming insistent. 'Have a look, see for yourself – see the column?'

'Deaths,' she read, and began to tremble as she followed his finger down the column, a long, neatly manicured nail. Too long, like a talon.

'Look, there!' His voice was filled with childish glee. 'Can you see?'

She froze.

'CURTIS. Tragically. Samantha (Sam) Ruth. Aged 32. Beloved wife of Richard and loving mother of Nicky. Funeral service private. Family flowers only.'

'The date,' she dimly heard him say. 'The only thing they left out.'

She felt a sharp draught of air, and a sheet of the newspaper suddenly blew away onto the floor, then another sheet, as if caught in a ferocious gust. She heard the roar of an engine, felt her hair whipping her face, saw the curtains crashing wildly. She looked up, petrified, at the ceiling. The fan was spinning wildly, huge, black and menacing, spinning and clattering, the noise turning into a deafening roar that made her put her hands over her ears.

No!

The wind ripped at the bedclothes and tore them off the bed, hurling them across the room like pieces of paper.

'No. Oh God, no!' she screamed, as the glass of water beside her exploded like a grenade, showering her in sharp stinging shards.

The doors of the wardrobe suddenly flew open and her clothes hurled out onto the floor. The light bulb on her bedside light exploded, and the room went dark.

'Oh God help me.'

'You little bitch. Think you're going to beat me with high tech? Think you could make me disappear just by thinking about it?'

She was flung out of the bed and smashed into the ceiling, then felt herself falling down, falling through a freezing swirling vortex, tumbling head over heels through a debris of glass and furniture which cut and stung, and then she crashed into the ground, hard; so hard, she was unable to move.

There was a brilliant white light, which dazzled her and she closed her eyes against it.

'Sam?'

She shivered. Cold, it was so cold.

'Sam?'

She smelt a strange, unfamiliar, dusty smell, and opened her eyes. She saw a beige fuzz. A strange beige fuzz, lying on top of her, crushing her. She was bitterly cold.

'Jesus Christ,' said a man's voice.

'Are you all right, Sam?'

Dr Hare, she thought. It sounded like Dr Hare.

She pushed the fuzz of beige, but it would not move.

'Have you hurt yourself?' said Colin Hare's voice.

I don't know, she wanted to say. I don't know. 'Please get this thing off me.' She pushed the beige fuzz again. Then she realised. It was the carpet.

She was lying face down on the floor.

'Jesus Christ.' Laszlo's voice.

'We'll lift her back onto the bed.'

She felt hands, awkward, fumbling hands, then the fuzz was lifted away and she saw the white ceiling. No fan, she thought vaguely, then heard the creak of springs and felt the softness of the bed. Hare's face was close to hers, searching, worried. Laszlo's dark-ringed eyes probed her with a strange incomprehension that frightened her.

'Are you all right?' said Hare.

She gave a weak nod.

'She looks cold, Laszlo. Let's put the bedclothes back over her.'

She watched him turn and walk across the room. Laszlo was still staring down at her. Why? He seemed to be saying. Why?

Hare bent down, scooping up a sheet from the floor, Christ. The mess.

The room looked as if it had been destroyed.

Glass, clothes, bits of furniture were strewn all around. The window was smashed and the curtain rail had been ripped away from the wall. There was a thin trail of something white underneath the wash basin. A chair was lying lopsided against a wall, one of its legs buckled under it, like an old man who has fallen and can't get up. Her bedside table was lying on top of the wardrobe.

No. It was not possible.

Hare came back towards her, dragging an armful of

bedclothes. He dropped them down, disentangled a sheet, then draped it over her gently.

Like a flag over a dead soldier.

I'm dead. I'm dead. That's why he's looking at me like that.

'Take the other end, Laszlo. Tuck it in firmly.'

'Am I all right?' she asked.

Hare was studying her carefully. She felt the bed tilt slightly, first one side, then the other, then Hare stooped down again, and she felt the weight of a blanket. Warmth.

'I want to wake up now,' she said, and she caught a brief nervous glance between Hare and Laszlo.

Hare smiled thinly. 'You are awake now, Sam. You had a bad—' He paused and raised his hands in the air.

'Lucid,' she said. 'I had a lucid dream.'

'Ah,' said Hare. 'Yes – I—'

'Toothpaste. He squeezed my toothpaste. Is it there?'

'Your toothpaste?'

'On the wash basin.'

He looked over at the basin, then down at the carpet beneath it. The trail of white toothpaste spelled out a word in large, clear writing.

AROLEID.

Hare knelt, touched the toothpaste with his finger, then picked up something and held it out. It was the toothpaste tube, empty, rolled flat.

'He was here,' she said, staring wide-eyed at the writing. 'He did that.'

'Who, Sam?'

'Slider.'

He gazed around the room again.

'I didn't do all this,' she said. 'Not on my own. And I couldn't have reached . . . not with the wires—' She raised her hands and felt the wires. They were all still in place.

Hare looked back down at her, his eyes darting about her face, then at Laszlo.

'How's the graph?' she said, feeling anger suddenly, anger and confusion and fear and shock battling it out inside her head. 'Everything's fine, is it? Showing sweet dreams? Any abnormalities?'

Hare turned to Laszlo. 'I think we'd better – ah – disconnect.'

Laszlo smirked and raised his eyebrows.

Sam watched them both.

What the hell's up with you two? Is this some kind of a game? Think it's funny? Great hocus-pocus? Christ. Then she realised: he was smirking, but it wasn't humour, no, not at all. He was grimacing. He just looked like he was smirking when he was grimacing. Hare didn't think it was funny either. He was shaking like a leaf, like a rabbit.

Like someone seriously shit scared.

She looked away, around the room, then back at Hare again. Could see the terror in his eyes.

And suddenly she understood why.

33

She'd stayed awake most of the rest of the night, in numb silence. Hare had sat in the room with her, hunched in a chair much like he was hunched in a chair now opposite her in the pub, by the window that looked out on the main road outside the university.

AROLEID.

What the hell did Aroleid mean? Was it an anagram? DIE LORA? DIE ORAL? Riddles. No good at riddles.

AROLEID.

You've got the really big fall to come.

Falling? Was it something to do with falling? Hare was blinking quizzically. God, the poor sod looked awful. Couldn't have slept at all. Not in a chair. He said something to her, but the pub was filling up with its lunchtime trade, and it was getting harder to hear his soft voice above the babble of conversation and the roar of the traffic outside. 'Pardon?'

'I hope you didn't mind coming here?'

'It's fine,' she said, relieved not to be in his bedsitting room, not in that room. That was clear. Clear as daylight. Jesus. Fine cold jets of water sprayed her insides; needle sharp they hurt, stung, flooding her with icy coldness that got into her blood and filled everywhere in her body. She looked at him, into his tired, frightened eyes, and took a deep breath.

'It wasn't your wife, was it, who smashed your room up?' she said.

He sat for a long time in silence, before he finally replied. 'No,' he said.

'It was someone – some *thing* that didn't want you to help me, wasn't it?'

He continued staring. Staring right through her. As if he was watching some private movie. Then he raised his shoulders and nodded lamely, eyes wide open, like a frightened animal. So frightened it scared her too. His mouth twitched, and he locked his fingers together, then pulled them apart, slowly, one at a time.

'There is a scientific explanation.' He picked up his glass shakily and drank some beer, then wiped his beard with the back of his hand. 'Disturbances . . . energy.' He nodded as if that was it. Simple.

'I'm not quite with you.'

He seemed reluctant to go on and hesitated, locked

his fingers again, then unlocked them. 'Our brain waves give out terrific energy. Incredible energy – particularly if we are in any state of excitement – I—' He stopped whilst a waitress brought over their lasagnes and set them down. Steam rose up between them.

'Anxiety – that sort of thing – can transmit. It's possible, of course, that I picked up your anxiety and the energy set off a chain reaction in the energy patterns of my room affecting the electro-magnetic polarisation of the – ah – molecules in . . . It's what is sometimes called the poltergeist phenomenon.'

'Doesn't poltergeist mean "angry spirit"?'

'Well literally it means "noisy spirit". In German.' He dug his fork warily into his lasagne, as if worried it might be booby-trapped. 'They do good food.'

'Looks delicious,' she said flatly. She lifted up a forkful of scalding microwaved pasta, but she had no appetite, and lowered it.

'If you come up again, I'd like you to meet other people who have premonitions – to know that you are not alone.' He put his fork down and sipped his beer, gazing at her with his worried eyes. 'I'd be grateful if you would come up, or I could come down to Sussex. I really would like to make further studies. Most fascinating – it could be most valuable.'

'Have other people had as many as me?'

He seemed to relax a fraction. 'Oh yes, I—' He paused – 'I would say yes.' He frowned. 'It's a question of logging your future ones now, isn't it? Seeing which of those come true.'

'What I want to know is where do premonitions – precognitions, whatever you call it – come from?'

'Ah. Well, that's the big one. That's what we are trying to discover here. We are working on three theories. We are not looking at anything that can be dismissed as coincidence, or self-fulfilling prophecy; we are studying case histories only of people who genuinely seem able to see into the future . . . Real time. Does that mean anything to you?'

Sam shook her head.

He turned a layer of cheese over with his fork, peering at the meat it uncovered, swivelled round to study the crowd of people behind them, a rag-bag mixture of businessmen, students, building labourers, then turned back to her.

'Real time is the theory that you tune into people's thoughts, telepathically – unintentionally, of course. You see, you may have tuned into the pilot, tele-pathically. Maybe he had a drink problem, or some other problem, and he knew the plane was going to crash when he next flew to Bulgaria. Perhaps he was going to do it deliberately – commit suicide. Perhaps you picked those signals up.'

'Read his mind?'

'Yes. Picked up his thoughts. Even the sort of dia-logue he knew he would have with his co-pilot.' He smiled. 'The child who fired the shotgun and the rapist in the underground station – you could have tuned into them, into their thoughts, in your dream state.'

She felt an uncomfortable tightening in her throat, and stared down at her fingernails. They were looking worse. 'If I'm picking things up telepathically, why don't I get more things – your thoughts, my husband's, people walking down the street?'

'The air is full of signals – radio signals, light waves, sound waves. We only pick up a narrow band of them. Either our brain is incapable of receiving the rest, or it filters them out, keeping only what we need. It's pos-sible something's gone wrong with your filtering system and in your sleep you're picking up bits of thought from other people.'

'Would they show on your graphs?'

'We're hoping so. We're hoping we may find some common irregularity in people who have premonitions.'

'What about mine, last night?'

'Unfortunately, we didn't record you for long enough. The only thing was you – when you went to sleep, you did seem to go into REM sleep quickly – but that often happens in a strange environment.'

'How does this telepathy theory explain my balcony dream?'

'Dreams can be very obscure. Premonitive or pre-cognitive dreams get mixed up with the dream processes and buried in symbols. It's one of our biggest difficulties, to separate it all out. The true meanings are often concealed, and need interpreting. I'm sure far more people have premonitions than ever realise it, because they don't analyse their dreams.'

'What symbols do you mean between the balcony and scaffold?'

'Well, falling – in a woman – often relates to falling to – ah – yielding to sexual advances—' He fidgeted with his hands. 'Ah – intercourse.'

Good old Sigmund. Knew you couldn't keep out of this.

She felt her face going bright red.

The dream was nothing to do with the scaffold.

Was it?

She saw him looking quizzically, saw from his expression that he realised he had touched a nerve.

'Symbolism . . .' he said, trying to move on quickly. 'It's not always correct, you see.'

'What are the other theories?'

'The supernatural, of course.' He prodded his lasagne

with his fork, pricking it all over, as if trying to let the steam out. As if trying to exorcise the steam.

'Do you believe in the supernatural?'

'Ah.' He turned the fork over in his hand. 'I'm a scientist. Officially we're not allowed to believe in the supernatural.'

'And unofficially?'

'It's a question of definition.'

'Do you believe in ghosts?'

He scratched his beard then his cheek and lowered his head a fraction. 'I don't have any – evidence – of a connection between ghosts and precognition.'

'What about Slider?'

'You think he's a ghost – a spirit – haunting you from the past?'

'What do you think?'

He plucked up sudden courage and put a forkful of lasagne in his mouth. A tiny morsel fell away and tumbled through his beard like an acrobat in a safety net. He chewed thoughtfully. 'I think he's very interesting. Most bogeymen get left behind in childhood. He could simply be an embodiment of your fears. That whenever you are afraid – whenever your brain picks up danger – it translates it into this grotesque image. It's saying to you "Slider, watch out," as if it was saying "Red Alert".'

'So when he appears in a dream, I know that I have to be careful – that something's going to come true?'

'It seems that way, doesn't it?' He dug some more lasagne with his fork. 'I think it's important for you to try to work things out, to find the meanings. There's a paper I've written on just this. I'll nip over and get you a copy. I think you'll find it helpful.'

'Thank you.'

He smiled. 'The other theory we are working on and

feel has currency is the time warp theory. Do you understand time, at all?'

'Vaguely, I suppose.'

'I won't blind you with science, but we believe there do exist different spheres and planes – different dimensions of time – and that in the dream state some people tune into those—' He raised his hands – 'by design or by accident we don't know.' He toyed with his shirt collar. 'You are frightened that our hooded man is a ghost of someone from the past, haunting you, but I would tend to take the view from what you have told me that he's not a ghost from the past at all. I think it is possible that he's someone in the present, now, who is bothering you, worrying you – someone that you are associating with this Slider.'

She felt the coldness again, much more now, spreading out around her body just beneath her skin. She saw that the table was shaking, then realised that it was her hands holding onto the edge of it that were making it do that. Her legs were crashing together. Everything seemed to have gone out of focus.

'What—' Her voice was trembling. 'What sort of person?'

He was looking at her anxiously. 'Someone you know, perhaps, who makes you feel uncomfortable? Someone you don't like, or don't trust? Someone who reminds you of this hooded one-eyed man? I don't know. I don't want to put thoughts into your mind. It's just a possibility that you're seeing something bad connected with this man.' He shrugged. 'It may be nothing.'

Andreas? she thought. Andreas? Tell him about Andreas? No, stupid. There's no connection.

'Maybe Hampstead?' he said. 'Maybe you saw him in Hampstead – or someone who resembled him? Reminded you of him?' He checked his watch. 'Just a theory, of course. You've got a train to catch. I'll just nip over quickly and get that paper for you. Two minutes.'

He drained his beer, stood up and hurried out of the pub. She watched him through the window as he ran to the edge of the pavement and waited for a gap in the stream of lorries, then she looked down at her lasagne, and cut a piece with her fork.

There was a fierce squeal of brakes, and a thud like a sledgehammer hitting a sack of potatoes. She spun around and looked back out of the window, and saw Hare hurtle up in the air then disappear. She heard slithering tyres and a dull metallic bang, then more slithering and another bang.

Someone screamed.

Herself.

Then someone else. She leapt up from her seat, sending her chair crashing backwards, ran, barged into someone, knocking their drink flying. 'Sorry, so sorry.' Out of the way! Oh please get out of the way! She lunged for the door. 'Excuse me, excuse me. Colin!' She burst out of the door, then stood and blinked.

Hare was standing on the pavement, waiting to cross.

'Dr Hare! Colin! Colin! Don't!'

There was a gap in the traffic and he sprinted out into the middle of the road.

'No! Dr Hare! No!'

She saw the truck. Heard the fierce squeal of brakes, and the thud, like a sledgehammer hitting a sack of potatoes, and Hare disappeared. She heard slithering tyres and a dull metallic bang, then more slithering and another bang.

'Dr Hare! Colin! No. No, please God, *nooo*.'

The door behind her opened and she heard footsteps.

Car doors were opening. Someone hooted. She heard the hiss of air brakes. The rattle of a diesel engine.

She inched forward, clutching her thighs with her hands, then sprinted over, pushed past the crowd that was already forming, looked, saw his body face down, his head somewhere underneath the massive wheel of the artic, a stain of blood and – something else – spreading out beside it.

She turned away, staggered, bumped into someone, apologised, knelt down and vomited violently.

34

The room was warm and the tea was hot and sweet, treacly sweet, and she sipped some down, felt it slipping down her throat and into her stomach, felt the warmth of its spreading out inside her, then she had to put the mug down because it was too hot to hold. She put it on the vinyl table top beside the words which looked freshly carved into it.

FUCK ALL PIGS.

She was surprised it hadn't been noticed and covered up or removed. Perhaps it happened all the time? Then as she watched them, they changed.

AROLEID.

The police officer smiled at her from across the table, a big teddy bear of man in his blue serge jacket and his silver buttons and a coating of dandruff on both shoulders, and a face that looked as though it would like to change the world but didn't know how.

'Drink some more, love, drink it all up. It'll make you feel better.'

Sam nodded and picked the cup up again, but she was shaking too much and hot tea slopped over the rim and scalded her hands. She put it back down and a puddle spread out around it. 'Sorry. So sorry.'

'Doesn't matter, love. Let it cool a bit.'

She fumbled in her bag, pulled out her handkerchief and wiped her hands, then dabbed her mouth. She'd rinsed it out, but she could still taste the bile. She looked around the room: small, dull, an interview room with hard lecture hall chairs, green paint on the walls, flaking, chipped, a big chunk missing on the far side – was that where they had banged some punk's head while they were interviewing him?

The police officer read through her statement again slowly out aloud to her. 'Anything else you'd like to add, love?'

Yes.

I caused it.

I killed Tanya Jacobson, and now Dr Hare. They both died because – because they might have been able to help me?

So why hadn't Bamford O'Connell died? Because he hadn't tried? Had Ken tried?

'All right, love?'

She sat up with a start, blinking. 'Sorry. I—'

'Would you like to lie down somewhere, for a while?'

She felt her stomach heave. 'I'll be all right, thank you. I should get back to – back down – to London.'

'There's someone come from the university to run you to the station.'

'Thank you. That's – very – kind.'

He pushed the statement across the table to her. 'If you wouldn't mind just signing that. I don't know if the coroner will want you for the inquest. He'll write if he does.'

She followed him out into the front of the police station and to her surprise saw Laszlo sitting, waiting.

He stood up, his face ashen, the black rings around his eyes even more pronounced, and as she saw him she began to cry. She felt the kindly pat of the police officer's arm on her shoulder and heard him speak.

'She's suffering from shock, I'm afraid. I have suggested we run her up to the hospital, but she wants to get back to London.'

Then she was outside in the bright cold light, climbing into Laszlo's beat-up 2CV Citroën. He clipped her seat belt and closed her door for her, then got in himself and started the engine. She listened to its high-pitched lawn-mower whine.

'Thank you,' she said.

'I think there are trains quite often.'

'Yes.'

He drove in silence for a few minutes. 'Terrible,' he said suddenly. 'This is so terrible.'

'Yes.'

'He was the whole department. He knew so much. It was all just beginning.'

'Nice. He was so nice.' She felt tears running down her cheeks and didn't brother to wipe them

'He was a very dedicated man. Maybe he was too dedicated.'

'What do you mean?'

He turned and glanced at her. 'You know what I mean.' He braked at a traffic light.

She looked at him, but there was nothing in his face, just an emptiness as if he'd put up a sign which said 'SORRY, CLOSED FOR THE SEASON, GONE AWAY.'

'I feel responsible,' she said. 'I feel that I caused it.'

'No,' he said, and the sharpness of his reply surprised her. The light changed and they drove on. 'You know

what they say, Mrs Curtis. You know the expression.
"If you can't stand the heat get out of the kitchen".'

'What do you mean?'

'If seeing the future frightens you, don't go looking for it.'

She stared numbly ahead. Her head was pounding and her stomach was heaving again. 'I'm not looking for it.'

'Why have you come here then?'

'Because I want to stop. I want to stop seeing the future. I don't want to see it any more.'

'You've gone too far down the road. You can't stop.'

'Why not?'

'Existence is full of crossover points, Mrs Curtis. Countries have boundaries. Life has a boundary of death. The earth's gravity has a boundary beyond which it cannot pull. When you start to look into the paranormal you remain a spectator up to a certain boundary. When you cross over that, you become a participant. Do you understand?'

She frowned at him, trembling.

'When you are looking into the future, you are look-ing beyond the earth's plane, Mrs Curtis. If you look long enough, you cross that boundary and you become part of the future.'

'I – I don't really understand.'

'I think you do. You understand the forces that are around you, that you brought into the laboratory last night. I could see on your face that you understood.'

'I didn't understand last night.'

'Didn't you?' he said, almost bitterly.

'Do you think I deliberately killed Dr Hare? Do you think that I—?'

They pulled into the station and she wished that they hadn't arrived. Laszlo wanted her out, out of his car, his town, his life, wanted her out as fast as he could make her go. 'I think you have a bad energy force around you, Mrs Curtis. It's . . . maybe making bad things happen because it's confusing things, confusing people.'

'What energy force? Where's it coming from?'

He switched off the engine and unclipped his seat belt. 'I think there is a train in about five minutes. If you hurry.'

She climbed out of the car and he lifted her overnight bag off the back seat and carried it into the station for her. 'You have your ticket?'

She nodded.

'That platform there.'

'Can I ask you just one thing, please?'

He said nothing.

'If this is how you feel about seeing the future, why have you been working with Dr Hare?'

'Because I thought that I wanted to know,' he said, and turned away. He stopped and half turned back round. 'I was wrong.'

She watched him walk out of the station without looking at her again, heard the slam of a car door and the lawnmower whine of a 2CV engine, and the crash of the gears. As if he could not drive away fast enough.

35

It was eight o'clock in the evening when she got back to Wapping. Richard hadn't come home yet; Helen was in her room watching television and Nicky was lying in bed, awake, looking miserable. She sat down beside him and hugged him hard, but his face did not change.

'I don't want you and Daddy to go away again, Mummy. It's not fair. You're always away.'

297

'It's only a week, Tiger. Mummy and Daddy have got to spend some time together.' She hugged him again, and kissed his forehead. It was a cold dry night and a strong wind was blowing, nearly a gale, and the water was slapping around in the river outside. She looked down at him, and wished she could tell him the truth: that she didn't want to go away either, that she was worried about leaving him alone, even though he would be staying with friends and would have a good time with them. She didn't want to tell him that she was scared to go.

Scared as hell.

She told him a story, then started another one and he finally fell asleep. She went out, closing the door behind her and walked through into the living area. The phone started to ring and she went over to Richard's desk and answered it.

'Yes? Hallo?'

'Sam?'

'Ken!' She felt excitement surging through her. 'Ken! You're back!'

'How's everything?'

'Oh – everything is – well – it's—' But suddenly she couldn't speak any more; her voice seemed to catch in her throat and her eyes flooded with tears. She began shaking, shaking so much she dropped the phone. It hit the floor and a bit chipped off the mouthpiece. She bent down and picked it up.

'Sam? Sam? What's up? Are you OK? On your own? Want me to come over? Want to come over here?' he asked when she did not reply. 'Or meet somewhere?'

'I'll—' She forced the words out – 'I'll come over. Be there as soon as I—' She hung up and sniffed, staring bleakly out through the window. Then she dried her eyes and knocked on Helen's door to tell her she was going out.

She sat at the traffic light at the edge of Clapham Common and the Jaguar's engine died on her. She pressed the starter button and it rumbled into life again, and she blipped the accelerator hard: there was a crackling roar and a cloud of oily blue smoke swirled through the darkness around her. Haven't taken the car for a decent run for weeks, she thought, blipping it again. It backfired with a loud bang, crackled and chucked out even more smoke as she accelerated when the lights changed, then she slowed down, turned into the driveway of the huge Victorian monstrosity of a house and pulled up behind the Bentley.

The front door opened as she climbed out of the car.

'Ken!' She flung her arms around him and hugged him hard, showering him in tears from her madly blinking eyes.

'Sam! What's—?' He held onto her tightly and hugged her back. She broke away and he looked at her. 'Christ, what's happened? You—' He hesitated. 'Come on, let's get you a drink.'

'Are you alone?'

He smiled. 'Yes. Only got back from Spain an hour ago. I rang you because I won't be in tomorrow – have to go down to Bristol.' He closed the front door and she followed him through the hallway, with its two suits of armour, glancing warily at the eye slits, past another waxwork of Ken sitting in a wicker chair – had he bought up a job lot? – and a ten-foot-high surreal picture of a wild pig leaping between two mountain peaks, past a juke box and into the drawing room with its minstrels' gallery and a Wurlitzer on the floor underneath, and more big paintings, a Hockney and a

299

Lichtenstein and a spoof Picasso portrait of Arianna Stassinopoulos Huffington by Georges Sheridan, and the roaring fire in the Adam fireplace which Ken had salvaged from somewhere or other. The television was on; *Miami Vice*, it looked like.

She sat down on a high-backed antique sofa that swallowed her up, and Ken went out of the room for a minute, then came back in with a tumbler in his hand. 'This is a really fine malt. Islay. You'll like it. Get it down you.'

She drank some, and then some more and it burned some of the churning out of her stomach.

'How was Spain?' she asked, looking down into the glass.

'Fine. Went well.' He lit a cigarette and sat down on the equally huge sofa opposite her.

'I shouldn't be here,' she said, 'it's dangerous, you see – for you—' Then the tears exploded as if a pipe had burst somewhere in her head.

Ken came and sat down beside her. She looked at him through her streaming eyes.

'I'm frightened for you, Ken. I think you could be – I think you've got to be really careful.'

'Careful of what?'

'I have a bad energy force around me,' she blurted.

He put his arm around her. 'Have you had another dream?' he asked gently.

'Sharp antennae,' she said, and she told him about the fall from the scaffold and her trip to Hull, told him everything that happened, and all she could remember of what Hare and Laszlo had said.

He sipped his drink and stubbed out his cigarette, blowing the last lungful of smoke up at the fresco of plump naked cherubs on the ceiling. 'You think this Dr Hare was killed because he was trying to help you? That

300

his flat got smashed up by some spirit, as a warning, and because he ignored the warning he was killed?'

Sam watched the flickering flames of the fire, and nodded. 'I'm not sure how much more of any of this I can take.'

'You're having a rough time of it, aren't you? The scaffold – all this in Hull.' He squeezed her shoulders. 'I think we've got to try to take a balanced view on everything. I know it all seems horrific, but the human mind is a strange thing, Sam; we're very susceptible. It's still possible that a lot of what's going on is getting over dramatised.'

'You're beginning to sound like Bamford O'Connell.'

He smiled. 'Not quite as bad. I do believe you've had some premonitions – the aeroplane and the tube station – but the balcony is pretty iffy, Sam. This man getting run over – Dr Hare – is horrendous, but you said how dangerous that road was, that he was flaked out after a night awake and had drunk a pint of beer. We have to try to keep a balanced view, that's all.'

She pressed her lips tightly together and said nothing. Ken leaned his head back against the cushions. 'Or I deal!'

'Pardon?'

'Or I deal!'

'Or you deal?'

'Aroleid? That word? "Or I deal" – it's an anagram.'

'Or I deal? Doesn't mean anything to me.'

He clicked his fingers. 'Got it! "I reload!" '

'I reload,' she echoed.

'This Slider – he was wearing a green motorcycling suit, and gave you an airline ticket? Chartair?'

'Yes. The same one he gave me in the taxi after we had lunch. You know, after the Chartair disaster. I remember the seat number. 35A. And he said that I was wrong to think the scaffold was the big fall.'

Ken looked hard at her. 'It seems that it's more likely a bad dream connected with the disaster and your fall. You're bound to keep thinking about it.'

'I can accept that, I suppose. I can accept that much more easily than—' She turned the glass around in her hands.

They sat in silence. 'OK. So what are we going to do with you now? Wrap you up in cotton wool until the dreams all go away? Putting you in a padded cell would seem the safest for everyone.' He grinned, then saw she was not smiling, not smiling at all, but nodding in agreement. He touched her cheek with his knuckles. 'You're going to be OK, Sam, you're one of life's survivors.'

'Oh yes?'

'Look—' He lit another cigarette. 'I think you may have made a mistake dashing off up to Hull so soon after your fall.'

'Why?'

'This may sound hard, and it's not meant to: I think you are panicking. You've got yourself into a state, and you've got to let yourself come down out of it. I think you need to go away. As I said last week, have a holiday. Try to forget about it all. Really relax.'

'I'm going on Saturday. Skiing for a week with Richard. I've sorted everything out in the office. Is that OK?'

'Of course. But you've got to relax, OK? Take a hard look at everything and see if it still looks the same afterwards – I think you'll find it won't.'

'I hope you're right,' she said.

'So do I. Come on, I'll buy you some dinner – I bet you haven't eaten. Are you hungry?'

'Not really.'

'You should eat something.'

'I'll take you. I'll treat you.'

'It's a deal.' He stood up and drained his glass. 'Be a great Scrabble word that.'

'What word?'

'Aroleid. Makes a lot of words. I thought of another: Redial.'

'That's not using all the letters.'

'Did your hooded motorcyclist tell you you had to?'

Sam looked at him anxiously. 'Please, Ken. Be careful.'

They went out into the hallway and he slipped up the visor of one of the suits of armour. 'It's OK, Sam. I've got my own hooded men with slits for eyes. They'll kick yours to pieces if he tries messing around here.'

He let go of the visor and it shut with a loud clang.

36

GATWICK AIRPORT.

The blue and white motorway sign with its symbol of an aeroplane flashed past.

'Out of the way, you prick!' Richard pressed the horn, flashed his lights, then accelerated hard as the car in front finally moved over. Sam watched the BMW's wipers shovelling the cold February rain off the windscreen. There was a loud slap and spray from a lorry blinded them for a moment.

The same dream. Thursday night, and again last night. The fan on the ceiling, rotating, getting faster, faster. The fan she had dreamed of in the laboratory. The fan that was like a propeller. Then she would wake, shivering, in a sweat. That was all. Just that. It had stayed with her all yesterday and all of today.

She'd sent flowers to Colin Hare's funeral. She

thought about writing a note, but in the end she'd asked them to put her name on the card and nothing else.

There was a deafening roar and a Jumbo sank down towards them. Flaps and undercarriage lowered, it passed slowly overhead and down out of sight behind some warehouses. She waited for an explosion, for a dull boom and sheeting flame; but there was nothing.

Richard braked, then accelerated again.

'You're driving fast,' she said.

'We're late.' He pressed the horn, angrily blasting at a car that pulled out in front of them. 'I got a couple of bucket seats. I couldn't get us on a schedule as everything to Geneva was booked. The whole world's going skiing these days. 'S all right – it's a good airline.'

'Which one?'

'Chartair . . . Come on, you arsehole, move over.'

Chartair.

Chartair.

She stared through the windscreen at the black blades of the wipers scything backwards and forwards.

Like propellers.

'Do airliners have propellers?' she asked.

'Only small planes do.'

'So the sort of plane we're going on wouldn't have any?'

'They haven't for about thirty years.'

'I thought they had tiny little propellers, inside the engines.'

'They have fan blades. To compress the air.'

Fan blades.

She heard the clicking of the indicator, and saw the turn-off ahead.

'I wish we were taking Nicky,' she said, 'He's old enough to start skiing now.'

'Next year,' Richard said.

Next year. Would there be a next year? 'I feel lousy leaving him alone again. All I ever seem to do is leave him.'

'He'll be OK. Fine. He's an independent little chap.'

Independent. That was what her uncle and aunt used to say about her. Their way of justifying ignoring her. *Oh you needn't worry about Samantha. She's an independent little girl.*

She thought of the plane taking off in the teeming rain, taking off into the swirling grey sky. The vortex. You swirled through the vortex into the void. You stayed in the void for ever.

The car slowed, then accelerated up the ramp. 'We're fucking late. I'll drop you. Grab a porter or a trolley and get checked in while I park.'

She wheeled the trolley through the jam-packed departure concourse, steered it through lines of people who were queuing in every direction, so many queues they all seemed to meet together somewhere in the middle in a solid wedge of baggage and anoraks and fraying tempers. An old man was driven through them in a buggy, leaning back under his panama hat, looking around with a bewildered expression as if he thought he was in a rickshaw in another century.

Please don't fly, she wanted to shout. Not today. You'll be dead. Some of you. It's dangerous today. She bit her lip. Relax, for Christ's sake. Millions of planes, every day. Everyone flies. Like a bus; only safer.

Beng-bong. 'Will Mr Gordon Camping please go to the Airport Information Desk.'

She saw the row of Chartair check-in counters, saw signs on the wall saying GENEVA, MALAGA, VENICE, and joined the shortest queue. Come on, come on. She looked at her watch. The queue moved forward a fraction and a man with a face like a nodding dog rammed her legs from behind. She turned round to glare, but he hadn't noticed and a moment later he did it again. She spun round, angrily, wincing in pain.

'Why don't you have a driving lesson?' she said.

'Can I have your tickets please, Madam? Madam? Madam?'

Sam fumbled in her bag and pulled out the small folder. She put it down on the desk top.

The girl pulled the tickets out and frowned. 'You're late for that flight. It closed twenty minutes ago.'

'I – the – traffic—' she said lamely.

The girl reached under her desk and pulled out a phone. 'I'll have to ring through.'

Sam stood, waiting, looking around to see if Richard had arrived yet. No sign of him.

'All right,' said the girl. 'You're lucky. How many pieces are you checking through?'

'Two.' Sam heaved the bags onto the conveyor and the girl glanced at the weight on her dial. She peeled two numbers off the chart in front of her, stuck them onto two orange and white boarding cards, and handed them to Sam.

Sam glanced down and saw the number on the top one.

35A.

No.

Joke.

The check-in desk came towards her, banged her knees. She stumbled backwards, tripped over the nodding dog's trolley, grabbed his shoulder and sent his cases flying.

The check-in girl was watching her strangely, oddly, hostile.

Sam's face was burning hot. 'I'm sorry . . . is it possible . . . different seats?'

'Absolutely not,' said the girl. 'The flight is completely full.'

Sam saw the bags beginning to move along the conveyor, and she lunged forward and grabbed them, pulling them back onto the floor.

'They're checked through, Madam,' said the girl.

Her mouth tasted as if she had bitten into a lemon, and she screwed up her eyes, feeling spikes shooting into her brain like splinters of glass, and held onto the desk top for support.

The girl was looking at her as if she was mad.

Don't you realise? You stupid dumb check-in girl? Your plane's going to crash? They're all going to be . . .

'You can have these back,' Sam said. 'I'm afraid – you see – we can't go.'

'We can't resell the tickets for you, and they are not transferable.'

'Fine, that's fine.' Sam dumped the boarding cards on the desk top, heaved the cases back onto her trolley, and started to battle her way back across the concourse.

She saw Richard, sprinting, dodging through the crowds, dressed as if he was off for a day's shooting, in his sleeveless puffa, striped shirt and green cords, his face sweating.

'Hi,' he said. 'What's up?'

She felt her face redden, then a tear roll down her cheek.

'Oh, shit. We've missed it?'

Sam nodded.

He looked at his watch. 'Forty minutes. It doesn't take off for another forty minutes. This is fucking ridiculous. I'll get the manager. I've met the fucking guy who owns this airline. Tom Chartwell – he's a friend of Archie's. I'll sort them out.'

'No.'

'What do you mean?'

'I don't want to.'

'Want to what?'

'I don't want to get on the plane.'

'What do you mean?'

She lowered her head, and pulled out her handkerchief. She squeezed her eyes shut against her tears, against her hopeless feeling of foolishness. 'I can't do it.' She waited for his explosion. Instead, she felt his arms around her, warm and gentle.

'You really are in a bad way, aren't you? I thought that – the two of us going away together, y'know?' He sighed.

Someone barged into them, and apologised. She scarcely noticed. 'I want to,' she said. 'I do want to. But I can't get on that plane. Something's going to happen to it.'

There was a loud pop and the sound of splintering glass, right behind her.

She shrieked and spun round. Then she closed her eyes and breathed in, as she saw a man kneel down and stare ruefully at the golden brown liquid gushing from his dropped duty-free bag.

'Are you going to tell them?'

'Tell them?'

'Yes,' Richard said, almost shouting. 'Tell them.'

She dabbed her eyes.

'Are you, Bugs?' he said harshly. 'Are you going to bloody tell them? Why don't you go and announce it over the tannoy? Tell them. Chartair flight CA29 is going to fucking crash?'

She tried to think it through. Tried to imagine walking up to Airport Information. 'Excuse me. I've had a dream a couple of times . . . well, actually about your plane that crashed – the one in Bulgaria. Well, you won't believe it, but I think this one's a-goner too. You see, Slider, this hooded bogeyman has turned up twice, in two dreams, with this boarding card. 35A. Well, you see – that's the card I was given for this flight, so it's obvious, isn't it?'

'We could drive, Richard,' she said. 'I don't mind, if you're tired, doing the driving.'

'Have you dreamed this plane's going to crash?' he asked.

'I can't get on it.'

'Is it going to crash?'

'I don't know.'

'Are you going to tell someone?'

'Something's going to happen, but I don't know what. I don't know if it's going to crash – or—'

'Bugs, I've got to get to Switzerland. I have to be there Monday morning. Things are getting—' He looked around nervously at a policeman who was standing near them, and lowered his voice. 'I could end up with everything bloody frozen; I've got to move quickly now. If you don't want to come, I'll go on my own.'

'I do want to come . . . it's twenty to three now. We could be in Dover in a couple of hours, take the ferry or the Hovercraft, drive through the night and we could be in Geneva by two or three in the morning. It's Sunday tomorrow, and you haven't got to be there until Monday.'

'Montreux,' he said.

'It's only a short way further.'

'I was looking forward to a nice day tomorrow. I was hoping we could take a boat out on the lake.'

'We can,' she said.

'Are we all right to drive?'

'What do you mean?'

'No weird dreams about driving?'

She wiped her eyes again. 'No.'

She waited whilst he went to fetch the BMW and watched the cars and taxis that pulled up, emptying out people who put their arms up against the sheeting rain and sprinted for trolleys. There was a mocking laugh right behind her.

Slider's laugh.

She turned around. A man's suitcase had burst open, spilling its contents over the floor. He knelt down to scoop them up, and his companion laughed again. An unpleasant gloating laugh that went on and on, getting louder, until it was so loud it was deafening her and she couldn't stand it any longer. She pushed her trolley away through the crowds, pushed it along the pavement, until she was past the shelter of the awning and on her own, a solitary figure drenched in the torrenting rain and in her fear.

37

The bed felt strange. Huge. Soft. Too soft. She moved slightly, heard the clank of a spring and felt a slight reverberation somewhere beneath her.

There was a warmth and brightness in the light that flooded into the room soaking up her waking fears. Headlights strobing past. Stiff policemen at the border. *Non!* You are the woman who dreams. You are not welcome in Switzerland. Why are you coming here? Please go away. Take your dreams away with you.

We are coming to ski.

You are not coming to ski. You are coming to fiddle with the great Swiss banking system.

Sunlight streamed in through the gap in the curtains and lit up a section of the wall to her right. There was a faint whirring sound above her and a gentle draught of air. She looked up and saw the blades of a fan turning slowly.

She pulled herself up in bed a fraction, watching the fan warily, then fumbled on her bedside table for her watch. She felt the base of a lamp, then the leather strap, and picked up the Rolex, holding it dangling in front of her face, staring at the twin dials. It took her a moment to work it out. Eleven-forty. She had a slight headache, she realised, heaving herself further up and taking a sip of water, the same ache she seemed to have had for weeks, a dull pain that sometimes got turned up and was sharper, but never stopped. Her back was aching too, from the soft mattress, far too soft. It felt as if the bed had half collapsed under her.

The noise of the fan altered slightly, became a fraction louder, and she looked up at it again. It seemed to be wobbling as if it were loose.

She wondered where Richard was. The door to the bathroom was ajar but she could not hear any sounds from in there. She sipped some more water and looked around the room. A huge elegant room, grand and comfortably old-fashioned. Louis XIV furniture. A frieze of a bas-relief moulding around the ceiling. Soft pastel colours. A glass chandelier over the dressing table.

The noise above her became louder still, and she was nervous suddenly that the fan was going to fall down on top of her. Great. Terrific. Get killed by a ceiling fan that falls on you. She watched it, feeling increasingly uncomfortable. It was spinning faster; the draught was turning into a bitter howling blast. Her top sheet began to flap.

Christ.

It was wobbling more now and it still seemed to be

accelerating. Lines began to appear in the ceiling all around it, like veins in an old woman's hands. They got thicker, wider, and the ceiling began to sag, to swell. It looked like a huge cracked eggshell. Bits of the plaster fell away, crashing down around her, spraying fine white powder all around. The fan lurched drunkenly, and dropped several feet.

She screamed.

It hung at a weird angle, the blades only inches above her head now. Wiring spewed out all around it, the ceiling sagging, more chunks of white plaster tumbling all around her, the icy wind from the blades whipping her hair against her face, making her eyes smart and her lips hurt; the blades sagged more, lowering every second, lowering down towards her.

She threw herself sideways, rolling in terror to get away, but the sheets wrapped around her like nets, winding tighter as she rolled. She flung her weight against the side of the bed, feeling the chunks of plaster dropping around her, damp, icy cold, striking her head, her neck; she pulled, twisted wildly and flung herself sideways again; she felt the bedclothes give, and then she was free, falling. She tried too late to put her arms out, and hit the carpet hard with her face, painfully, rolled across and kept rolling until she crashed into the skirting board.

Then there was complete silence.

She lay back, gulping down air, feeling the perspiration trickling down her face and her body. There was a jangle of keys, and the sound of a door opening. A deep woman's voice, embarrassed, said '*Excusez-moi.*' and the door was shut hastily.

A spring clanked, and she felt a slight reverberation somewhere beneath her. Something felt odd, strange, not quite right.

Bed? Was she still in bed? The fan was still clattering, but it was quieter now. She opened her eyes and stared fearfully around. The room was filled with soft warm light, diffused through the heavy curtains. Everything was normal, calm. There was no wreckage. Nothing damaged. She glanced warily up at the ceiling, frowned, blinked. There was no fan. No cracked plaster. Just a crystal chandelier and elegant moulding. But she could still hear a fan.

Puzzled, she tried to put her hand out to the light switch, but could not move it. It was caught up in the sheet. Her whole body seemed caught up in it, as if it had been tied around her like a straitjacket. She sat up with a start, panicking, then realised it was just trapped underneath her, and she pulled it free.

She heaved herself up a fraction then fumbled on her bedside table for her watch. She felt the base of a lamp, then the leather strap, and picked up the Rolex, holding it in front of her face, staring at the dials. Eleven-forty.

That had been the time in the dream. Had it been a dream? She looked around, feeling disorientated. Her head ached, she realised, heaving herself further up, and taking a sip of water. Her back was aching too, from the soft mattress, far too soft. It felt as if the bed had half collapsed under her.

The pitch of the fan changed slightly, and it began to make a clacking sound. She looked up at the ceiling again, then realised it was coming from the bathroom. She slid out of bed, padded across the soft carpet to the bathroom door and looked in at the massive white bathtub and twin basins. It smelled of soap and cologne and there was a warm damp haze. A huge white towel was lying on the marbled floor, and the bath was wet, as if it had recently been used. Richard's paisley dressing gown was hanging on a hook on the door. Then she saw the fan, a small extractor on the wall above the lavatory seat. It sounded much louder in here.

She glanced in the mirror at her face and was shocked how puffy and tired she looked. She switched off the light, and the fan's motor cut out; the blades hummed, clacked a couple of times then stopped.

The silence felt strange, uncomfortable. She wrapped a towel around herself and walked across the room, drew the curtains and looked out of the window. Quiet, everything's so quiet, she thought. She opened the window. It was mild, warm in the sunlight, more like spring than February. She leaned on the sill and stared out at Lake Geneva, at the vast expanse of water that felt more like an ocean than a lake, except it was completely flat, as if the water had been stretched taut between the shores, like a giant canvas. Beyond, through the hazy light, she could see the French Alps, snow-covered, with craggy brown patches. Somewhere over to the right, through the haze, was Lausanne. And beyond, out of sight, at the end of the lake, was Geneva.

Below her an elderly well-dressed man with a bright cravat was walking a tiny terrier down a wooden pontoon; he stopped to gaze at the speedboats and small yachts that were moored to it, motionless, like toys, then peered down at the water, studying it carefully, as if trying to spot something he had dropped. She smelt a sudden whiff of cigar smoke, then the tang of the lake, almost salty.

Her head twinged. What time had they arrived? She tried to remember. About three. They'd stood outside ringing the bell until an elderly, grumpy night porter had opened up, and grudgingly carried their bags in.

A church bell rang twice then faded away into the silence. Peace, she thought. Peace. She watched a boat, a long way out, a smudge moving through the haze.

They had listened to the BBC news on the car radio as they had driven down through the night, in case, just in case, and there had been nothing up to the last news at midnight. No air disaster. Nothing at all. Chartair Flight CA29 had probably taken off and landed, like any other flight.

But if she had been on it? What then?

She turned and looked up at the chandelier and where the fan had been in her dream. So real. God, it had seemed so real. Like all the others . . . she turned back to the lake. Its stillness unsettled her. She heard the rattle of a key and the door opening behind her.

'Hi, Bugs, you're awake.'

'Just woke up.'

'I've arranged a boat,' he said. 'This afternoon. I thought we'd go out for a row after lunch.'

'Fine. Nice.' She noticed the wodge of newspapers under his arm. 'Are those today's?'

'Yah.' He put them down. The *Sunday Times* and the *Mail on Sunday*.

'From England already?'

'The Swiss are efficient.'

She scanned the front page of the *Mail*, and began to leaf through it.

'There's nothing, Bugs.'

'Nothing?'

'No air crash. That was what you wanted, wasn't it?'

She stared hard, trying to find the traces of satisfaction on his face, so she could shout, get mad at him. But there was no satisfaction. There was nothing but worry in his face. For her.

38

The gentle splash of the oars was the only noise that broke the silence on the lake. She leaned back in the tiny boat and trailed her finger over the side through the water. Icy cold. She pulled it out and rubbed it, then looked up at the mountains in the distance towering high above them. Everything seemed huge against the tiny insignificance of the boat.

It had been warm when they'd started out, almost hot, but the afternoon sun was fast losing its strength and wisps of white mist were rolling over the lake. She shivered, and watched a duck paddling on its own, a few feet from them, as if it was in the middle of a village pond.

'How are you feeling?' Richard said, pulling on the oars.

'OK. Tired.'

He looked tired too. White. Like a marble bust. Like a waxwork.

Like a corpse.

He'd scarcely spoken at lunch; they'd sat like two strangers forced to share a table. She thinking it through her way, Richard thinking it through his way, twitching his nose, lighting his cigarettes, drinking too much; beer, then wine, then cognac. She was surprised he hadn't gone to sleep, had still wanted to go out on the lake, as if there was some mission in it.

Maybe he hoped they'd fall in love again out here? Maybe some dream in his mind, some image, lazy days punting on the Cam. Summer. Summer was fine for boating on lakes. Right now it was still high winter. High winter and it was bloody freezing.

She hunched her arms up around herself, not wanting

to break the illusion, not wanting to say, For Chrissakes
let's get back before we die of pneumonia. Not romantic
that, not romantic at all. Hell we're here to give it a
chance. Give it your best shot. Heal the wounds. So let's
shiver it out.

A thin white trail of foam slid past them.

Like toothpaste.

*You little bitch. Think you're going to beat me with
high tech?*

'Are you getting cold, Bugs?'

'A little.' Somewhere in the distance she could hear a
strain of music, Buddy Holly's 'Every Day', as if someone had suddenly turned the volume up on a radio.
Then it stopped as abruptly as it had started. The same
song had been playing on the radio in the dream lab. She
tried to remember whether that had been in her dream,
or when she had been awake.

'Want to head back?'

She stared at the mist. Thickening clouds of it rolling
towards them.

'Yes,' she said, her mind churning. 'Let's go back.'
She watched Richard rowing in his chunky sweater and
his Ray-Ban glasses; trying to look young and trendy.
He could never look young. She'd never have loved him
if he had looked young. He had always looked middle-
aged. Like a father. 'What time is your meeting tomorrow?'

'Nine.'

'Will it be long?'

'Just have to sign a few papers.'

'What papers?'

'Just some banking things.'

'What sort of banking things?'

He grinned slyly. 'My disappearing act.'

'Disappearing?'

'Yes, I – Andreas is – he's set up this whole nominee chain. Absolutely brilliant. The money's being shunted all over the world – from Switzerland to the Dutch Antilles, then to Panama, then Liechtenstein, then back to Switzerland. Goes to a different set of nominees each time.' He shrugged as he saw her frown. 'Everyone does it.'

'Everyone?'

'Yah. Covers it up. Bloody Fraud Squad couldn't find who really owned it in a million years – nor could Interpol. No one could.'

A ball of mist rolled between them, making him hazy, like a shadow. She felt its icy breath.

Like a ghost.

She shivered. In the distance she could hear a faint thumping sound, and she turned, peering into the mist that was thickening around them. Row faster, she wanted to say, but she did not want him to see that she was scared. 'When do you think you'll know about—?'

He completely disappeared for a second in the mist. 'They've arrested the senior partner of our US affiliate and offered him a reduced sentence if he talks.'

'I meant what I said. I could, you know, support us if—'

The thumping sound was getting louder, nearer.

'It's going to be all right, Bugs. It's really smart, what Andreas has come up with. We're going to be fine.'

The mist closed silently around them and she could feel its icy tendrils dampening her hair. Her voice trailed, sounding flat, dead. She felt afraid. Afraid of being in this tiny boat in the mist. Afraid of the thumping.

Then she heard the rustle of water and the thrashing of an engine; closing on them. Fast.

'Can you hear that?' she said.

Richard took his sunglasses off and tucked them into his pocket. He watched the mist with a worried frown.

'Can you row a bit faster?'

He looked around. 'I'm not sure of my bearings. This damned mist has come down fast. It'll probably clear in a minute – it's only patchy.'

'Row, for Christ's sake!' she screamed, half standing up, then fell back in the boat, rocking it wildly, so wildly some water poured in over the gunwale.

'Bugs, be careful, don't make any sudden movement like that.'

She felt the icy water soaking her feet. 'It's coming at us,' she said. 'It's coming straight at us. Can't you hear it?'

'Did you dream this too?'

'I don't know. I don't know what the hell I dream.'

The thumping roar became louder, and she saw Richard squint through the mist.

'It'll be all right,' he said, pulling again on the oars. 'We'll just keep going.'

She turned around, craning her neck, trying to see through the dense white cloud.

Propeller.

She shivered again.

Propeller.

Not a fan.

Not a plane's propeller.

A boat's.

Then she saw the huge black shadow, almost on top of them.

'Hey!' she yelled. '*Hey!*'

Water smashed over them, stinging, hurting, hard as bullets, the boat plunged sideways then pitched madly, catapulting her forward off her seat onto the floor. Her face slammed into Richard's legs. She heard the thumping roar of the engine, the thrashing of the propellers, grinding, churning the water into a mad wild spray, throwing up huge heavy chunks that crashed down onto them, like a waterfall. They rolled crazily.

We're going to turn over, she thought.

Then there was silence.

It had gone.

Vanished.

Complete silence, apart from the slapping of water as the boat rocked in the wake.

Water was streaming down her face, oily, filthy water that tasted of spent fuel and stung her eyes. Richard's cavalry twill trousers were sopping wet, and his hair plastered down over his forehead. 'Are you OK?' he asked.

The boat lurched sideways.

'Where is it?'

'What an arsehole. Going that speed through this.'

'I can't hear it. Where's it gone? What was it, Richard? What the hell was it?' She crawled back onto her knees, then carefully sat back down, wiping the water from her eyes and pushing her hair back.

'Some sort of speed boat.'

'Why can't we still hear it?'

'What do you mean?'

'It's – like – it's just vanished,' she said. 'Into thin air.' She peered into the swirling whiteness, shaking with cold, with fear. Then she heard the whirring of a starter motor, the sharp boom of a powerful engine close by, like thunder, and the sound of thrashing water.

A voice called out of the mist. '*Allo? Ça va? Allo?*'

The engine revved a fraction, then died again. '*Allo?*'

A massive dark shape appeared behind Richard, then the mist cleared and she could see it was the stern of a large smart powerboat. A man was standing behind the wheel in a tartan jacket and a baseball cap, looking anxiously down. '*Pardon. Je m'excuse.*'

Behind him was a cabin with smoked glass windows and wide-slatted Venetian blinds, and Sam could see a figure behind the blinds, a man peering at them.

'You fucking loony!' shouted Richard.

'*Je m'excuse – je m'excuse.*' The driver raised his hands. '*Ça va?*'

Richard waved his hand dismissively. '*Ça va, allez, allez, ça va.*'

Sam caught the eye of the man behind the blinds, caught the malevolent smirk, caught the features just enough to be almost sure.

It was Andreas Berensen.

The driver pushed his gear lever forward with a loud clunk, and as the boat burbled slowly away from them, the mist lifted for a moment and they could see the shore clearly in the distance. Then the mist dropped down again like a stage curtain and the boat and the shoreline were gone.

'Did you see him?' Sam asked.

'Him? Who?'

'Your friend.'

'My friend?'

'Yes, your friend. Did you see him?'

'What do you mean, Bugs? My friend?'

'Andreas. He was on the boat.'

'Don't be fucking ridiculous.'

'He was watching us. I saw him in the cabin.'

'You think he'd have just stayed in and not come out? Andreas?' He laughed. 'He'd have come out, wouldn't he? He's one of my best friends. Christ, Bugs, you've really got a thing about him. You don't like him, do you? There wasn't anyone else on the boat. It's your mind playing up again.'

'I didn't imagine it. There was someone in the cabin. I'm certain it was Andreas.'

Richard shrugged. 'You're being daft, Bugs. I really think that – maybe – when we get back you ought to go and see Bamford.'

She turned and stared angrily into the mist, and listened to the sound of the boat accelerating off into the distance. As the burble of its engine faded, she could hear another sound, like distant laughter that rolled slowly across the lake as if it had been carried by the wind.

Except there was no wind.

39

The sunlight strobed at them through the fir trees, and she watched the three-pointed star on the end of the bonnet flickering like a dancer in a silent movie. The scenery passed by soundlessly, as if she was in a cocoon. The air inside the car was thick with the smell of new leather and she caressed the soft hide of her seat gently with her fingers, ran them along sensuously.

The pass dipped sharply down to the right, and there were a series of warning signs – thick, squiggly lines, two arrows, one black, one red, and a large exclamation mark. Richard braked, and she braced her feet in the thick carpeting in the foot-well. Strange, to see him sitting on her left, driving, she thought, trying to remember the reason why they were in this Mercedes and not his own BMW. She stared again at the vivid green colour of the bonnet. Vile. A vile colour for such an expensive car. Yuck.

They squealed around a hairpin bend, passed a small hut with a sign advertising ice cream and Löwenbrau, then crossed over a narrow stone bridge. A yellow PTT bus passed going the other way.

'Don't you think the colour of this car is horrible?' she said.

'Haven't got time to worry about the colour,' he said, and accelerated hard, with an angry look on his face. She felt the tyres scrabbling on loose grit, heard them squeal as they bit onto a stretch of fresh tarmac and the Mercedes yawed slightly. The engine bellowed and the car surged up the hill, past a marker post and a row of trees with white rings around them. The trees ended and they hurtled up a section of twisting road with a rock face rising steeply up to the left and an unguarded drop to the right, down into the fast-flowing river that was getting smaller beneath them.

She looked at him anxiously, unsure why he was driving so fast, too fast for the road and the size of the car, as they moved over even closer to the edge making space for a massive truck that was thundering down from the opposite direction; she felt the blast of its slipstream rock the Mercedes.

They squealed around a double hairpin, and to her relief she saw there was now a low stone wall at the edge of the road. A few hundred yards further on the right was a small lay-by, with a sign indicating a panoramic view. She heard the faint blaring of horns. A red Volkswagen came fast down the other way, then a motorbike, its engine revving with a caterwauling howl, followed by a white van.

She heard the horns again, closer now, vicious, angry blasts, and something made her shiver. She could see the road curving out of sight ahead, and they passed a road sign with a black curving line and a warning 40 KPH underneath.

Her seat belt seemed to tighten on her, jerking her

back into the seat so hard she could not breathe. A juggernaut was hurtling out of the bend on their side of the road, straight at them, its horn blaring, trying desperately to pass another juggernaut on its inside. She heard the screeching of the Mercedes's braking tyres, saw Richard stare wildly, first at the rock face to their left then at the drop of several hundred feet to their right. The juggernaut was almost on top of them, she could see the driver in the cab wrestling with his wheel, the helplessness on his face as his vehicle began to slew out away from the one it was overtaking. A gap began to open up, and for a moment she thought they might be able to squeeze through it.

Might.

Then it swerved crazily back the other way, hit the juggernaut it was overtaking and rebounded straight at them.

The front of it seemed to rear up towards them, a huge shadow like the mouth of a giant hungry insect, and she tried to duck down under the instrument panel, but her seat belt jerked her up. She heard the thundering of its engine, the piercing banshee of its horn, its hissing squealing brakes, its slithering tyres, all orchestrated into a deafening terrifying cacophony of destruction.

She saw the three-pointed star flick backwards, then the massive bumper of the juggernaut exploded through the windscreen, and she threw her hands up in front of her face as if she was going to be able to push it away, hold it off with them. She felt herself catapulted up, forwards, and an agonising pain as her head smashed into something hard, sharp.

There was a grinding, grating roar, and a terrible screeching of rubber and metal, and then she was outside, standing at the roadside in the lay-by, she realised, puzzled, watching as the juggernaut careered on wildly down the road with the Mercedes jammed under its cab, like a beetle with a fly in its mouth. It slewed out towards the edge, the rear of the Mercedes smashing through the low wall, then they both plunged over, still locked together, tearing through the trees, banging like huge dustbins, crashing. Then there was silence as they fell, a long silence, and the light was fading around her, everything was going dim, until it became completely dark and she could see nothing.

Death.

This is death. Silence. Trapped in a dark void.

For ever.

The void.

For a moment, she felt sick. Sick and angry. Then she began to shudder. Help me someone. 'Richard!' she called out. 'Richard?'

Nothing.

There should have been sirens. Police. Ambulance. Fire engines. 'Help me someone!' She felt herself floating, suspended in something that did not feel like water or air. Void, she thought. This is the void.

'It's OK!'

A single whisper.

'It's OK, Sam!'

A figure glided towards her out of the darkness. Another figure in the void with her. Coming closer. Closer. She saw a glint of light on the metallic green racing suit, then his head.

No. Please God, no.

The head coming closer. The black hood. The livid red eyeless socket coming closer, closer, so close it was going to touch her cheek.

'*No!*'

'Bugs?'

'Help me. Oh God help me.'

325

'Bugs?'

Different voice.

Then the single bong of a church bell, and something stirred in the darkness beside her.

'Bugs? It's OK. You're OK.'

'Richard?' she said.

The room was cold, icy cold. Cold as hell. Her face was numb. There was a rustle, then the clank of a spring.

'OK, Bugs?' said Richard's voice sleepily. She heard another grunt then a louder rustle, and felt herself move slightly.

Gingerly she slid her right hand across and touched him, in disbelief. Warm flesh. Breathing. She touched him again and let her hand stay on him, squeezing the flesh, and he grunted again. Then she rolled over towards him, put out her other arm, and touched his shoulder with her hand. She held him tightly, trembling with fear, with relief, and kissed his back.

He stirred again.

'Make love to me,' she said.

40

She stood at the window and stared out at the lake, waiting for the porter to collect their suitcases.

A powerboat sped across the water, a long way out, so far she could scarcely hear its engine. She wondered if it was the one that had come out of the mist and nearly killed them.

There was a rap on the door, and she called out, '*Entrez!*'

The porter came in and picked up the cases and she followed him down the corridor to the elevator. The lobby was gloomy, chilly, with the same unruffled, faintly expectant air that the lobbies of grand hotels always seemed to have. A phone rang, muted, and was immediately answered. The hall porter stood at his station, eyeing his domain. A short neat man in thick glasses sat behind the cashier's desk, writing in a huge ledger. Behind the reception desk, one clerk was talking on the telephone and another was flicking idly through a brochure.

A young man in a sharp suit waited just inside the entrance, his shiny leather briefcase on the floor beside him, glaring impatiently at his watch. Near him a well-dressed elderly couple were sitting on a sofa, the man reading a newspaper, the woman working on a small tapestry. Sam sat down opposite them, and pulled her book out of her bag.

A tall elegant woman strode in through the revolving doors in a full-length fox coat with a string of pekinese dogs tangled around her feet. The hall porter stiffened deferentially, and addressed her in German. Sam wondered whether she was some actress she should have recognised, or the bored wife of a rich businessman. She watched her chat for a moment with the clerk who had been reading the brochure, then take her key and tow her train of dogs towards the elevators.

They'd made love last night for the first time since – since it had happened. Back to normal; it felt strange; everything had changed and yet nothing had. If he'd learned anything new from his office tart, he'd been careful not to show it. Same position, same technique, same dead weight. Same romantic words.

Shit, that was great Bugs.

Then asleep.

Well, it was three in the morning. Could you put back romance once it had gone? Romance, she thought, feeling a twist of sadness. She opened her book and turned to her place.

'We will meet again soon?' he asked, and she was quick to notice the question in his voice and could not resist the opportunity to tease him.

'Perhaps,' she said languidly, and was enormously pleased to see the frown that sprang across his forehead.

'Perhaps?' he said brusquely. 'Only perhaps?'

For her answer, she reached for his hand and kissed his fingers one by one.

'Hi, sorry about that,' said Richard breathlessly. She looked up and saw him hurrying across the lobby towards her, looking harassed. He kissed her on the cheek. 'What are you reading?'

She held up the cover. '*Daughters of the Storm* by Elizabeth Buchan. It's good. I'm enjoying it.'

'Are we packed?'

'Yes. You've been longer than you thought.'

'The car's broken down.'

'What's happened?'

'I got to the bank all right, then it wouldn't start when I left.'

'Is it OK now?'

'No. Something's wrong with the electrics, I think the computer's gone on the blink.'

'I've just checked out,' she said. 'Shall we check back in again?'

''S OK. Andreas has lent us his car.'

'Andreas?'

'Yah. He's going to come up and join us in Zermatt for a couple of days – says he knows some great off-piste runs. He'll bring the BMW if it's fixed, otherwise we'll pick it up on the way back.'

'That's very decent of him,' she said hesitantly.

'Yah's a good bloke. I told you.' He looked down. 'This all the luggage?'

'Yes. How did it go?'

'Fine.' He sniffed. 'No problems. As far as the Swiss banking system is concerned, Richard Curtis no longer exists.' He stooped to pick up the bags, and the porter sprinted across, snatching them away, then beamed triumphantly.

'Outside? Your car?'

They followed him out into the brilliant sunlight, and Richard pointed across the driveway to the car that was parked awkwardly with two wheels on the kerb; a shiny green Mercedes.

41

She turned and walked back into the lobby, sat down on the sofa and stared ahead, stared at nothing.

Richard followed her in. 'Bugs? What's the matter, Bugs?' He sat down beside her. 'What's up?'

'I – don't want to go in that car.'

'What do you mean?'

She continued staring ahead numbly.

'Why not Bugs? It's almost brand new.'

'The colour,' she said.

'The colour? Do you think I had a choice? It was fucking decent of Andreas to lend us it – his own car. It's only about a month old.'

'I had another dream!' she screamed at him, so loudly that everyone in the lobby heard. And she didn't care, thought they probably hadn't understood what she said and that it was just another couple having a row.

'Great. Another fucking dream!' He leaned over

towards her, and put his hands on the arm of the sofa. 'What did you dream, Bugs?'

'A – green Mercedes.'

'What do you want me to do? Go back to Andreas, tell him "thanks a lot for the car, but my wife doesn't like the colour"?'

She smiled. She wasn't quite sure whether it was because she thought it was funny or it was nerves, but she looked up at him and smiled again.

'Pull yourself together, Bugs. You didn't want to fly out here because you thought the plane would crash. Now you don't want to drive because . . . what do you want to do? Stay here for the rest of your life?'

She followed him back out to the car, and he held up the keys.

'Would you feel better if you drove?'

'No.' She climbed in and he slammed her door shut for her.

Neither of them spoke for a long time as they headed out of Montreux following the lake around, and then down into the Rhône valley. Everything that had happened in the past weeks churned over in Sam's mind, the advice she had been given, the explanations.

It's important for you to try to work things out. To try to find the meanings.

Green Mercedes. Disappearing into the mouth of the juggernaut.

Very Freudian.

You think so?

Bound to be.

Think it could symbolise a desire to rebirth?

Oh definitely.

I'm getting the sexual act very strongly, Sam. Does that resonate?

Regular ding-dong.

She watched the sunlight glinting off the three-pointed star on the Mercedes's radiator. The car even smelled the same as the dream. Leather. Thick, rich, pungent leather. Like Ken's Bentley. Like her uncle's Rover.

Like the dream. Like the dream. Like the dream.

The dashboard was wood, immaculately polished, new.

Like a coffin.

Richard was on her left. The hideous green colour. The same colour. Designer puke.

He stretched out his arm and laid his hand on her thigh, patting it gently. 'Andreas says the snow's terrific at the moment. He was up there last weekend.'

'Good,' she said. 'Good.'

The vine terraces rose steeply up from the Rhône valley to their left, and the Alps towered down on them from the right, like a fortress wall. A wooden fruit stall flashed past, then a giant furniture mart. She felt her throat tightening and a deep numb sense of dread building in the car. She wanted to stop, get out, but instead she sat silently, thinking; trying to work through everything, as Hare had told her.

Green Mercedes. Disappearing into the mouth of the juggernaut. Sure. Plenty of interpretations. Bamford O'Connell and Tanya Jacobson and everyone in the dream group could have had a field day on the dream.

Except.

Closer. All the time closer. Drawing her, reeling her in.

To meet the monster?

She opened the glove compartment and looked in, looking to see if there were any clues about Andreas. Nothing. Just an assortment of classical music tapes, an owner's handbook and a clean, neatly folded duster.

Andreas; she picked at a hangnail. Andreas who had no wife or family. Richard thought he had been married once, some time ago, and that his wife had died, but he wasn't sure. Andreas. The enigma. Was it you peering out from the cabin of that boat? Were you trying to run us down? Ridiculous; not before the forms had been signed. So why didn't you come out and speak to your friend? Why did you stand and smirk? If it was you?

Maybe Richard was right; maybe Andreas was a nice guy and she was maligning him. Maybe.

The road narrowed and ran along beside a shallow rocky river; she watched a man and a small boy standing on the bank with their fishing rods. A cassette was sticking out of the tape deck and she pushed it in. A Beethoven piano sonata tinkled from the speakers and made her feel sad, reminded her of autumn.

The road curved away slightly from the river, and was now lined on either side with trees bowing across towards each other in a guard-of-honour salute, and the sun, low down behind them, flashed through them like a strobe.

Like the dream.

She glanced at the road ahead. The trees ended. Different trees to the dream. They were firs in the dream. The scenery was different, too.

'How did you meet Andreas, originally?'

'Rang me up; said I'd been recommended – wanted me to do some dealing for his bank.'

'Why's he being so . . . helpful?'

He rubbed his index finger and thumb together. 'Dinero. The Swiss will always be helpful for dinero – and he's just a good bloke as well.'

'You don't think that he's being too helpful?'

'What do you mean?'

'You don't think he has any – I don't know – any other motive?'

'Like what? Christ, you're so fucking suspicious, aren't you?'

'Is he involved in this insider dealing stuff?'

He shook his head.

'He got you dropped in it, but kept out himself?'

'Wasn't—' He hesitated – 'wasn't just him, Bugs, you know. I suppose that's what I get paid for doing – taking risks.'

'You don't get paid to break the law. Or did he pay you?'

He went bright red.

'Is that where all the money came from? To buy the house, and everything?'

He sniffed nervously, fumbling for his cigarettes. 'No, I told you. We – I – did rather well on a few deals.'

'What sort of deals?'

'Oh, you know – had a couple of good tips. Take-overs,' he said evasively, sniffing again, then braking as they approached a hairpin bend.

As they rounded it she saw a small hut with a sign advertising ice cream and Löwenbräu, then they crossed over a narrow stone bridge. A yellow PTT bus passed going the other way. Her throat tightened more. Richard accelerated hard with an angry look on his face. She felt the tyres scrabbling on loose grit, heard the squeal as they bit onto a stretch of fresh tarmac and the Mercedes yawed slightly. The engine bellowed and the car surged up the hill, past a marker post and a row of trees with white rings around them. 'You're being bloody stupid about this whole thing. I'm doing it for us,' he said, picking up his cigarettes and shaking one out.

To their left was a rock face rising straight up from the edge of the road, and to their right was an unguarded drop down into the fast-flowing river that was getting smaller beneath them.

Unfolding.

The dream was unfolding now.

Exactly.

Calm. Stay calm. Stay calm.

They moved over even closer to the edge as a massive truck thundered down past them, and she felt the blast of its slipstream rock the Mercedes.

'Richard, please drive a little slower.'

''S all right. I'm not going fast.' He lit his cigarette. 'Got a long way to go, and we've still got the fucking train journey up into the village.'

We're not going to get there, she wanted to say. We're going to get wiped out by a juggernaut. In a minute or two's time. We'll be dead. All over. Fini. Curtains. Snuffed out.

She felt a curious sense of euphoria suddenly. Of power.

Of freedom.

As if someone was telling her to relax, that the next few minutes did not matter, that nothing mattered any more. That the choice to live or die was hers. That dying would be nicer. So much fun. Live out the dream! Go for it! Be free!

She laughed. Silly. Stupid. To have been so worried.

'What's funny?'

Funny, The word echoed around. Funny. Then the shivers gripped her and she felt as if a million hoses were pumping iced water straight into the centre of her stomach. They squealed around a double hairpin, and she saw the low stone wall at the edge of the road.

I'm going to wake up in a minute, she thought. This is a lucid dream. I can control it.

She heard the faint blaring of horns, then a red Volkswagen came fast down the other way, followed by a motorbike, its engine revving with a caterwauling howl, followed by a white van.

The ones she had seen. Identical. The same colours.

She was shaking with terror.

Richard. She tried to speak, but nothing came out. 'Richard!' she shouted, but it only came out as a whisper. She heard the horns again, closer now, vicious angry blasts. She unbuckled her seat belt.

Lay-by. They were coming to the lay-by.

'Stop!' She threw herself at Richard, grabbing the wheel, and felt the Mercedes swerving wildly. Richard stamped on the brakes and the car squealed to a halt.

'For Christ's sake, have you gone fucking mad?' he yelled.

'Pull off the road,' she said. 'For God's sake!' Her voice was a weird, croaking whisper. 'Quickly!'

He glared at her, then accelerated harshly, squealing the tyres again, pulled over into the lay-by and stopped, flinging her forward. 'What the fuck are you playing at?'

'Out! Out! Get out!' She opened her door, flung herself out, tripped, grabbed the swinging door and stared wide-eyes down the steep wooded gorge towards the river.

In the distance she heard the roar of a juggernaut. Two juggernauts, closer, coming closer, hurtling down; any moment they would come around the corner, one overtaking the other. Coming, coming, coming. She turned and saw Richard standing beside the Mercedes, staring at her.

They're coming. You'll see. You'll see that I was right.

Where are you?

The roaring continued. Closer. Getting closer.

Richard walked around the back of the car towards

335

her. A car came around the corner, then another, a red Porsche with skis on the roof, a small Renault, a BMW, an Audi piled high with suitcases.

Come on.

Still the roaring.

Then she realised that it wasn't the roaring of juggernauts. It wasn't coming from the road at all.

It was the roaring of water in the gorge below.

She walked along the lay-by, listening to the loose stones scrunching under her feet. A small truck droned up the road past her followed by a line of cars, then nothing again except for the sound of the gorge. She walked to the wall and stared down the sheer rock face through the trees at the frothing white water of the river. She heard footsteps behind her, then felt his arm around her waist.

'Maybe they should put me away,' she said.

'Maybe you should just forget your dreams, Bugs.'

42

They'd had to stop and put chains on the Mercedes for the last ten miles. Richard had straggled and cursed for the best part of an hour, whilst she'd hovered around in the freezing cold and tried to help, and not been much use. But it had been better than just sitting, waiting. Anything was better than that.

Maybe Ken was right.

'You've got yourself into a state, and you've got to let yourself come down out of it . . . Try to forget about it all.

Yes.

Take a hard look at everything and see if it still looks the same afterwards – I think you'll find it won't.

Yes. Yes, boss. Oh absolutely, sir.

Christ, I wish you were right.

Täsch was where the road ended. Richard lifted the cases out of the boot of the Mercedes and put them onto a luggage trolley. Sam stood in the snow and watched him drive off into the vast car park, the exhaust smoke trailing behind, thick and heavy in the bitterly cold afternoon air, the chains clattering and the tyres squeaking on the hard-packed snow.

The snow smelled good, smelled fresh and clean and lay everywhere. It was still falling, and tickled her face and made everything look like a Christmas card, made her think of snug log fires and roasting food, and wine, and laughter.

They were here. They'd got here. Got here because? Because the dreams had told her how? Because the plane would have crashed if they'd been on it? Because if she hadn't made Richard row like hell they would have been run down in the boat?

Because two juggernauts would have come round the bend if she hadn't made Richard pull off the road?

Sure they would have, Sam. By magic?

It was because we stopped that we survived.

Bullshit.

You know why you refuse to believe it, Richard? Because you're scared, that's why.

I'm not nuts, oh no. Slider's playing this game with me. 'Now you see me, now you don't.' 'He's standing right behind you . . . oh no he isn't.' 'Some dreams come true and some dreams don't.' It's a game, that's all; a game you have to win.

Because if you lose you die.

She stamped her feet to warm them up and dug her gloved hands deep inside her pockets. Richard hurried back towards her in his red anorak and his white moon boots, and they pushed the trolley together up the ramp to the funicular train to Zermatt.

The porter put their bags into the back of the electric buggy, then held the door open for them. They moved off from the station with a jerk, heading up the narrow Bahnhofstrasse, the buggy making a high-pitched whine. A stream of horse-drawn sleighs trotted past them the other way, bells jangling.

Money, she thought. You could smell it in the thick coats, in the fat chocolates and expensive watches that sparkled in the windows; you could smell it in the cigar smoke and coffee and *chocolat chaud* that hung in the frosty air along with the dung and the smell of horses; in the bustle, jostle, in the signs, Confiserie, Burgener, Chaussures, Seiler, Patek Philippe, Longines, in the smart skis rattling on smart shoulders, pink, green, Racing, Slalom, Géant and the clunking and crunching of unclipped boots. The Matterhorn rose like a monolith above the roofs of the hotels, the sun sinking down beside it, thin and dull, like a tarnished bauble in need of a polish.

Whymperstübe. Hotel Whymper. Named after the first Englishman to climb the Matterhorn. The graveyard under the bridge was full of them. So full they had run out of space. She shivered. Stone slabs sticking crookedly out of the snow like old men's teeth. Young Englishmen along with the local traders and local heroes, all just as dead as each other, all with their epitaphs. 'I chose to climb', she remembered on one, and she wondered what would be on her own.

'Hasn't changed much,' said Richard.

Nine years. It had been magical then. Like coming to a fairy tale. Snow and hot chocolate and soft pillows and laughter. Free. Taking the baker's sled and tobogganing through the streets at three in the morning. She had felt so free then. Free and silly and mad.

The buggy turned up the alleyway, braked to avoid two elderly women, then pulled up outside the Alex. They went to the reception desk and Richard filled out the forms, and the porter took their bags up to their room. It was simple and comfy with modern wooden furniture, plump pillows and a great thick duvet soft as snow. 'We ought to call Nicky,' she said.

'Yah.'

She went over to the window and stared out at a school opposite, the desks abandoned for the night. She could see a display of crayoned drawings pinned to a notice board. She tried to concentrate her mind. To think.

There were so many possibilities. Maybe that's why people ignored their premonitions: because once you started looking, trying to cover all the options, you would become a hermit, or go mad. Perhaps you couldn't escape. All you could do was delay, buy a few hours or days or weeks, a time of terror and confusion; a bonus not worth having.

The snow was falling more heavily, and she felt the warm air from the radiator on her face.

'How're you feeling, Bugs?'

She raised her eyebrows.

I'd feel a lot better if—

If you believed me; but you won't. Ken doesn't either; not really. Only two people do. One's dead; the other doesn't want to know.

Laszlo. Driving away from the station as fast as he could.

But you're not going to win, Slider. I'm not going to let you. She smiled wryly. I'm going to beat you. Doing OK so far, eh? I'm going to win. I promise.

Richard rolled over on the bed and pulled his cigarettes out of his anorak pocket. 'What are you smiling at?'

'How does that limerick go?' she said.

> ' "There was a young lady of Riga
> Who rode with a smile on a tiger. . .
> They returned from the ride
> With the lady inside
> And the smile on the face of the tiger." '

'Is that how you feel?'

'Life's a tiger,' she said. 'That's how I feel.'

'Cheers!'

'Cheers,' she said.

They clinked glasses. Richard swirled his wine around and took a large gulp. 'It's good being away on our own, don't you think?'

'Yes.'

'We never seem to talk when we're at home, do we?'

She sipped some wine. 'What would you like to talk about?'

He shrugged and yawned. 'Us, I suppose. We seem to have been through a bit of a thin patch—' He inhaled deeply on his cigarette and focused on something past her. She turned her head. There was a glitzy blonde sitting at a table with a portly man a good thirty years her senior.

'She's not that great,' Sam said.

'She's got good tits.'

'It's very flattering to sit here watching you ogle other women.'

He drank some more wine, then his face suddenly

became animated and he leapt up. 'Andreas! We weren't expecting you until tomorrow!'

She saw the banker walking stiffly towards them in a long fur-collared coat sprinkled with snow, his gloved hands by his side. She sensed a sudden chilly draught, as if he had left the outside door open, and felt goose-pimples breaking out on her flesh.

He nodded at her as he reached the table, a faint smirk on his lips; the same smirk she had seen through the slats of the blinds on the boat. She was certain.

'How are you!' Richard said effusively.

'Not much changed since this morning.' Andreas smiled coldly back at him, shook his hand, then fixed his eyes on Sam. 'Good evening, Mrs Curtis.'

'Good evening,' she said, as courteously as she could, staring back into his icy cold eyes that seemed to be laughing at her.

'So nice to see you again. I enjoyed meeting you at dinner very much. Such a pleasant evening.'

'Thank you. I'm glad you enjoyed yourself.'

'Sit down, join us,' Richard said, urgently signalling to a waiter for another chair.

'You have eaten, I think,' said Andreas. 'I have something then I join you.'

'No, absolutely not, you join us now,' Richard insisted. 'It doesn't matter. We're happy to sit while you eat. I'll get you a glass. Would you like some wine?'

'Thank you.' The banker pulled off his coat, and Richard scurried around, taking it from him then passing it on like a rugger ball to the waiter who brought the chair; he grabbed a glass from the empty table next to them, poured out some wine and put the glass down in front of Andreas. 'Just a local one, I'm afraid. Dole, nothing grand.'

'The local ones are the best to drink here,' Andreas

said, sitting down and locking his eyes onto Sam's again.

'Yes,' Richard said. 'Yes, of course, I'm sure you're right. We had some excellent wines last time we were here . . . Perhaps we should have a toast. To today! Let's have some champagne – bottle of Poo – we'll have some Bollers if they've got any. I'll get the wine list.' He grinned. 'Got to toast the – dematerialisation – of Richard Curtis.' He looked at Andreas for approval, and the banker looked away dismissively, like a dog bored with a puppy.

'They don't find anything wrong with your car.'

'What do you mean?' Richard waved at the waiter again. 'Could we have a menu – *un menu, et la carte des vins, s'il vous plaît.*' He turned back to Andreas. 'Nothing wrong?'

He shrugged. 'Maybe it is something – how you call it? – loose in the wiring or something. It's fine, now. Drives very nicely.'

Nothing wrong.

Sam felt the goosepimples crawling up her neck. Nothing wrong. Like the Jaguar in Hampstead. She shook, as if she had had an electric shock. Both Richard and Andreas looked at her.

'You all right, Bugs?'

'Fine. Just a bit cold.' She caught Andreas's eyes again, the cold blue eyes in that flat featureless face that appeared so unassuming until you looked closer; neat, dull, fair hair, but lost most of it on top, almost bald except for the light fuzz; he'd probably been quite handsome when he was in his twenties, in a rather stiff sort of way. He looked a fit man now, fit and athletic, and flashily dressed in his pink cashmere sweater, cream silk shirt, and the small silver medallion on his chest.

'Extraordinary,' Richard said. 'I suppose that's the

problem with these electronics. Get little glitches in them which come and go. Almost impossible to find.'

Then she saw it.

Saw it and realised.

Saw it as Andreas curled his gloved fingers around the bowl of his wine glass, the quick almost imperceptible flick of the thumb and the little finger, which she would have missed if she hadn't been looking hard, the click he had devised to make the middle three fingers move, to make them curl around the bowl.

To make them look as if they were real.

43

She thrashed violently, trying to free herself from the bedclothes that were over her head, heavy as sandbags, smothering her, trying to free herself and escape from the blades of the fan that were coming down towards her and the ceiling that was cracking like eggshell. She heaved the bedclothes away frantically, but they fell back, crushing her body, crushing her face, blocking her mouth, her nose. She was gulping, gasping for air, twisting, helplessly.

Trapped.

She tried to scream but the sheet came into her mouth.

Too late, she realised the sheets were holding her.

Preventing her from falling.

She was slipping free of them now, slipping out into the swirling vortex below her. She grabbed the corner of one, desperately, but it held her weight only for a fraction of a second, and then tore.

'Help!' Her voice echoed around her as if she was in a cave. Then she plummeted downwards, hurtled through

the freezing cold air, bouncing, falling, spinning towards a tiny hole of darkness. She put her hands up,
trying to ward it off, trying somehow to swim away
from it.

'*No!*'

She hurtled into the hole, trying to grip the walls, but
they were covered in smooth ice and her hands slid
down them, burning from the cold, from the friction.
There was whiteness below, and she could see the
blades of the fan scything through the air, clattering
louder as she tumbled down towards them, waiting for
the impact, waiting to be cut into a thousand pieces.

'Fifty-five and a half seven. OK, hit that fucking bid.
Sally, that's Mitsubishi Heavy five hundred at fifty-five
and a half I sell. OK, now buy back the bloody stock!'

Richard's voice in the darkness.

'I'm talking big noughts, Harry. Big noughts. No.
Serious. He's a major player, a triple-A client. We
should hedge with futures. Five hundred contracts.
Could be a squeeze on the market. I'm seven and a
half bid for as many as they've got. Shit. It's moving
away from us. Take the offer. For Christ's sake take the
offer!'

His voice rambled on. She had never heard him talk in
his sleep before. Never heard him talk in such a faltering, nervous voice.

The she heard children chanting.

> Humpty Dumpty sat on a wall,
> Humpty Dumpty had a great fall.
> All the King's horses and all the King's men,
> Couldn't put Humpty together again.

The children laughed, and she heard the laughter echoing, as if it was echoing around an empty classroom. It

continued, getting louder. She slipped out of bed and immediately it stopped.

Puzzled, she walked across the room. Richard stirred and grunted behind her. She lifted the curtain and stared out. The whiteness of the snow on the ground filled the night with a strange translucence. A church bell chimed three o'clock. The school opposite was dark, silent, empty. She turned and went back to bed, pulled the duvet up around her and lay staring into the darkness.

A cold breath blew into her ear, and she heard a voice, soft, whispering, taunting. Slider's voice. Just one word.

'Aroleid.'

Then silence.

44

It was snowing hard as they trudged up the hill towards the Furi lift station with their skis over their shoulders. They passed a cowshed then a row of old chalet-style buildings, PENSION GARNI said the sign on each one.

'I thought you'd always been keen on Japanese warrants?' Richard said.

'Swiss franc ones only,' Andreas replied.

It was another language. As foreign as the languages of the country they were now in. French. German. Switzer-deutsch. Snatches of foreign languages all around. Two lanky men strode in front of them, one wearing a fluorescent yellow ski suit and bright yellow boots, the other in white, with bright pink boots. They talked loudly, their feet clumping, skis slung over their shoulders. They roared with laughter. Normal people. Out for a day's skiing. Going for it.

Going for it. Living in the fast lane. Flying at the sharp end. Style.

Death. Lying in a cellophane bag on a mortuary slab. Floating in the void. In the void where you could shout and no one could hear you. For ever.

For a moment, she did not care. She was tired of walking up the hill, tired of the snow tickling her face. Tired of being scared. She wanted to sit down. To sit down and sleep and not dream.

To sleep: perchance to dream: ay there's the rub. For in that sleep of death what dreams may come?

Did you go on dreaming after you were dead? In the void?

'You're quiet this morning, Bugs,' said Richard.

She blinked away the snow and trudged on, saying nothing, and looked again at Andreas's padded green skiing gloves.

I think it is possible that he's someone in the present, now, who is bothering you, worrying you – someone that you are associating with this Slider.

He's a banker, that's all. A banker with a bad hand. He's dry and arrogant; so are most bankers. What are you afraid he's going to do? Eat you? Turn you into a frog? Jump on you when Richard's not looking and rape you and slit your throat? Just because you imagine you saw him on that boat? He's doing you both a favour, be nice to him.

They crossed the wooden bridge over the river and then climbed up the steep steps to join the jostling queue into the ski-lift station. She shuffled slowly forwards behind Andreas and Richard in the air that was thick with garlic and suntan lotion and lip salve and perfume.

'Sony,' Richard said. 'Their seven-year warrants are a fucking good buy at the moment. Five times geared and a four percent premium.'

'I prefer Fujitsu,' said Andreas.

She could hear the machinery now, the whirring of the motors driving the massive cable, the scraping, sliding sound of the six-man gondolas unhooking, slowing, the metallic thump of their doors opening, the clatter of skiers pushing their skis into the racks then clambering in, the clunk of the doors shutting and the sudden roar of acceleration as the tiny cabins, like eggs, slid down the cable, gaining momentum, and through the gantry that locked them to the cable. She felt afraid of the gondolas, suddenly, afraid of the mountain, wanted to go back to the hotel.

Something hit her hard in the small of her back, and she spun round.

'*Entschuldigung.*' A woman was leaning forward, trying to push her skis back together, smiling apologetically, a flustered, messy-looking woman with two small girls in matching pink outfits.

She felt her skis being lifted out of her hand. She turned and saw Andreas placing them in the rack at the back of the gondola. He took her arm and propelled her in.

She looked around. 'Richard? Where's Richard?'

'He is going in front.'

There were four little Japanese boys in the gondola, watching them wide-eyed. Someone shouted outside, urgently, a torrent of Japanese, and the boys scampered out seconds before the door closed.

The gondola accelerated, unbalancing her, and she sat down hard on the plastic bench. Andreas sat down opposite her, holding his ski poles, fingers neatly curled around the handles, as they swung suspended on the cable just outside the mouth of the station, then began to glide upwards.

She looked out of the window. Flash bastard. His

ultra-modern ski suit, a metallic green racing suit, and goggles pushed up on his head. Wonder if you ski as flashily as you look? Probably do, damn you.

It was snowing even harder. The wind buffeted them and the visibility seemed to be going as the weather closed in around them. The gondola juddered and she looked anxiously around, listening to the rattling of the cable and the patter of the snow hitting the windows, and caught his eye. He was watching her and smiling drily to himself.

'The weather is not so good,' he said, his eyes still staring, penetrating.

'Not a nice day for boating,' she replied.

He did not flinch.

She looked away. 'Do you sail, Andreas? I should think Lake Geneva is a great place for sailing, or for power boating.' She looked sharply back at him; still no reaction.

'I am working too much. Skiing is my only relaxation.'

'If I lived in Montreux, I'd be out on the lake all the time. Very exhilarating on a cold Sunday afternoon to roar across water, wouldn't you think?'

'I would not know,' he said, turning towards the window as if he was bored with the conversation.

'It was Ratty in *The Wind in the Willows*, wasn't it, who said "There is nothing – absolutely nothing – half so much worth doing as simply messing about in boats." *The Wind in the Willows*. Did you ever read *The Wind in the Willows*?'

'I don't believe so.'

She searched his face, trying to read it, trying to read the signs from the way he shifted his position, from the way he turned his head to look out of the window again, from the way he clenched his fists just a fraction.

348

'Higher will be better. I think perhaps it will be above the cloud,' he said.

She glanced up nervously again as the cable rattled loudly through the runners of a pylon, and the gondola swayed. Through the window she could see the tops of the fir trees below.

There's more to come. So much further to fall. You've got the really big fall to come.

Who the hell are you, Andreas? Or is it me? She looked again at the fingers, then at his green suit; something seemed familiar about the suit.

The gondola stopped with a jerk, and swayed wildly. She felt the fear surge through her. A gust of wind caught them and tossed them sideways. The snow and the mist seemed to be getting even denser; she heard the wind wailing mournfully through a pylon, felt it shake them again and there was a creak above her head, then a sickening rending sound, like metal tearing. Andreas was smirking again, smirking at her fear.

The cabin lurched violently, twice, then the gondola began to move forwards. There was another tearing sound above them, and the gondola lurched again. There was a loud bang. A dark shadow fell across them and her heart jumped. There was an even louder bang and a tremendous jolt, and they swung backwards.

Then the doors opened with a hiss and a dull thump, and the banker stood up.

They had arrived at the station.

He lifted her skis from the rack and stood waiting for her. She swung herself out and jumped onto the ground. There was another bang as the next gondola arrived, crashing into their empty one. 'Thank you,' she said, and followed him over to Richard who was standing in the queue for the exit.

Richard turned around. 'I thought you were right

behind me. Got in a gondola with a bunch of Krauts. They didn't speak a word of English. Did you have a nice chat?'

'Your wife is very charming. Such a well-read lady.' Andreas smiled again at Sam, and she looked away, up at the ceiling of the lift station, at the dark churning wheels of the machinery, listening to its rattling and grinding. There was a clang as the next gondola arrived and thudded into the rear of the one in front.

It was here, she knew. Here on the mountain. Waiting.

45

'Sam!'

She heard Ken's voice echo around the mountain and turned with a start, looking up, scanning the slope she had just skied down. But there was no one. No one but Andreas in his metallic green suit waiting to start his descent, waiting until she had stopped so she would be sure not to miss it. She looked at Richard, but he did not seem to have heard anything.

Clear.

It had sounded so clear.

Like a warning.

'The sun's trying to break through,' said Richard.

She nodded and stared up again at the slope. At least they were in the lee of the wind here. Beyond the peak she could see the silhouette of the sun smouldering behind the clouds, like a cigarette burning through a tablecloth.

In the last hour, since lunch, the snow had stopped and the mist was starting to clear. They had gone higher at Andreas's suggestion, up to the top of the glacier to get above the worst of the weather, and he had been right. She heard the drone of the piste basher grinding up the glacier behind her, close, too close, and she turned and watched the huge red machine with its caterpillar tracks and rotating blades chomping through the snow. PISTENBULLY was emblazoned in large letters on its side. An orange warning light flashed on its roof, and its siren wailed, a short, monotone pulse, like a door hinge creaking in the wind.

Andreas launched himself off the top of a mogul, crouched low, dug his pole in, straightened his legs then bent them again, turned neatly, too damned neatly, straightened and bent his legs again, repeated his pole action and turned again, neat, snaking, even turns, his body flowing, rhythmic, exaggerating each movement as if he was giving a lesson. He headed down towards the rotating blades of the Pistenbully, in zigzagging tightly carved turns, his speed staying constant, keeping his head down.

As if he had not seen it, she thought, with a tremble of horror and excitement.

He turned again, accelerating hard away from it, then back again, straight into its path.

Straight towards the blades.

Then at the last moment he made one sharper even more stylised turn, crouched down low into a racing tuck and accelerated out of its path, straight at her, grinning demonically.

She stepped sideways, crossed her skis, lost her balance, and flailed out with her poles.

He swung into a sharp braking turn and skidded towards her, showering her with shards of cold snow.

She fell on her side with a jarring thump, and heard him roar with laughter. She dug her ski poles into the ground, and pushed herself upwards. Her skis slid away from under her and she fell back down, hard. Bastard; she glared up at him, then at Richard, who was standing with his glove off and his finger up his nose.

Andreas seemed to have come alive here on the slopes; as if he could make up for what he lacked in conversation by a virtuoso performance on his skis. He pushed his goggles up onto his forehead. 'Here, I help.' He leaned over, grabbed her arm in a vice-like grip, and heaved her back up. 'Hurts, doesn't it, to make the fall?' He stared, a piercing hard stare. 'We make a traverse here, into a very good powder bowl I will take you down. Not many people know it.' As he replaced his goggles, she looked at the hand he had used to pull her up, his right hand with the three useless fingers, and she remembered another time she had felt a grip like that, only once in her life, a very long time ago. He stretched his hands behind him and pulled the green hood up over his head, then launched himself off down the mountain and disappeared into a bank of mist.

Sam dusted the snow off her trousers. 'I don't want to ski with him any more, Richard.'

'He's a good skier,' he said defensively. 'Knows this area well. It's good to have a guide with this mist.'

'I don't care.'

'Actually, I think he rather fancies you.'

She stared at him in stunned silence. 'What am I, Richard? Part of your deal?'

He blushed, and scratched his ear. 'Don't be ridiculous. Just keep him sweet, that's all.'

'God,' she said. 'You used to be such a proud man.' She turned away, unable even to look at him, and began to ski down following the direction of the banker. She made a stiff, awkward turn, then another and stopped, her eyes smarting, anger and fear churning her up, fuzzing her brain.

She watched Richard hurtling down too fast as usual, in his hunched, slightly out-of-control style, and disappearing into the mist. She heard the rustling of more skis, and watched another couple ski past, the man slightly stiff, the woman elegant, flowing. The mist swallowed them as well, then there was silence. She was alone, suddenly, on the slope.

She looked around nervously. Her thigh hurt from the fall, and she was cold and wet. She wished she was home, in front of the fire, with Nicky playing on the rug.

Home was a cosy place. A safe place. Somewhere that no longer existed.

She blinked hard, pushed herself forwards half-heartedly, made a poor, jerky turn, then another, trying to get the rhythm, trying to get the enthusiasm. She felt the jar of an edge catching, and her skis crossed. The ground raced up towards her and hit her hard in the stomach, winding her.

'Shit,' she said. She was lying face down, one leg still in its ski jammed behind her, the other free. She crawled back to her feet, put her ski back on, and stared down into the mist that was fast rising up towards her.

Where were they?

'Richard?' she called.

Silence.

'Richard?' she shouted louder, but the mist sucked in her voice like blotting paper.

She eased her skis downhill and made two more turns, then stopped again. She saw a figure a short way below her, a dim silhouette, and skied down towards it. She got closer and saw the metallic green of Andreas's ski suit moving off again, turning sharply to the right. There was a shadow just below her, a piste marker post, with an arrow. She skied down. It was black, a black run, pointing the opposite direction to which Andreas had gone. There was something written on the marker, the name of the run, as there always was, and she peered closer.

AROLEID.

She stared, blinking in disbelief.

AROLEID.

The snow seemed to be swaying underneath her. Rocking her as if she was standing in a boat.

AROLEID.

Sweet Jesus, no.

AROLEID.

It was flashing at her, strobing, corning closer, closer, then it smacked her in the face and knocked her to the ground.

She lay there and stared up at it, numb with terror.

DIE ORAL!

DERAIL.

AIR DOLE.

OR I DEAL.

ORDEAL I.

REDIAL.

She heard a sound like a snigger and spun around. But there was nothing.

She scrambled back onto her skis and stared at the sign again.

AROLEID.

Pointing to the left. The solitary marker in the mist.

She stared into the mist, shaking. Terrified to stand here alone by the sign. Terrified to go. In any direction.

'Richard!' she shouted again, but no sound came out.

The cold gnawed at her fingers, her face, gnawed at her insides as if it was trying to eat its way through her. The mist was thickening and there was a weird dream-like quality to it.

It's OK.

Lucid dream.

I'm going to wake up in a minute.

Please God, I want to wake up.

She thought she heard a sound behind her and turned around. There was a silhouette just above her, like a person, but it seemed to disappear as she watched. The mist, she thought. Tricks with the eyes. 'Richard! Is that you?'

Nothing.

The mist was thickening again and the green suit had disappeared.

AROLEID.

To the left.

The sign Slider had shown her.

No way. No which way, thank you. She turned right, pushing herself off after Andreas, pushing herself away from the sign as quickly as she could. She was gathering speed now down an incline, then felt herself jerk forwards and almost fell as her skis ran from the firm piste into deep powder snow.

The green suit had disappeared completely, but she could see his tracks, and skied in them. 'Wait for me, you sod,' she muttered, turning with difficulty and nearly falling again, trying to remember her powder technique, but the snow was heavy and she missed the tracks, heard a sharp scraping under her skis, and almost lost her balance as she went over a buried rock. Christ. Wait. Wait for me!

The slope fell away and she shrieked as she accelerated sharply. She turned frantically, then turned again, hurtling down a steep unskied gully. She heard the scrape of another rock then slewed on a patch of ice, peering ahead, trying to see where she was going, to see the next bump before it rose up under her and threw her off balance. She stopped, inches from a massive bare rock, backed away, turned, skied over a bump that threw her up in the air, and she came down into deep wet powder, and started shooting up the side of the gully. She tried to turn. She hit another bump and swung around, bounced up hard, then saw Andreas's green suit just ahead. She turned again, then again and stopped, exhausted, gasping for breath, right behind him.

'Christ,' she said, panting. 'That was steep. Are you sure this is right?'

'Yes, this is right,' he said. 'But from here it gets even steeper. It's a good run, but you have to be a little careful.' He pushed his goggles up onto his forehead, and turned around.

Sam screamed.

The backs of her skis crossed and dug into the wall of the gully and she slid forward and jammed the points of her ski poles into the snow, gripped the handles hard, shaking her head, staring in wild disbelief.

Staring at the black hood with slits for the eyes, nose and mouth that he had over his face.

Staring at the metallic green suit.

Slider.

In the dream laboratory.

The metallic green suit.

That suit.

She turned around looking for Richard. Christ, where are you? Then she stared back at Andreas afraid to take her eyes off him, afraid in case—

He was smiling, enjoying himself, enjoying watching her shake. He touched the hood with his ski glove. 'Silk balaclava – very good for keeping the face warm. We go into deep powder soon. It sprays up and makes the face cold.'

Calm down.

For Christ's sake, calm down. Just a balaclava. Lots of skiers wear balaclavas.

Only a bloody balaclava!

Only a green metallic suit.

Coincidence. That's all.

He tugged his goggles back on and beckoned her with his hand.

She stared, not wanting to move, but her skis began to slip, and she had to jam her poles into the snow again to stop herself from skiing straight into him. She turned her head, staring back up the gully.

Richard. Please come.

The mist lifted a little and she could see how steep and narrow it was.

'It's lucky for you I stopped here,' he said, still smirking. 'You could have had a nasty fall.'

She saw a shape appear at the top. It was Richard. Her heart leapt with relief.

He started down, turned, crossed his skis and fell head first. She watched anxiously as he lifted his face out of the snow, then he waved at her.

She looked back at Andreas. Was this a dream? Was this a lucid dream?

I'd really like to wake up now. Except she knew this time she was awake.

'Come!' Andreas said. 'Come slowly, be very careful. I want to show you.'

I think it is possible that he's someone in the present, now, who is bothering you, worrying you – someone that you are associating with this Slider.

She edged forward, unable to take her eyes off his face, until she was beside him.

'Now look.' He pointed down.

She peered over the ledge she was now standing on; the gully opened onto a narrow couloir which dropped away almost vertically. It was filled with rocks and loose snow, and its sides were rounded and covered in smooth ice, like the barrel of a cannon. It became narrower as it went down, finishing in a shelf that she could not see beyond.

'You must be very careful down this couloir, and not fall,' he said, grinning again. 'You won't stop if you fall. There is a bad drop at the end. You must turn immediately right and make a traverse. If you fall, you will go three hundred metres onto rocks.' He jump-turned and skied gleefully down as if he was on the nursery slope, swaying his arms, pumping his legs, leaping almost like a dancer, gaining speed, ignoring his own warning.

She turned and saw Richard getting ready to start down towards her again.

'Richard, be very careful here,' she called. 'Stop where I am – don't go too fast.'

He raised a hand in acknowledgement, and she set off down, slowly, petrified, turning awkwardly through the rocks and the rubble. She halted at the bottom, and froze. The slope below her became a sheer ice wall that fell away down into the mist below; she felt her head swim with vertigo, and inched back, away from it, turning around to warn Richard. He had stopped several yards above her. 'All right?' he shouted.

'Be careful. Be really careful here, it's a sheer drop.' She edged further backwards, afraid to turn around until she was several feet back up the couloir. Richard was still waiting for her to get clear. Silence, she thought. A frightening, terrible silence.

Where the hell was he taking her, this man? This creature. This thing. Whoever he was? She stared back up at the couloir. Christ, it would be a nightmare to climb that. It was four o'clock. The light would be going soon, particularly if the mist got worse again. The runs would be closing, and the pisteurs would be making their sweeps of the pistes. But not here. This wasn't a piste. They'd never get back up there before dark. The only way was to keep going down.

You have to meet your monster, Sam.

I'm meeting him, she thought, starting the traverse across the icy narrow ledge, with the sheer drop to death two feet away. She was gathering speed, she realised, and the ledge was too narrow to turn. She stemmed the skis outwards in a snowplough and began to slide out towards the edge.

She eased them back, parallel, and the icy ground was hurtling past faster, the wind whipping her face. Out of the corner of her eye she saw Andreas, laughing through his hood, then the ledge opened up into a huge slope and her skis ran off the ice into deep soft powder snow. She stopped and looked down. It was steep. Far steeper than she normally skied. The slope went down for several hundred feet then eased into a more gentle gradient, down to a lip. Beyond that seemed to be another sheer drop.

Somewhere above was the clatter of a circling helicopter; ski patrol, she thought, straining her eyes with sudden hope, but she could not see it.

A savage gust of wind blew, whipping the surface snow up into a bitter stinging mist that she had to turn her face away from. She stared up at the sky again, dark blue through her goggles, like deep silent water. The clattering was fading into the distance.

Behind her Richard's skis scraped on the ice; he had stopped at the lip and was peering down at the sheer ice wall.

'Where the hell are you taking us, Andreas?' he

shouted. 'We're not bloody mountaineers. Are you try-ing to fucking kill us?'

Andreas grinned at Sam, ignoring him. 'This snow is sitting on ice. You must not traverse. Make your descent straight down. Short turns. Follow in my tracks exactly. If you traverse, you could cut it away and it will avalanche. Follow me exactly. If you are not turning in the right place, you go over the lip at the bottom. There's another ice wall. Sheer.'

She stared down, then looked at him. The fear was paralysing her.

Andreas launched himself, compressing his body, exploding in a spray of powder, compressing again, ex-ploding again, turning, sharp tight turns, controlling his speed. He compressed again, but came up oddly, twisting, tried to recover but he fell face forward, somersaulted and disappeared completely for a moment in a spray of snow. One hand emerged, then his head. He lifted himself up a fraction, and put his hands over his face.

She knew what she had to do, knew that she had to go now or she never would. She launched herself gingerly down, making the first turn, in Andreas's tracks, too slowly. She had not enough momentum and her upper ski caught in the heavy powder and nearly pulled her over. She jerked it free, panicking, and turned again, gathering speed now, too much. She turned again, then again, surging; she saw Andreas fifty yards below her, and beyond him the lip, a long way down. Don't look down. Don't fall. Her muscles were so clenched she was turning all wrong. She was trying to slow, but she was not slowing; she was accelerating.

Twenty feet above him she turned out of his tracks and began to traverse across the slope, accelerating fiercely now.

'Bugs!' she heard Richard scream. 'Don't traverse! Bugs! Turn, for God's sake, *turn*!'

The lip was rushing up.

She was going too fast to turn now.

'Bugs! Turn! Turn, Bugs! Fall over, for God's sake! Fall over!'

It was getting closer.

She screamed; tried to force her skis to turn. Tried right. Then left. The lip was hurtling towards her.

Then the snow exploded around her. Her neck cricked painfully and she was lying flat on her back, staring at the sky.

She heard Richard's voice, anxious.

'Bugs? You OK?'

She felt her heart thumping. She rolled over and the snow moved under her. 'Fine,' she shouted. 'I'm fine.' She pulled herself up, brushed the snow off her goggles and saw Richard looking fearfully down, first at her, then at the long cut she had made in the snow. Andreas, a hundred yards above her now, still had his hands over his face, and she saw blood running down his gloves.

'Andreas!' Richard shouted. 'Are you all right?'

The gradient was more gentle here and she was still some way from the lip. Both her skis had come off, and she hauled them out of the snow, laid them down, and reset the bindings. Richard waited. Andreas was sitting, his hands covering one eye, and she looked again at the diagonal line she had cut above him as she pushed her foot back into one ski, and trod down hard, trying to get the lock of the safety binding to snap home, her hands numb, her mind numb.

There was a sound like a clap of thunder, and she felt as if someone had kicked the soles of her feet. Cracks began to appear in the snow above her. They spread out, like veins.

Like eggshell, she thought.

There was a loud rumble, and the ground began to shake. The cracks spread out all around her, with a strange, terrifying sound, like a giant sheet of parchment being torn.

Like a giant eggshell cracking.

Like the ceiling of the hotel room.

She heard Richard's voice scream at her: 'Go, Bugs. *Go!*'

She tried to move, but she was frozen with fear.

Frozen as if she was in a nightmare.

'Go, Bugs!'

There was a whiplash crack and a chunk of snow slid away right beside her. She heard the roar of a breaking wave above her, and looked upwards; saw the cloud moving down the slope towards her, saw it in slow motion, boulders of ice and the foaming spray of snow.

She pushed herself forwards, trying to skate with the one ski she had on, her other foot sinking into the deep powder.

The roaring was becoming deafening now and she heard a mad howling wind, felt it blasting her. She was almost at the edge, almost, then the snow slid away under her and she was falling.

The wind tore at her face, its wailing banshee howl in her ears, then she felt the pressure pushing in on them.

She heard the drumming and thudding of falling rocks and ice all around her, a crazed, accelerating, terrifying cacophony, like a million footsteps racing down a tunnel. The clatter and rattle and howling, echoing, getting louder.

Swim. Try and keep to the surface.

She moved her arms. Something hit her on the head, blinding her with pain, then she was tumbling again.

She felt her hands sliding down something bitterly cold that was burning them.

The ice wall.

She was spinning.

Vortex, she thought.

The mad dark roaring was all around her. Something smacked into her cheek and hurt, then she was falling, free for a moment. She bounced off something hard, then something else again.

Then she stopped moving. She could hear the mad noise continuing all around, the drumming and rattling and howling, becoming more muffled, slowing down. Distant.

And then silence.

She lay in darkness. She closed her eyes tightly, then opened them again. But she could see nothing at all.

She tried to move her hands. They would not move.

She tried her legs – her head. It was as if she had been set in cement.

She began to tremble.

The void. The void that she had dreamed of when the Mercedes had crashed, and gone over the edge.

The void where she would never see Nicky again.

Nor Richard.

Nor anyone.

She felt the terror surge through her. Half an hour.

Half an hour was all you had if you were trapped in an avalanche. After that you were virtually given up for dead.

Where was she? How far down? How deep?

She felt the cold all around her.

And the silence.

This is death.

She tried to move. Her right hand felt loose, but something was trapping it.

The strap of the ski pole. She wriggled her hand, and it came free. She was able to touch her face. She ran her fingers over her forehead, her nose, her mouth. It is me. I am alive. She touched her cheek. It was stinging.

Which way up am I lying?

They had talked about avalanches so much in the past. Joked about them. Discussed what to do. They said that you crapped yourself in the fear. That was how the dogs found you. From the smell.

She wondered if she had done that.

How embarrassing. If they found you like—

Spit. Someone had once said that you should spit. If the spit landed on your face you knew you were lying on your back. She spat. Damp spots landed on her forehead.

'Help me!' she shouted. 'I'm here! I'm here!' But she could tell, from the flatness of the sound, that her voice was trapped with her inside the tomb.

At least I could be unconscious, she thought. At least I could have been knocked unconscious and allowed to die without waking up.

A drip fell on her face; then another. Melting snow.

Where was Andreas? Richard? Was Richard buried in it too?

They were way off the piste, down the side of the mountain. Would anyone even have seen the avalanche? She put her hand up and pushed. Hard as rock. She tried to scrape with her glove. It slid, uselessly.

Ski pole, she thought, putting her hand down and grasping the top of it. But it would not move.

Something sharp, metal. There must be something.

She pulled her glove off with her teeth, feeling another drip as she did so, and scraped at the snow with her fingers. Cold shards dropped onto her face, into her eyes. Her goggles must have come off, and she was suddenly annoyed that she had lost them. Maybe they'll find them? Maybe they'll find them even if they don't find me?

Identified by my goggles.

Her hand was getting cold. Conserve heat. She wriggled it back into her glove, then tried again to free the ski pole, yanking it, twisting it around, but it was jammed. She closed her eyes and punched the snow above her head, listening to the muffled thuds. It felt good to make a noise. To break the silence. The dark silence.

Could you breathe through ice? How much air did she have?

She heard a sound, like a handful of pebbles flung against a window. Right above her.

Her heart raced. They had found her. Found her!

Then nothing. She heard a faint echo. It could have been a footstep a few yards away, or an explosion way in the distance.

She punched the snow again, in anger, despair, closing her eyes against the falling slivers. It seemed to give a fraction, or was she imagining it? She punched as hard as she could, and suddenly her hand broke through. She felt a shower of snow over her face and down the inside of her sleeve. She wiped her face and opened her eyes.

Daylight.

Brilliant white daylight.

She stared at it through a small hole, barely wider than her fist.

'Hey! Help me!'

The daylight seeped into her tomb and she could see around her.

Could see that she was not alone.

That there was someone else in here with her.

Could see the livid red eye socket staring sightlessly through the slit in the blood-stained hood. Inches above her face. As she looked, another drop of blood fell from the socket down onto her cheek.

She screamed. And screamed again.

Andreas's hooded face inches above her, squeezed out of the roof of the tomb like a gargoyle. His mouth was open in a twisted smile and the eye socket gaped, stared at her, seeing as much as his good eye which was also staring at her from its slit, staring blankly, not moving or blinking.

Oh sweet Jesus no. No.

Then she saw the hand at the strange angle above her, as if it did not belong to the same person as the face; the hand, stripped of its glove, the deformed hand, withered, with just the thumb and the little finger, sticking motionless out of the snow like a claw.

She shook her head, trying to turn away, trying to look up through the tiny hole she had made at the daylight. Then the daylight darkened, and for a moment it vanished completely. The ground around her seemed to be drumming, shaking.

Oh God don't avalanche again. Don't move. Please.

She saw blades rotating above her.

A fan.

Black blades.

Descending down towards her, whirring madly.

Propeller.

The fan.

The ceiling cracking.

Eggshell.

The black blades.

Helicopter.

Then they began to move further away. The drumming stopped.

Helicopter.

Oh please come back. I'm here. Please come back.

But it had gone.

'Help!' she screamed. 'Help! Help me!'

She heard a scrabbling, rattling sound above her, and voices, excited. '*Ici! Ici! Ici!*'

There was a sudden, deafening rumble, and a shower of snow and ice fell onto her face. Andreas's face was shaking, vibrating as if he was laughing, the black hood lifting up and down as if he was still alive, still breathing, still mocking. The head was coming closer, nearer, inching down to her, inching down as if he was trying to kiss her.

No. No. No. No.

There was another rumble. Then the light went and she was in pitch darkness again.

Entombed in darkness and silence.

In the void.

In the void where you could scream for ever.

Her eye lashes touched something, soft, cold, damp, flicked backwards and forwards, making tiny scratching sounds as the face came closer, started pressing against her face.

She pushed her head away, swivelled it backwards and forwards, trying to drill into the ice behind, but all the time she could feel the face pressing more and more, the hard cheekbones through the silk pushing into the side of her own mouth, pushing harder and harder, grinding, as if their two heads had been put together inside a vice which was slowly being tightened.

The pain was getting worse. It was getting harder to breathe, she was gulping and choking, trying to think through the terror that was blinding her even more than the darkness.

You're smothering me.

367

You're crushing me.

You're hurting me so much.

Then she felt the explosion inside her head.

Like a light bulb.

And everything stopped.

46

A bald man smiled at her out of the darkness, and stretched his arms down towards her.

She shrank back, tried to kick out at him, but her legs wouldn't move. 'Leave me alone!' she screamed.

He blinked, startled, then smiled again, a gentle reassuring smile. Sam frowned. Different, she realised, quite different. Large warm eyes and a bushy black beard. 'It's OK, please, it's OK,' he said.

She watched him, puzzled. Puzzled by the vibration and the dull roaring din that echoed around as if she was inside a tin drum, and the curious smells of rope and oil and grease and exhaust fumes. She heard the snap of a shackle, the clank of a chain, and a voice shouting; the man with the beard shouted something back which was drowned. Someone squeezed her hand.

'It's OK, Bugs. You're fine. You're going to be OK.' Richard.

She turned her head a fraction and saw fir trees slide past, then a blue wall of ice, then nothing but a grey haze, as if she had just caught the end of a home movie.

'How you feel?' The man with the bushy beard was leaning over her again.

'My leg hurts.'

'We give you something for it. Do you have allergies to any drug?'

She shook her head. It hurt to do that. 'Where am I?'

'In the helicopter. We will have you in hospital in Visp very quick now. Just we wait a few more moments.'

Her hand was squeezed again, and she felt her forehead being caressed. She dosed her eyes and immediately felt sick. She opened them and saw Richard standing over her. He stroked her forehead. 'You're OK. You're going to be fine.'

Beside him she noticed the silhouette of the Matterhorn spin past in the distance. She sat up a fraction, ignoring the pain, remembering.

'Lie down, Bugs. Don't try to sit up.'

She could see a sheer wall of ice, steely blue, dropping away below a long gully. Near it, a wide strip was missing from the side of the mountain.

That was where she had been.

It went out of sight for a moment, then she could see it again clearly, just below her. They were level with the couloir, and she followed it across and down. The top part of the slope which had been covered in powder snow was now rock and mud. To the right, the rock and mud continued all the way down to the lip, and then gave way to the ice wall. To the left, the mud turned into snow, great chunks, like white boulders strewn across, piled up at the bottom making a wall several yards high that stopped just short of the lip; and further to the left, where the ice wall ended and there was a lesser gradient, the ice boulders carried on, stopping short of a second lip below.

On both the higher and lower lips men in brown clothing were trudging through the boulders, fanned out, taking short steps forward and pushing thin metal rods into the snow between each boulder. They raised their heads, moved forward and pierced again.

'Crazy,' said a voice behind her. She turned and saw

the man with the bushy beard look first at her, then at
Richard. He shook his head and looked angry, angry
and hurt. 'Crazy. You English. Crazy. Why you go
skiing down there?' He tapped the side of his forehead
with his finger. 'Crazy.'

'I—' But there was no fight in her. 'I'm sorry,' she
said.

'I think you have very lucky.'

'Lucky?'

He gestured to the window, and shook his head
again. 'You see there? The ice, the walls? It's impossible.
Look where you are coming down.'

She could see clearly now. The whole side of the
mountain dropped away sheer. If they had succeeded in
getting down the slope that had avalanched, they would
still . . .

The lip where Andreas had told her to turn ran on
around the side for a few yards, then dipped steeply.
They wouldn't have seen it from above when they were
on it. They wouldn't have seen it until their skis had left
it, and they were tumbling down the rock face that fell
away sheer beneath it, down a thousand feet or more,
into the rolling mist.

47

There was a knock on the door of her hospital room.

'*Entrez*,' she said.

A policeman came in, in his dark blue uniform and
black holster, holding his cap in his hand. He closed the
door behind him and nodded politely at her. He was
short, trim, precise-looking, with neat dark hair and a
neat thin moustache.

'Meeses Curtis?'

She nodded.

'Kaporal Julen from the Walliser Kantonspolizei,' he said.

'Hallo.'

'How are you feeling, Meeses Curtis?'

'OK, thank you.'

'You have the ribs broken, and the leg?'

'Two ribs, and my ankle.'

'I hope you do not mind, I would like to ask you some questions?' he said.

'No, of course.'

He pulled up a chair near the bed, and sat down, placing his cap in his lap. 'It is a bad thing, to get caught in an avalanche. We try to make safe on the pistes, but when people going away from the marked routes, without a guide—' He raised his hands in the air.

'Yes.'

'You know – this place where you were, there was no way down? If you 'ad not been taken wiz the avalanche, you would have moz certainly been killed. You could not have skied down further. Impossible to ski. Why did your 'usband take this route, down this couloir?'

'It wasn't my husband. It was Andreas.'

'Andreas?'

'A business colleague of my husband's. A Swiss. He claimed he knew the area well.'

He frowned. 'I do not understand.'

Something in the policeman's face unsettled her. 'He lives in Montreux and skis in Zermatt a lot, he told me.'

'Who is Andreas?'

'Andreas Berensen. He's a director of the Fürgen-Zuricher Bank, based in Montreux.'

'I don't think so, Meeses Curtis. The ski patrol helicopter see you at the top of the slope, juz before the avalanche. There were only two people.'

'Myself and Andreas. My husband was behind us. We got separated, you see, in the mist.'

He shook his head. 'Only two people,' he said firmly, raising his voice a fraction.

She felt a sudden frisson of fear. 'There were three of us—' Her mouth twitched into a nervous smile. 'There were three of us. Andreas was trapped with me – dead. I'm sure he was dead; his eye was all—' She saw the strange expression on the policeman's face and faltered.

He stared down at his hat, then up at her. 'Are you trying to make a joke with me?'

'A joke?' She flared in anger. 'A joke? You think I'm joking? That I think this is funny?'

He stood up and walked over to the window. 'You come from London?'

'Yes.'

'Nice city. I was there. On holidays. I visit Scotland Yard. Good. Very efficient, Scotland Yard. Always raining in London, yes?'

'Not always.'

He sat down again and placed his hat in his lap. 'You were skiing down this mountain with your husband and with Andreas Berensen?'

'Yes.'

'Broken two ribs; and you have the multiple break of the ankle?'

'Yes.'

'Otherwise you are all right?'

'Yes.'

'Concussion?'

'I don't think so.'

'I think perhaps concussion. Concussion or you are making jokes – or making excuses? You are trying to make blame on someone other for your stupidity.'

Her face was smarting. 'I'm sorry, I don't understand.'

'Don't you?' He thumped his chest, angrily. 'Me, I understand. Every year people dead in the mountains, stupid peoples, who ignore the piste markings, who think they can go off the piste without having to pay for the guide.'

'I'm sorry – I really don't understand what you are saying.'

He glared at her, furious now. 'I think you understand, Meeses Curtees; I think you and your husband understand very well.'

She closed her eyes. Riddles. Riddles. Was this some crazy new riddle? Some new game? 'Could you please explain to me exactly what you are saying? What you are insinuating?'

He drummed his fingers on his hat, then stopped abruptly and looked directly at her. 'Andreas Berensen, director of the Fürgen-Zuricher Bank . . . You and your husband were skiing with this man, yes? He was your guide, yes? You tell me this and your husband tell me this, yes?'

'Yes. Christ, he was buried with me in the avalanche. We were under the snow together. He'd – he must have fallen on his ski tips. His eye was gouged out. He was trapped with me – dead.'

'There was no one with you. I have spoken with the men who rescued you: nothing. They said there was no one with you when they found you. I have spoken to the Fürgen-Zuricher Bank, Meeses Curtees.' He looked at his hat then at Sam again and shook his head. 'They don't know any man of this name. They have never heard of Andreas Berensen. There is no one called Andreas Berensen who lives in Montreux. There is no one in Switzerland who is a director of a bank with this name. There is no one in Switzerland who even has a passport in this name.' He tapped his hat. 'You know why, Meeses Curtees? Because he does not exist, that is why.'

48

'Dead men don't climb out of avalanches, Sam.'

But dreamers wake up from dreams, she thought, glancing round the restaurant. Four businessmen sat at the next table studying the lunchtime menus. Although it seemed empty, there was an air of expectancy about the place. It was still early. In half an hour it would be full, Julio would be turning away the punters with a smile, a raised eyebrow, a humble peasant shrug. Scusa. Sorry. So sorry.

Ken leaned forward, in his crumpled denim shirt, studying her face carefully, and broke a roll in half, spraying crumbs over the tablecloth. The waiter swept the Orvieto from the table and poured it into their glasses with flourish, as if he was watering a couple of plants.

Ken shook out a cigarette and tapped the tipped end hard on his watch. 'Richard saw him swept away?'

'Yes.'

'And you were trapped with him?'

'I – thought so.'

'And he was above you?'

'Yes.'

'So the rescuers would have dug him out first?'

She nodded.

'And they saw nothing?'

She picked up her glass and drank some wine. 'No.'

He lit the cigarette, inhaled, and slowly blew smoke

374

out of his nostrils, rolling the cigarette around between his finger and thumb at the same time. 'So you imagined it?'

Her brain did not seem to want to work, did not seem to want to tackle the problem; the insides of her head felt flat, inert. 'Andreas must have been swept off the precipice – I suppose – and I was just imagining I was trapped with him. The bash I had on my head – perhaps that's what – it's just that it—'

Tiny crows' feet appeared either side of Ken's eyes as he smiled.

She shrugged. 'It seemed so real.'

'Being buried in an avalanche – must have been very frightening.'

'It was freaky. I thought I was going to die. I really thought, you know, that was it. When I saw his face – Andreas – I felt – I—' She glanced down at the table cloth, then across at the door where a knot of people were standing; Julio was helping a short fat man off with his coat, with clinical efficiency, as if he was peeling a large orange.

Ken raised his glass. 'It's good to have you back. I've missed you.'

'It's good to be back – I've missed—' She hesitated and blushed, and glanced away; she heard the clink of their glasses, and took a mouthful of wine, cold, steely, then winced as it touched a cracked filling.

'When are you planning to come back to work?'

'After lunch.'

'You're joking.'

'I'm serious. I'm starting again this afternoon. Ten days in a Swiss hospital is enough sitting around. I'm pretty nippy on my crutches.' She smiled. 'And I don't want Claire getting my job.'

He sniffed his wine, took a large sip, drew on his cigarette and carefully knocked the ash into the ashtray. He studied the tablecloth thoughtfully, then looked up at her. 'Claire's left.'

Sam stared at him, numb with surprise. She shivered, feeling cold, suddenly. Cold, damp; she wondered for a moment whether the heating was on in the restaurant. She eyed him carefully. 'Left? Claire?'

'Uh huh.'

'How – when?'

'She never turned up the day after your avalanche. I got a note two days later.'

'What – did it say?'

'Nothing. "I regret that I shall not be able to continue working for you." Signed, Claire Walker, brackets, Miss.'

'That was all?'

'Uh huh – really dumped us in it – you were right – I should have listened to you. The bloody cow.'

'And she hadn't said anything to you before?'

'Nope.'

'How on earth have you been coping – I mean – so you've had no one there—?'

'Drummond's been a good lad. We've got by.'

'Bloody bitch. God, she might have waited until I'd come back. You've always treated her fairly – just to walk out like that—'

He drew hard again on his cigarette, nodding, and blew the smoke away from her. 'That's staff, isn't it?' He picked up his glass and leaned back. 'So what's Richard going to do about his money?'

'He says the bank – in Montreux – is lying. He's had several meetings during the past few months with Andreas, actually at the bank – there's no question he was a director. It was obviously all part of the covering of tracks – it's been a bit too thorough – it seems that Andreas covered the tracks a little too well.'

'So Richard's hoist on his—?'

She nodded. 'His money has vanished. Gone.'

'What's he going to do?'

'He'd set all this up because he thought he was going to lose his job and that he might have his accounts frozen. But it looks as though that won't happen now – the case against him is being dropped. His solicitor told him last night.'

'What's the reason?'

She raised her eyebrows, and smiled a thin smile. 'Richard's not sure. It seems that one of the key prosecution witnesses has vanished.'

Ken looked hard at her, then dug his hand into his breast pocket and pulled out a buff envelope. 'This one?' He handed it across to her, and she took it, her eyes locked on his, frowning.

The envelope was not sealed; she slid her fingers inside and pulled out a black and white photograph, which she laid down on the tablecloth. It was a page of a book divided into three panels, a large one at the top and two smaller ones beneath. She glanced up at Ken and down again. Then she saw him. The bottom right hand panel. She leaned down, closer and felt a creeping sensation up the back of her scalp.

She saw the hand first, the small deformed hand, with just a thumb and little finger, the middle three fingers missing; then the face, the cold, rather correct face, with the high forehead, the fair hair neatly groomed either side of the head but thinned to a light fuzz on top. The only thing different was that he was wearing spectacles, round, metal rimmed, that had a dated look to them. He was standing in front of a building, in a suit with all three buttons done up, and looked as if he was unhappy about the picture being taken.

'Andreas,' she said. 'That's Andreas.'

'How old is your Andreas?'

'Late forties – early fifties.'

'This one would be about ninety-five, if he was still alive. He hanged himself in a prison cell in Lyons in 1938.'

Her legs hit the underneath of the table, jolting it; her head suddenly felt boiling hot and for a moment she thought she was going to be sick. She put her hands flat on the table for support.

'I was watching a documentary on the box a couple of weeks ago, about evil, and black magic, and they showed a picture of this bloke – the hand – it reminded me of your chap you told me about.'

'Who is he, Ken?'

'Claus Wolf. He was a very weird German – heavily into black magic – got involved in several covens around Europe in the Twenties and Thirties. He had something going in Italy and got kicked out when Mussolini had a clean up, and moved to France. He married someone equally weird and they got into ritual sacrifice killings. He was arrested in Lyons, in 1938, on several murder charges, but his wife, Eva, who was eight months pregnant, fled, and is believed to have come to England, posing as a Jewish refugee. They had a four-year-old son she had to leave behind, who was eventually adopted by relatives in Switzerland.'

'And he's Andreas?'

'There can't be too many people with the same deformity.'

'This was all in the programme?'

'No. I know the producer – at the Beeb – so I rang him

378

and asked if he had any more gen – and he had a word with the researcher – and let me have the photo.'

She sat in silence for a moment, staring at the cold arrogant face. 'It's Wednesday, today.' She looked at her watch. 'Claire said she's always there on Wednesdays.'

'Who?'

'Bloomsbury – can we go to Bloomsbury?'

Ken stopped the Bentley outside the Whole Mind and Body Centre and Sam hobbled in. The woman with the pulled-back hair and pulled-back face was sitting behind her cash register.

'I'd like to see Mrs Wolf.'

'She's not here,' the woman said, with virtually no movement of her lips.

'I thought she always was on Wednesdays.'

'She's ill.'

'Do you know when she'll be here next?'

'She's very ill. I don't know if she'll ever be back.'

'I need to see her.'

'She doesn't want to see anybody.'

'Is it possible to have her address?'

'No,' said the woman. 'It is not possible.' She lowered her voice. 'Go away. Just get out, go away; don't come back. We don't want you here again.'

Sam hesitated. 'I – it's very important – I must—'

The woman half stood up, and for a moment Sam thought she was going to lunge at her. She backed away, stumbling, tripped on the doorstep and dropped a crutch. She leaned down, scooped it up, and looked again at the woman, who was standing upright now, her face filled with hatred, and hurried outside. She climbed into the Bentley, shaking, her face smarting. Ken put her crutches on the rear seat then closed her door. 'Any joy?'

'Christ, they're strange in there. She's ill and they don't think she's coming back – and they wouldn't give me her address.'

He was silent for a moment. 'I think I know it,' he said.

Sam looked at him in amazement. 'How? What do you mean?'

He started the car, without speaking.

'What do you mean, Ken?'

He raised a finger, and eased out into the mid-afternoon traffic.

They crawled up Tottenham Court Road, then turned left into Marylebone Road. She watched the lights and the silver flying spur mascot on the bonnet blankly, her mind fogged, unfocusing, a part of her still in the icy underground tomb. They went up the ramp of the Paddington overpass, and she glanced again at Ken, trying to find some clue in his expression. They turned off towards Shepherds Bush, came to the end of the expressway and joined the slow heavy traffic.

They went through Acton and into Ealing. Ken stopped twice and checked the A–Z, and they navigated a maze of back streets, finally stopping outside a crumbling Victorian mansion block.

He opened the door for her and helped her out of the car. 'I'll come with you, be your minder.'

'How do you know this is—?'

'I don't; but I think I'm right.' They looked at the names on the entryphone. It was written in pencil and faded so badly it was barely legible. '2 Wolf' was all it said.

She looked at Ken again, puzzled. 'I don't understand.'

'I think you will.'

She was about to press the buzzer, but Ken stopped her and, instead, pressed one for another flat.

'Harry? That you Harry?' said a grumpy old woman's voice.

'Parcel – special delivery,' Ken said, then the latch buzzed and he pushed open the front door, holding it for Sam.

The corridor was dark and dank and smelt of boiled cabbage; the linoleum on the floor had rucked up and was uneven to walk on.

'Wait here,' Sam said. 'It'll be better on my own.'

'You sure?'

She nodded and carried on into the gloom. She squinted at the first doorway on the right, which was number 1, then reached the far door, smelled a strong smell of cats, and saw the faded brass number 2 on the door. She hesitated for a moment, and listened. Somewhere behind her she could hear a television turned up much too loud. She glanced around, and pressed the buzzer; there was a grating metallic rasp which echoed around. Then a long silence. She was about to ring again, when she heard footsteps, firm, quick.

The door opened, and Claire stared out at her.

Sam blinked in disbelief.

Claire.

Claire staring at her, matter-of-factly, no trace of surprise.

As if she had been expected.

Sam stumbled back, confused. 'Claire?' she said.

'Why have you come here?' she said, icily.

'I – I thought – I – I wanted to see Mrs Wolf.'

'My mother has had a stroke and can't see anyone. Go away and leave us alone.'

'Your *mother*?' Sam shook her head, trembling. 'Your mother?'

'She had the stroke when she saw her son fall in the avalanche. She saw it all.'

'Saw it?'

'My mother sees a lot of things.'

'Where did he fall?'

'He went over a drop, fell a long way down, then through deep snow and onto a frozen lake. They will find him in the spring.'

Sam stared at her, unable to speak.

'You've killed both of her sons. Isn't that enough for you? Why don't you leave my family in peace now?'

The door closed firmly and she heard the sound of the safety chain. She stood in silence too shattered to move.

'Sam? You OK?'

She saw the red glow of Ken's cigarette. Slowly, she hobbled down the passage towards him.

'OK?'

She stopped in front of him. 'You were right,' she said. She tried to read his face in the dim light, then she heard a noise that sounded like a door handle behind her, and turned fearfully. But there was nothing.

She climbed into the car and sat in silence as they drove away, watching the lights of the traffic and the darkness.

'You've had no more dreams, since?' he said.

'No.'

'I wouldn't talk to anyone else. I wouldn't dig any further, Sam. Try to forget about it. It'll heal in time.'

'I wish I could believe that.'

'Don't you?'

She shook her head.

'If the mind's got the ability to see the future, Sam, then I'm sure it's got the ability to forget the past.'

'Maybe.'

'Forget it all. The hooded man's dead and buried.

Both of them are now. Bury him in your own mind, too.' He tossed his cigarette butt out of the window. 'Forget it. Forget the past. It's over. You've met your monster – isn't that what someone said to you?'

She nodded.

'You've met your monster – all your monsters – and you've beaten them.'

'Life's full of monsters, Ken.'

'Life's full of survivors, too.'

Maybe it was an hour later that Ken dropped her off at Wapping. Maybe it was several hours. She seemed to think they'd stopped and had a drink, or perhaps she was confusing that with another time. Her head was a blur of burning pain and she was shaking all over.

She went into the lift and pressed the button for the fourth floor and the door slid shut and the light came on and they began to move upwards, slowly, shuffling and clanging, it seemed to be going slower than ever. It stopped, with the same jerk that always unbalanced her, but this time it seemed even more vicious and she was thrown against the side.

There was a sharp pop, and the light went out. She felt the sting of glass on her face, and yelped.

Then there was silence. She waited for the door to open, but nothing happened.

She fumbled her fingers down the control panel, trying to find the round 'Door Open' button, her heart thumping. It ought to be at the bottom of the panel, she knew. She felt the indents of the floor selectors, reached the bottom one, then nothing. Just cold smooth metal. She moved her hand up, counting. Ground, First, Second, Third, Fourth, then smooth metal again. She pressed a button at random. Nothing. Tried another. Nothing. She gave the door a thump with her fist and heard the dull metallic boom echo around. She thumped it again.

Alarm bell, she thought. There was an alarm bell. Higher up; or was it the last button? She pushed each button in turn. Nothing. Nothing. Suddenly the door began to open, slowly, scraping, and her heart leaped with relief.

Then she screamed.

Screamed and fell back across the tiny lift.

Pressed herself hard against the wall as Claire came in through the door with a sickle in her hand, raised above her head.

'No! Claire, no!'

She flung her hands up and felt a raw terrible pain as the grimy, muddy blade sliced into her arm. She tried to fend Claire off with a crutch, but the demented woman tore it out of her hand and flung it, clattering, into the corridor.

'Richard!' she screamed, 'Oh my God Richard, help me!'

The blade smashed into her hand, slicing off fingers, then into her chest.

'Richard!'

It gouged into her chest again, searing her with pain, then it crashed into her head; she heard the clang; felt the agonising pain, closed her eyes, opened them again, saw Claire's face right up against hers, her eyes bloodshot, flooded with crazed pleasure, saw the hand rise up again, then a million red hot spikes were being ground into her skull.

Claire jerked sharply backwards; Sam saw her dimly, skidding across the floor, a hand holding her hair, shaking her head like a rag doll, saw her flung against the wall, a startled look in her eyes, saw the sickle smash into the wall, then drop out of her hand. Richard.

Richard shaking her, wild with rage, smashing her head into the wall, again, then again, until she slumped senseless onto the floor. He turned towards her.

'Bugs?'

Sam stumbled forwards, reeling. Richard was now a dim blur. She fell towards him.

'Bugs?'

There was silence.

'Bugs? You OK?'

The blood covered her face, poured down it, poured through her clothes.

'Bugs?'

Light came on. Brilliant dazzling white hospital light, a doctor staring into her face, and beyond him she saw the painting of a nude on the wall, and she realised it wasn't a doctor, but it was Richard.

'You're OK, Bugs, it's all right. You're OK.'

She ran her hand across her face and stared at it. Water. Perspiration; it was only perspiration. She stared at her hands; counted her fingers, slowly: they were all there; not a mark.

'Was that another?' he said. 'Was that another of your nightmares?'

She shook her head. 'No. It was different. Different.'

He leaned forward and kissed her on the forehead.

She was panting, she realised, panting and gulping down air. She lay back and listened to the sound of her own heartbeat pounding inside her chest that was as tight as a drumskin. 'It was different, this time. It was fine. Just a dream,' she said, loudly, clearly, as though she wanted the whole world to hear; as though, if she said it loudly and positively enough, she might even believe it herself. She closed her eyes for a moment, and saw Claire's head smash into the wall again, and again. Saw the glazed beaten expression in Claire's eyes as she slumped to the floor. Then she looked back at Richard and smiled.

'It was just a dream.'

available from
THE ORION PUBLISHING GROUP

———————

☐ **Dreamer** £6.99
PETER JAMES
978-0-7528-7678-8

☐ **Alchemist** £6.99
PETER JAMES
978-0-7528-1729-3

☐ **Host** £6.99
PETER JAMES
978-0-7528-3745-1

☐ **Faith** £6.99
PETER JAMES
978-0-7528-3711-6

☐ **Sweet Heart** £6.99
PETER JAMES
978-0-7528-7677-1

☐ **Twilight** £6.99
PETER JAMES
978-0-7528-7679-5

☐ **Denial** £6.99
PETER JAMES
978-0-7528-2688-2

☐ **Prophecy** £6.99
PETER JAMES
978-0-7528-1737-8

All Orion/Phoenix titles are available at your local bookshop or from the following address:

Mail Order Department
Littlehampton Book Services
FREEPOST BR535
Worthing, West Sussex, BN13 3BR
telephone 01903 828503, *facsimile* 01903 828802
e-mail MailOrders@lbsltd.co.uk
(Please ensure that you include full postal address details)

Payment can be made either by credit/debit card (Visa, Mastercard, Access and Switch accepted) or by sending a £ Sterling cheque or postal order made payable to *Littlehampton Book Services*.
DO NOT SEND CASH OR CURRENCY

Please add the following to cover postage and packing

UK and BFPO:
£1.50 for the first book, and 50p for each additional book to a maximum of £3.50

Overseas and Eire:
£2.50 for the first book plus £1.00 for the second book and 50p for each additional book ordered

---

BLOCK CAPITALS PLEASE

name of cardholder ....

address of cardholder ....

delivery address
(if different from cardholder)
....
....
....

....

....

postcode ....   *postcode* ....

☐ I enclose my remittance for £..............................

☐ please debit my Mastercard/Visa/Access/Switch (delete as appropriate)

card number ☐☐☐☐☐☐☐☐☐☐☐☐☐☐☐☐☐☐

expiry date ☐☐☐☐   Switch issue no. ☐☐

signature ....

prices and availability are subject to change without notice